DROWNED SEA

A DARK FANTASY ADVENTURE

TRISTAN MIRANDA

BLAISE MIRANDA

MW PRESS, LLC
MWPRESSBOOKS.COM

MW Press, LLC
mwpressbooks.com

This book is fictitious. Any references to real events, persons, or places are used fictitiously. Any resemblance to real persons (living or dead), places, events, or businesses is coincidental. Other names, characters, places, events, and businesses are products of the authors' imaginations.

Published by MW Press, LLC
Edited by Katerina Krizner
Cover Images © Steven Stahlberg
Seas of Kaidas Map © MW Press, LLC

1st Edition, May 2024. Published in Mission Viejo, CA. Printed in USA.

Library of Congress Control Number: 2024931356

ISBN 978-1-959587-01-9 (Hardback)
ISBN 978-1-959587-00-2 (Paperback)
ISBN 978-1-959587-02-6 (E-Book)
ISBN 978-1-959587-03-3 (Audiobook)

To Us

It's been a long, fun journey... And it's only just begun.

"Love is a religion, and its rituals cost more than those of other religions. It goes by quickly and, like a street urchin, it likes to mark its passage by a trail of devastation."

- From *Father Goriot* by Honoré de Balzac

Ice Barrens
Borova
Skystone
Aritrasta
Sungate
Arden
Farcliff
Alira
Crimson Reef
Greenrun
Straitfell
Exetis
Golden Strait
Drowned
Valak
Black
Endall
Tavrak
Werm
Noble
Ruvval
Glass Tides
Jernak
Vulcanus
Syrnius
Heraceus
Atremon
The Seas
of
Kaidas
N
W
E
S

Eliston
Deadlands
New Linfeld
Poison Gulf
Aenu
Casanought
Renford
Sea
Norland
Trench
Stotan
Tibur
Russet
Nessus
Dark Shallows
Midius
Cassius
Solanus
Corinthus
Damned
Depths
Frigid Wastes

PART ONE

URCHIN

CHAPTER ONE

A shark with sails crept across the whitecaps, hunting its prey. The two-masted brig's hull cut the obsidian sea like a blade through skin. From the mainmast flew its dorsal fin: a turquoise flag embroidered with the crossing white cutlasses of the Avowed—loyalist pirates sworn to obey their king and the Cutthroat Code. Not that the Code made them good men. Such laws only made the Cutthroats more dangerous.

On the main deck of the *Widowmaker*, these piranhas grinned and gasped for the blood to come. They wore an uncoordinated assortment of vibrant fabrics, leather hats, and golden jewelry—all of which had been stolen. Each loaded flintlocks and unsheathed cutlasses, anxiously awaiting the night's raid as the ship steered toward a lantern bobbing in the darkness, a bright light surrounded by dim stars.

Where there's a lantern, there's a ship. Where there's a ship, there's power, Raskel thought. He stood at the bow, the paragon of Avowed captains: stoic, staunch, and savage. His black tricorn hat sat askew, and a yellow overcoat hid a red vest, blue shirt, and black breeches underneath. The storied white cutlass remained sheathed at his side, though its colored blade had worn gray with heavy use. Raskel's hand never strayed far from the ivory hilt.

Especially not during a raid.

His prey came into view: a single-masted sloop whose rigging was in disrepair. Not dismasted, despite the hurricanes that plagued the east, but not unscathed either. Holes riddled the sails and widened with each gale. Yet the ship was still afloat, so the damage was fixable. With new sails, the sloop would once again carve the sea and capture slower vessels, which meant more money, more ships, more *everything*.

"Small ships have small crews," Raskel said, licking his chapped lips. "We'll take them quick."

And if we're lucky, there'll be some women to take too. The thought gave way to a hungry smile. Few women sailed, fewer still on sloops, but it was still a possibility. Last year, Raskel had found two hiding within a sloop bound for the northern island colonies. *That* had been a great raid, and an even better night—

"But, captain, there ain't anybody to take," said a nasally voice too close to Raskel's shoulder.

The thought of women fell to the depths below as Raskel snapped out of his reverie. He spun, facing a Cutthroat whose narrow face was accentuated in all the wrong ways by a golden septum ring. "Jacobs," Raskel said in a cold greeting. His right hand clenched the hilt of his cutlass as he added, "Sneaking up on a man like that is a good way to get yourself killed."

"Mayhap, captain, but... *look*. There ain't no one on that ship," said Jacobs, wearing soiled Aritrastan clothing stolen during previous raids: a white frill shirt and a black leather vest. Both were more fashionable than functional, revealing his northern blood and blue skin.

Raskel pushed Jacobs away and studied the sloop through his spyglass. Though the lantern rested precariously on the railing of the crow's nest, no one trimmed the sails or climbed the ratlines. Nor were there any men walking along the deck or holding the helm. The vessel skulked through the sea as if commanded by Eo, the night Goddess.

Raskel shook his head, though it didn't change what he saw. "That ain't possible. That ship would've sunk by now."

"Mayhap it's a ghost ship," Jacobs said before murmuring a prayer and cutting his knuckle with the edge of a knife to ward away evil spirits.

"It's just planks and timbers, Jacobs. Nothing more." Raskel frowned as other Aritrastan Cutthroats made complex hand gestures and tossed coins into the ocean for safe passage. Even the minority of gray-skinned Corinthian Cutthroats clutched at gold pendants and bowed their heads in silent prayer to their sun God, who held little sway over this Godless, monstrous sea.

Ignoring their foolishness, Raskel turned to the four Aritrastan sentinels, whose job it was to stand by the port and starboard gunwales to watch the sea for syrens. The sentinels held daggers, but all Cutthroats knew a blade wouldn't stop the deep terrors from attacking. Weapons were false hope—fool's gold.

The Drowned Sea would always take what it wanted.

"Any sign of syrens tonight?" Raskel asked, refusing to stand too close to the rail. He'd seen those horrid monsters before. All Cutthroats had. Syrens were attracted to corpses, as were all deep terrors whose names were lost in the sea. Creatures of the Black Trench and the Damned Depths.

"Nothing yet, captain," they replied successively, adding *yet* in hopes of avoiding a fatal jinx—not that the precaution was ever a guarantee.

Nothing was.

As clouds surged from the east and strangled the night sky, plunging both ships into deeper shadows, Captain Raskel discovered another omen in the dead space between stars: Eo's smile. On the far horizon, the crescent moon formed the Goddess's crooked smile, mirroring the scowling reflection in the waters beneath. Superstition foretold of great fortune or great danger, because the Goddess always smiled when She watched mortals closely.

Raskel wasn't smiling, but he wasn't about to succumb to superstition either. Not when a ship was so close at hand.

"Nobody's at the helm, but it's sailing straight, captain," Jacobs said. "We should give it a broadside. Sink it and—"

"Nobody's sinking that ship," Raskel said, his hand moving from his cutlass to a flintlock pistol.

Jacobs thrust his chin up. "We should vote on it."

"We don't vote during raids, Jacobs," Raskel said, staring down at him. "I'm captain, and *I* say we're taking that ship."

Eyes narrowing, Jacobs stepped closer. "I have as much a voice as—"

Raskel's fist smashed into Jacobs's jaw, and the Cutthroat crumbled to the ground near the captain's feet. "Your voice is as small as your prick, Jacobs. Next time, keep your squalling mouth shut."

Jacobs gasped like a fish, spitting a tooth into his outstretched palm before pulling himself to his feet. "There ain't gonna be a next time, *captain,*" Jacobs spat, snarling as he reached for his flintlock.

Raskel raised his own pistol, but a knife slit Jacobs's throat before he could fire. Gurgling, Jacobs sank to the ground and grasped at his torn flesh even as the blood spilled between his fingers. Not a sound was made as he choked to death, eyes rolling back into his head before his body stilled.

As crimson dripped from his dagger, Marius stood solemnly over the dead man. The first mate didn't shiver despite his simplistic Corinthian garb: sandals, a leather skirt, and an orange-and-white headdress. With a flourish, he sheathed the dagger at his belt, where several more just like it waited for blood. Quietly, Marius said, "You are quite right, Jacobs. There will not be a next time."

Nodding to Marius in thanks, Raskel addressed the accusatory glares surrounding him. "Nobody disrupts a raid. Everybody knows that. Jacobs knew that, too, because *that's* what we voted on before we left Port Noble."

Begrudging mumbles and nods revealed the crew's acceptance, and Raskel let out an uneasy breath. To Marius, he said, "You saved my life again."

Marius put a hand on Raskel's shoulder and squeezed. "You'd have done the same for me, captain."

"I *have* done the same for you," Raskel said, which only made the Corinthian smirk. To a couple of Cutthroats nearby, Raskel added, "Chum the waters with that corpse. Bless our ship."

They grabbed Jacobs's body and spat on it, ensuring that he wouldn't endure a half-life as one of the damned, one of the Drowned. Then they threw him overboard. It was too dark to see if hands yanked the corpse beneath the waves, or if it sank of its own accord.

A howling wail rose from the decrepit sloop across the water. It was sourceless, echoing off the mast, the sails, the winds above, and the waves below as it formed into words. A song as raspy and beautiful as it was haunting.

The Gods forgot, but She did not,
The promise They made to Her.
Her tears fell, storm and rain.
Her wails echoed thunder.

Forgotten by, She said on high,
Forgotten by the sea.
You'll pay the price for your deeds.
You'll pay eternally.

Raskel's men all fell silent. Eagerness ebbed from their still bodies only to be absorbed by that chilling voice.

"Undo's song," a Cutthroat said, breaking the silence. "A wraith's singing Undo's song."

"It's nothing but a sham." Raskel's voice was lined with lead, his throat devoid of moisture. He swallowed hard. A few Cutthroats muttered prayers to Undo, but Raskel only tensed his jaw. "Are you men so craven that a voice would scare you away? You made an oath—a *vow*—when you became Avowed. Fulfill it and prepare to board. *Now!*"

Stealth forgotten, the crew shouted in excitement and horror as their ship pulled alongside the smaller sloop. Four Avowed hefted a long, thick boarding plank above the gunwale to span the gap between vessels. They secured the plank with rope, and Raskel was the first across it, flintlock and cutlass raised as he jumped onto the sloop's deck. Others followed, carrying lanterns which revealed thick trails of dried blood and gunpowder residue that even the waves had failed to wash away.

Lots of men died here, Raskel thought. *But who killed them?*

A shrieking laugh echoed beneath the deck, so chilling that even Raskel felt fleshless hands grip his spine. Several Avowed shrank back, their fingers quivering as they pointed their flintlocks in all directions.

"Stay the course, men." Raskel walked along the deck, passing the bloodstains and the gunpowder tracings to stare up at the lantern in the crow's nest. The light was positioned so it could be seen for dozens of miles on a clear night in the open sea.

A beacon. A harbinger.

"I don't like this," Marius whispered, now standing at Raskel's side. "Feels like a trap."

"Something tells me that the trap was already sprung." But for all the iron in his voice, Raskel's stomach sank below his navel. He unsheathed his cutlass and pointed its edge at a group of Cutthroats. "You lot! Down the hatch. We're searching the ship!"

Raskel followed his men down the ladder, overwhelmed by the growing scent of gunpowder. "Only steel until we find the crew," he said, watching as the other Cutthroats holstered their pistols. "Any shot could set the entire hull ablaze."

The shadows lengthened and withered as the Cutthroats swung their lanterns, finding nothing except crimson stains and emaciated rats whose empty eyes glowed from the shadows. On the gun deck, they found barrels of gunpowder between cannons, but as Raskel pushed one with a boot, it rolled away with ease.

"Empty," he said, his voice dying in the darkness. "Why are they empty?"

Glass shattered above, followed by erupting cries from the main deck. Shots rang through the air, and the screams silenced. The deck grew warmer, hot even. Raskel turned and stared up the hatchway, seeing a strange glow intensifying.

It's not just a trap... it's a tomb.

Forgetting the others, Raskel raced to the main deck and emerged into an inferno.

Ash swirled through the air, and glass fragments from the broken lantern glittered across the planks. Bleeding men burned and sizzled as licking tendrils trapped and consumed them.

Raskel backed away until he hit the gunwale. "What happened?" he sputtered as smoke choked his lungs.

"The shadows, captain! They came alive!" an Avowed said. His eyes widened as he pointed behind the captain. "Look! There it is!"

Raskel whirled around, staring across the plank at his brig to find a dozen of his crew dead on the deck with their eyes glazed, throats torn, and entrails spilled. "By the Gods."

Two red eyes emerged from the dark mainmast of his ship. A shadow stepped forth, tore away the mooring knots at the gunwale with clawed hands, and kicked the plank into the frothing waves below.

Raskel stiffened as the shadow stared at him. He took an instinctive step backward before the fire's heat forced him to stop. The moment he raised his flintlock, the shadow was gone, indiscernible from the masts and the rigging. Raskel kept his gun raised, though there was nothing to shoot.

Behind him, fiery ropes snapped, and the ship lurched. Raskel stumbled away from the flames as a strip of sail fell on Marius, who burned with it. The first mate frantically ripped at the cloth and screamed for Raskel, who was too far away to do anything but watch him die.

"Marius..." Raskel trailed away. Nothing he said would reach Marius now—the flesh of his ears popped, sizzled, and melted as the fire consumed him. Mouth, nose, face—all gone. Strange that, after having spent so long fighting side by side, Marius had died out of reach. Painful was too simple a word for it.

More ropes frayed and cut loose, swinging wildly like the tentacles of a kraken. A crack of thunder exploded beneath them, a deposit of gunpowder catching fire and blowing a hole through the hull. The sloop groaned, crippled and sinking, as Raskel's brig pulled away.

"No, *no!* How dare you take my ship! Damn you! *Damn you!*" Raskel shouted, firing his flintlock at the shadows, though the bullet made no difference. He tossed the gun aside and drew a loaded one from his holster but didn't shoot again. He couldn't afford to waste another shot.

The sloop continued to burn, listing to the starboard side, further from the safety of Raskel's ship. He stumbled, only to be caught by an Avowed teenager who looked too confused to be afraid.

"Captain, what do we do?" the Cutthroat asked.

"Jump for it!" Raskel shouted as he sprinted through the raging fires and leaped over the gunwale. His head slammed into the hull as his fingers curled around the ratlines.

A dozen Cutthroats followed the captain's lead and leaped for the *Widowmaker*. All but two lost their grip and slipped into the sea below. Then there was laughter, which bubbled up from the abyssal waves. High-pitched, like the laughter of children. Except it was maddening and ceaseless.

The unending laughter of syrens.

Though he did not see their horrid, misshapen faces, Raskel saw the silhouettes of their humanoid forms as they broke the water's surface—and the necks of the Cutthroats. Gray, long-clawed, and webbed fingers raked through flesh and pulled the Avowed beneath the surface. One drowning Cutthroat fought back, stabbing at the gray horde with a cutlass while treading water, which only made the syrens laugh harder. They ripped him to pieces, and his blood turned the whitecaps crimson.

The syrens never stopped laughing, but the sea swept away their voices as they slunk back into its depths. In their wake, the silence was worse.

Raskel had no time to grieve. Instead, he clambered up the ropes. So did the other two Avowed near the other mast, but as they climbed, the red-eyed shadow reemerged. Gunshots rang through the scream-filled air, and both Cutthroats fell from the side of the ship, dead before the sea could drown them.

The syrens took those corpses too.

Alone but unscathed, Raskel hefted himself over the gunwale and pulled himself to his feet—only to feel a sword slip between his ribs.

Raskel stared in disbelief at his chest as red eyes gleamed before him. The shadow kicked him backward, twisting the blade as it slid from his flesh. The captain's legs buckled as he gasped. Tears spilled from his eyes. His back slammed into the gunwale, and he fumbled for his last flintlock just before the sword skewered his hand against the deck.

Raskel screamed for what felt like minutes, hours even.

Then the moon cleared the darkness from the shadow's face, revealing black paint covering leather armor, bow, arrows, blades, flintlocks, and bare skin.

For the first time, the adrenaline that had carried Raskel through countless battles subsided, and mortality weighed heavily on his screaming chest. He slumped against the gunwale as his lungs filled with blood. "Ain't a shadow at all, are you? Not a monster, just painted to look like one."

It stared at him, silent as it stole his white cutlass and leveled a flintlock pistol at his head.

"You tricked us. Lured us in so you could take my ship, kill my crew." The world dimmed as Raskel's blinks lengthened. More blood dribbled from his lips as he asked, "But... *why?* You already had a ship. Why burn yours to take ours?"

"Why not?" it sneered, voice containing more fire and rage than even the wreckage glowing behind him.

"Damn you," Raskel coughed between rattling half-breaths. "Damn you to the Core."

"We are all damned."

The gunpowder ignited, and a lead ball shattered Raskel's skull.

CHAPTER TWO

The shadow left the Avowed captain's corpse to rot on the main deck. She descended the ladder with a cutlass in one hand and a lantern in the other. The darkness sneered at her from crevices as she made her way toward the lowest deck. Yet the shadow hadn't needed the light to find what she was looking for. She only had to follow the smell.

Shit, piss, and bile permeated the air as the shadow opened the door to the slavehold. She raised the lantern, revealing thirty-six chained slaves shoved into cages. Some scrambled back from the light like rats. Others mumbled and prayed amidst growing sobs.

Pathetic, the shadow thought without an ounce of empathy. *I need killers. Not rats.*

She almost turned around and abandoned the men, but one slave—isolated from the others and kept in a private cage—made her hesitate. A hulking man with ripcord muscles, he was filthy and covered in rags. His nails were long and grimy, and his feet bled from where the rats nipped him. White dandruff flakes salted his greasy black hair, and open sores oozed across his scaly skin. Scars marred his body, some from scurvy but most from blades and knuckles. It wasn't his appearance that she focused on, but the way the slave held himself—he didn't back away from her as the others had. Instead, he tried to stand straighter, would have if not for the chains that bound him to the floor. A killer?

The shadow smiled, offering a crooked expression filled with patient rage—a mockery of a crescent moon. It only made the slaves cower further.

"Are you Eo?" one slave asked as fear, thirst, and death clung to his words.

Eo. The name echoed around the compartment, the slaves' voices a mixture of hope and awe. Some sniffed and wiped away tears, but a few of the weaker ones openly wept.

The shadow ignored them. Her eye twitched, though none could see it. She hated the Gods, Eo foremost among the pantheon. *The Gods are silent,* the shadow thought. *That is why your precious Goddess is unseen and unheard. But I will speak for Her. I will make you all believers—my believers. So long as you all can be of use.*

Her grin widened as she approached the isolated slave and asked, "Are you a killer or a rat?" Her voice was grim and quiet, yet as loud as a cannon in the silence between words and breaths.

"I'm Greeley," he said, still straining against his chains.

"Greeley," the shadow echoed, rolling the name across her tongue. She liked the taste of it. "A killer, then." She inched closer. "But what use is a killer in a cage?"

"Open it and find out," Greeley said, maintaining eye contact.

I can use this one. Her grin didn't waver, but the darkness around the lantern constricted tighter. As did the silence. Then metal clinked as the shadow pulled out a ring of keys, dangling them in front of Greeley while standing out of his reach. "You are strong, Greeley, but you could be much stronger."

"You think you're stronger than me?" Greeley asked, baring his teeth.

"I know I am," the shadow said, dropping the keys at Greeley's feet. "Give me your strength, Greeley, and I will make you a warrior. Give me your loyalty, and I will make you a leader. Give me both, and I will make you a Champion. It is what you want most in life, is it not?"

"How do you know what I want?" Greeley asked, kneeling to grab the keys before fiddling with his manacles. The metal chains fell from his hands as Greeley turned his attention to the door.

"All men want the same thing." The shadow watched Greeley's eyes, expression, and movements. He was determined and focused, but he didn't look like one who was grateful for freedom. *He is going to attack me,* she thought coldly. *Good.* Quietly, she took two steps backward and opened the lantern with painted fingers in preparation. *Come at me, Greeley. Face your master.*

As Greeley turned the lock and threw open the door, she extinguished the light and stepped to the side, ducking low. The wind whooshed above her shaved head as she turned and stood behind the killer. Silently, she drew her talan and held the curved dagger against his throat. "All men want *control*," she whispered, jamming a flintlock into his lower back without pulling the trigger. "But only a Champion has that. Others do as they are told. *Walk*."

Greeley walked, and together, they ascended to the main deck. There, he saw her level of control.

Blood-soaked corpses laid on the deck. Most had torn throats, but the dead captain had a bullet between his eyes. A pillar of fire, smoke, and ash rose in the distance as a sloop—*her* sloop—sank into the frigid waters. Several small figures ran along its deck, trapped both by the flames aboard and the laughing syrens waiting for them to dive into the sea. Rather than await their slow deaths, some pressed pistols to their heads and pulled the triggers. Gunshots rang out as their bodies tumbled into the outstretched arms of the deep terrors who ate them merrily. Before long, only the burning crow's nest was all that remained of the sloop. But even that was claimed by the Drowned Sea.

"You did... *all* of this?" Greeley asked as the menace vanished from his voice.

"This is what it means to be a Champion, Greeley. To *control*. But strength is nothing without loyalty. Loyalty is nothing without strength. I need both. Will you give them to me?"

Greeley relaxed, somehow calmed by the mayhem. "Yes."

"Good." The shadow removed the gun from his back and the knife from his throat. "Now face me."

Greeley did as he was told.

"Go, Greeley," the shadow said. "Release the other killers, but leave the cowards—the *rats*—to rot."

Greeley nodded, turned, and was swallowed by darkness once more.

The shadow smiled as she waited, having found her first follower. Greeley would be a strong and loyal warrior, but a Champion? Never. He'd be a useful tool, as would the rest. They'd play their part as long as she kept them busy and exhausted. Just as she'd been taught.

Eventually, Greeley returned with others, but not all. The shadow smiled in satisfaction as she heard the wailing screams of cowards left to rot below deck. Had all the prisoners been released, there'd be no reminder of their enslavement. No anchor. No iron spike to drive the memory through their skin and into their hearts.

Good. Let them scream. I have no use for cowards.

The killers assembled before her, picking their way through the bodies left in her wake. Each took a moment to gaze upon the dead but not spit, leaving them to the fate of the Drowned. Their bodies would drift into the black depths, and their souls would remain anchored to the bloated flesh, never finding rest.

Let them have their hatred as I have mine, the shadow thought, seeing the lust for violence grow in their eyes just as it had in Greeley's. *Let it drive out everything else. Let it exhaust them.*

Then she spoke in Aenuite, the tongue of the eastern jungles, because the slaves wouldn't understand her words. Though the torrent of ebbing and flowing syllables sounded mystical and musical, she uttered a trail of obscenities against the silent Gods who had been deaf to her pleas. "Damned be the Gods. Cursed be Their Swords, Belts, and Crowns. Drown Them in the depths. Burn Them in the Core. Let Them know my pain." She waited, allowing the echo to fade, before switching back into the common Aritrastan tongue. "Praise be to You, Eo. My patron, my Unseen Lady."

"You're... not Eo?" one man asked. "Then who are you?"

"I am Lilyth the Red—Eo's Champion. The Unseen Lady came to me many moons ago and offered me Her blessings. Now, I am here to purge these seas in Her name. Praise be to our Goddess."

Lilyth reached down, dipping two fingers into the Avowed captain's blood before walking to Greeley. In a solemn, practiced gesture, she smeared the blood across his forehead into a sideways crescent moon. After, she offered another quick, blasphemous prayer in the ebbing Aenuite tongue.

"You are first to be freed, and you stand apart from the rest." Lilyth grabbed Greeley's right hand and pressed it into the blood at their feet. "For your strength this night, I name you the Red Hand—my lieutenant."

Red Hand. The name was meaningless to Lilyth, but she knew the weight of such titles: the promise of respect, of glory, of control. Yet she hadn't sworn a Drowned Sea oath for this promise, so she had no intention of keeping it.

Lilyth turned to the rest of the freed slaves and asked, "Who will be next to carry the Mark?"

Mark. Another name. Another empty ritual. Another anchor to exhaust them.

One by one, the men approached until all but the cowards below had received the crescent mark on their foreheads. Yet all of them stared wistfully at Greeley's red hand, which marked him as higher than them. It was the beginning of a hierarchy. Good.

As Greeley stood at Lilyth's right hand, she spoke to all of them. "You are my Red Legion. The Chosen of the Unseen Lady. You are as much mine as I am yours. Just as we are all Hers."

Chosen. Another title. Another lie.

Lilyth gestured grandly at the fading visage of the burning ship. "Together, we will be a scourge upon these seas and bring ruin to these Cutthroats. Together, we will be stronger than any chain. Together, we will be unbreakable. Together, we are the night!"

Lilyth the Red grinned at each of her legionnaires. They grinned back as she shouted, "Strength and loyalty!"

"Loyalty and strength!" the Red Legion shouted back.

Good, Lilyth thought. *Very good.*

Then she ordered the legionnaires to complete various tasks across the ship—they obeyed without question. One piloted the helm, three navigated by constellations and star charts, a dozen tended to the sails, and the rest looted the corpses before hurling their bodies overboard.

Though she could not see the syrens, Lilyth knew they were there. Just beneath the surface. Waiting. Always waiting.

"There will be plenty more soon," Lilyth said to them, gripping the rail tighter even as splinters stabbed her palms. She fought to keep the past at bay, but the sight of the waves, the smell of brine, and the sound of creaking planks dredged up memories best left forgotten. Those of drowning. Of cannons. Of blood. Of Cutthroats. Of being trapped in a wooden coffin floating across this endless sea—

Lilyth bit down on her tongue hard enough to draw blood, and the sharp pain returned her to the present moment. *Remember why you are here,* she thought. *Remember why you are doing this. It will all be worth it in the end. It has to be.*

Lilyth pulled out the necklace she always wore beneath her armor: a leather string with brown clay beads and a single worn feather. Her fingers brushed it as she remembered the daughter who had worn the necklace, lost it. A young girl with brown hair and eyes, a mischievous smile, and chubby legs and hands. The spitting image of her father. Both of them, together. Separated from Lilyth.

By Cutthroats.

By *Rolf.*

The image of her daughter and husband fell away as Lilyth envisioned the Cutthroat's sunken brown eyes, razor-thin mustache, and cruel smile. Rolf the Bloody, the Skull of Wrath. A captain who didn't bow to the Cutthroat King but kneeled only to his own sins. A breaker of men, of children, of *mothers.* Rolf was the embodiment of all she hated.

Releasing the rail, Lilyth's hands gripped each other, nails cutting skin like snakes devouring one another. She imagined wrapping her fingers around the man's throat and hearing him choke as he tried to scream. Lilyth grinned at the thought, but the smile didn't reach her eyes—twin funeral pyres that burned in a black corpse.

Then Rolf's face slipped away. Only darkness remained.

Hollowness overwhelmed Lilyth. She ground her teeth to keep from screaming, grabbed the gunwale to keep from collapsing, closed her eyes to keep from seeing the ocean she'd feared since her first voyage. *Just hold on for a little longer. I am coming. Gods be damned, I am coming as quickly as I can.*

"Gods be damned," she said in Aenuite, hoping Eo would hear her and finally respond.

But there was only silence.

The pyres in Lilyth's eyes blazed brighter.

CHAPTER THREE

Jameson Ash stood on the gunwale of the *Constable*, a three-masted frigate, and held onto a taut rope above his head for balance. The sun shined at his back, illuminating the hundreds of wooden ships docked and anchored just off of Port Alira's coast. All had arrived early for the Five-day Celebration, an Aritrastan holiday which had become an increasingly raucous occasion with each passing year. Those five days of merriment hid the other three-hundred-and-sixty days—forty ninedays broken into ten equal months—of sweltering life in this cauldron of disease, famine, soot, and pain. Five days of excess followed by hunger. Five days of boxing and gambling followed by murder and theft. Five days of drinking followed by drowning. Five days—

A hand slapped his back, and Jameson jumped from the gunwale onto the cathead. He whirled, unsheathing his cutlass and uttering a low growl. Jameson regretted both immediately as he noticed Captain Ink, the one-eyed Aritrastan man who'd snuck up behind him. Though his left eye was hidden behind a leather eye patch, the other one was piercing and aware enough for both of them.

"Is that any way to greet your captain?" Ink asked. He wore a loose-fitting white shirt, his exposed chest and hands covered in black tribal patterns from the island natives south of the Aritrastan mainland. His indigo overcoat was folded over the gunwale, taken everywhere but seldom worn. Despite being captain, Ink was never one to sit around and watch work being done.

"Sorry, captain." Jameson bent his head, hopping back down onto the deck. "Alira always brings out the worst in me."

"You'd think that the Fiveday would make a man forget even his name, but that memory of yours always comes back to haunt you, eh?" Ink asked.

"I'm not one to forget." Jameson scratched his scalp, trying to rid himself of childhood memories and dandruff. No such luck. After running his hands through his long dark hair, he sighed and fingered the red bracelet on his right wrist. It was a ratty cloth he'd stitched back together countless times—more stitching than cloth at this point. Yet he didn't dare part with it. The bracelet was as much a part of him as his beating heart—the last vestige of his childhood family. Quietly, Jameson added, "It would be easier if I could forget."

Ink snorted. "Life could always be easier. At least we'll have some time to drown our sorrows during the Fiveday—that is, if you're done brooding."

Ink pointed over to the *Pelican,* a three-masted barque, which the *Constable* had been guarding and escorting between the mainland and the island colonies for the past four months. When Jameson had last looked, dozens of ferrymen in rowboats were helping *Pelican* merchants and *Constable* mercenaries to deliver cargo—which could be anything from southern Corinthian sugar to eastern Stotan whale oils—to the dockyard. No boats circled the hull anymore. No syrens either. *Yet.*

"The cargo's all unloaded, my boy, and the merchants have paid me handsomely for our services," Ink said. "No need to be standing in these gales when we could already be three sheets to the wind."

Ink whistled sharply at a passing ferryman piloting a rowboat, and they haggled over price. When an agreement had been made—an absurd six copper sickles for a hundred-yard, one-way trip—Jameson and Ink climbed down a rope ladder to the water. Careful not to scrape against the sharp barnacles that clung to the hull, they stepped into the awaiting boat and sat on the bench thwarts as the ferryman rowed them to shore.

When they touched dry land, Jameson inhaled the salty air as his legs adjusted to the sand, which didn't sway with the rhythm of the seas. The ocean was so lively compared to such dead dirt.

Jameson's gait slowed as he admired the abandoned Wright, the strip of coastal land dedicated to the construction of new ships. Amidst iron and plank sheds, saw pits, and piles of fresh timber imported from the inland forests, the skeletons of partial hulls looked like the decaying bones of forgotten monsters whose ribs had been splayed open and picked clean.

Inland of the Wright was the Smithy district, which housed the shops of independent blacksmiths, shipwrights, and carpenters. Those Alirans normally waged price-wars with each other, but all had signed a temporary ceasefire during the Fiveday Celebration. Their businesses, too, were closed for the day.

Jameson and Ink left the beach and buildings behind, entering the southern market that was bustling with activity as merchants, farmers, and artisans sold their Fiveday wares. It was less a street of storefronts and more a maze of rickety, vibrant stands jockeying for attention. Glass baubles in all shades of color twinkled in displays like western Tavrakian gems. Silk, satin, and taffeta dresses that would have turned paupers into princesses hung from metal racks. Spiced apples, honeyed hams, and cinnamon pastries wafted from clay pans. From each vendor, voices cascaded like waves, crashing against Jameson with the sounds of laughter, haggling, and ecstasy.

But beneath the sights, smells, and sounds, Jameson could still detect the underlying stench of death that polluted the port. Unconsciously, his fingers touched the red cloth bracelet, and then the memories came rushing back.

Street urchins, clothed in rags thrown out by even the poorest Alirans, running barefoot through alleyways to escape larger urchins and chard addicts, who preyed on urchins of all sizes. They were known to sell children's corpses to butchers for that orange powder.

Street urchins, wearing colored scraps to differentiate their gangs, wielding broken glass and stabbing each other over scraps of meat and coins. Blood splattering stone. Fists shattering bone. Corpses left alone. So many dead for pitiful copper sickles. Many more over silver lunes. Nobody he'd known had ever even seen a gold crescent.

Street urchins, shivering and cuddling together to survive the cold winter, inhaling chard to feel a spark of warmth before it burned them from the inside out. Blackened noses that crumbled to dust along with their minds. A bad death, even by Jameson's standards, having known the depths of cruelty by age eight. Inflicted it by age ten.

There was no peace or rest for ashkids. Jameson's childhood gang—his family—was no exception. Death claimed their names and faces.

Daisy, the older rogue who'd taught Jameson how to pick pockets and cut purses. A gaunt face, hollow eyes with a spark of lunacy, mouth twisted in a grin that spoke of equal loss and laughter. Daisy had swung from the gallows for stealing in the Cloud District.

Posey, the caretaker who'd sewn up all of Jameson's wounds. A diamond face with warm hazel eyes and a sweet smile—beautiful enough to have been a courtesan if she hadn't been abandoned to the alleys. Posey had caved in her own skull after being driven crazy by the Whispering Madness, an incurable illness spread by rats.

Eliza, the lover who'd kept Jameson warm in the cold months. An angular face with a cleft chin, auburn hair, and a small scar across her left cheek that had wormed when she laughed. Eliza had disappeared one day after becoming addicted to chard.

Josh, the best friend who'd gifted Jameson his red bracelet. A smashed face with jet black hair, green eyes, and a too-quick mouth. Josh had been ambushed by a rival gang and left to die alone in the grimy alleyways with a shiv in his stomach.

Jameson let go of his bracelet, took in a deep breath, and forced his eyes open. *Don't think about the past,* he thought. *Stick to the present. Ground yourself. What do you see, smell, hear, feel?*

Around him, fishermen sold trout, bakers displayed glazed pastries, and artisans sold faux silks. *I lost Ink,* Jameson realized with a frown as he turned in a circle. Dread gripped his chest as he strolled deeper into the marketplace to find him.

Erin Rose hid in an alleyway as sailors and merchants mingled with the Aliran locals in the southern market. Soot-faced, her eyes darted from faces to pockets as she shifted her weight, ready to run at a moment's notice. Shoeless, her hardened soles could absorb the pain of the pebbles and dirt as long as she avoided the broken glass. But she didn't need to run.

In the splendor of the Fiveday Celebration, Erin remained unseen and unheard.

Spices, rums, and other expensive, exotic imports were on display in stands across the marketplace. Made of driftwoods and timbers from the northern forest, the stands were decrepit but displayed fine colored powders, shell necklaces, glass-blown figurines, beautiful garments, and jewelry that glinted in the sun.

So many pretty things that meant so little to Erin. What use was colored powder when urchins were after her? Or, a shell necklace when chard addicts cornered her? Glass-blown figurines could be smashed for a quick getaway, but even then, only used once—better to use an empty bottle for that than a nice figurine. Showy garments and jewelry only made her more visible, as well as less piteous. She couldn't be wearing a nice dress and earrings while begging for spare coins—not successfully, anyway.

It was far more difficult to ignore the bakers nearby, who were watching for hungry little urchins with hawk-like eyes. The smell of sweet pastries caressed her face, kissing her nose. Erin stamped her feet and plugged her nose even as her stomach protested.

Dad told me to find a mark—not food, Erin thought, driving away her hunger. *If we can get some coin, we can eat later. Just have to focus.*

Merchants shouted their wares and prices as others passed by, often exchanging copper sickles and silver lunes with buyers. Though she kept an eye out, gold crescents weren't exchanged in the outer markets. Only in the walled inner city, where denizens of the Cloud District and the Jade Parliament couldn't comprehend hunger. Even during the Fiveday, they kept to their district and their own celebrations. Rumors had reached Erin's ears of elegant balls, where wealthy couples danced beneath chandeliers made of rubies and diamonds, and banquet halls, where elites gorged themselves on exotic animals of the eastern Aenuite jungles. Erin would have given anything to see inside, but she didn't even have a single sickle to give.

Find the mark and steal a sickle, Erin thought. From the shadows, she examined mannerisms of buyers. The length of gait, formality of tone, alertness of eyes, hunch of shoulders, and speed of hands were all indications of potential targets. Best of all were the movement of lips—even from her distance, Erin could read them. Some spoke of politics, others of ships and spices, but most were haggling for prices. She paid special attention to those who could afford anything worth a lune.

Erin's focus crumbled as the smell of nearby cinnamon bread invaded her nostrils again. Her stomach rumbled, and she winced, biting her lip. *I can steal one. Just one. Then I'll find a mark.*

Erin looked at the baker, whose flour-dusted apron flapped in the wind as she barked out prices while leaning on a cane. Her skin was blue leather,

her hair white wisps. Reflections of the sea and sky—old as dirt. The woman took a breath between calls before sitting in a teetering chair that threatened to collapse.

A frown tugged at Erin's lips. Her stomach grumbled again, though this time she ignored it and the bread both. *Dad says we can't steal from the elderly.*

Erin forced aside the cinnamon temptation as her eyes trailed a twenty-something sailor, lean instead of strong. Long tattoos of serpents, ships, and stars twisted around his arms and disappeared into his rolled-up sleeves. A sword hung on his hip, but his hands were far from it. Instead, he kept fidgeting with a ratty red bracelet on his wrist. He walked slower than most, stopping to stare at market displays with a wistful eye and a phantom smile. Erin memorized his rectangular face: wild black hair, green eyes, thin lips, and a scarred cleft chin.

That's him. That's the mark, Erin thought, stepping out of the alleyway and following the sailor farther into the market.

◆◇◆

While a young baker's back was turned, Jameson stole a pastry. Its sweetness pushed away his bitter memories as he walked deeper into the market. Baked goods and fish vendors transitioned to jewelry, fabrics, and colored powders with which Alirans dusted the city. Blues, whites, yellows, greens, browns, and reds—all to honor their Gods. But never black, never Kuma.

On a hastily constructed platform in the center of the market, fiddlers, lyrists, and lutists played songs while dancers competed for prizes: bundles of food, soaps, and trinkets. The music filled the air as paupers, who were usually stoic and dirty, joined in the merriment and danced between the market stalls. Husbands danced with their wives, brothers with sisters, and fathers with daughters. Even a few urchins danced, though most still clung to the alleyways rather than venture into the bright market stalls.

Jameson watched the celebration with a smile and stomped in time with the beat of the music. He ripped off another part of the bread and popped it into his mouth, closing his eyes as the sugar gnawed his gums. When he opened them again, an urchin appeared between the merchant tables. A young girl with straw arms and legs, watching him with an eye of desperation.

Jameson flinched at the uncanny similarity between the girl and Posey.

The girl was no older than twelve, though she could have been as young as nine. Malnutrition made it difficult to know her exact age. Her feet were bare, probably cut and scarred from running through the ashkids' paradise: the ruins of old Alira just east of the outer wall. Dirt clung beneath her nails, and soot gripped her face and hair. She probably hadn't bathed in weeks—not with freshwater, anyway.

A bath in these waters is as good as swimming in mud, Jameson thought.

Beneath the urchin grime, he could see the young child underneath: the blonde-white hair, the shocking blue eyes, and the missing baby teeth. Her attention flicked from Jameson down to the pastry in his hand.

Trying to put fresh vigor into his voice, Jameson kneeled in front of her and said, "Hey, come over here, little one."

The girl took a step backward, but before she could run, he tore the pastry in half. Her feet hesitated as her eyes and nose were glued to the sweet bread. Jameson held out the larger half toward her. "My stomach can't handle sweets very well, and I've been looking for somebody to help me eat this pastry. Can you help a sailor out? I'd be in your debt."

The little girl looked at him, intelligent eyes glimmering with confusion. Jameson opened his mouth to ask again as her fingers darted out, snatching the sweet bread almost as fast as he could blink.

Jameson could have kicked himself for being surprised. *She has to be fast to survive here.* He looked around for other urchins, knowing they'd fight her for the bread. Off behind a table, several kids watched the two of them with parched lips and hardened eyes. He glared at them, baring his teeth. They darted a little farther away but remained in sight.

As Jameson turned his eyes back to the girl, she'd already wolfed down the pastry and was now sucking at her fingers.

Eat whenever possible, he thought. It had been one of the first rules he had learned in Alira. As with everything, he had learned it the hard way. By the look of things, so had she. *If she's smart, she'll get out of here as quickly as she can. Quicker than I did.* More memories of torn feet, fistfights, blood, hunger, and fear. So much fear—

"Good lass," he said to stop the memories, shivering despite the blazing sun overhead. "You best take care of yourself now. And run the opposite way, you hear? The others are still—"

Bumping into his side, the girl took off away from Jameson and the boys.

"Watching," Jameson finished. He checked his pockets, noticing that a couple of spare copper coins were missing but only laughed. "She'll need it more than me, I think." A smile crossed his face, albeit a bittersweet one.

Then he realized that the red bracelet, the sole reminder of his urchin family, was also gone. The smile fell and anger blazed. "Wait!" Jameson shouted, standing. "Give that back!"

The girl ran faster.

Jameson sprinted after her.

Chapter Four

Jameson knocked into a couple of vendors, yelling back apologies as they cursed and raised their fists. He jumped over tables while the girl scurried beneath them with all the speed and agility of a practiced street urchin. Breathing heavily, Jameson followed her east until she darted through an alleyway into the Chasm District—his old home.

"*No!*" Jameson stopped at the alleyway's edge, unwilling to enter because he knew *exactly* where it led: to the ashes, which were all that remained of his family.

I can't be here. Hand at the pommel of his cutlass, Jameson took a few steps back. This was the closest he'd come to the Chasm since leaving it a decade ago. Instinctively, his eyes darted around, peering into the dilapidated alleyways for any signs of an ambush. While he didn't see any urchins, Jameson knew better than to look away. Rats and men lurked in those shadows, just waiting for him to turn around so they could drag him back into that hell.

Jameson's eyes flickered between buildings, windows, and alleys. Countless shacks and lean-tos had been built around and on top of the original brick homes that had long ago been condemned. These newer dwellings were made of driftwood, stolen lumber, and even cobblestones, which had been pried from the very streets. Roofs were connected with long wooden timbers and blankets that blocked out all light, shrouding the alleys in shadow even at the sun's highest peak.

Instead of a city district, the Chasm resembled an urban jungle, whose animals—rats, addicts, and urchins—had bites worse than those of the eastern tropics. Not even fire could conquer the Chasm, for grime covered the buildings so thoroughly that the district couldn't be burned—Jameson had tried twice after all of his friends became ash but to no avail.

The bracelet is all I have left of them, Jameson thought, desperately. "I'll make a trade for the bracelet!" He shouted just outside the alleyway. "What do you want? More money? Fine! Just... Just give me the damn bracelet!"

Nobody within the Chasm responded, but a voice behind him said, "You there! What's the matter?"

Jameson turned to see three men in purple cloaks and leather-and-metal vests approaching from the market: gallowmen, the Aliran city guard who patrolled the outer city with swords and truncheons.

"Urchin took my coin," Jameson said. "Already scurried away."

"Just like the rats, they are! Damn them!" the chief gallowman said. "Best to cut your losses and enjoy the Fiveday. You'll forget all about it after a couple of drinks and a girlie or two."

Jameson gritted his teeth, knowing better than to insult the men. The gallowmen were stationed in the city to protect the rich from the poor—not to protect sailors from urchins. While they never ventured more than ten feet into the Chasm's depths and lived to tell the tale, they would certainly beat him to death in the middle of the street.

After the gallowmen left to patrol the market, Jameson looked into the Chasm again. "I'll give you a silver for the bracelet, kid!" he winced, hearing the word in his own ears. Saying a word like *copper* aloud was asking to be mugged. *Silver* and *gold* invited murder. But Jameson needed that bracelet. He even pulled a lune from his purse and raised it so anybody within the alley could see it, despite the danger of the gesture. "Give me the bracelet, and it's yours!"

I'll give you another bracelet, Jameson, a familiar voice whispered from the darkness. *But you can keep the lune. All you have to do is come a little closer.*

Taking several more steps away from the Chasm, a chill crawled up Jameson's spine. He felt small and weak as he'd once been. "Josh?"

Wrong way, Jameson.

It *was* Josh. There was no mistaking those green eyes, black hair, and anvil face as he limped out of the alley toward Jameson. Josh was different now, though. His skin was ash, his smile sinister. One hand clutched his stomach while the other held a red bracelet dripping with blood. *His* blood.

Jameson's legs buckled. He stumbled backward and landed on his ass, dropping the lune. Josh tittered with laughter—dark laughter. He lifted the red bracelet toward Jameson with both hands, even as his entrails spilled out from his stomach and dragged across the dirt.

Don't you want it, Jameson? I made it special—just for you.

"I... I—" Jameson's voice broke, and his legs refused to move. He could only watch as Josh limped closer. Ten feet... eight feet... five feet... "You're dead, Josh. You've been dead for years."

But you remembered me, Jameson—that makes me alive. We're all *alive.*

Dead children appeared at the alley's exit, all the corpses of the past. Some with shanks sticking out of their chests and necks. Others with black noses, orange lips, and oozing sores. Several with eyes missing, clawed out by their own fingers because of the Whispering Madness. A few with broken, hanging necks and nooses around their throats. All wore red bracelets and beckoned to him with the insidious smiles and laughter of syrens.

Come back with us, Jameson. Josh said, kneeling beside him as the dead children formed a semicircle around Jameson. *We can be a family again. All you have to do is take my hand and follow me—just like you used to. Remember that?*

Jameson remembered, but he shook his head anyway. "You're not real. *None* of this is real." As Josh reached toward him with the bracelet, Jameson leaned back only for a hand to grab his shoulder.

Jameson looked up to see a blonde, barrel-chested sailor whose breath smelled of sour beer and mutton. His right arm held Jameson, and the left, a crutch, for his left leg was missing. He flicked the lune to Jameson and said, "Hey! What d'you think you're doing, boy? Waving money around like that'll get you killed in these parts!"

Jameson didn't answer. Instead, he turned back to Josh and the other dead ashkids, but they were all gone. Disappeared as if they'd never existed. Perhaps they hadn't. Not knowing whether to laugh or cry, Jameson sat in the dirt, too stunned to reply.

The man let go of Jameson's shoulder and said, "Say, looks like you've seen a ghost—maybe even a wraith or two. You feelin' alright?"

"Better now," Jameson said, swallowing the rising fear. He was slow to his feet and slower still to take his eyes off of the alleyway. "Thanks."

"Easy to be a helping hand during the Fiveday, it is," the sailor said. "John Steward, I am. Belonging to the *King's Ransom*, I be."

"Jameson," he said, hiding a trembling hand. He still felt eyes watching him, unsure if they were alive or dead. "First mate aboard the *Constable*."

"No surname, son?" John asked.

Jameson bit his tongue. Having no parents, being called *son* or *my boy* was something only Ink was allowed to do. And even then, sparingly. But Jameson held his words, if only for fear of alienating John and being alone again. "Not one of consequence. Ash."

Ash. A name shared by orphans, as much a sign of respect among their kind as it was an insult by others. One of the few traditions that Jameson had kept. That and the bracelet, which had now been returned to the ashes.

"An ashboy turned straight as I live and breathe?" John asked. "Meaning no offense, of course."

Jameson nodded, eyeing the alley. "As much as a bent nail can be straightened."

"Why, that's a tale I'd pay to hear!" John said, his face alighting with a grin. "How's about we get ourselves a drink and swap stories? I'm parched, and you look like you need something to settle the nerves."

"As long as it's not anywhere near here," Jameson said, too grateful to escape the Chasm to be particularly suspicious of John. Being that he had only one leg set Jameson further at ease. Unlike the girl, John couldn't run away from him—not fast, at any rate.

"That's a good man." The crippled sailor clapped him on the back and limped away from the alleyway. "Come on, I know the best spots."

Jameson followed him down the narrow path between market stalls and lean-tos. John still talked, but Jameson didn't listen, looking back over his shoulder for any signs of the girl and his bracelet. He almost ran into John, who'd stopped to watch two young sailors push their way out of a nearby tavern, unsheathe their cutlasses, and bark insults at one another like dogs fighting for scraps. A crowd of locals gathered to watch, several gallowmen among them, circling to cut off escape into the Chasm. As was the custom, they'd intervene only after somebody died. That was for murders *outside* the Chasm, anyway.

"My money's on the tall one," said John.

Jameson appraised both men. The taller man was lanky but graceful, the stout man more bullish—likely to run headfirst into a blade. "I think I'll hold off on that bet."

"Not a gambler, I take it." The sailor's gut shook with his bellowing laugh.

"Not when I'm sure I'll lose." Jameson said, no longer watching the fight. He was more interested in the urchins working their way through the crowd, as likely to steal as they were to watch. They picked at least five pockets before the stout man threw himself on his enemy's blade, and they slipped away unnoticed as the gallowmen apprehended the lanky sailor.

"Well, so much for that—over too quick, if you ask me, but men don't duel like they used to. Come inside. I'll treat you to a drink!" John threw open the door to the tavern, and Jameson followed him inside.

Though several patrons had passed out in the corners of the tavern, more were still raising their tankards to their lips. A fiddler played in the background, and in drunken-kindness, a couple of customers threw copper pieces into his open case. Limping around the intoxicated patrons, John approached the bar and ordered two steins of ale. When the mugs were filled, Jameson grabbed one without a word, as John only had one free hand.

By the time they'd navigated through the crowd toward an empty table in the back corner, John's light beard already glistened with foamy ale. "So, you're aboard the *Constable*, you said?" John asked, his eyes widening with interest. He flashed a toothy grin, revealing more gums than teeth. "Heard she's a Guardian. A mighty fine escort on these seas."

"And I've heard the *King's Ransom* is a fast barque—carries a lot of coin," Jameson said, comfortable now that his back was to the wall. Nobody could sneak up behind him, least of all the ghosts.

"Enough to be considered a king's ransom, mate." John winked with a blue eye.

"You have enough protection?" Jameson asked, only half-joking because Guardians like the *Constable* were always looking for a better payout. He took another sip of his drink, trying not to wince at the putrid taste. *Worse than I remember. But so is everything else.*

"Ha! Could always use more protection. If I'd done it right, I wouldn't have any youngsters, would I?" Jameson couldn't suppress his grin, and John shared in the laugh. "Oh, you meant for the ship? Suppose you can never have enough protection with men like Captain Rolf around."

Several sailors stopped mid-conversation to stare at John, muttering under their breaths and making warding gestures with their fingers.

"Phah!" John spat at them, though he lowered his voice. "A superstitious lot, sailors be. They think that just by saying a man's name, you're invoking a curse on yourself!"

Jameson winced, thinking of Rolf the Bloody, who'd murdered the prior Skull of Wrath to become one of the seven rulers of Port Tibur near the center of the Drowned Sea. Unlike the Cutthroat King of Port Noble, the seven Skulls ruled Tibur as a coalition, each defined by their chosen sin: sloth, gluttony, lust, avarice, envy, pride, and wrath. Rolf's cruelty was unmatched—as was his skill with the cutlass. That made him powerful even among the other Skulls. Rolf might have been able to depose the Cutthroat King himself, if not for his insatiable appetite to pillage the seas. According to myth, Rolf the Bloody would attack ships and kill all but a handful of the crew, forcing them to fight each other to the death for entertainment. Then he'd hang the dead bodies from the gunwales to chum the waters—intentionally attracting the syrens to his ship.

Jameson shuddered at the thought of such a madman. "Can't say I disagree with them."

"Ah. A superstitious mate, are you?" John asked, leaning in.

Jameson shifted in his seat and said, "No. Just cautious."

"Then I'll tell you something, mate. Just between you and me." John grabbed Jameson's shoulder. "There have been strange tales from the sea as of late."

"There're always strange rumors on the seas, John," he said with a smirk as he leaned backward, out of the stout man's reach. "Which story is it now? Krakens? Ghosts? Drowned? Or is it one of the nameless deep terrors?"

"Wish it were just a story," John said solemnly, tilting his head to the left. Jameson looked over and saw a haggard man sitting in the corner, not quite in a drunken stupor, but close to it. His beard was long and unkempt, his shirt soiled. Still, the man looked powerful enough to fight the entire tavern. "That's Bareknuckle Bruce, mate. Been telling me things, he has."

"Drunken truths are sober lies, John," Jameson replied, though amiably.

"So you'd think, but that man used to have confidence... and *balls.* They call him *Bareknuckle* for a reason." Jameson looked at Bruce's fingers. Even from this distance, they were pillars of stone. "Now look at him. Drinks himself stupid every day."

"Not uncommon for a sailor," Jameson said, raising an eyebrow and his cup.

"The man never drank before last month," John said, his attention never leaving Bruce. Jameson looked at John with a dubious eye, so the sailor added, "The man never drank. Swear to it, I do."

But not on the Drowned Sea, Jameson thought. *That's the only swear that matters.* Looking down at his drink, he chided himself. *The man's a gossip.* He sighed, resting more comfortably in his seat. *At least I'm getting a drink out of this nonsense.*

John looked around to ensure they weren't overheard before whispering, "You ever heard of the *Jewel*, son?"

Jameson twitched at the name. *Son.* He only let Ink call him that. Politely but firmly, he said, "Son of James, not of John. But no, I haven't. Should I have?"

"Wasn't of note until four months ago. The *Jewel* was a merchant barquentine, much like the ones you Guardians are always escorting down the way. Except this captain wasn't near superstitious enough. Forgot, or maybe even flat out refused, to pay his respects to the sea. No meat, no rum, no gold, no *nothing.* Now, as I heard, everything was well for the first day or so, but after that? A storm befell the *Jewel*, it did, and the syrens came with it. First, they destroyed the rudder—left 'em like gulls without wings, they did. Then harpoons and tridents came flying from the depths, catching men's flesh and dragging them back down into the waters, screaming all the way. Laughed, the syrens did. Laughed as men screamed. Starved the rest of them out. Stuck on that sea for months, they were. And when they ran out of food and water, the survivors cracked, turned on each other until only a few remained."

"Never heard of a syren leaving survivors. Just empty ships," Jameson said, polishing off his stein despite the horrid taste of the swill.

"Right you are, son of James. They would have died, too, but it just so happens that Bareknuckle Bruce found them on the waves, he did. Told me he found the last of those cracked men eating each other from ankle to neck."

Jameson had heard far scarier stories, but a chill crawled up his spine. His stomach felt queasy, and his hands were sweaty. Jameson stared down at his drink as the edges of his vision blurred. He blinked all-too-slowly, and it took a lot of strength to open his eyes again.

"I've... I've gotta go," Jameson whispered. He tried to stand up, but his legs trembled weakly as he did so. Falling back to the seat, John grinned and laughed as if Jameson had just told him a funny joke.

"Starting to affect you, has it?" John asked with a theatrical grin.

"What... what'd you do?" Jamson asked, looking from his hands to the stein and back.

"There seems to be a little sleeping powder in your drink. Won't tell you how it got there, though. A magician never reveals his secrets," John replied, laughing again. "But it works quick, my boy. Won't do nothing except give you a nice bit of rest—"

"Jameson!" a voice shouted behind him. *Ink.* "Bring your friend over here and join us!"

"Of all the squalling luck," John said, his grin never leaving his expression.

Jameson fumbled for his knife, but his movements were slowing. John caught his hand and forced the blade back down into the sheath.

"No need for that, lad." He reached into Jameson's coat, feeling for the wages Ink had given him. When he found it, John slipped it into his waistband. "Hope you enjoy the Fiveday. There'll be plenty more stories to be heard. Some may even be true." With a wink, John got up from the booth and shouted to the other sailors, "Been deep in the cups, he has! You might need to take him over to the inn. Spent all his coin on alcohol!"

Jameson could feel the rough hands of men around him, helping him up. If he could have spoken, he would have cursed himself for being so foolish. He made it only five feet before his vision became night.

CHAPTER FIVE

Erin held her father's hand as they walked through the Merchant District, having snuck through the market to escape from any friends of the sailor he'd robbed. It seemed unnecessary, as Erin hadn't seen anyone following her dad, but it was still safer to get to the opposite side of Alira.

Dad hummed beneath his breath as Erin walked in time with his crippled gait. She stared up at his face, catching the glimmer of impish glee in his expression. Like her, there was a layer of grime underneath his nails and dirt in his blonde hair and beard.

"You did so well, my rose," Dad said, dropping his fake accent and squeezing her hand. "But I don't want you taking more risks than you have to, okay? There're many people that can hurt you out there. Especially in the Chasm."

Erin rolled her eyes but said, "Okay, Dad." She rolled a copper sickle along her fingers, the same sailor's red bracelet twisting as she turned her wrist to perform a more difficult sleight of hand.

Rising above the other structures was Eo the Unseen's temple, a fifty-foot-tall columned structure made of concrete and fluorine, which made the temple glow like thousands of stars after dusk. In front of the dozens of stairs leading to the tall entrance doors was a twenty-foot-diameter fountain. At its center, water arced from the raised sword of a ten-foot-tall stone warrior and splashed into the shallow pool at his feet.

Aritras the Red, she knew. From the stories her dad had told her, Aritras was the only person who'd ever found a Sword of the Gods. He'd used it to kill the Forgotten King of the Deadlands to the east, conquer the northern lands, and become the Champion of Eo, the Unseen Lady.

How easy would life have been with a magical Sword containing the power of a Goddess? Erin marveled at the thought, imagining her face on the statue. *If only Eo gave me the chance, I could be just as powerful as Aritras. With that power, I could do anything. Dad would never have to worry about money, and I'd never be hungry. A Sword would solve all our problems.*

Except, Erin knew that there was no chance at finding a Sword. Ever.

Disappointed, she turned her gaze to the small congregation of Eo worshipers gathered near the fountain. Among them was a pale man with long black hair and red robes—an Eonian priest. He caught Erin's gaze and smiled as she waved sheepishly back at him. Then the priest returned to tossing copper sickles into the basin at Aritras's feet. There were hundreds—if not thousands—of sickles glittering in that water, and it was easily within reach.

If I could just get a handful every day, it wouldn't be long before I could get a gold crescent—enough for me and Dad to leave the Chasm and Port Alira forever, she thought before she felt the statue of Aritras the Red scolding her. Erin's cheeks reddened, and she kept her head down out of shame.

Like the elderly, priests and their temples were off limits out of respect and love for the Gods—Eo chief among them. Erin had only broken that rule once. Years ago, she stole a single copper sickle from Aritras's pool to buy a loaf of bread she shared with her dad. When he realized where she got the sickle, her dad was so horrified that he dragged her back to the fountain and made her throw two sickles back in. Erin still felt guilty about that and didn't dare to do more than dream about stealing the coins. Even then, she was ashamed of herself.

They walked further through the district, passing two smaller temples. One was dedicated to Eo's twin: Io the Bright, Goddess of the day and the sun. Her temple was also made of concrete, but its columns were of living trees. The surrounding area had been de-cobblestoned so that sunflowers could sprout from the dirt.

The other temple was claimed by Kovu the Wise, God of the skies and storms. His resembled a cylindrical tower with oddly shaped holes and complex architectural patterns. When the winds blew through the structure, it vibrated and whistled with music that reminded Erin of wind chimes.

Together, those three major deities were worshipped by sailors and merchants who sought protection on the Drowned Sea. While five others were worshipped privately in homes and in shops, none dared speak of the ninth and final God, Kuma the Chained—He who created the Drowned Sea and its monsters.

Temples gave way to higher-end inns and boutiques. The brick-walled stores attracted patrons with dazzling lamps, glass displays, and painted signs. Erin slowed her gait to gaze longer at the stores carrying dresses and shoes. Sometimes, she aligned her reflection with that of the mannequin, just so she could imagine what she'd look like in one of those crescent-priced red dresses.

How would it be to wear that and dance the night away at a Cloud District ball? Erin failed to imagine it. She'd only ever danced with Dad in their shack. Though he tried his best, he wasn't a good dancer. Being one legged, Dad often joked that he didn't even have two left feet—let alone one.

The other problem was that Erin couldn't afford a dress like that. Nothing close to it. Erin stared at the ragged clothes she'd grown out of almost a year ago but still wore because she'd been unable to buy new ones. Her eyes trailed lower to her scarred, shoeless feet. They were a shade darker than the rest of her light blue skin because of the layer of grime. *Who would ever want to take me to a ball?*

The question crushed her spirits as much as the wealthy couple who walked toward her. The man was in a blue three-piece suit with long coattails and silver buttons shinier than most lunes. The woman was wearing the same dress that Erin had been eyeing as well as crystal earrings shaped into waning moons. Both sneered down at her through their noses.

"I thought I smelled rats," the man said as he passed, causing the woman to laugh.

Erin opened her mouth to say, *And your girlie snorts like a pig,* but stopped herself when Dad squeezed her hand more firmly. He shook his head, and Erin shut her mouth, even as she gritted her teeth. *They act like they're so much better than us—like they're better than Dad...*

After they disappeared down the street and around the corner, Erin said, "We should go. We stand out too much here. The gallowmen—"

"Won't see us because we won't be long," Dad said as he shrank against the side of the building to be less obvious.

Amidst ornate shops and extravagant inns, the taverns also catered to the wealthier patrons. Instead of tankards of ale, glasses of red and white wines accompanied the pompous talk and laughter.

"See anyone?" Dad asked.

A couple of younger men walked into the tavern, moving with a confidence that suggested money-filled pockets. Their white wigs, tan suits with knee-high socks, and golden bracelets all supported this theory. The man on the left had a lurching gait. If things went wrong, he'd be easy to outrun—for Erin, at least. The man on the right was tossing an apple into the air and catching it with ease. Youth and daring glinted in his eyes as he tracked the apple.

"Guy with the apple," Erin said without gesturing. She'd learned that pointing led to trouble.

"Oh?" Dad asked. "Why's that?"

"He seems like the type to never turn down a card game," Erin said, eyes glancing toward the tavern and then at the other storefronts on the opposite side of the cobblestone street. No eyes were watching them. Yet.

"Why would you choose him over the gimp?" Dad arched a quizzical eyebrow. "If it helps, I think I could outrun him—the Gods would love a cripple race, I think."

Erin smiled despite her darkening mood. "Not that. Most gimps don't make it to his age unless they've got something going for them. He's probably smart. Just like you, Dad." She frowned. "So, if they're together, targeting either of them will get us into trouble. The gambler is too fast, the gimp too smart."

"Good, good. You're learning so much quicker than I ever did," Dad said with a genuine smile, which was impressively similar to his performative one. "If I had been as smart as you, I'd have probably never lost my leg."

Erin smiled mirthlessly, as she stared at her father's wooden leg, which had been all but a death sentence for him when he'd lost it fifteen years ago. He'd lost all job opportunities to young, spry men who worked faster for half the wage. Erin and her dad were left with one option to survive: lie, cheat, and steal—to marks, anyway. Never to each other.

Pursing his lips, Dad scanned over the crowd again. "What about the older man? He's also got a cane."

"We don't cheat the elderly," Erin said without bothering to look again.

A proud grin came to his face. "Right again, you are. Always remember that's the line even we shouldn't cross, my rose. Let's keep going. We'll find a mark around here somewhere."

When they came to another inn, Erin looked around. No gallowmen. No wealthy patrons either. In case she was wrong, she re-memorized the alleyways and escape routes they could use to flee if things went wrong.

Winking at her, Dad asked, "I'm thinking we use the *Sick Girl* gambit for this one. Are you ready?"

"Ready," Erin said, holding tighter to her dad's right arm to seem sicklier, though she was careful not to pull too hard for fear of making him fall.

"Then away we go!" he said in an excited whisper.

As Dad used his shoulder to open the door, Erin hacked. Her entire body shook with effort as her father dragged her behind him. Writhing under her father's grip, her teeth chattered as she convulsed.

"Excuse me?" the innkeeper said. A thin man in a tweed jacket peered around the log book he held in his hand, watching them with thin arched eyebrows. Though he wore gilded spectacles, Erin could see the softness in his eyes and the small wrinkles around them—a worrier. *If he can worry, he has the money to worry.*

"Oh, baby," Dad said, his eyes filling with tears. "Daddy's here. Daddy's got you."

"Excuse me!" the innkeeper said a little louder. "Is everything alright?"

Dad dragged Erin farther into the establishment, right up to the innkeeper. She leaned against her father, but not enough to unbalance him. This close, Erin could smell the lilac and jasmine scent covering the innkeeper's musk, indicative of high-quality soap.

"Please, sir. My daughter... she's sick. I don't know what to do!"

"What's wrong with her?" the innkeeper asked, peering closely at her and then suddenly backing away. "It looks like the Whispering Madness. Is there another outbreak?"

"I don't know!" Dad shouted, pulling at his hair as he looked between Erin and the innkeeper. "She just started coughing and shivering. Then she collapsed! I've never seen anything like it!" The innkeeper shrank back, pushing himself against the back wall, but Dad took another step toward him. "Please, help her."

"Have you seen the doctor?" the innkeeper asked, ignoring Dad's pleas.

Erin could see the controlled stream of concern on her father's face, the shame clouding his eyes. Even she almost believed Dad's act. He whispered, "I don't have the money, sir."

"What? And you think I do?" the innkeeper asked, trading wide-eyed glances between Erin and her father.

Yes, you do, Erin thought as she continued to cough and shiver.

"Are you really going to make a one-legged man get down on his knee and beg?" Her father shrugged helplessly. "Can you at least give her some soup, sir? Please? What about a blanket to keep her warm? *Please!* Don't help me, help *her*."

The innkeeper's face was stained with pity as he put a quick hand into his pocket and pulled out a few coins. He held them out to Erin's father and dropped them before their hands could touch. Then he immediately shrank back again. "It's not much, but it's all I can give you."

Her father's faced brightened, though it was still expertly torn between hope and worry. "Oh, thank you, sir! May Eo bless you all of your days!" Still holding Erin, Dad turned to the door and said, "Come on, baby. Stay with me. We can go see the doctor now. Soon, you'll be right as rain!"

When the door closed behind them, Erin heard the *snick!* of it locking from the inside. Still dragging her, Dad moved around the edge of the building. Then he let go and chuckled. Erin looked up at her dad, stifling a laugh instead of forcing a cough.

"Great job, sweetie," he said, ruffling her hair. He opened his palm, showing her the two copper sickles and one silver lune.

"Wow," Erin said, staring at the coins. "We got a silver piece?"

"Not just one." Dad pulled out the sailor's leather coin purse, revealing seven sickles and another lune inside. "Eo showers us with her blessings." He placed one lune in her hand and said, "A family that shares together..."

"Stays together," Erin finished, looking up at him with bright blue eyes. She pulled out a few copper coins she'd snatched from loose pockets, placing them into the purse.

"That's my rose." Dad took her hand once more. "How about we celebrate?

Erin and her father sat in a corner booth in the Second Hook Tavern, holding weapons underneath the table in one hand even as they ate with the other. Dad had a flintlock, Erin a four-inch folding knife. There was little to worry about, though. The other patrons were too busy gambling, drinking, and singing shanties to pay attention to Erin and her father. The same could not be true of Dad, whose eyes kept creeping over to the gambling tables where debt-ridden sailors cursed their fortune and lucky ones collected their take.

Erin didn't let the gamblers sour her mood, though. The warm, meaty soup filled her stomach, and she savored every bite as she forced herself to eat slowly. It was difficult to not gulp down her stein of milk—it was a delicacy they could only afford after big scores like today. Even the bread was delicious, made with rosemary, garlic, and cheese. *Cheese!* Erin moaned and dramatically leaned over the table. "I love cheese."

"That good, huh?" Dad asked, letting go of his spoon to rustle her hair. "Better than my cooking, I take it?"

Erin gave him a pointed stare. Between bites of bread, she said, "You've burned *water* before."

"I have not," he said in mock offense. "I'll have you know that water burned itself."

Erin giggled and swung her feet underneath the table. She accidentally kicked her dad, but rather than complain about it, he just kicked her back. Then they both broke out into laughter so loud that they drowned out the songs and gambling.

For a moment, the outside world fell away, and Erin saw only her father. She watched him lovingly, noticing all the small details. How his blonde beard danced when he laughed. How his smile created small dimples in his cheeks. How his blue eyes sparkled with hope and excitement even when life was at its worst. Somehow, Dad always made everything okay.

Despite her young age, Erin knew the secret of life: finding someone to share it with. Dad was that person to her, and as long as they were together, she needed nothing else. Not the money. Not the dresses. Not even the cheese. Just this moment with her dad. A time to smile and laugh, to enjoy each other's company.

Erin wished it would last forever.

Erin and her dad sat cross-legged on the dusty floorboards and huddled by their fire pit. A storm had blown in from the coast far faster than either had expected, and they'd walked a mile in the rain through the Chasm to return to their home: a small room on the bottom floor of a crumbling brick building that had been subdivided into tiny compartments to house the growing population. It didn't feel like a home.

With neighbors above and to either side, the sounds of violence and death—coughing illnesses, domestic violence, and muggings—were never far away. Because the front door's lock was broken, a chair was wedged underneath the door handle to keep it from being forced open. As the room was so small, they had little space for personal items aside from the fire pit Dad had won while gambling and a small bookshelf without books. Instead, it contained bottles of water, a thin pot, a deck of cards, and dice. No food, though.

Wrapped in a threadbare blanket, Erin shivered and leaned closer to the fire pit. No matter how close she leaned to the fire, she still felt cold.

A crack of thunder caused the room to shake and dust fell from the rafters above. *We're in for a bad one,* Erin thought, eyeing the rags that had been stuffed beneath the door to keep both the water and the rats out.

As if noticing her worried expression, Dad said, "Don't worry about that storm, my rose. It will pass, and the sun will shine through. It always does." He smiled. "You should be proud of yourself, you know. You did great today. You've got a gift for the grift—the *eye*. You see *through* people—see what they're like on the insides. Far wiser than I ever was at your age. You're growing up to be just like..." Dad trailed off with a wistful expression. He cleared his throat, and the expression faded, but not quickly enough for Erin to miss it.

He's thinking about Mother again, she thought as fury welled inside of her. Mother had abandoned them four years ago. Worst part was, Erin still didn't know why. Probably never would. But she hated Mother for it.

"Always remember rule number one: be *aware*." Dad pulled a small, plastic flower from the air and handed it to Erin, whose eyes were quick enough to see through the parlor trick. He'd pulled it from his sleeve. Still, she held the pink rose close. "That's the only way you stay safe in this life—you control perception, and you control the world, Erin. You must always remember that."

Lightning cracked, and Erin jumped. The room shuddered again. Dad winced and gave her an uneasy smile. "We'll be okay here," he told her as he began rummaging through his backpack. "Besides, I think I've got just the thing for a night like this." His brow knitted as he searched deeper. "Where did I put it?"

From under her blanket, Erin revealed the apples from his pack. "Looking for something?"

"Oh, such a rascal you are! Just like your old man!" Dad exclaimed, laughing with his entire body. He took one apple and bit into it. Another laugh shook him. Grinning with him, Erin bit into her own apple and savored the taste.

"Thank you," she said between mouthfuls.

"Anything for you, my little rose," he said with a wink. "I'd give you the moon if I could—if Eo would be so kind."

Erin didn't remember falling asleep by the fire, nor did she remember her dreams. Yet her body ached when she awoke. Taking a shallow breath, she scooted closer to her father. Huddling for warmth, she closed her eyes again until she felt him shift beside her.

"You're shivering," Dad said, frowning.

"N-no, I'm n-not," Erin said, unconvincingly.

"You've gotta stay warm, Erin." Dad took off his own blanket and wrapped it around her. Then he pushed her closer to the rusted fire pit. "You'll get a cold if you don't warm up, and then we'll really have to go to the doctor."

"I-I'm okay," she said, her lower jaw trembling with effort.

"I know you're okay, sweetheart, but I want you to be better than okay, *okay?*" he said, putting a rough hand to her soft cheek. His palm was so large that Erin could use it as a pillow.

"I'm okay." Erin stifled a cough and wiped her nose.

Dad's eyes narrowed as he glanced over at her and put a hand against her head. "No fever. Good. But we've gotta do something about that cough." He scratched his beard before snapping his fingers. "I'm sure I can find a remedy for that—just need to rustle up a little more money for it."

"I'm fine," Erin said, resisting a chill that ran through her. "W-we don't have to get medicine."

"We don't *have* to do anything, my rose. But that's what I'm going to do."

"But I w-want to c-come with—"

"Oh no," her father said. "You need to rest up. Sleep off the aches. Then, when I get back, you'll take that medicine. We'll bask in a warm fire and get some more soup. I don't know a better remedy than a hot bowl of soup, do you?"

Erin could smell potato soup in her nostrils as she imagined a warm night inside. She nodded vigorously. Erin would have given a lot to go help her father get the money, but she'd give even more for another dinner at the Second Hook Tavern.

"Good. Good!" Dad grinned. "Then we'll do it," he added with a wink before kissing her forehead and walking to the door. He paused, turning toward her, his eyes serious and grim. "Now, what do you do when I leave?"

"I lock the door and put the chair back in place."

"What about when I come home?" Dad asked.

"I wait for the secret knock," Erin said.

Dad nodded. "What if the secret knock is wrong?"

"Then the door stays closed."

"And if somebody else tries to get inside?" Dad asked.

Erin pulled her folding knife from under the folds of the blanket. "I protect myself."

"And?" he asked, the morbid gleam still in his eye.

"I run."

"Where?"

"To Eo's temple."

Dad crossed his arms. "Why?"

"Because the temple will protect me, and you'll come looking for me there."

"That's right," Dad said, opening the door. "I will always come looking for you, sweetheart. Don't you ever forget that." He smiled before stepping through and closing the door behind him.

Chapter Six

The night caressed even its worst monsters, and Lilyth leaned into that icy embrace. Wreathed in shadow, she stood just ahead of the *Crescent's* mainmast as her newly stolen brig sloshed between the waves. Heavy ropes bound the furled sails tightly, and the anchor kept the ship from drifting away further into the Poison Gulf—the curse of the Deadlands supposedly tainted those waters. More storms, fewer fish, no sailors. Only Lilyth and her Red Legion braved the blighted gulf, making it the perfect place to train.

Almost perfect.

Though the ship was safe from the harsh waves in an uninhabited island's cove, the deck still rolled ceaselessly from starboard to port. The movement, compounded by the unyielding darkness, made the bile in Lilyth's stomach slosh around and crawl up her throat. Yet she refused to throw up. She'd endured far worse pain than this, so she bore it without complaint. To these thirty-six freed slaves, Lilyth would never show weakness.

Especially not to Greeley.

Yes, Lilyth knew that brute's mind better than he did, but she wasn't concerned by his ambition or sadism. Those traits worked to her advantage. The key to breaking Greeley—to breaking them all—was simple: more training sessions, less food, and far less sleep to make their minds more malleable. Keeping legionnaires aboard her ship was another tactic. So long as they were at sea, the crew would have no contact with the outside world. Their individual identities would crumble, and Lilyth would bind them back together with her ideology, rules, and bloodlust. Lilyth would become their Champion. As long as they learned and obeyed, they would be her puppets. Otherwise, she'd cut their strings. And throats.

Silently, Lilyth paced along the main deck, appraising her legionnaires as they dueled in pairs with dull cutlasses. They swung wildly, parried poorly, and stumbled often as the deck shifted beneath them. Despite being sailors, they still didn't know how to *fight* at sea.

These are supposed to be my warriors? Lilyth thought, masking her disgust behind a veil of confident indifference. *They know nothing of death. Not yet. But they will.*

Lilyth stopped pacing as she noticed Greeley hacking and slashing at an older teenager, who only seemed to parry the Red Hand's furious, unending barrage. Why wasn't he attacking? Lilyth continued to stare, her eyes abandoning Greeley to dissect the young man's stance. His front leg was too far forward, spine leaning too far back, and arms too rigid. But his eyes were calm and calculating. They focused on Greeley's body instead of his blade and reacted faster than Greeley could swing.

Kendrik, Lilyth thought, remembering his name because it was an essential tactic to breaking and mending these slaves. *He's letting Greeley tire himself out... Cunning boy.*

Noticing Lilyth's presence, Greeley attacked with even greater ferocity. When Kendrik didn't weaken, the Red Hand huffed, spat curses, and swung with both hands. Kendrik blocked with both. As their blades locked together, Greeley stepped close and decked him. Kendrik's head snapped sideways, and he crashed to the deck.

Not cunning enough, Lilyth thought.

"Brother!" a younger teenager shouted, abandoning his own duel and running to Kendrik's side.

Jericho. He and Kendrik were nearly identical with their lighter blue skin, aquiline noses, and long blonde hair, despite being several years apart in age. Lilyth would need to break their tight bond sooner rather than later. That, or kill one of them. Probably Jericho. He was the weaker of the two.

As Jericho helped Kendrik to his feet, Lilyth stepped forward, offering a small, calculated smile to express maternal pride. Then she placed a hand on his chin, tilting his head to the side and pretending to inspect the bruise. His pain didn't matter to Lilyth, but the gentle touch and attention reinforced herself as a motherly figure, which lowered Kendrik and Jericho's defenses.

"Patience is a virtue, but so is aggression," Lilyth said. "Wait until you find an opening, but strike. Otherwise, you will only ever wait, Kendrik. Then you will die, and your brother will have to bury you at sea. Is that what you want? To make your brother weep?" Kendrik looked to Jericho, flinched, then shook his head. "I need to hear you say it, Kendrik," Lilyth added, the smile slipping into an intense, maternal scowl.

"No, Champion," Kendrik said, sullen. That he addressed her by *Champion* was a good sign of obedience, further establishing the leader-follower relationship she strove to instill in each legionnaire. But words alone were not good enough. Lilyth needed results.

"Then you must *improve*," she said, offering an empathetic smile. "It does not matter where you begin so much as it matters where you end, Kendrik. And the only way to improve is to train until you cannot lift a blade. Day after day after day."

"Yes, Champion," Kendrik said, coughing before spitting out a bloody tooth. He rubbed his jaw where a bruise was already forming from Greeley's haymaker.

Lilyth whistled once, and all the duels ceased—easy as a master summoning a pack of well-trained dogs. Just as they were trained to stop, they could be trained to kill. It was merely a matter of time.

And reinforcement.

"Gather around, legionnaires," Lilyth said. The crewmen obeyed, forming a wide half-circle and sitting cross-legged on the deck. "I am going to teach you to spill blood—drink of this knowledge greedily. Red Hand, stand beside me." When he had, Lilyth added, "The Red Hand is the strongest among you—the best with a blade and even better with his fists. Is that not correct?"

"Yes, Champion," Greeley said, puffing out his chest further. "I was a cage fighter. Undefeated."

"An undefeated cage fighter," Lilyth repeated mechanically as her mind assessed various scenarios. She needed to humble Greeley in a way that wouldn't alienate him. Yet Greeley would only listen to strength. Like offering a treat to a dog, the trick was to offer him a trophy that would serve as a constant reminder—a reminder of *her*.

When she came up with a solution, Lilyth said, "Between a cage fighter and a Champion, who do you think is stronger, Red Hand?" Before he could answer, she added, "Let us find out."

Greeley immediately reached for his battered cutlass, but Lilyth instead raised her hand. Greeley stopped, more out of confusion than obedience. She would have to correct that behavior later, if this bout of fighting didn't do just that.

In a magnanimous gesture, Lilyth untied the knots securing the Avowed captain's white cutlass to her belt. Then she handed Greeley the sheathed blade. "The man who held this was your enslaver, was he not?"

"Yes, Champion." Greeley stared at the blade in his hands as if he were holding the moon itself.

"You were enslaved by this very blade," Lilyth said, pointing at it. "I have purified its edge with blood and sharpened it to cut even a falling strand of hair. Yet a sword is only as sharp as its wielder. Are you sharp enough to cut me with this blade, Red Hand?"

Only the crashing waves and the creaking planks of wood answered as Greeley stared at the blade. The rest of the crew waited with bated breaths for a response that never came.

Lilyth picked up Kendrik's dull-bladed cutlass. "This blade, though, is so dull that it would be difficult to cut a rope." Lilyth flicked her wrist, slashing at one of the unused coils of ropes hanging from the gunwale. Hacking at it only severed a few fibrous stands of its hundred. "Yet this blade could still be sharp in the right hands."

Lilyth slid into a forward-leaning stance with her sword hand outstretched. Her empty left hand waited behind her back. "Attack me, Red Hand. Let us see whose blade is sharper."

Greeley ran forward, slashing in wide, arcing movements as Lilyth knew he would. The Red Hand may have been undefeated in boxing, but pure physicality mattered little when blades were involved. Steel was far stronger than flesh and bone.

As Greeley smashed into her, Lilyth deflected his blade, slapped him with the flat side of her cutlass, and stepped out of reach as he slashed at the shadows where she'd been standing. Then she tapped his blade to elicit a reaction. He swung again as she feinted left, right, then left again. Greeley's blade found only air as Lilyth's sliced his cheek.

So easy, she thought. He touched a hand to his face, stunned as it came away red.

"Again, Red Hand," Lilyth said.

Greeley rushed forward, the white blade cutting wickedly close as Lilyth ducked, danced, and deflected. Yet as her body reacted, her mind wandered far from the fight and toward the stars. Each second wasted on this point-less show of swordsmanship was another spent far from her husband and daughter. How much longer until she would see them again? How many more nights would she spend alone on the hardwood planks?

The Cutthroats will pay, they will all pay... Lilyth felt her body lurch effortlessly, even as her mind remained in an abyss darker than the depths below the ship. Were the syrens still there?

Of course they are, they're always watching. Waiting for me to slip and fall. Waiting to eat. But they will have to be patient. I will not die here. I will find Rolf. I will find my family. Ash filled Lilyth's nose, screams scratched at her ears, and fire brimmed in her eyes. *I will turn their port to cinders. Bleed them dry as they burn.*

Lilyth could see the carnage more clearly than the deck of the ship: the erratic flames of burning buildings, chaotic duels in the dirty streets be-tween Cutthroats and legionnaires, and rivers of blood that were dammed by corpses. And there, on the other side of the street, was Rolf the Bloody. He was whispering to her about where he'd kept her family, goading her to attack. So be it.

Lilyth unsheathed her talan and rushed forward. Rolf raised his sword to swing, but Lilyth was far faster. She darted, feinting in both directions and lunging as she swung. Rolf backed away, eyes stained with terror. Lilyth only laughed. Rolf was right to fear her.

Lilyth snarled and slashed harder, faster. Her laughter grew louder as her hands blurred with speed. She feinted left before diving right, cutting Rolf with her cutlass as she passed. The so-called Skull faltered as Lilyth threw the sword. It sailed just past Rolf's head as the Cutthroat ducked to avoid it. But dodging pushed Rolf off balance, and Lilyth pounced on him with a wild shriek.

They collapsed to the ground in a heap, both wrestling for control. While Rolf was stronger, Lilyth was faster—and armed. She slid out of his weak grip, slicing his arm and face as he reached for her. When Rolf recoiled, Lilyth kicked him in the jaw. The Cutthroat groaned and fell into the dirt face-first as Lilyth straddled his back, grabbed him by his hair, and pressed the talan against his jugular vein.

This is it, Lilyth thought. *This is the moment.* What to do first? Slit his throat? No, too easy. Cut off his fingers? No, too slow. Rip his lungs out through his back? She would have to sever his lower spine first to ensure that he couldn't run away. Brutal. Painful. Perfect.

Lilyth raised the blade to stab him in the lower back, but the gasps of several nearby bodies brought her to her senses. Lanterns, legionnaires, and the planks of a ship replaced the fire, corpses, and dirt of the port. She glanced down to see the body beneath her wasn't Rolf's, but Greeley's.

Taking a deep breath, Lilyth released him and stood, glaring at the other legionnaires who had leaned away in fear. They murmured to themselves in strangled bits of conversation:

"That laugh. Sounded like the syrens, she did," said one legionnaire. "By the Gods, I ain't ever heard anything like it."

"How can she move so fast?" asked another. "It ain't human..."

"...really is the Champion of Eo. That talan must be her Sword. That's the only explanation," Jericho said, his eyes shining with genuine hope.

Lilyth saw her opportunity and took it.

"It is never enough to make a Cutthroat bleed," she said, donning a mask of composure, confidence, and wisdom while silently cursing herself. Small mistakes like these could destroy all her meticulous plans. She couldn't lose control again. "Cutthroats are too familiar with blood to be frightened by it—even if it is their own. You must make them afraid in other ways. Through camouflage, traps, and unconventional warfare. Through darkness and *laughter.*" Lilyth paused, letting the information sink in. It wasn't completely true, but she needed an explanation for her loss of control. "Fear is a tool we must use to bring Eo's truth to the world. Do not be afraid to harness it."

After demonstrating several more efficient sword strokes, Lilyth commanded the legionnaires to continue training with new partners. As they did, Lilyth turned to see that the Red Hand had retrieved the white cutlass and was feasting his eyes upon her skin.

Despite the lacerations on his face and arms, Greeley wasn't afraid. He was *hungry* for her. It was a look Lilyth was too familiar with. Her arm twitched, and she fought the urge to disembowel him. Hunger, like most emotions, was something she could leverage. A gentle touch here, a kind remark there, and some individual attention would be enough to ensnare his feeble mind.

As Greeley approached, Lilyth gently placed a hand on his shoulder and smirked. "You did well, Red Hand."

"But I lost," Greeley said, confused.

"You lost as a *cage fighter*," Lilyth said. "If you wish to win, then you must stop thinking of yourself as such. Instead, think of yourself as a Champion. With strength, loyalty, and training, you will improve. There will come a day when you will be unstoppable. A Champion in your own right—but not today."

Greeley nodded, holding the white cutlass out to Lilyth. "I will obey."

So you say, she thought. In a warmer tone, Lilyth said, "Then you will be rewarded, Red Hand." She pushed the cutlass back against Greeley's chest, letting her fingertips briefly kiss his skin. "Keep the blade. Learn to kill with it, and you will never again be enslaved. Be sharp and be free. Be the night."

Greeley's wide smile threatened to split his skull.

Sharpen your hunger, Red Hand, Lilyth thought, displaying a mirthless smirk. *Become my blade. Become my slave.*

After several more hours of back-breaking work, sparring, and lessons, Greeley sat in a hammock swaying in the ship's berth. Between the endless whorl of activities, Lilyth was all he could think about. Just staring at his white cutlass made him think of her eyes. They were seductive in conversation but flat, apathetic, and remorseless in combat.

When they had sparred earlier, Lilyth hadn't fought so much as danced with the night. Her movements were fast yet elegant, unlike his own wild strikes. As she lunged and leaped, he remembered her muscles shimmering with sweat. But her tackle had been the most vivid of all. She'd pounced like an animal on all fours without sound. He'd felt her—all of her—as they both grappled for control.

It was unlike anything he'd experienced. Lilyth's embrace was far different from the twirling-skirt girlies of the brothels he'd visited in port cities—passionate but cruel. She was just as violent as he was. Always ready to cut, stab, and kill. Gods, how he wanted her.

As he stared at the new trophy in his hand, Greeley thought, *All these possessions are trinkets. But Lilyth? She's the real trophy. And I will have her. I will make her mine.*

CHAPTER SEVEN

Wearing an ornamental robe dyed red with Cutthroat blood, Lilyth preached from a dais. Nailed to the wall behind her was a blood-stained wooden crescent––a crude altar to Eo. While her congregation kneeled in meditative prayer, Lilyth read from Eo's Tome: a book Lilyth had bound in human skin—courtesy of the dead Avowed captain. The Aenuite symbols she'd written in blood were unintelligible to anybody else. Because she alone could read it, nobody could disagree with her regarding the Word of Eo. And that made it divine.

"In darkness, there is light," Lilyth said.

"We look to the moon and stars," replied the now thirty-five legionnaires. One had fallen overboard last week during the night watch. At least, that's what Lilyth had led her crew to believe. She'd thrown the legionnaire overboard for whispering his doubts about her. Such dissonance couldn't be allowed to bloat and fester upon her decks, not when she had so much more to accomplish.

To achieve those ends, the number of legionnaires would soon become thirty-four.

Picking up her tome, Lilyth paced across the temple in the middle of the orlop deck. Her temple served as the macabre spiritual center for worshiping Eo while also eliminating an area for the crew to congregate, rest, and relax. On Lilyth's ship, comfort was as much the enemy as Cutthroats because it gave legionnaires time to think critically.

In the temple, the legionnaires couldn't speak except during responsive prayers. They all had to kneel on the deck with their eyes closed and foreheads touching the planks. Lilyth expected them to stay awake during the night and to sleep only a few hours during the day. Save for her own lantern, no light was allowed.

Being the Red Hand, Greeley had special privileges. His job was to ensure that other legionnaires stayed awake. When one fell asleep, he would grab them by the collar, drag them from the room, and beat them into submission. None dared interfere, but few liked Greeley for his treatment. They associated him with pain, her with mercy—despite Lilyth having ordered Greeley to violence.

They're all just dogs, Lilyth thought, looking out at her congregation. *And smart dogs are far easier to train than stupid ones.*

Her lantern shined across the kneeling men's backs as she slipped between their ranks. Quietly, she kneeled beside Kendrik, resting a hand on his back. He flinched, but not like one startled out of sleep. Good. She moved from him to Jericho to find that he was also awake. Smiling, she said, "In darkness, Eo watches us."

"Her eye is our guide," replied her congregation, the loudest voice being Jericho's.

"In darkness, Eo knows us," Lilyth said after inspecting the rest of the row.

"Her eye is our judgment." This time, the congregation spoke with only thirty-four voices. The thirty-fifth was silent. Hector—the rotten apple of an otherwise healthy tree—had drifted into unconsciousness.

Lilyth pointed at him.

On cue, Greeley stalked toward him. He grabbed Hector by the collar and threw him onto his back. Hector's eyes opened slowly, painfully. Before Greeley could grab the legionnaire by his foot and drag him out of the temple, Lilyth raised her hand. Greeley stopped abruptly.

It wasn't Hector's fault he was tired, Lilyth knew. It was the milkweed poison running through his veins. She had slipped it into his meager allotment of food an hour earlier along with mandrake root, which caused severe hallucinations. When combined in the correct amount, mint powder masked the bitter taste. By knowing the age, height, and weight of the mark, the timing of symptoms could be predicted. *Prophesied.*

"Ours is the path of Eo," Lilyth said.

"Ours is the path of the righteous. Ours is the path of the night."

Lilyth continued with the recitations, watching Hector for other symptoms. He was losing control of his muscles, kicking and physically reacting to her voice. Within minutes, he would hallucinate just before permanent-ly losing his vision. Then he would experience total muscle loss—including the ability to expand his lungs. The key to her miracle was to predict his demise before the illness overtook him completely.

Just a minute more.

"Eo blesses us and curses our enemies—even those within our own ranks," Lilyth said, her voicing taking a colder tone as she broke from the recitations. The room chilled with her words, and the legionnaires broke from their trance. They opened their eyes and stared at Lilyth as she added, "Eo knows who among the Chosen truly believes. Just as She knows who does not. Eo has divined the contemptuous heart of one legionnaire who has repeatedly refused Her guidance."

The horrified legionnaires shared glances, but none dared destroy the sanctity of the silent temple.

"As punishment, Eo has cursed this nonbeliever with the Night Plague—the living darkness. It is an illness that devours one's very soul, and it burns like the Core itself... Isn't that how it feels, *Hector?*"

Legionnaires gasped as Lilyth turned toward Hector, who staggered to his feet with a cry. He tried to run or turn, but his legs gave out beneath him, and he crumbled back to the ground.

"Get away from him," Lilyth said, and the legionnaires distanced them-selves. "He is filled with the Night Plague. A single touch could kill you."

As the legionnaires mumbled to themselves, Hector swayed where he kneeled as he stared back at Lilyth with horrified eyes. He twitched, seeing and hearing nightmares that didn't exist. "What... what have you done to me?"

"It is not me who is at fault," Lilyth said. "You have nobody to blame but yourself. You have sown discontent among Eo's Chosen. You have tried to sway them from Her embrace. That, She does not forgive—nor forget. You are cursed to see what awaits you in damnation, to see the nightmares lurking *behind* the stars. You can see their faces can't you? Hear their voices? *Feel* their screams?"

Lilyth stared at Hector, whose arms were shaking and feet were useless. It was taking all of his effort just to remain on his knees.

"Now witness Eo's truth, Hector!" Lilyth shouted, using his mind against him, guiding his hallucinations into a form that she could leverage. "See Eo standing before you! Be exposed to Her true might! See what only the dead and damned can truly see! Witness Her glory! *Witness Her true face!"*

"No... *no...* It can't be." Hector's eyes widened as his pupils dilated, and he screamed. Though he had no control over his muscles, he writhed across the floor. "It's true! It's all true! Oh Gods, the Unseen Lady is here!" He sobbed, blood pooling from his eyes in place of tears. "My Goddess, forgive me!"

"Eo has touched him. He is Hers," Lilyth said to the entire congregation, whose mouths were agape in various forms of awe, shock, and horror. If only to temper their fear, Lilyth added a touch of sympathy to her voice.

"Make it stop," Hector whispered, leaning toward Lilyth and losing his balance. He crawled forward to grovel at her feet. As his hands touched her boot, Greeley drew his white cutlass back to stab Hector, but Lilyth stopped him. "Please, forgive me, Champion. I will do all as you require. Just make this stop."

"I cannot stop the Night Plague, Hector. It is irreversible," Lilyth said truthfully. "But I can hasten it, though you will find no solace in the fate that awaits you."

"You can't?" Hector asked, grief-stricken. "I'll do anything. *Anything!* Just name it, Champion. *Please.*"

"But I already asked you for something, Hector," Lilyth replied. "I asked that you believe in my teachings—believe in Eo—but you could not do that. All I wanted was for you to accept Her truth, but you refused me. You refused the Unseen Lady. You refused our *Goddess.* Now, I fear, it is too late."

As the crimson tears spilled down his face, Lilyth stepped toward Hector, putting a hand on his head just before his entire body began to spasm. She closed her eyes in false concentration and mumbled nonsense beneath her breath. With sleight of hand, she slipped an ordeal bean into her mouth, swallowing it whole. The natural emetic would induce vomiting within fifty seconds, having practiced it countless times.

Masking the movement by kissing her fingertips and pressing them to Hector's chest, Lilyth added, "But I will alleviate the pain by taking a piece of your burden—even if you do not deserve it. I do that for you, Hector, because even when you do not believe in me, I believe in you. *I believe in you."*

Legionnaires wept, blessing Lilyth as she continued with her ramblings. After ten more seconds, Hector's spasming stopped. Then Lilyth collapsed beside him as the emetic took effect. Greeley took a step forward, as if sensing her weakness. Jericho did, too, if only out of compassion. Kendrik held him back. The rest of the legionnaires cried out in alarm. Some tried to come to her aid, but Lilyth waved them away. "Stay back! *Stay back!* I am filled with the Night Plague! The liquid darkness! If it touches you, you will die!" Taking a rattling breath, she whispered, "Bring me a bucket. *Hurry.*"

When they did, Lilyth retched into the pail, purging her stomach of water and charcoal that she'd forced down earlier. When it splashed into the bucket, the liquid was black as tar.

"The Night Plague," Jericho said, leaning over to look in the bucket. "It's real."

"Of course it is real," Lilyth replied, spitting the remnants of charcoal from her body. "Do you still doubt me? Doubt Eo? If you do—"

"No," Jericho said, too excited. "I believe. I believe with all my heart."

"Good. At least there is one true believer among Eo's Chosen," Lilyth said as she got to her feet. She glanced at each of her tired, hungry believers before asking, "Is there one among you who still doubts all I have shown you? All I have taught?"

No one dared to respond. By the looks on their faces, there were still some legionnaires who didn't know what to believe. Unlike before, though, they were all finally *listening.* From here, obedience was a matter of simple repetition.

"I must dispose of the plague, legionnaires, but while I am gone, you must pray to Eo. Pray for Hector—and for yourselves." To Greeley, Lilyth added, "Keep watch and make sure that they pray. I do not want any more cases of the Night Plague."

Taking the bucket to the main deck, Lilyth squinted in the harsh sunlight, having been below deck in the dark for so long. As sight returned to her, Lilyth lugged the bucket toward the gunwale, stopping to stare into the pail's reflection.

Though she hoarded the food to keep it from the crew, Lilyth was skinnier than she'd ever been. Her face was a jumble of scars, her head shaved for the tactical advantage. A smashed and curved nose sat beneath her bloodshot eyes, having been broken too many times to heal properly. The consequences of cumulative sleepless nights gathered in bags beneath her eyes. Her face bore no wrinkles from smiling—only scowl lines between her eyebrows.

Hard to understand how the love of her life had once called her beautiful.

Disgusted with herself and pained by the memory, Lilyth tossed the vomit overboard and retired to her quarters to sleep, only to see her daughter's face as she closed her eyes.

I am coming with an army, Lily, Lilyth thought. *The Cutthroats cannot keep you from me much longer. But I need zealots—not sailors. When the Red Legion is ready, I will unleash damnation upon Port Tibur's shores.*

Kendrik focused on striking more efficiently and timing his parries to force opponents off-balance as he sparred. The movements had a rhythm to them—a beat that filled him as the stars did the night. He felt it in his bones. *Step, feint, parry, shove, stab. Step, stab. Step, feint. Step, feint, parry, shove, stab...*

The rhythm was repetitive, not immediately simple, though it had become simple in the months of practice. That beat matched the tempo of the day's activities, which were much the same every day. Wake up for roll call. Spar for three hours. Pray for an hour. Eat. Spar for two hours. Pray for two hours. Chores. Spar for one hour. Pray for three hours. Eat. Spar for four more hours. Pray for an hour. Sleep for four hours. Wake up for roll call...

It never ended, and the exhaustion eroded his mind. There was just always so much to do and so little time to do it. And even when he had time to sleep, he struggled to *stay* asleep. He had nightmares of Jericho contracting the Night Plague, which had killed two more legionnaires in the last month, bringing their number to thirty-two. Kendrik couldn't get the memory of the Champion puking up that black sludge out of his mind. There was something about her that bothered him. But it was something he couldn't quite put his finger on, especially while he was in the rhythm.

Step, feint, parry, shove, stab. Step, lock. Shove. Step, feint. Stab...

The scarcity of food was painful, too, but as the Champion said, pain always had its uses. She had yet to be wrong, so Kendrik trusted her in this. He leveraged the pain to sharpen his skills with a cutlass, just as the lack of sleep offered more time to train. He didn't believe in the Champion's religious tutelage as fully as his younger brother did, but who could? Jericho worshiped the planks that the Champion stood on. Not in the metaphorical sense either. He was always the closest to her during prayer and had the audacity to crawl closer when he thought none were watching. Whenever Jericho did, Kendrik had the urge to pull him back. Not out of embarrassment, but to protect him from her.

Why am I so uneasy? Kendrik thought, distracting himself from the question by stabbing his opponent. Despite the monotony of the rest of his duties, cutlass training was undeniably exhilarating. His arms fought and stabbed based on visual cues he was hardly conscious of. Tense legs? *Parry, stab.* Shifting shoulders? *Parry, shove, stab.* Careful retreat? *Lunge, feint, step, shove, stab.*

The key was to never move backward, never give ground.

The Champion's tutelage had improved his fighting prowess a hundred-fold in these short months since being freed from the Avowed. Kendrik no longer had to fear the cutlass. He *was* the cutlass.

But Jericho wasn't.

The training isn't helping him. He's too young, too small, too trusting to be strong, Kendrik thought. Then he flinched, stirring out of the rhythm and, thus, misreading a shove as a feint. Kendrik raised his blade as the other legionnaire sent him sprawling to the deck. Kendrik's head hit the ground hard, and he laid there for a moment, mentally trying to stumble back to that horrid thought.

"Jericho's strong," Kendrik whispered as the Champion—who'd been watching him spar—helped him to his feet.

"Yes, he is." Leaning close, her breath tickled his neck as she added, "But I understand your need to protect him. He is your brother—there is strength in that bond. Loyalty too. Never lose it." She patted his shoulder. "As for sparring, *parry* next time."

Kendrik nodded, still off-balance even as he tried to force himself back into the rhythm, which now seemed so far away.

After the last bout of sparring, long past sunset, Kendrik stumbled toward the temple, where they would eat their meals in silence before falling to sleep for a few brief hours. Yet before he could climb down the ladder, Jericho caught up to him and asked, "Hey! What'd she say to you earlier?"

Kendrik didn't have to ask who *she* was. Lilyth was the only woman on this ship, and the only person who Jericho cared about these days. Yes, they were still brothers, and yes, nothing would ever change that, but the relationship *was* changing. And not necessarily in a good way.

Do things really have to change? Kendrik thought, noticing the awestruck glint in Jericho's eyes. He used to worship Kendrik that way, but he was no longer Jericho's role model. That hurt far more than Kendrik expected.

Having to protect him so often had always been annoying—even when they'd been mere fisherman before being captured by the Avowed—but the Champion filling that role was far more difficult to stomach. Jericho was *his* brother. *His* responsibility. Why did that have to change? Why did Jericho have to grow up?

That was the real problem, Kendrik knew, even if he didn't want to admit it. Jericho was becoming a different person. More accurately, becoming his *own* person—no longer Kendrik's shadow. He'd long wished for the day Jericho would become independent, but now that the time was here, Kendrik longed for the past—those long days spent fishing with Jericho, who was more likely to hook a seagull than a sea bass.

Why didn't I appreciate it?

"...Kendrik? Are you still there?" Jericho asked, waving a hand in front of his brother's face.

Kendrik's eyes fluttered, and he shook his head as if to clear away the cobwebs. It didn't help. The exhaustion was dragging him into a realm of semi-consciousness. "Sorry, what'd you ask?"

"What did the Champion say to you?" Jericho asked again. "She said *something.*"

"Oh." *What had she said?* Her words were already starting to blur and fade. Kendrik scratched his head and said, "Just that it's good to have a brother who cares about you." Admittedly, that wasn't what Lilyth had said—he couldn't remember her exact words—but it was close enough to the truth that Kendrik didn't consider it a lie.

"Brothers forever," Jericho said, staring up at the stars. "In this life and whatever comes next."

Kendrik refrained from rolling his eyes. "Let's just focus on dinner first." Wrapping his arm around Jericho's shoulder, they retreated below decks and joined the Champion, whose unsettling eyes watched him closely.

Chapter Eight

J ameson awoke in an uncomfortable bed. His head pounded, and his face hurt. He grimaced as his fingers caressed a swollen bruise on his cheek. *How did that happen?*

Fully clothed and lying on top of the sheets, Jameson sat up and grabbed at the hilt of his cutlass, but it wasn't in his sheath. Then he reached under his pant leg for his ankle dagger, which was also gone. In its place, an iron manacle chained him to the bed. "What the…"

"Looking for your blades?" Ink asked, his voice rumbling like echoing thunder. "Perhaps your wit, too? Be glad you've still got all your fingers and toes after what you pulled."

The one-eyed captain glared at him from a seat in the corner of the room. Ink's face was a weathered plank, prickly and unreadable, equally likely to be amused or angry. Judging by the bandages covering the captain's forearms and two blades resting in his lap, Jameson knew it was the latter.

"Ink? What happened?" Jameson tried to stand before recalling the manacle. He settled back on the bed.

"Oh? You don't *remember?*" Ink asked venomously, his stoic facade cracking beneath his anger. "Strange. Thought you had a knack for remembering things."

Jameson only grunted.

"Maynard and I dragged you out of that tavern and brought you here, but when you woke up, you started shouting. Didn't think you had the Whispering Madness, but we couldn't let you leave until we were sure. Can't have another outbreak in a city this big—not after last time." Ink scratched at his leathered cheek. "I came in here to talk you down—not that you did much talking. You got a couple of swipes in before Maynard caught you with a left." Ink pointed at his bandages with one knife. A flash of lightning crackled in his brown eye. "You weren't kidding about Alira bringing out the worst in you."

The tavern, Jameson thought, feeling as though he'd been gut-punched. "That cripple... John Steward was his name. He drugged me and took my purse."

Ink ran a thumb along the edge of the knife. Dangerously quiet, he asked, "That's all you got to say for yourself after the trouble you caused me?"

Jameson opened his mouth and immediately closed it. Being robbed was embarrassing, but being robbed by a cripple in front of his role model was humiliating. Having made a fool of himself afterward and not being able to remember it infuriated Jameson. He felt a simmering rage burning hot in his throat. Had he been alone, he would've screamed. Instead, Jameson rubbed a hand against the back of his neck guiltily and said, "I'm sorry, Ink. Truly. It won't happen again."

The storm of anger left Ink. He sighed and said, "I hope so, boy, because if it *does* I'm taking an eye." He tapped the knife against his eye patch before tossing Jameson a key to the steel restraint.

Meekly, Jameson undid the manacle. He took the knives from Ink when he offered them, but he couldn't meet his captain's eye.

"How much did the bastard take from you?" Ink asked, walking to the door.

"A nineday's earnings and half of my Fiveday bonus," Jameson said, sheathing his blades before standing. He winced as he stretched his back, feeling bruises he didn't remember receiving. Then he joined Ink in exiting the room.

"That's a bit of coin," Ink said, walking down a narrow flight of stairs. "An expensive lesson then: never trust a man who offers you a drink for free. Nothing's ever free."

"Don't I squalling know it," Jameson said, before he could stop himself.

Ink stopped halfway down the stairs and glared at him. "What'd you say to me, lad?"

Jameson sighed. The captain wasn't one for cursing, especially not *that* curse. "Sorry, Ink. Just... frustrated."

"Frustration, I can understand, but a loose tongue is like a loose sail. It's either reined in, or the wind takes it."

"And you're the wind?" Jameson asked.

"Aye. So don't make me cut out your gift, weaver."

Weaver, the Aritrastan nickname of all storytelling sailors. Often a compliment, but in this case, Jameson knew it carried a lashing. He nodded, slouching as he followed Ink down the stairs and into the main room of a small inn. A few patrons ate stew and drank ale at tables, but the inn was otherwise empty.

"Don't be looking like a bruised girlie, son," Ink said as they reached the entrance. "I ain't even hit you yet. If you get soft, then I'm gonna have to rough you up." Ink put a hand on Jameson's shoulder. "So, if this cripple got half of your earnings, where're the rest?"

Jameson grimaced from the headache. "I'm not stupid enough to hide my money all in one place, Ink. Much as I like you, I'm not telling you where the rest is. Don't need another lesson in that, I think."

"Good." Ink's eyes laughed, but his mouth made no sound. "I'll tell you a secret, lad. Cowards who steal silver and gold? They always end up with iron and lead."

They walked out into the street, following the throng of people who were enjoying the Day of Creation, the second celebration of the Fiveday. Hungover sailors and citizens wandered through the tables as bright-eyed tinkerers displayed their inventions and artwork for the creation contest. Toys danced atop tables. Music boxes played resplendent sounds. Glass figurines showed beautiful myrfolk sunbathing on rocks. No syrens, though, which were too grotesque for such a happy day. Other figurines depicted Aritras the Red conquering his foes with his Sword, Eo in her hooded red cloak, Io touching the sun, and Kovu sailing on the clouds. It was decent work, but far from the best. The greatest artisans were selling their crafts in the inner city to the wealthy aristocrats at high prices. A single sculpture could cost upwards of a dozen gold crescents, each coin being more than most citizens made in a year.

The thought of coins reminded Jameson of John Steward, and his mood soured. *Can't believe I was duped so easily. Damn that crippled bastard.*

"If I ever get my hands on him..." Jameson said, touching the cutlass at his side. "I'll take his other leg."

"Maybe in your stories, but not in life, weaver. Too many people, too many places," Ink said, grim. "If he's smart, John Steward is long gone. Or waiting us out until after the Fiveday—if he's not dead already. Bite the bullet and enjoy yourself."

"You wouldn't bite the bullet."

"Wouldn't have gotten drugged, either," Ink replied, pushing through a few onlookers who were blocking the path through the stalls. "You need to get your mind off of it. Go find yourself a girlie and drain the sea monster... Still got enough money for that, don't you?"

"I'd rather grab a drink," Jameson said, rolling his eyes. For all the old captain's wisdom, his solutions too often involved girlies.

"That so?" Ink asked in a suspiciously eager tone. "Then you can buy for both of us."

"But I already lost half my wages," Jameson said, pleading.

"And I almost lost both my arms saving you," Ink said, showing his bandaged arms. His eyes shone with shadows and blades. "You're buying."

Jameson knew there was no point in arguing. And it was the least he could do to truly apologize. "Fine."

"Then away we go, lad." Ink veered from the marketplace and toward the Chasm. Seedy taverns lined its edge, and rough-and-tumble sailors drifted between the pubs. Even in the early afternoon, most stumbled and swayed like they were still toiling on ship decks.

Jameson was quick to join them, drinking beside Ink while swapping stories and shanties with the other patrons. Knowing more songs than most, he even led those of Aritras the Red, the Deadlands, the Borovan Wars, and an assortment of forgotten monsters with which luckless Aritrastans always seemed to cross paths. Patrons paid for his drinks as encouragement to continue, and as ale filled his belly, he transitioned to bawdy tales—the worst of which made even Ink roar with laughter. By the end, he stood arm in arm with strangers of the saltwater, his anger nearly dissipating.

Gradually, they shambled like tortoises from tavern to tavern until they reached a cozy gambling bar named *Luke's*.

Ink stopped just inside of the doorway, grabbing a fistful of Jameson's shirt. "Damn me to the Core, weaver," he said, pointing to the far corner of the room. "How's that for a squalling story?"

"You hypocrite... What about your rule against cursing?" Jameson asked, grinning drunkenly.

"Just *look*, son," Ink said, shaking him.

Jameson followed Ink's finger, glaring at the blonde-haired, one-legged bastard sitting at a card table.

The cripple's hands drifted over a deck of cards as he dealt five to each of the four other men at the table. His stack of money was small, but Jameson knew the man was pulling another con by the damn laugh that hadn't left his memory for a moment.

"John Steward... I'll kill him!" Jameson said, reaching for the cutlass at his hip and making far too much noise.

The cripple looked up, locking eyes with Jameson. Gasping, his hand slipped on the cards during his deal, and the bottom card he dealt in his own hand drifted a moment too long.

"What in the Core?" one of the drunken gamblers asked. He reached for John's cards and flipped them over, revealing a winning hand.

"You're cheating!" shouted another.

"Kill the squall!" said a third.

John held up his hands. "No, I—"

A bullet slammed through John's teeth. Enamel shattered as lead tore his throat. He slumped to the table, clutching at his face as blood dribbled from his mouth. The bar went silent as all sailors put hands on their blades and pistols but didn't pull them out. They listened to the cripple wheeze and choke until he went still. Blood pooled around John's body as the burly tavern keeper shouted for the gallowmen, who arrived too late to arrest the fleeing gamblers. Those armed guards dragged the cripple's corpse away, and immediately after their departure, the bar erupted back into music and conversation as if nothing had happened.

"So much for biting the bullet," Ink said as the tavern keeper cleaned the blood and gray matter from the floor. "Looks like the cripple did it for you."

Erin woke to the sound of a gunshot.

Startled, she examined the room. She was still shivering despite the blankets, and nausea spun the world in circles as her head thumped in rhythm with her beating heart. It was difficult to think but more difficult to sit still.

Rocking back and forth, she stared at the door, wishing to hear her father's secret knock. It didn't come.

Something's wrong.

"Just wait for Dad to come back," she told herself after coughing. "He'll be back any minute now."

Hugging her knees, her throat burned, raw like fire. Water dripped into the corner of the room before seeping through the cracks in the floor, reminding her of the itching, tingling sensation at the back of her mouth. Erin smacked her lips and walked to the bucket of fresh water in the corner. Drinking from it, the taste of iron overwhelmed her, but she thought of potato soup. She winced as her stomach growled. *Focus on something else until Dad gets back.*

Erin stared at the door again before grabbing the cards from the ground. She practiced dealing both the bottom card of the deck and the second card from the top, shuffling without changing the bottom cards, and shuffling without changing the top cards. Tongue out in concentration, she cut the deck and attempted to deal from the center, but the cards always slipped from her hand. Erin worked on that deal for an hour before moving to other forms of card manipulation.

After a convincing card switch, Erin grinned. *Dad will be so proud.* She couldn't wait to see the look on his face when she showed him the trick, and she grinned in anticipation.

The grin faded as more hours crept by.

"He should've been back by now," Erin said, watching the door.

He said to wait, a naive part of her said. It was the same nagging voice that had urged her to stay under the blanket and to fall back asleep.

"But he should've been back." Erin argued. She stayed put for a few more minutes before abruptly getting to her feet and removing the chair from the door.

Erin slipped from the room, carrying the pack of cards. Her fingers fiddled with them as she snuck between the shadows and into her father's usual haunts. They bustled with energy and coin, but there was no sign of her father in the first few. As she walked further along, the fear rose. Her steps became quicker until she was sprinting between taverns and alleyways.

He's not here... he's not there... where is he?

Erin went to the final tavern, a smaller building at the edge of the Chasm. Wooden letters hung above the door, revealing its name: *Luke's*. From the layers of grime, Erin could still see where the letters had once spelled *Mark's*. She couldn't read well, but she at least knew that much. Erin stepped inside, and the smell of lilac overpowered her. She hesitated before a sailor knocked her to the ground.

"Watch yourself," he slurred and stumbled away.

"Watch your coin," Erin said as she picked herself up, pocketing the coins she'd stolen in that half-second of contact. A few sailors eyed her with curious glances as she approached the bar top.

So did the tavern keeper. Wearing a soiled long-sleeved shirt and a clashing apron, he was one of the biggest men she'd ever seen. A foot taller than Dad and three times as muscular, though he had a giant beer belly. "Won't find any handouts here, urchin. Be on your way," he said behind a long black mustache and a pointed beard. As she drew closer, she could smell the bourbon on his breath, which was partially masked by lilac.

Erin hesitated, her tongue forming the words *have you seen my father* before thinking better of it. Asking that would only invite more trouble. It would reveal that she was alone and vulnerable, and by the appraising looks of the patrons, some would take advantage of that fact. But what else could she say? The worsening headache was making it difficult to think.

Repressing a shiver, she sneezed, wincing as a couple of sailors made gestures to ward off the Whispering Madness.

"You sick, kid?" the tavern keeper asked.

"No," she said, trying to keep her voice low and guttural to mask her age.

"Well, you ain't deaf either. Get out of here, if you know what's good for you," the tavern keeper said, his voice roughening like sandpaper. He straightened his back and squared his shoulders, rising to well over six feet, closer to seven, his face as dark and cragged as a mountain.

Erin swallowed but didn't move, still failing to form her question.

"I ain't gonna tell you again. Go on. *Get!*"

Erin shook her head and took another step forward. "I'm looking for a sailor with one leg. Blonde hair. Blue eyes. Have you seen him?"

"Oh," he said in a much softer voice. The tavern keeper twisted a tarnished ring on his finger, ignoring calls for drinks from other sailors. Keeping his eyes downcast, he asked, "Don't suppose this man played cards, did he?"

Did? Erin hesitated, her hands gripping the cards. "Yeah. He *does*." She said, emphasizing the word. "You saw him then? He came in here?" She looked around, not finding him. "Do you know where he went?"

"I think you ought to sit down, kid." The tavern keeper gestured to a barstool, and Erin sat, swinging her feet. He poured some heavy liquor into a shot glass, threw it to the back of his throat, and slammed the glass down on the bar.

The sound rang out like a gunshot, and Erin flinched.

The waiting patrons called to the tavern keeper again, but he gave them a sobering glare. They recoiled with murmurs. "This man you're looking for... Who was he to you, kid?"

"Was?" Erin asked, not understanding. Panic flooded her mind, and she looked around nervously for any signs of danger. Everybody seemed so happy, but she felt like she'd swallowed an icicle—the cold spear stabbed her throat and stomach. Something was terribly wrong, but she was too afraid to move.

"He was your father, wasn't he?" The tavern keeper winced, leaning down on the bar to make himself eye-level with her. "What's your name, little one?"

"Irene," Erin said, glancing at the far corner of the tavern. Compared to the rest of the room, it was much too clean. The floor and table over there had been scrubbed with lilac soap, explaining the smell.

Somebody died here, Erin thought, her fingers gripping the stool as the fear reached her eyes. *Somebody died here, and I don't know where Dad is, and I don't want to be here anymore. I want to find Dad, and I want to go home, and I want to show him my card trick—*

"Alright. Well, I'm Mark. Mark Tulich... Listen, Irene—"

"Can you just tell me where my dad is? *Please?*" Erin asked, interrupting him. She fidgeted on the stool. It felt as if everybody was watching her. Her skin tingled, and she couldn't feel her legs. To distract herself, she pulled out her decks of cards and shuffled them. "If you just tell me where he is, I'll go. You'll never have to see me again, okay?"

"Look, Irene. I, uh, I ain't too good at this stuff, but... you've the right to know..." Mark cleared his throat as he broke eye contact with her before adding, "Your dad was in here. Came alone. He, uh, he asked one of our men to play a game of cards, but this man he played with... he was a man of violence, you understand?" Mark stopped, looking at her apologetically. "Your father, he played with a cheating hand. Pulled one card too many."

Erin's fingers fumbled as she cut the deck, and cards spewed from her hands onto the bar. Her vision blurred. "But where *is* he? Please just tell me!"

"I'll be your daddy if you pull up them skirts!" a drunk man sitting on the stool beside her said. With a sleazy laugh, he tried to grab Erin's arm, but she flinched away and jumped off her stool. "I'll be your daddy if you just let me—"

Mark's giant fist collided with the drunkard's jaw, dislocating it with a spray of blood. The man slumped, cracking his head against the bar before falling to the floor.

The music paused, and the patrons stared at Mark in shock. He shouted something to them, but Erin's mind was too muddled to hear what he said. Her ears rang, her head hurt, and her nose ran. She kneeled down and picked up her poker cards as Mark dragged the drunk out of the bar. Some had fallen into puddles of beer and were soaked. *Dad's going to kill me for ruining these.*

Erin felt a hand on her shoulder. Mark. He was now slouching on the stool beside her. "Did you hear what I said, Irene?"

Erin shook her head, lifting her hands to show the ruined cards. "These are my dad's. Do you have a new pack? I have the money to buy them from you. I just don't want Dad to be mad at me when he gets back." She shoved the cards into one of his hands, ignoring the look of pity in his eyes. Erin shoved all the coins she had into Mark's other hand. "Take everything, okay? Just tell me where my dad is."

"Irene... I can't take this," Mark said, pushing the cards and coins into her hands. "Understand something, alright? Your father's at the cemetery, Irene."

Relief flooded over Erin. "Dad's visiting the cemetery? Why didn't you just say so?" She immediately jumped up to go, but Mark grabbed her. "Hey! Let me go!"

Pained, Mark said, "No. You don't get it, Irene. Your father's *gone.* He paid a steep price with those cards. Paid with his life. He's dead."

"Dead?" Erin froze. The tavern music and laughter of the patrons seemed far away, as if a chasm separated her from them. Though Mark was still holding her wrist, she couldn't feel his touch either. She couldn't feel

anything. When had everything become so cold? Erin shivered and, in a small voice, whispered, "No..."

Mark put his free hand over her restrained one, trying to reassure her. "I know it ain't easy to accept, but it's the truth, Irene. Just breathe, okay?"

Erin did, and slowly, everything came back into focus. The music, the laughter, the heat of the room. Even the pressure of Mark's hand on her wrist. The lilac too. She hated that smell. She hated that laughter. She *really* hated this tavern.

And then there was Mark. Who even was this man? Why would he be trying to help her? Nobody tried to help her or Dad. *Ever.* So, what was his angle? What was he trying to take from her? How could he *really* know what happened to Dad?

Maybe Dad pretended *to get shot,* Erin thought, feeling stupid for not thinking of it before. *Of course, that's what must've happened. It's just another grift. He's playing dead, but he's really alive and probably already back home.* Erin flinched. *But I'm not there. He's probably out looking for me, worried sick.* She racked her brain, trying to figure out what to do. *If we ever got separated, he told me to go to Eo's temple. That has to be where he is!*

"Good, Irene. Keep breathing, alright? I'll get you a glass of water and—"

"No!" Erin shouted, and the music stopped again. Patrons turned toward her angrily as she frantically clawed at Mark's hands. He didn't let go. "Dad promised me he was coming back! He *told* me that! He doesn't break promises! And if I can't find him, I'm supposed to go to Eo's temple! So let me go!"

Mark didn't. "Irene, he didn't *mean* to break a promise. He died and—"

"You're lying! You're a liar! My dad doesn't break promises!" Erin screamed, hurling her cards at him.

Mark raised his free hand to keep the cards from hitting him in the face. He still hadn't released her. "Irene, stop! You gotta—"

"Let go of me, you liar!" Erin lunged forward, biting his hand. Mark screamed and released her. She bolted for the door even as a couple of patrons tried to stop her. Erin threw the coins at them, which started a free-for-all and gave her space to escape through the door.

"Irene! *Wait!*" Mark shouted, his voice only catching her as she rounded the corner and sprinted away. As the moon rose higher in the night sky and shadows loomed longer, Erin fled across the city toward Eo's temple.

Chapter Nine

Erin sat beside Aritras's fountain outside Eo's temple. Fluorite specks glowed within the concrete, glinting like stars in the night sky above. Fluorite also glowed in Aritras's statue, and his Sword shined brighter than the rest of his body. The bottom of the fountain glowed, too, illuminating the hundreds of copper sickles resting at the bottom. Despite refusing to steal any, one of Erin's hands floated gently in the water, casting ripples.

Erin had been waiting for what felt like hours, though she had no accurate way to tell the time. All she had was hope. *Dad will just be a couple more minutes. It's just taking him longer because he's only got one leg.*

After another hour, Erin stood and paced by the fountain, muttering to herself. But when doubt started creeping into her mind, she got on her knees and clasped her hands together as she'd seen Eonian worshipers do.

"Eo, I've never asked you for anything, but I'm asking you now. Please, *please* bring back my dad." Erin looked up at the night sky as a gale cooled the sweat gathering on her forehead. When no response came, she added, "Eo, if you do this for me, I'll be your servant for the rest of my days. I'll... I'll do whatever you want, whatever it takes."

The hairs rose on the back of Erin's neck as a patronizing voice asked, "My child, what is it you require?"

"I... I just want my dad back, Eo." Erin closed her eyes tighter, worried the Goddess might disappear if she looked at Her. "Bring him here, and I'll be your servant forever, if that's what it takes."

The voice laughed, not quite mocking but not gentle either. "My child, I'm not Eo. I am but a humble servant of our Unseen Lady. My name's Clifton. And yours is?"

Erin opened her eyes and turned, seeing the familiar swaths of red cloth. The Eonian priest stood over her, only an inch shorter than Mark but far thinner. His black hair was long and braided, nose thin and straight, mouth pale and smiling.

"I—" Erin stopped herself from saying *Irene* because Dad had taught her it was a sin to lie to an Eonian priest. "My name is Erin." She wiped the snot from her nose with her hand and rubbed it against her shirt. "You can help me, can't you? You're a priest. You have to help me."

"I don't have the power, my child, but the Mistress of the Moon certainly does. Come, walk with me. I'll bring you to Her altar so that you may speak with Her directly." He held out a long, thin hand, but Erin didn't move.

Clifton smiled, his eyes appraising Erin's body as his hand remained outstretched. "Perhaps we can even get you a set of fresh clothes if you wish to speak with Eo at the temple. How does that sound?"

Erin wiped away more tears and snot before nodding. "Okay." She followed the priest but ignored his offered hand.

Passing the water fountain and ascending the steps, Erin walked beneath the giant columns of glimmering stone before passing into the main chamber of the temple, where two men in black shirts and red vests stood with their shaved heads bowed.

"Our temple is open to all of Eo's chosen people, though it is unusually quiet tonight," Clifton said, making a sweeping gesture with his hand. "But the temple will overflow with believers on the Day of Death, I'm sure."

A gigantic, rectangular stone altar to the Goddess stood in the center of the room, laden with offerings of bread, wine, cheese, and flowers—tithings from merchants, sailors, and Fiveday vendors. Behind the altar stood a thirty-foot-tall statue of Eo the Unseen Lady, whose hands were cupped beneath a small moon. She wore a shining cloak, but her face was swathed in darkness despite the torches that lit the interior.

Erin approached the altar, preparing to plead with the Goddess before the priest's light hand pressed into the small of her back.

"Where are we going?" she asked as he guided her around the altar.

"To give you fresh clothes and clean you up, Erin," Clifton said, still smiling.

Erin stopped. "I like my clothes."

Clifton stopped beside her. "Of course, my child. If you wish to keep them, you may, but I believe you will find the clothes I give to you to be a little more comfortable." Sensing Erin's hesitation, he continued. "Erin, you needn't worry. You are in the House of the Unseen Lady. You are safe here. You are *welcome* here."

Once more, Clifton's hand pushed Erin forward to a door behind the statue of Eo. It opened into a pitch-black expanse.

Erin stopped, shaking her head. "But I can't see."

"The Unseen Lady will guide your steps."

Erin didn't budge. Dad had always taught her to avoid shadows like these. Muggers and thieves were always hiding within the darkness, and despite being in a temple, Erin's instinct was to run. She glanced backward at the statue of Eo, whose back was to her now. Was the Goddess still watching her?

"Eo will only end your suffering if you trust Her, Erin."

I need to talk to Eo. I need to get Dad back, Erin thought, swallowing her fears. She stepped inside, and Priest Clifton followed, closing the door behind them.

Erin could see nothing, hearing only the soft breaths of Clifton. "This is the hallway of the disciples of the Unseen Lady. Brothers of the faith live in this darkness every day as part of their training, as do I. Just continue forward for another fifty steps, and we'll reach our destination."

Erin counted her steps, having only learned her numbers so she could gamble and play poker with her dad. But thinking about that only made her feel worse. She shoved the emotions aside and thought, *I'll go get my clothes, talk with Eo, and get Dad back. Then everything will be okay.*

Because her legs were shorter, Erin ended up counting to sixty-one before reaching the door at the far side of the hallway. Clifton opened it, ushering her inside. Candelabras revealed a lavish interior complete with a wardrobe, a wide bed with a black comforter, a rich mahogany desk, and a shelf of religious tomes. Small flames jumped erratically on the desk as if trying to escape the priest's lilac-scented chambers.

Lilac, Erin thought, freezing again. Her breathing quickened. Something was wrong about this place, something *worse* than the tavern. Erin turned to reach for the door, but Clifton was there. He removed his red robes, hanging them against the coat rack. Beneath them, he wore the traditional red vest over a black shirt and pants.

"I must admit, it's quite stuffy in this room, Erin. Much too warm for my tastes." As he said the last word, he licked his lips and glanced at her. It sent a shiver down her back.

All of Erin's instincts told her to run, but the door was closed, and Clifton blocked her path.

"I've… I've changed my mind." Erin said, her hand reaching down to the knife that was hidden under her clothes. "I don't want to pray to Eo."

"But Erin, you're already here. Don't turn your back on the Goddess now."

She turned Her back on me first, Erin thought.

Clifton reached down and took her hands in his. His palms were both sweaty and cold like fish in a frozen river. "I know this must be a difficult time for you. I want you to know that I am here for you. If you need anything, *anything* at all, my child, all you need to do is ask." He licked his lips again.

"I don't *want* anything!" Erin tried to pull back from his grip, but he held her tighter than Mark had. "Let go of me!"

Clifton's smile stretched into a grin as he crushed her fingers between his. "Erin, you must listen to—"

Erin's foot connected with something between his legs. Clifton keeled over in pain. She yanked one of her arms free—

The back of Clifton's hand sent Erin sprawling against the edge of the desk, and she fell to the floor in a heap. Erin whimpered, scooting away as the Eonian priest drew closer. Her heart felt like it was going to explode, and everything ached. Whenever she was hurt, Dad was supposed to be there to make it better. But he still wasn't here. *Where is he?*

Trembling, Erin reached for her knife, which had fallen to the floor, but Clifton grabbed her foot and dragged her away. She screamed and flailed as he threw her onto her back and kneeled on top of.

"Shut up!" Clifton put a wet hand over her mouth. "You will do as *I* say, Erin, and right now I am telling you to—"

He screamed as Erin bit his hand, tearing through his palm. His fist snapped her head to the left. Her jaw instinctively released, and he pulled back his hand.

"You *squall!*" Clifton screamed. "I'm going to send you to the gallows when I'm through with you!"

Erin spat at him weakly, the bloody saliva barely leaving her chin. The shaking room settled just long enough for her to see the door open behind Clifton. The light was too dim to see anything but a shadow.

"Dad?" Erin asked, hope swelling in her chest. Tears spilled from her eyes. "I knew you'd come."

"Dad?" The priest turned as the shadow lunged. A fist echoed like thunder, pushing Clifton off her. The shadow grabbed him by his hair and slammed his head into the wardrobe twice. Teeth fell from Clifton's mouth, bloodying the wooden floor, as the shadow picked him up and threw him across the room. Clifton crashed into a bedpost and moaned, trying to crawl beneath the bed.

The shadow took two steps toward Clifton but hesitated, turning toward Erin. In the light of the candles, Erin could clearly see the shadow: a mountain of a man with long black hair and a pointed beard. Mark the tavern keeper.

Dad didn't come. Why didn't he come? Erin's heart broke, and she wept.

Between breaths and tears, she whispered, "Dad... Dad isn't coming, is he? He's really dead. He's gone, and he's not coming back."

"No, he ain't coming back, Irene," Mark said, kneeling by her side. He put a hand out to grasp her shoulder but pulled back when she flinched. Lifting his palms up in a calming gesture, he said, "Easy, Irene. Let's just get you out of here, okay?" He peered at her swollen eye and inspected her superficial wounds. "Can you stand?"

Erin nodded, pushing herself to her knees as Clifton moaned again. Her eyes widened, and she scrambled backward, whimpering. Her heart pounded as she tried to force air into her lungs.

"It's okay, Irene. I won't let anything happen to you," Mark said. "But I need you to take a breath and stand up. Can you do that for me?"

Taking a calming breath, Erin closed her eyes and nodded. She could taste the blood in her mouth—Clifton's blood. She spat and shuddered. Holding a hand against her bruised ribs, Erin stood.

"That's a strong lass," Mark said. He jerked his head toward the exit and drew a curved dagger from a sheathe. "Can you walk out that door for me, Irene? Just wait out there for me? There're some things in here that I need to take care of. Things I don't want you to see."

"I... I don't want to be alone," Erin said, her voice hoarse. Her eyes flicked to the edges of the room, where candles had been knocked over onto the stone floor. Their lights flickered, casting terrifying shadows. "Please don't make me be alone."

"I'll only be a minute. Swear it on the Drowned Sea, I do."

"Okay," Erin said, sitting just outside the door and hugging her knees to her chest as Mark closed it and left her in the darkness. Little could be heard with the thick door closed, so the screams were only a whisper. After a time, there was no sound at all.

Mom left and now Dad's gone, too, Erin thought. *And I'm all alone.*

"Eo, you're all powerful, aren't you? You can bring my dad back to life, right?" she asked aloud. *"Please?"*

More silence.

From what Dad had taught her, Eo experienced everything within the realm of darkness, shadow, and night. Every conversation. Every moment. The Goddess was here with her, just as She'd been in Clifton's room when he'd tried to...

Erin flinched, distracting herself with conversation. But no matter how she asked, how hard she begged, or how much she cried, Eo remained silent. Unseen and unheard.

"You don't care, do you, Eo?" Erin asked at last. "You could have helped me. You could have saved my dad. But you didn't. You didn't do *anything.* Not even when your own priest hurt me. I thought you were supposed to be better than people. Kinder. But you don't care about any of us."

Cold clarity flowed like ice through her veins, making her thoughts and senses sharper. She felt hollow and yet stronger than before. Another part of her felt weaker, too, but she ignored it. Erin focused on her anger instead of the pain. "Damn you, Eo. Damn you to the Core."

Erin hugged her knees in silence for what could have been days. She was too angry, too lost to do anything but think. And her thoughts were blacker than even Eo's darkness.

When Mark returned, Erin didn't look over at him. Instead, she stared into that dark abyss as she asked, "Is he dead?"

"Yeah," Mark said, deadpan.

"Good." Some of Erin's anger faded, but not nearly enough. "If you hadn't come, he'd have killed me... How did you find me?"

"We were talking about the temple when you ran off. Figured you'd come here, so I followed you. That's when I saw you talking by the fountain with that priest."

"Oh." Erin slowly curled and uncurled her fists. "Thanks for saving me."

"You never have to thank me for something like that, Irene," Mark said. "Come on, we need to get out of here before they find him."

"We can't just leave," Erin said, retracing every moment that had led to that horrific room. "The two disciples at the entrance saw us in here. They'll realize what happened when we leave."

Mark swore under his breath. "I forgot about them."

Erin thought of Clifton's face, his disgusting smile. How different were his disciples? Were they just as willing to hurt children? *More* willing? There was only one way to deal with them and stay safe. "We have to kill them, don't we?"

Erin couldn't see Mark's face in the darkness but heard him gasp. Shifting uncomfortably, he said, "I think you're exhausted, Irene. You ain't thinking straight."

"I'm wide awake."

"That ain't what I mean," Mark said. "Listen, killing's a thing you can't take back. It causes more problems than it solves."

"You killed that priest," Erin said.

"That was different," Mark replied. "Killing was a necessity."

"But this is a necessity too. Those disciples saw us. They'll figure out who killed Clifton, and we'll swing from the gallows. Unless they're dead too."

Mark was silent for a long time. When he spoke, his voice was hollow and slow, as if he were talking to a dangerous criminal, not Erin. "I know you're angry. Gods know I am. But those disciples have done nothing wrong. We're not killing them, Irene."

"Okay." Erin frowned as her mind churned to think of an escape. What could she do? What tricks?

"What if *you're* the priest?" Erin asked. "The priest is probably only an inch shorter than you. You could pass as him. His robes are in there." She pointed to Clifton's room before realizing it was too dark to see the gesture. "But we'll need a distraction to draw their attention away from you." Erin thought of the various ways that she and her father set up grifts for their marks, and she fought back the tears that threatened to fall. "A fire will work. The disciples will put out the flames while we run away."

Mechanically, Mark asked, "You want to burn the temple? That's…"

"Our only option. We dress you in his robes, start the fire, then escape. Either that, or they have to die." Erin said, shoving open the door to Clifton's room.

"Don't!" Mark tried to stop her, but she already saw what he'd done.

The priest was lying on his bed, looking peacefully asleep if not for the deep gash across his neck and the pool of blood around his body. Without hesitating, Erin grabbed a candle and threw it onto the bed, watching as Clifton burned.

Beside her, Mark slouched forward, even further, bowing his head. "Forgive us, Eo."

There's nothing to forgive, Erin thought with a snarl.

Within a minute, flames devoured the room—Clifton's bed, desk, and wardrobe all burned. Smoke curled along the wooden ceiling. Despite the stone, the fire wouldn't stop burning.

Erin ran with Mark, whose identity was concealed by the hooded red robes, down the hallway and into the main altar room. They pushed themselves through the door, Erin breathing harder than necessary and hacking out a cough. The tears came easily because they were real. Had it really only been yesterday since they'd swindled the innkeeper?

The two disciples at the entrance to the temple stood straighter and rushed toward her. Before they could ask questions, Erin coughed harder and squeaked, "*Fire!* The others are still in there. Please, you need to help them!"

"By the Goddess! Priest Clifton, are you alright?" one said, coming forward to check on him. "Thank Eo you're alright!"

Mark pushed him back and pointed down the hallway without speaking.

"We're fine!" Erin said. "Help them! We'll be outside waiting for you. Just make sure everybody else gets out!"

"What about the other visitor? Did you see him in there, too?" Mark stiffened as the disciple added, "He came in, but neither of us saw him leave. We thought he might have gone inside the alcove—"

"He's probably still in there," Erin said gravely. "Go! Help him!" Her voice contained blind panic, a partial truth but for a different reason. *They're going to figure it out. They'll blame this on Mark. On me. They've seen our faces. They remember who we are.*

The two disciples rushed past them into the dark corridor.

They need to be silenced, Erin thought, closing the door behind the disciples, knocking over a stone pillar, and sealing the door shut.

"Irene, what in the Core are you doing?" Mark asked, eyes wide.

"Saving us!"

"I don't need saving," Mark said, scooping up Erin in one arm while simultaneously pushing the fallen pillar out of the way.

Erin fought him but didn't scream, knowing even in her fury that any noise would be a costly mistake. In silent rebellion against Eo, she grabbed a wicker basket of bread, meat, and flowers from the altar as they passed it.

At the door, Mark dropped her, still clutching her hand as they descended the steps. Erin smiled to not draw attention from onlookers but was numb, wishing for her father's hand instead of Mark's. And as they passed the fountain, Erin reached into the pool and grabbed a fistful of coins.

That's for you, Dad, Erin thought as they disappeared into the shadows.

◆〇◆

Erin carved a rose into the headstone. Then she placed it back on the ground.

When she'd arrived in the cemetery at midnight, she'd searched for signs of fresh dirt, new gravestones, and newly trodden grass—anything that could help her identify her father's grave. After an hour of searching, she determined six possible locations but hadn't been able to narrow it down from there, short of digging up each grave.

Erin had already tried that, but Mark stopped her. She might have done it anyway, if he hadn't told her *how* Dad died. A bullet to the teeth. Erin had imagined digging through the dirt and uncovering his face. His blonde hair and beard would be dirty and bloody—no longer blonde but black. His smile would be ruined. She'd seen enough bodies in the alleyways of the Chasm to know that his blue eyes would be milky. Erin didn't know if she could survive seeing that—imagining it was bad enough.

So she'd stopped digging. Erin had finally accepted the fact that Dad was dead, his grave was lost, and there was nothing she could do to fix it.

"I'm sorry, Dad," Erin whispered, as she finished carving the headstone and stood. "I'm so sorry. I *tried.* I tried to bring you back, but I failed."

Eo failed us.

As tears scalded her cheeks, she asked, "Why did Dad have to die? What did he do wrong? What did *I* do wrong?"

Mark, who'd been standing behind her, took a step forward and gently placed a hand on her shoulder. This time, Erin didn't flinch. "I don't know. I ask myself that question every day, but I still ain't got an answer."

"My dad didn't deserve to die. He... he was a good man. He gambled, but he took care of me. He was just trying to make money so we could have food, so we could be warm." Erin wiped at her eyes with dirty hands. "Now he's gone, and I'm all alone. What am I supposed to do now?"

"There's only one thing you can do. You keep living. You become the best person you can be. Not for yourself, but for them. Because they can't. You do everything you can to make them proud."

Erin sniffed, nodding.

Mark stared at the moon as it began descending to the horizon. "But we should go soon."

Erin shook her head. "I don't want to go."

"I know." Mark squeezed her shoulder gently. "Listen, Irene—"

She turned and buried her face in his chest, ignoring the smell of lilac lingering on the clothes. Wrapping her arms around him, she said, "Erin. My name isn't Irene... It's Erin."

Mark's body stiffened under her touch, but after a few moments, Erin felt the weight of his arms across her shoulders and back, bringing her closer. "Quiet now. It'll all be okay, Erin. It'll all be okay."

Though Erin couldn't be sure, she thought Mark was crying with her.

CHAPTER TEN

E rin awoke from a nightmare in a panic and reached out for her father, only to realize he wasn't there. The past rushed back to her as quickly as a bullet. She wasn't sure how long she'd sobbed, but when she stopped, Erin realized she was in an unfamiliar room. A small kitchen, table, and bed shared the space. Erin couldn't remember the last time she'd slept in a bed. So used to the hard, splintering floor of her home, the softness of the mattress was uncomfortable and only made her aches worse. Wincing, she sat up and swung her legs over the edge.

A throat cleared, and Erin looked over at Mark, the tavern keeper, who was sitting in the chair across the room with a steaming mug in his hands. Bergamot tea by the citrus smell. "Erin, I, uh, I hope you don't mind, but I, uh, I brought you back here after... last night."

Last night, she thought, remembering. *Could it have only been last night that my father was still alive?*

"Was that okay?" Mark asked when she didn't respond.

Erin nodded, afraid she'd cry if she spoke aloud. She stared at the floor before her vision shifted to the dirt and blood that encrusted her finger-nails. *Clifton's blood. The dirt from Dad's grave.* She gritted her teeth and focused on that pain and anger. It helped to push away her tears.

"Hey, uh, Erin? Do you..." Mark scratched his head and took a sip of his tea. "Do you have a place to stay?"

Erin shook her head.

"Well, if you want to stay here, even if only for a couple of days, you could. I could get you some extra clothes, some food. Could probably take care of that sickness you've got, too," Mark said, scratching the back of his neck and refusing to look at her. "If you, uh, wanted to stay longer, I'd ask for your help keeping this place up-and-running, but I think it could work well for, uh, both of us." His shoulders remained slumped and his head bowed as he added, "That's only if you want to, of course."

Words of negation started on her lips as a gentle voice asked, *My rose, what do you have to lose by saying yes?*

Erin knew she had nothing left to lose. No money, no food, no shelter—nothing except for the clothes on her back and the dull knife at her belt. If she stayed with Mark, she could have a better life. Enough food to eat every day. A place to live without the fear of being kidnapped or killed in her sleep. A place she could be happy.

Erin's eyes traveled to the wall, past it, on the other side where she knew her father's blood still stained the tavern floor. *I can't be happy here. Not in the place you died, Dad.*

"I'll stay a couple of days," Erin said. "Until the Fiveday is over, but then... my dad..."

"Okay," Mark said, unable to keep the disappointment out of his voice. "Guess I can't fault you for that." He exhaled, and the room seemed to shake with him. "I know you already know this, but I gotta tell it anyway. The world... the world don't care about you. The world don't care about anything. Most people don't either. And it'll just keep taking from you if you let it... You have to protect yourself and the things you care about. You gotta be tough, you gotta be fast, and you gotta be willing to make the tough choices others won't. You gotta be willing to kill if it means surviving, because that priest ain't the only one who's gonna try to hurt you. The world's filled with worse things than him. And I, well, I ain't gonna be there to protect you."

Mark stood and crossed the small distance between the chair and the bed. He uncurled his giant fingers and revealed the knife laying on his palm. The black blade was curved, resembling the claw of a wild beast. A small ring was carved at the far edge of the wooden handle, the grains stained dark with blood.

"That's Clifton's blood?" Erin asked.

"Uh, yeah." Mark's eyes drifted around the room before settling on the floor. "Not sure if you've ever seen a blade like this before, but we"—he winced—"*I* call this a talan. Used them all the time in the Wright and on the ships before the Armada banned them. Guess they thought we'd start a mutiny." He tried to laugh, but his awkwardness made Erin hesitate, her hands not yet reaching for the blade. "Uh, look, if you don't want the blade, I understand, but I... I'd like you to take it. To know that somebody was using it would mean a great deal to me."

Erin ran a thumb across the smooth wood before wrapping her fingers around the handle, avoiding the ring.

"The ring's made so nobody can take the weapon from your hand. You can't drop it either. So long as you use the ring, the world can't take it from you. Ever." He pushed her pinkie into the ring, and the blade curved outward from the top of her palm. "This is a forward grip. You need to grip a talan like this if you're trying to cut rope, carve wood, or gut a fish." Mark reversed the blade, slipping the ring onto her index finger. This time, the blade protruded from the bottom of her fist. "This is a reverse grip. Hold a talan this way when you get into a fight. Always remember: in a fight, a blade is supposed to be felt, not seen."

The world can't take it from me, Erin thought. *I have something that I can keep.*

"But you must also remember that the true strength of any blade is control. You need to know when to use it and when *not* to use it. You can't just kill everybody you don't like or whoever gets in your way. That's an easy way to get hanged. Learning control is the only way to survive." He pulled out a second, larger talan and inserted his index finger into the ring before flipping it across his knuckles and jabbing downward. The knife's point stopped within a hair's width of her arm. "Kill only when you need to, because it will always only create more problems. Avoid the situation altogether when you can."

Erin looked between the two blades—a matching pair. Gesturing to the one in her hand, she asked, "Was this one yours, too?"

Mark stiffened. "No. My son's. He, uh, he doesn't need it anymore."

"Luke?" Erin asked.

Mark stared at the floor. "Yeah. How'd you know that?"

"You renamed your tavern after him. Where is he?"

A glistening tear fell from his cheek. "Luke, he died three years ago. Right around your age, I reckon. Caught the Whispering Madness during the last outbreak. No rhyme or reason for it, but it took him and left me." He sighed, and his shoulders hunched forward more as if his burden had grown tenfold heavier. Eyes red, face stoic, he added, "Used a funeral pyre to make sure he'd, uh, reach the heavens. Kept the ashes. I keep him close, you understand? It's... it's all I've got left."

Mark turned from her, picking something up from the floor. A bundle of clothing with shoes and a worn bowler hat. Mark hesitated before handing her the bundle. "Luke was a scrawny kid, so the clothes should fit. The hat too. There's a bucket of water by the door, so you can clean yourself up before you put them on." He turned and wiped away the moisture on his cheeks. Sniffing, he added, "I'll, uh, let you change. Not many people here yet, so I'm going to clean the place up. Join me when you're finished."

Alone, Erin discarded her shabby clothes on the floor and cleaned the dirt and blood from her skin until the water was brown, the rag red. Feeling cleaner than she had in years, she cast her clothes aside, donning the set that Mark had given her, baggy enough to hide her growing curves.

Erin stared at her reflection in the talan, noting the oval shape of her head and the rounded, soft chin. Boyish features. "That's what I need to be to survive," Erin said as she cut her hair close to the scalp. The blonde locks fell away as she pulled the hat low over her brow.

"A boy," Erin said in an intentionally low voice as she searched for the right name to use. It was a simple choice. "John. I'm John Steward now."

The Fiveday Celebration passed in a blur.

The Day of Plenty was next. It was a celebration of feasting and merriment, of bawdy tales and laughter. The tastes and sounds were ash in Erin's mouth and ears. She spent most of the day curled up on Mark's bed, recuperating from her sickness with Mark's homemade soup. Unlike Dad, he hadn't burned the water. Because of that, the soup was delicious, but it still brought tears to Erin's eyes.

The Day of Life was the fourth celebration. A time of appreciation for family and friends. But Erin had nothing to appreciate. Feeling better than she had the day prior, she sat at a corner booth by herself, watching sailors singing shanties and clinking mugs. Twice she caught gamblers cheating at cards and twice she squeezed her eyes shut. The third time, Mark told them to gamble somewhere else for the rest of the day. He checked on her more times than she could count, bringing food and drink that she ate mechanically while her eyes burned with anger. *They're acting as if Dad hadn't died. Like he meant nothing. How can they be going on like nothing's happened?* she thought more than once. *Dad meant something to me. He meant* everything *to me.*

The fifth and final celebration was a slap in the face. The Day of Death. A time of remembrance and honoring the dead. As if Erin didn't spend every day remembering.

The only positive thing about it was Clifton's death. As the Eonian priest was supposed to lead most of the day's funerary festivities, Alira floundered without him.

A public outcry had burst from the inner city's powerful statesmen—aristocrats with pudgy fingers and fleshy jowls whose iron barks were far worse than their glass bites. Their sorrow reached the Mercantile and Smithy districts but was only shared by devout Eonian followers and middle-class merchants looking to cry their way into the inner city. The Chasm was unpitying, its people too busy starving to notice one man's death.

Much to Erin's relief and Mark's remorse, the statesmen hanged an innocent man from the gallows for Clifton's death. From what Erin overheard in the tavern, he'd drunkenly fallen asleep near the temple when Mark killed Clifton. Mark had felt bad enough to close his tavern and attend the public execution, but not bad enough to turn himself in. Erin had elected to stay behind and watch over the empty tavern. With her sickness having faded after three days of good rest and food, Erin felt well enough to move around. She even swept the floor while Mark was gone, though she avoided the corner of the room that still smelled of lilac.

By midday, Mark returned. He watched her clean for a few moments with a serious, albeit pitying expression before gesturing toward the door. "Let's go."

Erin leaned the broom against a weathered table. "Where?"

Mark didn't answer as he locked up the tavern. Together, they left and moved against the flow of pedestrian traffic toward the northern cemetery, instead walking to the southern docks.

Erin marveled at the giant half-built ships in the Wright and asked, "Why are we going down here?"

"The cemetery's a place for private mourning. Nothing private about it today." Mark sat down on a strip of sand farther away from the Wright and closer to the Chasm's deadly sea cliffs. There wasn't another soul in sight.

Erin sat beside him, still fiddling with her stained cards even as the winds made sleight-of-hand tricks more difficult. Only when Mark pulled out a small bronze urn did she focus on him. The urn had no embroidery, no gildings. Nothing to show great worth aside from the way Mark clutched it to his chest.

"For the past three years, I've come here to mourn my son," Mark said, squeezing the sides of the urn. "Each year, I wonder if I should spread his ashes and let him be free." Mark took off the cap of the urn, reaching in to take out a pinch of ashes. He sprinkled them into the wind before replacing the cap. "Each time I come, I let a bit of Luke go. Though I'm saying goodbye, it ain't a *true* goodbye, not really. I know that one day soon, I'll see my boy again—just like you'll see your dad." Sniffing, he stood while gesturing for Erin to remain sitting. "Take a moment to yourself, Erin. Say what needs to be said. Tell the sea your story. And, if you can, start to say goodbye because someday there'll be a time to say hello again."

Instead of encouragement, his words only renewed Erin's pain. What she spoke to the sea was not her story but an oath. "I swear upon the Drowned Sea that I'll never say goodbye. Not to you, Dad. Not to anyone else. Not ever." Despite knowing full well that a broken oath would bind her soul to the ocean's depths, she added, "And, upon the Drowned Sea, I swear that you'll regret your silence, Eo. You refused to give my father his life back, so I'll take Yours. Somehow, someway, I'm going to be the last thing You'll ever squalling see."

An hour before sunrise on the first day of the new year, Erin awoke. In the dark, she prepared to leave before Mark would notice, only to find that he was already awake and cleaning the tavern by lanternlight. They watched each other without speaking. Though Erin wanted nothing more than to hug him, she didn't.

I can't say goodbye, she thought, for more reasons than one.

"Guess it's time?" Mark asked after a minute of silence had fallen between them.

Erin looked away. "Your son was lucky to have a dad like you, Mark," she said, walking past him toward the door.

"Erin—"

Withholding tears, Erin turned and ran toward him, burying her face in his chest and wrapping her arms around him. Her spine popped as Mark curled his massive frame around her and squeezed. He let go before she did.

"If you, uh, ever need my help, you're always welcome here," Mark said. "Break in, if you have to. Anything in here can be replaced, except you, you understand?"

"I understand."

"Good." He squeezed her shoulder and smiled for the first time since she'd met him. "You take care of yourself, you hear?"

"I hear."

"Then don't forget it. Goodbye, Erin."

Erin swallowed, throat closing and burning as she fought away tears. Before she could break down, she walked out of *Luke's* and joined the sailors approaching the dock to board their ships and depart.

At a safe distance away, Erin turned back and stared at the tavern. *Where do I go now?*

You could go back, my rose, her father's voice said in a passing sea gale. *Live a happy life. A good life.*

"I don't want a good life, Dad. I want you, but Eo took you from me," she said, hardening her gaze. "And She'll regret it."

In the morning light, Erin traveled back home through the darkening alleyways. But when she arrived, she found the door open.

Erin stopped, hearing somebody mumbling inside. Her heart pounded, and she took a step back, pebbles scattering under her feet.

The mumbling ceased.

"Do the pretties hide the powder?" a cracking, rasping voice asked.

Erin took another step back as a haggard woman leaned her head through the doorway, her mouth smiling with only three teeth. A small scar across her left cheek wormed with her panting grin. Orange powder lined the edges of her nostrils, and her nose was black and deteriorating. A chard addict.

"Hello, pretty. Do you have powder for Mommy?"

"You're not my mom." Erin took two more steps back.

The drug-addled woman's smile fell, the eyes hungry and snarling. "Does the pretty hide the powder from Mommy?"

Erin opened her mouth and closed it again. She took another step into the alleyway and pulled out her talan as Mommy limped toward her on a crooked ankle.

"The pretty hides the powder!" the woman shouted, extending her hands.

Know when to use a talan and when not *to use it,* Mark's voice echoed.

Erin bolted, faster than the woman but slower than her words.

"Come back to Mommy! Bring the powder back to Mommy!"

Erin lost herself in the Chasm's maze. Shadows loomed in the streets while total darkness hid worse: blades, eyes, and the burning powder. The alleys became strange, often hitting dead ends where a hastily constructed lean-to blocked the way. People shouted around her, gangs skirmished, and though she couldn't see it, she knew that at least one person died from the way his moans quickly quieted. Others rambled to themselves and spasmed as if controlled by a puppeteer—more chard addicts.

In the distance, sometimes closer, sometimes further, Erin still heard, "Come back to Mommy!"

I should have stayed with Mark, she thought, pumping her arms and lungs. *I should have stayed.*

Erin turned a corner and heard footsteps echoing behind her. Hands grabbed her shoulders and threw her to the ground. Her elbows and knees slammed against the stone as somebody kneeled on top of her. But the talan remained in her grasp, the ring still on her index finger.

Mark's words rang in her ears. *You gotta be willing to kill if it means surviving, you understand?*

Erin screamed as she stabbed. The blade met skin, ripping through tendons and muscles. The body fell away from her, scrambling back as Erin launched herself onto the mugger, stabbing and clawing as she climbed up the body until she reached the head. Erin thought she heard a scream, but it was too difficult to separate her own scream from any other.

In the darkness of the inner Chasm, Erin was glad she couldn't see the aftermath, having already felt the warm blood as she crawled off of the feeble corpse. Too small to be Mommy. Another starving child, she somehow knew. Erin sobbed, alone and on her knees, surrounded by shadows.

"Bring the powder to Mommy!" the chard addict shouted, much closer now.

"Go away!" Erin screamed. "I don't have any squalling powder!"

"Liar, liar, nose on fire!"

Erin scrambled to her feet as the laughter drew closer, stifling a yelp as her knee ached from the fight. Feet scuffled behind her, and Erin limped faster through the alleyways. The paths widened. She could see the twinkle of light as the sun rose over the cliff—

"No," Erin said, sliding to a stop near the hundred-foot drop off.

Behind her, Erin heard a maddening laugh. She turned as the chard addict shambled out of the shadows and drew nearer to the cliff. "You run. Mommy chases you. Now Mommy has you. You give Mommy the powder, pretty. Give Mommy the powder!"

"Leave me alone!" Erin's eyes darted around but found nothing helpful. On the cliffs, she had no hiding places, no distractions. Erin took a step back, feeling the ground give way beneath her, and she hastily took a step toward Mommy.

As the chard addict reached for her with deformed hands, Erin turned and jumped over the cliff.

When she slammed into the water, her right arm was wrenched from its socket. Bubbles spewed from her lips as the blood on her clothes dissipated into a cloudy mist. She grasped for the surface with only one arm as the tide tried to smash her into the cliff rocks. Erin reached the surface long enough to take a single breath before a wave sent her back to the depths.

Erin kept her eyes open, looking for something, *anything,* to grab. Nothing—

Then gray shapes. Moving ones. They darted through the water, too slim to be sharks, too long to be fish. Something in between. Humans without legs, tails where their feet should have been. Scalps without hair or eyebrows. Faces without noses or ears. Eyes without sclera, completely black. Giant mouths without lips. They smiled, revealing rows of concentric teeth.

Erin screamed. Water rushed into her lungs as she reached up to the fading surface with an outstretched hand.

PART TWO

SAILOR

CHAPTER ELEVEN

Lilyth lied on her back, sheathed in darkness. She kept her eyes closed and listened to the boots stomping across the deck inches above her. Eight of her followers had volunteered as bait and surrendered to the boarding Cutthroats. They'd been enslaved and taken to the other ship, trusting Lilyth to save them when the time came. Jericho had asked to a part of that group, but she had bigger plans for him. He and the remaining twenty-three legionnaires lied beside her. All of them were much stronger and more loyal than they'd been a month ago. Even a nineday ago.

But some of them would still die within the next hour.

The boots retreated, the Cutthroats not having noticed the shorter ceiling of the orlop deck or the newly constructed floorboards underfoot. After a second sweep, they still found no traces of additional crew. Instead of murmuring, the Cutthroats laughed and jeered, celebrating the capture of the new ship with a drink. And a second. And a third. It wasn't long before the rum roused them with laughter, then lulled them with sleep, confident that this ship had been a gift from Eo.

How wrong they were.

A growl formed in Lilyth's throat as she touched her necklace, and her Red Legion stirred at the noise.

"Go," Lilyth said, replacing the necklace within her painted armor. Her painted crew broke cover, crawling out from underneath the false deck like ants from a corpse. Lilyth was the last out, and she appraised the painted legionnaires armed with flintlocks, cutlasses, and knives. Greeley grinned excitedly. Kendrik kept a hand on his cutlass determinedly. Jericho's eyes darted around, looking ill at ease. Like Jericho, most of the legionnaires weren't ready for war, but they were as ready as they'd ever be.

"Time to show them strength," Greeley said with a grin. Like the rest of them, he'd shaved his head, painted himself black, and marked his forehead with a sideways crescent. The mark of the Chosen, as they believed. Uniquely, Greeley's right hand was stained with blood.

Lilyth flashed a vulpine smile, echoed by her followers. *Time for their first test.*

"No flintlocks until they know we are here. We keep silent as long as we can, kill as many as we can. Hold nothing back." After her legionnaires holstered their pistols and unsheathed their blades, she said, "Strength and loyalty."

"Loyalty and strength."

The Red Legion swept out of the sail room near the stern, making their way across the lower deck to clear it of any Cutthroats. A light reflected against the far wall of the corridor, just before Lilyth reached the corner. She held up an open hand, and the Legion stopped behind her. Her hand formed a fist. Greeley and three other legionnaires stepped in front of Lilyth and unsheathed their blades.

"This ship... It was too easy. Only eight crew? Syrens will be stirring in these waters, mark my words," a Cutthroat said in a hushed whisper, coming closer as the light brightened. "The sooner we get to port the—"

Greeley shoved his blade through the Cutthroat's heart as he turned the corner. The lantern dropped from his hand, but a legionnaire caught it and snuffed out the light as another carved the second Cutthroat's throat into a grim smile.

The Red Legion continued forth in darkness.

They cleared each compartment as they crept along until Lilyth spied five Cutthroats playing cards by lanternlight in an open area near the bow. They all sat at one table, talking more than playing. One had passed out with cards in his hand, which his neighbors switched with their own in full view of the others. When they laughed, Lilyth swallowed the bile in her throat.

One might scream before I can kill all four. Not a risk I'm willing to take. Lilyth pointed to a nearby ladder and motioned upward. The Red Legion followed her onto the gun deck, which had been turned into a berth. Cannons had been pushed against the walls and hammocks hung from the ceiling. Dozens of sleeping Cutthroats lied within.

Legionnaires slipped between them, holding out daggers as they waited for Lilyth's signal. She stared at the man lying beneath her talan: a blue-skinned Aritrastan with a golden earring, a half-shaved head, full lips, and a starched white shirt half-way unbuttoned, exposing the swell of breasts.

A woman, Lilyth thought, hearing Rolf's laughter in the back of her mind. *Your name, your family, your reasons. It doesn't matter who you are, what you are, or why you did it. All that matters is that you became a Cutthroat. That is reason enough.*

Lilyth slit her throat before slamming the blade into her heart. She stared down into the woman's eyes as they opened in confusion, pain, and fear. Her mouth moved, but blood spilled in place of words.

Look at me, Lilyth commanded silently, twisting the talan to rend the woman's heart. *Look at me while you die. This is your destiny. This is your punishment. This is what you deserve.*

As blood bubbled from the Cutthroat's lips and her last breath escaped, Lilyth ripped the talan from her chest. Her anger burned brighter. Her heart blazed colder.

The Red Legion slaughtered the Cutthroats in their sleep as Lilyth inhaled the carnage. A few awoke at the sound of the massacre. Their eyes opened only to see black blades rip through their crimson hearts.

Lilyth dipped her fingers in the dead Cutthroat's blood, smearing it across her forehead in a crescent. Religiously, the legionnaires followed her example.

Walking between the swaying hammocks, Lilyth examining the corpses' faces. Their deaths were on her shoulders—light feathers on her unrelenting body. Yet a few bodies caused Lilyth to pause: several young boys, ranging between ten and fourteen. Cabin boys.

Lilyth's hand crept to her daughter's feathered necklace, and her hesitation evaporated like smoke. She left the cabin boys behind, refusing to spit on their bodies and cursing them to the half-death of the Drowned.

More feathers to weigh on her, but theirs were lighter than her daughter's feather.

Alone, Lilyth stalked to the stern, where a door led into the captain's private quarters—*her* quarters. She opened it to find two sleeping Cutthroats lying naked beneath a blanket on the barren floor. Imagining Rolf's cruel smile, she slit their throats and cut apart their hearts. She abandoned their bodies to stain her floor and returned to her legionnaires.

Lilyth split the legionnaires into the three groups. Half were told to wait for her on the gun deck and remove any Cutthroats who traveled below deck. A quarter were ordered to sneak to the bow and descend back to the orlop deck. The other quarter followed Lilyth down the stern ladder back to the orlop deck, intending to surround the gamblers.

Staying unseen in the darkness beyond the lanternlight, Lilyth pulled the bow from her shoulder, grabbing for the arrows she'd strapped to her side in place of a quiver. With a practiced hand, she aimed at the Cutthroat farthest from her. Then paused, redirecting her aim to the lantern.

Cause confusion. Sow panic. It will take them longer to scream. And by then, it will be too late.

Lilyth loosed the arrow. The painted tip shattered the glass lantern and extinguished the flame. Cutthroats sobered and whirled in confusion as both groups of legionnaires converged. The Cutthroats died in a storm of steel.

"Let them know fear and pain. Let them know death," Lilyth whispered as she collected the arrow she'd loosed and returned to the gun deck. At her order, the Red Legion stayed put as she ascended the ladder leading to the main deck. She lifted the hatch to see out, but not enough to draw attention to herself.

A dozen Cutthroats carried out ship duties by lanternlight. Her eyes shifted to the moon and stars before catching the silhouette of the larger three-masted frigate sailing directly ahead of her vessel. The ship loomed like a titan, filled with more men to fight despite the dozens she'd already dispatched.

I will make it my flagship, Lilyth thought, looking for a way to board it. She eyed the thick, weathered ropes used by the Cutthroats to tow her ship through the choppy seas. Those towlines were tied from the gunwale of their ship to the foremast of hers. That was her way across.

But these Cutthroats had to be removed before she used it.

Lilyth closed the hatch and descended the ladder. She split the legionnaires into three groups of eight, sending each to a different ladder along the gun deck.

They climbed and slipped through hatches onto the main deck. Creeping silently through the darkness, they killed the Cutthroats and took their place on the deck as Lilyth picked off others in the rigging with silent arrows. Their bodies splashed as they hit the water, cursed to the depths.

When the deck was purged, Lilyth slunk toward the ship's bow, walking past the youngest member of her Red Legion. Sixteen-year-old Jericho stared at his blade, face stoic but hands shaking.

This is the first time this boy has had to kill. She frowned, unable to sympathize. Her first time had been many years younger. *He is afraid, but he wants to prove himself.*

"Jericho," Lilyth said softly. Maternally. "Are you ready?"

"Yes, Champion," he said, standing stiffly.

Kendrik stepped forward and squeezed his brother's shoulder. Jericho seemed to relax at the contact, comforted. But he was still unsure of himself.

Jericho will never be a warrior, Lilyth thought, leaving him and grabbing the towline. As others crowded near her, she said, "Strength and loyalty."

"Loyalty and strength," said the legionnaires in unison.

Saltwater sprayed Lilyth as she swallowed her fear of the sea and crawled across the rope with chafing fingers. The water beneath was black and churning, a monster with a thousand mouths and no eyes. It called to her, but she ignored its pleas. Instead, she dropped onto the stern balcony and slipped inside the Cutthroat captain's quarters.

Beautiful Corinthian rugs and pelts lined the floor. On the walls hung detailed paintings of medieval Aritrastan wars. An ornate armoire held coats and suits. A lavish mirror with a gilded frame laid opposite the four-post bed, which was unmade and empty. The captain must still have been on deck.

Copperheads, Lilyth guessed. A faction of Cutthroats with questionable loyalty to the Cutthroat King. They worked with Skulls and Avowed as pirates, but they also collaborated with the Aritrastan and Corinthian governments as privateers. They obeyed whoever paid them the most and always carried expensive cargo: gold, spices, and slaves. Lots of slaves.

The image of her daughter whimpering with manacles around her tiny wrists made Lilyth tremble with rage. *This is why Cutthroats kidnapped my family? Enslaved my child? For money and mirrors?* She exhaled and forced the anger aside. She couldn't allow it to consume her until victory was assured. *They want gold? I'll give them steel and lead.*

With her legion following, Lilyth left the captain's quarters and crept along the gun deck, filled with more sleeping Cutthroats. Almost a hundred. Their spilled blood was warmer than the ocean spray—immensely more satisfying.

Lilyth wanted to search the lower decks for her eight captured men, but she didn't. The other slaves might have cost her the element of surprise. Instead, Lilyth walked to the bow, climbed halfway up a ladder, and looked down on her gathered legionnaires. She said, "This night, you have proven yourself to Eo. But there is still more to prove. Above you is the enemy. Men who enslaved you, tortured you, *defiled* you." She paused, locking eyes with various legionnaires, who became angrier with each word. When her eyes landed upon Jericho, she added, "Eo saw greatness within you. That greatness lies in the enemy's blood. You must take it from them." Around her, legionnaires murmured, stirring into a frenzy. Slowly, Lilyth pulled out a flintlock, and others did the same. "You are legionnaires. You are Chosen. Become the night. Become their *death.*"

Lilyth was first onto the main deck, Greeley second. Behind them came a stream of legionnaires who cursed, screamed, and laughed. They swarmed over the first of the bewildered Cutthroats, and Lilyth led their charge. She ducked beneath blades, used human shields to avoid bullets, and emptied her quiver of arrows and supply of flintlocks. Then she relied on the cutlass and talan alone, whirling and stabbing, a maelstrom of paint, blood, and death.

After she slew the last Cutthroat at the bow, Lilyth turned her attention to the stern on the far side of the ship. Some Cutthroats had barricaded themselves by the stairs leading up to the raised quarterdeck. On it stood the grizzled captain, shouting orders, hurling curses, and holding a copper flintlock aloft—the mark of a Copperhead captain.

He was squat and black-haired, though his face was too far away to see clearly. Lilyth imagined his face to be Rolf's. Dark, pitiless brown eyes, a thin mustache, and scarred lips pressed into a line.

"Bring your strength," Lilyth said to Greeley, her body moving forward even as her mind reeled with dissonance.

Duels broke out across the deck, but Lilyth leaped through the chaos.

Greeley followed at her right side, Kendrik and Jericho at her left. Together, they fought in the moonlight, screaming like wraiths, banshees, and syrens as they cut a swath through the enemy lines.

Until Jericho fell.

"No!" Kendrik shouted, tackling the Cutthroat who'd stabbed his brother. He shoved his knife into the man's neck a dozen times.

Lilyth hardly heard Jericho's screams, leaving him and continuing her blistering assault with only Greeley at her side. Between the two of them, the Cutthroats fell to fists and steel.

As she reached the quarterdeck stairs, Lilyth plunged through the rows of Cutthroats. She parried swords and slit throats just before an exploding grenado killed the remaining Cutthroats barring her path.

In the chaos, another grenado rolled to a stop near Lilyth's feet. Before she could kick it away, a legionnaire threw himself onto it and shouted, "For the legion!" just before the explosive detonated. Shrapnel ripped the legionnaire to pieces.

Remorseless, Lilyth continued forward. She trampled the bodies of dead Cutthroats as she charged up the steps, ducking low beneath the railing to avoid getting shot.

As the captain fired the last of his flintlocks, Lilyth emerged from cover and ran straight at the old man. He raised his cutlass against her, but she went left as Greeley flanked right. The man blocked Greeley's first sword thrust only for Lilyth to slam her blade into his back, severing his spine.

With a moan, the Cutthroat crumpled, conscious but bleeding out and paralyzed from the waist down. He feebly tried to raise his blade, but Greeley hacked his arm off.

As the Cutthroat screamed, Lilyth said, "End him, Red Hand."

Greeley stalked forward and crushed the captain's head under his boot. Brains, blood, and bone scattered across the deck.

"Victory is ours!" Lilyth shouted. As legionnaires cheered, the remaining Cutthroats threw down their weapons and raised their hands in surrender, but Lilyth only sneered at them. To the legion, she said, "I need only two men alive. Kill the rest."

As the legionnaires obeyed, Lilyth laid a hand on Greeley's shoulder and said, "Come, Red Hand. There is still more work to be done."

Chapter Twelve

Rain fell like tears onto Greeley's bruised and bleeding face—so did fists. A boy kneeled on top of him, howling furious insults between each strike. Despite the noise of the fight in the narrow alleyway, nobody came to Greeley's aid.

If his eyes weren't swelling shut, Greeley might have cried. If a hand wasn't strangling him, he might have screamed. If this scenario hadn't happened every day—every hour—of his life, he might have been afraid.

Instead, Greeley shouted his own curses as he deflected punches with one forearm. His other hand reached for a rock in his periphery. Its sharp edge nearly cut him as he wrapped his fingers around it.

"Squall you!" Greeley shouted as he slammed the rock into the boy's skull. It caved in with a sickening *crunch*. With a pathetic gasp, he crumbled to the dirty cobblestones at Greeley's side. After he'd wiped away the blood from his mouth, Greeley crawled over to the boy. Through rain, blood, and swelling eyes, it was impossible to tell if he was still alive.

Better to be safe than sorry.

Clenching his broken teeth, Greeley bashed his rock into the boy's face until he could no longer tell cheek from chin, rain from blood, brain from mud.

"Now you're dead." Greeley said, rising from the ground before falling back to his knees. Breath hitching, his eyes darted for any signs of approaching scavengers but saw none. Hand shaking from adrenaline and pain, Greeley snatched the copper necklace from the dead boy's throat and clasped it around his own. It was yet another trophy to add to his growing collection. With a grim, satisfied smile, Greeley escaped into the twisting alleyways to lick his wounds.

Tomorrow, he'd search for his next victim. Somebody with a trophy, be it jewelry, coins, or clothes. Didn't matter, so long as it was something that Greeley could take.

Long years had passed, but his strength never left. Not when Greeley fled the alleyways. Not when he sought out the Cutthroats. Not when they betrayed him, replacing his trophies with chains.

Greeley looked down at his wrists and rubbed the white scars where those old manacles had marred his flesh. His strength hadn't been enough to break the manacles that had bound him, but Lilyth's loyalty had saved him. She had been his rock, glistening with paint and blood.

In return, Greeley became her rock. The Red Hand. The fist that broke bones.

But he still wasn't satisfied—wouldn't be until he had Lilyth in his grasp. Until then, this bloodshed would have to suffice.

Slick with blood, the swaying deck moaned beneath Greeley as he entered the slavehold to find sixty men shackled to the floor. Most carried the marks of slaves: ragged clothes, emaciated bodies, and festering sores. Only the eight captured legionnaires looked strong and unbroken.

Greeley's mind flashed back to his cage. He remembered being chained to the floor, kneeling in his own piss and shit, and wincing as scampering rats bit his toes. He'd spent so long in that darkness that he'd once wondered if he'd ever see light again. They'd made him fight for scraps of food and sips of water just to pass the time.

Him. The Red Hand. Being treated like a lowly dog.

Greeley's gut wrenched. His fingers twitched. *I'm no slave. I'm a free man. I'm Chosen.*

He looked at Lilyth, his eyes softening yet still predatory. Dripping with blood, sweat, and rage, she had treated each thrust like a dance only she knew. So elegant. So deadly. So strong.

So squalling attractive.

His eyes took her in. The slender ankles, thick calves, toned biceps. Her facial features were sharp like the blades she carried. He stared at her waist, wishing he could rip off her armor and wrap his arms around her—

"Red Hand."

Greeley stood straighter, eyes shifting from Lilyth to the legionnaires, who waited to be unshackled. With the key in hand, he undid their manacles before returning to her side. He stared at her as she marked each legionnaire with the blood covering her painted skin.

"Let this be a symbol of your courage for volunteering when many wouldn't. You are among my most loyal," Lilyth said to the freed legionnaires. "Go. Join the others. Enjoy our victory."

Among her most loyal? Greeley wondered as jealousy rose in his heart. *No. I am her most loyal. I am her first, her equal, her Red Hand. Compared to me, they are nothing.*

The slaves, sensing freedom as the legionnaires left the hold, raised their heads to stare at Lilyth and her Red Hand. A murmur echoed amongst the crew.

"Can somebody tell me what the squall is going on?" a short slave asked, his voice hoarse from dehydration. His arms were beefy, black tattoos darkening his blue skin. Long hair tied into a single braid, his face was clean-shaven. Being in his twenties, he should have had a scraggly beard by now.

"What is your name?" Lilyth asked, ignoring his question.

"I'll tell you after you unshackle me," the slave said stubbornly, crossing his arms over his chest. Or trying to. There wasn't enough slack in the chain, so he could only cross his wrists.

A low growl emanated from Greeley's throat. "Answer the Champion's question."

"I will speak for myself, Red Hand," Lilyth said, glaring at him.

Greeley looked away first, not understanding what he'd done wrong. He was the *Red Hand.* Lilyth's first. Lilyth's equal. That's why he was here. That's why she'd chosen him. So why rebuke him and entertain the slave? *I fought alongside Lilyth. I killed the captain.* Me. *This slave is weak. I could break him like a toothpick.*

"You're a Champion?" asked the slave. "You don't look like much."

A ripple of unease coursed through the other slaves. Lilyth stiffened. Her stoic expression didn't change, but the room grew colder. Greeley held back a shiver. *Now she'll kill him.* He stared at her, wishing her to give the order. *Tell me to crush his skull. Let me break him. Let me—*

"These chains haven't broken you yet. Good," Lilyth said, her voice deafening in the silence beyond. "But what do you think will turn to dust first? Your bones or your shackles?"

The slave's eyes flicked between them, saying nothing.

"I can give you freedom," Lilyth said. "I can break these chains that bind your wrists. But to do so, I will need your strength and your loyalty."

"That's it?" the slave asked, grinning despite the filth. "Alright. Sure. You have it. Just get these squalling things off of me."

Such weakness... Greeley glanced at Lilyth again. What could she have been thinking? This slave would *never* be a legionnaire. Better to kill him—kill them all. Was she toying with this slave? Greeley desperately wanted to see inside her mind. Instead, he said nothing.

"Not good enough," Lilyth said, turning her back and taking two steps toward the door.

"Wait." The sailor stared down at his chains, hunching over and shrinking into himself. "Arya. That's my name, alright? Release me, and I'm yours."

Lilyth turned back around. She stared at the slave, who squirmed under her gaze. "You expect me to release you after such disrespect?"

The slave winced, rubbing his chafing wrist. He murmured an apology so quietly that Greeley couldn't hear the words.

Lilyth seemed to hear, though. She handed the keys to Greeley and nodded to him. "Do as she says."

Greeley paused. He must have misheard. "She?"

Arya sat straight up. Her eyes widened in horror. Around her, the slaves glanced between Arya and Lilyth in confusion. "How did you know that?"

"Eo knows all," Lilyth said. "And She welcomes you as you are, whatever and whoever that is."

Another woman, but nothing compared to Lilyth. Just a pale imitation—a shadow, Greeley thought, staring at Arya before leaning forward and unlocking the manacles. They fell from her arms to the ground.

Arya looked down at them and let out a shuddering breath. "I... I didn't think I was ever getting out of those. Just in my dreams."

"What about the rest of us?" another slave asked.

"Join my Red Legion and stand by my side as we fill the Drowned Sea with fire and corpses," said Lilyth. "Otherwise, we will drop you off at the first port we come across."

Greeley glanced at Lilyth. Had she hit her head during the fight? How was *dropping them off* an option?

"You're... *not* gonna kill us?" a third sailor asked.

"There's been enough killing tonight." She paused, the words lingering in the air like glittering keys.

The slaves looked between each other and back at Arya.

Of the fifty-two, all stood and held out their manacles. But of those, four wished to be sent to port. Greeley glowered as he released the forty-eight newest legionnaires and watch as Lilyth marked them. At her instruction, the other four remained manacled.

"You said you'd free us," one of the four said, shaking his shackles. "You told us you'd let us go!"

"You were given a choice of freedom, and you refused it," Lilyth said, cold as the darkness that surrounded her, and turned her back on them. "Come, Red Hand. We are done here."

Relief flooded through him. Lilyth had been lying. Of course she'd been lying. Yet Greeley hadn't been able to tell. Strange just how good of a liar she was.

"You can't just leave us here!" another shouted as Greeley turned his back on them.

"Why not?" Lilyth asked.

"It's wrong!"

Greeley laughed. Lilyth didn't. "Arya's stubbornness is a strength, but your cowardice is a weakness. This is where you belong."

"I change my mind!" the first slave shouted. "I'll join you, alright? Just free me."

"Too late." Lilyth's voice was colder even than her gaze, snuffing out the whimpers of the remaining slaves.

Arya took a step forward. "Uh, Champion—"

"Arya, I will tell you this only once," Lilyth said. "Aboard my ships, all warriors are welcome. Men *and* women. But only warriors. Only those with strength and loyalty. You have shown me your strength. Now show me your loyalty."

Arya looked at the four men before dropping her eyes and taking a step back.

"Always remember: those who are not with us are against us," Lilyth said as she left the slavehold. Arya followed, as did Greeley, who savored the screams of the slaves as he closed the door behind them—loving Lilyth all the more.

◆◇◆

Rising from the darkness of the slavehold, Lilyth admired the pile of corpses rotting at the bow beside a pile of coin purses, pistols, and cutlasses—supplies for the ruthless war ahead. She turned her attention to the bodies of four sacrificed legionnaires laid to rest behind the foremast. A fifth leaned against the mast: Jericho. Blood spilled between Kendrik's fingers as he tried to hold his brother's wound closed.

"He's going to be okay, right?" Kendrik asked as Lilyth kneeled beside him. "This... this is just a flesh wound, isn't it?"

Lilyth assessed the stab wound with lanternlight. The crimson river gushed but was not dark, arterial blood. The blade seemed to have hit below the heart, the wound looking more severe than it was. By the way he breathed, it had missed his lungs too. Probably by less than an inch. Still a terrible wound, but Lilyth had cleaned and sewn together worse. Jericho could survive.

If Lilyth wanted to save him, that was. But to hone Kendrik into the zealot she needed, Jericho had to die.

"I am afraid the blade nicked an artery," Lilyth whispered, thinking of her daughter to bring herself to the verge of tears. Shoving Kendrik's hand back onto the wound as Jericho groaned, she added, "Hold the wound and staunch the blood flow while I pray to the Goddess. She's the only one who can save him now."

Closing her eyes, Lilyth pressed her hands against Jericho's head. In Aenuite, she whispered, "You can still save him, Eo. I know You can, but I also know that You won't. You could stop me, too, if You wanted, but You won't do that either. So now, I'm going to kill him. His blood is on Your hands."

Lilyth waited for Eo's response. It didn't come. Not that she'd expected one.

With a sigh, Lilyth opened her eyes and reached for one of Jericho's hands, feeling the fear in his shaking fingers. "Eo has spoken. It's your time to go into the night."

"I don't want to go," Jericho whispered to his brother. Then, to Lilyth, "Please don't make me go."

Kendrik looked at her helplessly. Perfect. "Can you do anything to save him?"

"Eo has already saved him, Kendrik. Her arms are wrapping around him even as we speak," Lilyth said. "Jericho has given us his strength. Grab his hand, and we shall give him ours."

Kendrik looked down at his dying brother. He seemed to want to say something more, but nothing came. Eventually, he grabbed Jericho's other hand, still pushing against the wound.

"We are with you, Jericho," Lilyth said, loud enough for the other legionnaires to hear. Many kneeled beside Lilyth, even those new to the legion. Isolated, Arya stood alone by the mainmast, arms crossed over her chest uncomfortably.

Lilyth put a hand on Jericho's cheek, smearing the paint and tears together. "I once told you that we are the night—that is Eo's truth. Your journey is not over, Jericho, nor will it ever be. She will take you and place you among the stars. Forevermore, you will watch us. Forevermore, you will guide us on our path. In darkness, we will know you and see you, just as we do now. We give you our loyalty and strength, as you gave yours to us. May the night take you, and may you suffer no more."

Lilyth plunged her talan into Jericho's heart without breaking eye contact. *You should not have given me your loyalty, boy,* she thought as he jerked, spasmed, and stilled. Beside her, Kendrik sobbed, and she placed a hand on his back to comfort him. *But even in death, you will be of use. It will make your brother that much easier to control.*

Sniffing, Lilyth closed his eyes and placed her mark on his forehead. "Jericho is among the first to join the night, to join the Unseen Lady. He will not be the last. But make no mistake. Jericho is not gone. He will never be gone. Each night, he will return to guide us, as will the others. These men's sacrifice are not, and never will be, in vain."

Five sacrificed so that I can save two. How many more will die? Lilyth wondered, touching her daughter's necklace. *As many as it takes.* She rose in silence, her shoulders square and her chin held high as she faced her followers.

"Legionnaires, from this night forward, this ship will be called the *Jericho*. Let us never forget the strength and loyalty of our brethren. Of Jericho, Keven, Nathaniel, Alfred, and Trevan. All of them great men and greater warriors. Let us send them into the night, into Eo's awaiting arms!"

Legionnaires prepared a rowboat as a makeshift funeral pyre. Along with the four others, Jericho rested in the boat with his hands crossed over his chest. Lilyth's mark remained on his brow as Kendrik removed his younger brother's flintlock and cutlass, fastening them to his own belt. In their place, he slid a knife between his brother's interlaced fingers. Kendrik sprinkled gunpowder over his body and spat on his chest to bless his soul before stepping away. As the boat was lowered into the Drowned Sea, Lilyth handed Kendrik a lantern. He hesitated before taking it, hands shaking the light. Kendrik lifted it over the gunwale but didn't release it. "I can't do this."

"Grief is heavy, Kendrik, but it is not a burden that you carry alone," Lilyth said, placing a hand beneath his forearm to steady him. "I will keep you strong. So will Jericho, for this night and all to come."

When Kendrik released the lantern, it shattered on the rowboat, igniting into a blazing pyre. The boat and bodies burned for several minutes before the waves swallowed them.

Lilyth faced Kendrik, who trembled silently as tears streamed down his face. She put a hand on his shoulder. "Close your eyes, Kendrik."

The legionnaire obeyed.

"Jericho is with us," she said, lightly resting her other hand on his shoulder for a half-second before removing it. "You can feel both of our hands on your shoulders, can't you?"

"I can." Kendrik lifted his head, and his eyes opened. Tears streamed between them. He let out a small laugh. "I *feel* him. He's there, in the night, guiding us. You were right, Champion. You *are* right."

"I would never lie to you, Kendrik," Lilyth said as more legionnaires gathered around them. She dipped her hand in the blood that stained the deck and pressed it against Kendrik's chest. A red handprint remained after she removed hers. "For your loyalty in this battle, I name you the Red

Heart—my second lieutenant. Whenever you charge into battle, my mark will be carried with you." Then she walked over to the pile of loot near the bow and picked up the captain's copper flintlock, which Greeley had been eyeing. Lilyth returned to Kendrik and placed the gun in his hand, adding, "Let this be a sign of your greatness. Let no one forget your sacrifice."

Kendrik nodded beneath the tears.

Lifting her chin upward, Lilyth staring at the sky and shouted, "My Red Legion! I want you to remember this night for all time! Forevermore, when you howl into the night, the night howls with you! Strength and loyalty!"

"Loyalty and strength!" the Red Legion screamed—Kendrik's voice louder than even Greeley's.

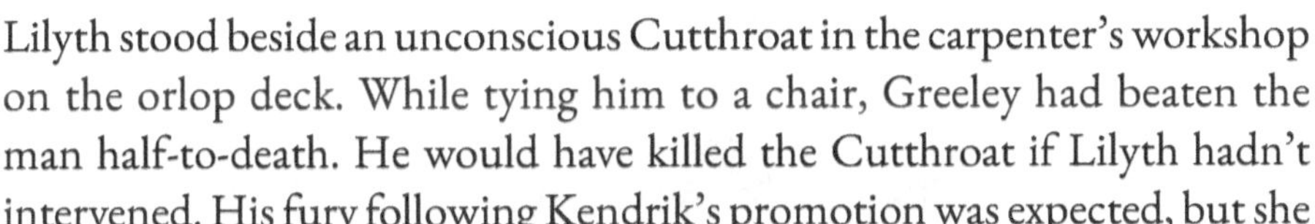

Lilyth stood beside an unconscious Cutthroat in the carpenter's workshop on the orlop deck. While tying him to a chair, Greeley had beaten the man half-to-death. He would have killed the Cutthroat if Lilyth hadn't intervened. His fury following Kendrik's promotion was expected, but she couldn't have him killing her captives until she had the information she needed. Until then, Greeley waited outside the workshop and paced across the deck, probably thinking she couldn't hear him.

He is but a dog—a feral one. A frown creased her brow. Lilyth wasn't yet worried about Greeley's loyalty, but his jealousy and lack of emotional control would become a problem if left unchecked. She considered slitting his throat again, now that she had Kendrik as another lieutenant.

No. Greeley's ruthlessness and cruelty are too valuable to waste so early in this war. I will keep him alive for now, but I need to keep him exhausted, break his ego, and give him a distraction, Lilyth thought, staring at the compartment's door. Earlier, when he'd thought nobody was watching, Greeley had been eying Arya. *She would work, but how to balance the three of them?*

Lilyth returned her gaze to the Cutthroat, mind churning with possibilities. She couldn't demote Greeley—his pride couldn't handle such disrespect. He'd slaughter Kendrik, Arya, and anybody else who came close. But something more subtle could work.

I will start neglecting Greeley to make him think he has upset me. Then I will promote Arya. They will both be on an even playing field. Greeley will try to intimidate her, but Arya seems too head strong to yield...But how to handle Kendrik?

Lilyth pondered the question. Kendrik was naive but intelligent. Now that Jericho was dead, he would be completely devoted to the Red Legion. He would need more guidance and tutelage, but Kendrik could become a great warrior. If only Kendrik could learn to be ruthless, he'd be the perfect adversary for Greeley. His superior, even.

Three lieutenants beneath me: Greeley, Kendrik, and Arya. For the next few battles, I will have Arya and Greeley fight together. Then I will promote her, have all three of them pining for my attention. I will focus on Kendrik and Arya at first, and then only Kendrik. Arya and Greeley will team up to remove him and regain my favor. They will all be too exhausted, divided, and confused to depose me. My authority will remain absolute.

Lilyth grinned, knowing before she'd even made the first move that she'd won this game. On to the next. On to Rolf.

Lilyth examined the bound Cutthroat more closely. Where once he'd been a handsome young man, his face was now split by dozens of cuts and purple-black bruises. Short black hair fell across his closed eyelids, mouth slack-jawed and partially open as he snored. Instead of the Aritrastan fabrics, he wore simple leathers unfit for nights at sea.

A Corinthian Cutthroat, Lilyth thought. Not an entirely peculiar sight, though uncommon as his people warred more over land than sea. From what she'd seen after years at sea, only a Tavrakian or Aenuite would have been a stranger sight.

Metal glinted beneath the man's shirt. A necklace. Upon closer examination, its pendant was of Deitan, the Corinthian God of the sun. She snarled, unable to prevent the coming flood of rage or memory.

A burly husband with curling brown locks and matching eyes played at the edge of a jungle river with his young daughter, his splitting image. He laughed as she squealed, neither aware of the approaching danger. Cutthroats flew down the river with their flags and sails and cannons and—

Lilyth twitched, ripping the necklace from the Cutthroat's neck as her heart pounded with ceaseless guilt. *I should have been there sooner.* She stared at the golden pendant before letting it fall to the floor. *But I'm coming now, and nobody will stand in my way.*

When the Cutthroat stirred, Lilyth circled behind him, waiting. As he came to his senses, he looked around the room, seeing nothing, hearing nothing. He fought against the restraints, thrashing in the chair and almost tipping it over several times.

Let him think there's hope.

The Cutthroat began biting the rope that secured his left hand to the armrest. After several attempts, the knot loosened. He wiggled his arm, beginning to pull it free.

Then take it.

Lilyth stabbed her talan into his hand, impaling it to the wooden arm. The Corinthian screamed as she rounded the edge of the chair and faced him. A soulless absence lingered in his widened eyes. A howling scream that was stifled by fear alone. She'd broken him already.

Such was the danger of hope.

Now give it back.

"Look at me," Lilyth said, touching his cheek with an open hand even as the Corinthian flinched away from her touch.

He didn't respond, only licked his chapped lips and flicked his eyes between her and the floor.

Lilyth switched languages and spoke in Corinthian. "I have seen the coin chalice and serpent on your ship's flag. A Copperhead, are you not? You are accustomed to negotiating. So, here is my offer: answer my questions, and you live."

The Corinthian's eyes widened in shock. "You know our language?"

Lilyth turned her lips in a small smile. "Yes, and if you tell me what I want to know, I swear to Deitan that I'll let you go."

Relief and hope flooded his eyes. He nodded.

"Good choice." Lilyth walked around him, her fingers drifting against his skin. Then, when she was behind him, she put her hands on his chest. "Tell me, what is your name?"

"Quintus. Quintus Rutilus."

"Very well, Quintus," Lilyth said, dragging him and his chair toward a table. On it rested an incomplete map of Port Tibur. Lilyth had drawn the general shape of the port but little else. "I need information about Tibur. All Copperheads should know it well. You are going to fill in this map for me. Everything that you know." Lilyth slid the paper toward him before setting out a feather quill and inkwell. The smile dropped from her lips as she added, "I will know if you lie, because other members of your crew have made similar maps. If your notes don't line up with theirs, I will hurt you in ways you can't even imagine. Do you understand?"

"Yes," he stuttered.

"Good." Lilyth cut the bonds of his right hand without undoing the other restraints. "Begin."

With a shaking hand, Quintus gripped the quill and added information to the map. Fortified garrisons outfitted with cannons and muskets littered the coast, providing support in case of an invasion. South was the Copperhouse, a bank used by the Copperheads to move cargo and money. East was the Fleshery, the auction house where Fleshlords sold men, women, and children into slavery. North was the Thorn, the headquarters of the Roses, a sect of Cutthroats who supposedly only stole from the rich. But west was Flotsam Hill, the fortress from which the seven Skulls ruled over Tibur.

Lilyth loomed over Quintus as he added more information to the area surrounding Flotsam Hill: streets, businesses, and important people. "Is Rolf the Bloody still there?"

"The Skull? I think so. Maybe?"

Maybe? Lilyth's eye twitched. She glared at him. "Maybe is not an answer, Quintus."

"Uh, I mean, yes," Quintus said, nodding his head vigorously. "He's definitely still there." He blathered on about the Skulls, explaining that most Copperheads knew better than to venture up to Flotsam Hill. Skulls didn't always follow the Cutthroat Code, and they killed and stole from anybody who wandered there.

Lilyth listened to his ramblings, face stoic and unsmiling, and when he no longer spoke, she continued to stare at him, her gaze unflinching and uncomfortable. Quintus squirmed and eventually spoke about every person and landmark he knew. Her questions became more directed, more pointed, and his answers unraveled.

Lilyth pointed down to the map, finger drifting along the ocean south of the port. "And how do I get to the port?" Quintus flinched, looking down. "Yes, I know all about the Battered Reefs. There's a secret way to sail across them, which only a Cutthroat knows. Tell me how."

Quintus looked down. "I don't know. Only the captain knows."

Squalls, Lilyth thought. "He's dead, so write what you know."

"But—"

"Write what you know," Lilyth repeated, stabbing the talan into the table.

Quintus tried, but his path through the reef contradicted the other Copperhead's answer. Neither knew the way through. *I will just have to capture more Cutthroat ships until I find somebody who does.*

When Quintus laid down the quill, Lilyth said, "You've been most helpful, Quintus. Thank you."

"Now let me—"

"Red Hand," Lilyth said, raising her voice. "You can come in now."

The door immediately opened, and Greeley stepped inside. "You knew I was there?"

The fool is as quiet as an ox. Although... he has been waiting there for quite some time. He is more patient than I give him credit for. I will have to remember that.

"Eo has given me many gifts," Lilyth said with a serene smile. She jerked her head to Quintus. "Do with him what you will."

Greeley grinned.

Quintus's face fell. "But I answered your questions!" The Cutthroat struggled in vain. "But you said you'd let me go!"

"I lied," Lilyth said.

"But you swore to Deitan!"

"You should have had me swear an oath on the Drowned Sea," Lilyth said, ripping her talan from his left hand as he shrieked. She left the room, but just before the door closed behind her, she added, "Rip out his tongue first, Red Hand. He screams too much."

Chapter Thirteen

Jameson paced along the *Constable's* main deck as the sun rose on the morning after the Fiveday Celebration. He'd been trudging along the deck for hours, stopping periodically to stare at the horizon. The waves reflected the sun's radiance, twinkling like glass. From a distance, the sea was calm, the clouds wispy and light. A beautiful day. Except trash and feces polluted the water, the air smelled of tar, and the sense of merriment had disappeared.

Alira had returned to normal, its citizens to poverty and starvation.

Jameson busied himself by watching other ships depart. Most of the merchant ships had a Guardian like the *Constable* as a protective escort on the high seas. However, one fleet of merchant ships didn't. They raised anchor and sailed away in a tight pod. All but one were three-masted cargo ships. The last was a scapegoat: a towed sloop that would be abandoned to Cutthroats at the first sign of trouble. It carried just enough treasure to bribe Cutthroats from chasing the rest of the fleet. But the strategy often backfired. While Avowed, Copperheads, Roses, and Fleshlords took the scapegoat as a free victory, Skulls were more interested in blood and mayhem than riches. They destroyed fleets along with scapegoats.

As much as Jameson hated to admit it, Rolf the Bloody was good for business. So long as there were Skulls, there would be merchants hiring Guardians for voyages across the Drowned Sea.

"Figured you'd be the first one back, weaver!" Ink called from below, pulling Jameson from his musings. The captain stood at the bow of an approaching ferry, grabbed the rope ladder thrown over the gunwale, and pulled himself up to the deck. He tossed a coin to the ferryman before walking over to Jameson and clasping his shoulder.

"Hadn't seen you all of yesterday, my boy. Thought you'd found a girlie last night, but I should've just come here first. You're the only man I know to enjoy the sea breeze more than a woman's velvet." Jameson shrugged his shoulders, and Ink added, "You're still upset over the gambler, then?"

"No. To live by gold is to die by lead." Jameson shook his head and clenched his jaw. "It's Alira. This whole squalling place. I hate it. Growing up in these alleyways was tough, Ink. We joined gangs to survive, but even that wasn't enough. Most urchins died in gutters with shanks in their necks, and that was one of the better ways to go." Jameson wrinkled his nose at the thought of the burning powder—a fate worse than death. "I sailed away the first chance I had. Didn't matter who I worked for. Didn't matter what I had to do. Anything was worth it to get away from this place. Even killing." Jameson removed his hand from his sword, unaware that he'd reached for it. "Made a lot of bad decisions before you found me. A lot of things I regret. But, coming back here? I don't know. People look at me different, talk to me different. But I'm not stupid enough to think that things *are* different—the people are the same, the streets are the same, and the Chasm is the same. People die the same." He clenched his jaw. "I just want to go and stay gone."

"You know, weaver, you may have lifetimes of stories, but I've *lived* a lifetime. I've chased the winds for decades, had a dozen battles at sea, and more than my fair share of girlies. Shouldn't have made it this long, but the sea keeps me around for entertainment, I think. You know what I've learned in all that time?"

"What?" Jameson asked, keeping his eyes on the horizon.

"We all choose the ship we sail. Some sink and others weather the storm, but we choose all the same." Ink turned to look at him. "You survived because you looked out for yourself. Same way I did."

Jameson pointed up at the sea cliffs, which were a quarter-mile down the coast. "You really think the ashkids in the Chasm get a choice? They don't even have parents, let alone food or drink."

"No, being born ain't a choice, and that ain't what I'm trying to say, weaver. They can choose to leave the Chasm. Start over. Be better. Like you did. That, or let somebody make the choice for them..."

Even as Ink digressed, Jameson's focus was on the sea cliffs. Up on the jagged rocks, Jameson saw two silhouettes fighting at the edge. A kid and an adult, he surmised by the height difference. Jameson was too far away to make out any details, but it was an easy guess: an urchin and a mugger.

Gods, it doesn't stop, does it? Always another day. Always another fight. Death begets death.

As Jameson watched, the urchin jumped from the ledge and fell a hundred feet into the frothing waves. He gasped as the urchin hit the water, the sound echoing like cannon fire. He flinched, thinking of Daisy, Posey, Eliza, and Josh's faces as the sound of the splash echoed in his mind.

"Don't see a death like that every day," Ink said, shaking his head.

Jameson watched the waves for any signs of movement, but he was too far to see anything. "Can I see your spyglass?"

Ink gave him the small telescope, and Jameson looked through it for several moments. No movement. He exhaled, frustrated. *Death begets—*

A small hand reached above the water.

"By the Gods, he's still alive," Jameson said, stripping off his boots, blades, and most of his clothes.

"What are you doing?" Ink asked as Jameson handed back the spyglass.

"He's alive, Ink!"

"Just because I lost an eye doesn't mean I'm deaf." Ink sized him up and down. "You can't seriously be thinking of *swimming.*"

"He's going to die if we don't help him. The water will smash him into those rocks." Jameson squatted, preparing to jump over the gunwale, but Ink pulled him away.

"I didn't save your life just to let you get smashed into the cliffs, weaver." Ink whistled, and a passing ferry stopped beneath the hull. He descended the ladder to the boat, jumping in as Jameson followed behind.

Ink pointed to the cliffs. "Take us there!"

The ferryman looked at Ink incredulously. "Over there? No! You'll turn my boat into splinters!"

"You don't want to go?" Ink grabbed the ferryman and tossed him overboard. "Then you're just dead weight!"

Jameson grabbed the oars as Ink navigated them around the ships. Where there had been soft swells and gentle winds only minutes ago, a storm had risen on the horizon. The tide pushed against the boat, threatening to capsize it, and Jameson rowed harder still as gusts slowed his progress.

A small hand still struggled above the waves.

Damn the Core, Jameson thought, rowing faster as he tried to reach the kid. *Eo, lend me Your strength.*

The words didn't affect the storm. If anything, it grew worse.

"Heave, Jameson! *Heave!*"

The hand disappeared beneath the water just as they reached the spot. Handing the oars to Ink, Jameson dove into the frigid sea. The deeper he swam, the more his bones chilled. Jameson opened his eyes, ignoring the sting of the salty brine. Turning in a circle, he caught shapes darting through the darkness with long tails and hands instead of fins.

Please let them be myrfolk, Jameson thought repeatedly. He reached for a knife at his belt before realizing he'd taken it off. *Squalls.* Below him, Jameson saw the outline of an outstretched hand. Heart pumping, he chased after the urchin, who had stopped thrashing and was gently sinking.

Grabbing the kid by his shirt, Jameson changed direction and struggled back toward the surface, swimming slower this time with the urchin's dead weight. His lungs moaned. His body shook. His mind raced.

The surface was too far away.

We're not going to make it, he thought.

Then the surrounding shadows grew larger, closer. Hands grabbed his back and legs, their slimy scales and sharp nails digging into his skin. *No! Oh Gods... I don't want to die. Not like this.*

Jameson waited to feel a harpoon in his back. It never came. Instead, the hands *pushed.* Jameson jettisoned to the surface, the light growing brighter as he exploded into the air. He slammed into the gunwale as the child tumbled into the boat.

Ink pulled Jameson aboard as he looked back at the water, seeing dark shapes dart away. They were out of sight before he could tell if they were syrens or myrfolk.

Had to be myrfolk. We'd be dead if those were syrens.

"Thought I was gonna have to find myself a new weaver, but I guess sharks don't like the taste of stories!" Ink said, grabbing the oars and rowing back to the docks.

"M-Myrfolk," Jameson said, shivering. "I-it was the m-myrfolk."

"Belay your mutterings and help the poor lad!"

Not a lad, Jameson thought, staring at the child. Purple bruises covered her face, and her right arm seemed to be dislocated. Blood stained her clothes.

Then he noticed the red bracelet on her wrist. *His* bracelet.

"That sneaky little... Of all the squalling luck!" Jameson took the bracelet from her and wrapped it around his own wrist. He briefly debated dumping her back into the sea before shaking his head. He pressed his hands down on her chest and began compressions. Though her body fluttered, she didn't breathe. Jameson pushed air into her mouth as the boat crashed into the dock. Together, they dragged her onto the flat planks, and Jameson continued with compressions. He winced when he heard a rib crack. "Come on, kid! *Breathe!*"

Finally, a geyser of water jettisoned from the girl's mouth. Her eyes flew open as she rolled over on her side and expelled more water before dry heaving.

"That's a good lad!" Ink shouted.

"A drowned man's gasp is a life regrasped," Jameson said. "She's a child of the sea now."

"She?"

The girl grumbled something unintelligible under her breath as she pushed herself to her feet. She swayed for a moment, and Jameson offered a hand to steady her.

"Take a breath—"

Her arm flashed down toward him, a blade extending from her fingers. Jameson pulled back just quick enough to avoid losing his thumb. "Don't touch me!" Her eyes were piercing, staring through him.

Jameson froze. *Like she's seeing into my soul.*

"Tiny ungrateful urchin," Ink said, reaching for the cutlass at his hip. "We just saved your miserable, rotten life, you—"

"Ink," Jameson said. "I'm fine."

Ink stared at him for a moment before grumbling more obscenities under his breath.

"What's your name?" Jameson asked as Ink regained his composure.

"John," the urchin said after a moment's hesitation. "John Steward."

Jameson's heart dropped. *That can't be coincidence.* Thoughts snapped into place. *She took the bracelet because she wanted me to chase her to the Chasm, so I'd run into the cripple and lose half my purse.* Guilt seamlessly replaced his anger. *But that means that he's her dad, and if he's dead, then that makes her an ashgirl. An orphan. I made the girl into an orphan.*

"Isn't that..." Ink exchanged a look with Jameson. "Your father's name?"

The girl flinched and stared at the ground. "It's mine now," she said, words flat and emotionless. They chilled Jameson's spine more than the cold depths of the Drowned Sea.

"Why'd you jump, Steward?" Ink asked.

The girl clutched her limp right arm. "It was the only way out."

Another pang of guilt coursed through Jameson. *She's like me. Just another kid trying to escape.*

"Your arm's out of place," Ink said. He leaned forward to grab it, but Steward snarled at him and raised her blade. Ink fixed the urchin with a withering stare. "You want to be a one-armed coward for the rest of your life, lass?"

"You want to be a no-eyed asshole, old man?" Steward asked.

A gleam of amusement twinkled in Ink's eye. "You talk as well as any sailor, I'll give you that, but it ain't gonna be easy walking around like a cripple the rest of your life."

After briefly deliberating, Steward lowered her blade. "Fine."

Ink leaned forward and delicately grabbed her arm. "I'm going to put that arm of yours back in place on the count of three. One—" Ink rammed her arm into place as fast as a trevally swallowing a seabird.

Steward shrieked, squeezing her arm after Ink released her. "What happened to three?" Her eyes carried daggers, but she didn't lunge forward to stab him.

"You'd have tensed up. Think the words you're looking for are *thank you.*"

Steward huffed, glaring at him while carefully holding her arm against her chest. Eventually, she said, "Thanks."

"Have any place to go?" Ink asked.

Steward's eyes darted around the dock and flicked back to Port Alira with a frown. She shook her head.

She hates it here as much as I do. Just a girl looking to escape. Choosing *to escape,* Jameson thought. To his captain, he said, "Ink, a word?"

They shuffled a couple of paces away from Steward, though her eyes never left their faces.

With his back to her, Jameson asked, "What do you think of the kid?"

Ink scratched his head. Flakes of white dandruff floated towards the ground. The tribal lines along his neck wriggled as his jaw clenched. "We saved her life, much as I'm regretting it." Ink stroked his beard, staring out at the storm that was brewing toward the south. "You notice how quick the weather changed? Felt like the sea wanted to swallow her up. Perhaps the Gods didn't want us to intervene. Maybe it'd been best to let her drown. We can still make things right, you know. Throw her back."

Jameson stared at him. "You can't be serious."

Ink stared back. "I am."

"Says the man who fished a Cutthroat from the sea and made him his first mate," Jameson said.

"And even then, I wondered if I should have let you drown," Ink said bluntly. "Glad I didn't, but I still wondered. Knew I made the right choice when I saw how those waters scared you straight. But her..." Ink glanced back at Steward, whose eyes still hadn't left them. "There's something different, something off. You can see it in that grave stare. Looks through you instead of at you—like a dead man who still breathes."

"She did drown, Ink."

"But that look, it ain't right."

"So you're going to throw her to her death for staring at you?"

"The sharks—"

"It was *myrfolk*. Not sharks."

"Myrfolk? But they haven't been seen in a hundred years... You really saw them?" When Jameson nodded, Ink added, "You sure it wasn't syrens?"

"I'm sure."

If there was one thing Jameson was sure of, it was that. The myrfolk were benign creatures, with the upper body of a man and the lower body of a dolphin. They were similar in height and weight to Aritrastans. Rumors told of their glorious underwater kingdoms in the depths below the Aritrastan islands with very limited interactions between the two. Tales always circulated in taverns of sailors falling overboard during storms only to be saved by myrfolk, and myrfolk getting trapped in fishing nets only to be saved by sailors. Whether or not they were true, Myrfolk stories had happy endings.

The same was never said of syrens. They were myrfolk who'd gone mad and evolved into far faster, far stronger creatures. Built more like orcas than dolphins but with scales instead of skin. Rather than mindless savages, all sailors knew syrens were strategic, cunning, and merciless. And if the worst myths were to be believed, the syrens had destroyed the myrfolk kingdoms and driven the myrfolk to extinction.

Or so Jameson had thought.

"Hated by the Gods but beloved by the myrfolk," Ink said, wary. He ran a hand through his hair. "And for you to find her... What a twist of the talan this is, son."

"It can't be coincidence," Jameson said.

Ink grunted in displeasure. "Been listening to too many stories, you have."

"I can't just let this go, Ink." Jameson peeked over his shoulder back at the girl. She stared back, gaze as intense as before. He turned back to Ink, lowering his voice. "I got her dad killed. She wouldn't be in this mess if it wasn't for that."

"The man made his own choice and died by it."

"Maybe," Jameson said, unconvinced. "But I can't just leave her."

"What then? You want to bring a near-defenseless girl on a ship with two hundred men?" When Jameson was silent and unyielding, Ink ran his tongue along his teeth. "You're serious about this, then. You think she'd even want to learn the ways of the sea?"

"I think she'd do just about anything to get out of this port," Jameson said, remembering the desperation he'd felt trudging from the Chasm to the docks and begging five captains to join their crews before a sixth finally took him in. Copperheads. It'd been far from an easy life, but he'd survived where others died. Again.

"*The Constable* ain't exactly a luxury ship." Ink crossed his arms. "And she's a bit young for hard work."

"Not that young. She's eleven or twelve by my guess," Jameson said. "That's around the time I left." He shifted uncomfortably, remembering life among the Copperheads. Little food. Lots of pain. Still better than the Chasm.

"Twelve?" Ink asked, looking back at Steward. He shook his head. "She looks no older than eight."

"Urchins look younger than they are—that's what a hungry belly'll do to you." Jameson glanced at Steward again. "She's at least eleven. I'd bet my wages on it."

"Half your wages, you mean," Ink said. His face was stoic and unreadable. He rubbed his chin. "If she's eleven, she's old enough, I reckon..." Then his face darkened like a storm. "But know this, Jameson. Steward's a *boy*. If he's joining us on the ship, nobody can know otherwise. For *his* sake."

"So the deck sways."

"Aye," Ink said. With a huff, he turned and shouted, "Steward! Come here!"

Steward inched closer, a hand ready on her belt.

"Ever been aboard a ship?" Ink asked. "Part of a crew?"

Steward shook her head.

"Well, you want to be?" Ink asked. "We'll start you out as a cabin boy and see how it goes, yeah?"

"Not a cabin girl?" Steward asked.

"It ain't safe to be aboard a ship as a girl, Steward," Ink replied. "My crew's better than most, but just because something ain't shit don't mean it's good eating."

"I can take care of myself," Steward said with a menacing glint in her eye. "When do we leave?"

"Then you'll come with us? That's a good *lad*," Ink responded, forming the last word carefully. "Was to be first light, but these sailors are slow to return. You can come aboard the ship now. More of the crew will trickle in over the next hour and then we'll set sail. Need anything from the city? Any belongings, any—"

Steward was already shaking her head.

She doesn't have anything to bring, Jameson thought, remembering how destitute he'd been before joining the Copperheads. All he'd had was his red bracelet and bad memories.

"You!" a voice shouted.

Jameson turned to see a soaked ferryman raising a fist and walking toward them. "You threw me into the water! Took my boat! I demand—"

"Belay your screaming, coward! And row me back to my ship, else I'll take more than your dingy!" Ink threw a lune, hitting the ferryman in the forehead. It dropped to the dock and landed flat on a plank of wood. Steward's eyes were glued to it, as if the coin held all the hope and evils of the world. Before she could rush forward to grab it, Jameson shook his head. Steward frowned, but she didn't disobey.

The brief trip to the *Constable* was silent and cold. Jameson scanned the water from the starboard side, glimpsing dark shapes that jerked and twisted beneath. He nudged Ink, who looked at the silhouettes and frowned. Neither said a word for fear of spooking the ferryman.

They're myrfolk. They don't hurt our kind, Jameson thought, unconvinced. *But myrfolk aren't known to follow ships. Syrens do...*

Unwilling to finish the thought, Jameson leaned forward and looked at Steward, who was sitting with her eyes closed and hands clenched. Fighting seasickness, probably. That would take a while to get used to, Jameson knew.

As they neared the *Constable*, a small group of sailors peered over the gunwale. Hands helped them aboard and gave Jameson and Steward blankets as Ink addressed the crew.

"Listen well and good, lads. This here is Steward. Fished him out of the waters, we did, and that makes him a part of our crew. The kid's got a bark to him—and a bite. Watch your fingers."

The crew laughed, but Steward was silent, watching them with the talan clutched behind her back. She watched them more like a shark than a little girl. *Like a syren,* Jameson thought, repressing a shiver.

Chapter Fourteen

Erin absentmindedly swabbed the deck with a mop. She wore another cabin boy's clothes, which were too big for her, and had rolled up the baggy sleeves and pant legs. By the dust and stiffness, she knew they'd belonged to a dead boy. Erin shivered from the knowledge more than the cold, though her shoes and hat—*Luke's* shoes and hat—were still wet. But Erin had faced worse things than cold and hunger, and she used her discomfort to focus on the haze of activity across the ship.

Jameson had already explained a lot of the terms, but Erin had forgotten them. What she needed were escape routes, not ten different names for a deck. Why were there so many names, anyway? She'd already forgotten the name of this one, which was at the rear of the ship. Did that make it the bow or the stern? Oh, and why was left always *port?* The Aliran port was currently to their right. And stars were overhead on both sides, so *starboard* made little sense. And why not just call the gunwale a railing?

"Stupid sailors and their stupid words," Erin muttered as she dunked the mop in a bucket of water. "This whole ship's just a bunch of wooden sticks."

Three vertical sticks that scraped the sky. Many more horizontal, smaller sticks that held sails—which also had special names aboard ships for no apparent reason. A square sail was square shaped, but a *jib sail* was triangle shaped. Why not just call it a *triangle sail?* Jameson hadn't known, and neither had Ink. Just a tradition, apparently.

Then there were the ropes. Seemingly infinite coils of rope were used to position those stupid sails. She counted two dozen ropes dangling from each, and the ship had a dozen sails. *Hundreds* of ropes for the sails alone.

More ropes to raise the anchor and hoist barrels of food, water, and equipment onto the deck.

Men scurried along like ants, pulling on seemingly random ropes and carrying supplies down ladders into the decks below. Somehow, they all knew what was what and where was where, even if they were too stupid to know why was *why*.

Dad and I would've made a fortune on these idiots, Erin thought, which only renewed her pain. She briefly debated running for it, returning to Mark's tavern and forgetting about a life at sea. Leaning on her mop, she mentally mapped the ship's layout but failed to think of any escape routes.

Out here, it's just an endless sea, Erin thought, her stomach sinking like an anchor. She thought of diving off the side of the ship before remembering the grinning, splitting faces she'd seen in the water. Erin couldn't leave. She was stuck here, like it or not.

Hands from behind shoved Erin to the deck. Rough splinters bayoneted her forearms as her head collided with the planks. She blinked away the dark spots at the edge of her vision.

"Oy! Done tugging your prick, are you?" a large boy in sweaty clothes asked with a sneer, standing over her with a bucket in one massive, callused hand. Though they were the same height, he was as thick as she was wispy. His size made him look sixteen or seventeen, though his face looked a lot younger with his disheveled brown hair, angry brown eyes, and caterpillar-thick eyebrows. His thin, colorless lips turned upward in a snarl, and the nostrils of his squashed nose flared like a bear's.

Erin stared up at him, dazed and unable to answer. "What?"

The boy tipped the bucket toward her. Seawater splashed across Erin's face and into her mouth. As she coughed and spluttered, the boy said, "Stay out of my way, you got that? I'm gonna pound you flat next time." Then he stepped over her and walked away.

As saltwater dripped from her cropped blonde hair, Erin rose to her feet and clenched her mop like a sword. She took one step in the boy's direction only for a hand to land on her shoulder.

"I wouldn't do that if I were you," an impish voice warned.

"You aren't me." Erin said, turning with a snarl.

A shorter boy with wild red hair, green eyes, and freckles met her glare with curiosity. He had the biggest ears she'd ever seen. "Easy now, didn't mean you any harm. Just a word of warning is all. Taran's a brawler, and well, a light breeze could push you over. You wouldn't last long with the likes of him."

Erin looked the spindly boy up and down. "And you'd last longer?"

The boy leaned forward flippantly. "It depends."

"On what?"

"On how much of a head start I have," he said with a laugh. The red-haired boy flashed a lopsided grin—the left half of his mouth frozen in a permanent line. "My name's Will, but everyone calls me Mouse. Suppose it's because I listen good. That or because I run fast. Not sure which." He shrugged too quickly, looking even more like a mouse with his big ears. "What's your name?"

"John Steward."

"Steward, like a cabin boy? Well, that's as good as any nickname I've heard, and it's your actual name!" Mouse laughed. "Guess that means I don't have to make one up for you—some people are just born lucky, I guess."

Born lucky. Erin frowned. "What's Taran's nickname then?"

Mouse shrugged. "Nobody ever gave him one—not to his face, anyway." He leaned closer and whispered, "But he's always looked like a Terry to me. Just something about his expression. Always frowning. Always terrifying. Always... *Terry.*"

Erin laughed, her shoulders relaxing.

Eyes alight with excitement, Mouse pointed behind her. "Look, Steward!"

With the last of the cargo finally stored, Ink, Jameson, and three other officers assembled at the bow in a solemn procession. Ink held sickles and lunes, Jameson a talan. The three others bore a fresh loaf of bread, a cup of wine, and a bucket of blood, respectively.

"Respect the waves and seas!" Ink shouted. "Offer up your prayers!"

Across the ship, sailors stopped, turning to look at him without speaking. They closed their eyes and mumbled to themselves.

"What's going on?" Erin whispered out of the corner of her mouth.

"Captain's making an offering to the sea," Mouse replied, mimicking without meaning to. "A 'please don't eat us' bribe for the syrens and Drowned, and a 'please protect us' blessing for the myrfolk, if you will. Not like we have Gods on this sea to protect us. We have to take what we can get."

Ink raised the coins above his head before scattering them. Erin wished she was close enough to guess his words by his lips as she'd done back on the dock. She hadn't been able to read Jameson's lips, though, because he'd faced away from her.

Ink had wanted to throw me back into the sea, but Jameson wouldn't let him. Not even after Dad and I stole from him. Why?

Erin watched as Jameson followed Ink's lead, tossing the talan into the water. He prayed longer than Ink, probably would have prayed far longer if he hadn't been told to finish and let the other three waiting to make their offerings.

"Coin is for good fortune, talan for protection, bread for fair winds, and wine for calm seas," Mouse said before she'd even asked. "But I've never seen the chum used before. Not for this, I mean. Blood for... blood, I guess? A life for a life? A sacrifice, maybe?"

A sacrifice for me, she thought.

"Either way, it's not a great sign," Mouse said.

"Why?"

"It means that there are bad omens afoot."

With the ceremony completed, another moment of silence passed before Ink shouted, "Alright, lollygaggers! Get a move on! Haulers to the lines, riggers to the sails! Have us ready to leave before the *Pelican* sets off! Ain't much of an escort if we keep 'em waiting!"

Sailors—the riggers, Erin guessed—climbed ropes and unfurled sails dozens of feet above the deck. How they kept their balance was beyond her, but she marveled at their skill as they moved deftly between sails and sticks. One even climbed to the top of the biggest vertical stick and shouted observations down to Captain Ink.

Others—the haulers—lined up on the deck of the ship and began untying and pulling the ropes connected to the sails. Several teams of haulers heaved ropes together, chanting shanties to keep them in rhythm. Their feet found purchase on the swaying deck even as Erin stumbled.

"Ahoy, captain!" came a shout from the right side. A sailor stood on a ferry below, hands grasping upward. "Throw me down a rope and let me up!"

Ink crossed to the gunwale to look down at him. "Stevens! You're late!"

"Sorry, captain, lost track of time! Let down a rope, won't you?"

"Can't do that, Stevens! We already gave our offering."

The sailor's mouth opened wide. "But, captain, I've been working for you for years! Let me up!"

"Been late for years!" Ink responded with a disappointed shake of his head. "Can't let you up, Stevens! We'd be risking the sea's wrath."

"But, captain—"

"Sorry, lad, but I ain't your captain anymore. Good luck to you."

Stevens continued to call up to Ink, but he'd already walked away from the gunwale.

"Why won't he let him on the ship?" Erin asked.

Mouse shrugged. "Can't. Once the offering is made, the ship is protected. If more people or cargo come on afterward, the ship loses its protection. Don't matter if it's a sailor, a mother and a wee babe, or a member of even the Jade Parliament—they'll be tossed off the ship quicker than a crate of nanners."

"Nanners?"

"Nanners. Bananas. Same thing, same curse. All the cargo ships that used to carry them just disappeared in the Drowned Sea one day. Not sure why, maybe the deep terrors took to the nanners, or maybe it was just plain bad luck. Either way, no one will carry them across the sea. It just ain't worth the risk."

A scream followed as a rigger fell from the ropes and crashed onto the deck, snapping his leg at the knee. His screams made Erin flinch.

Mouse remained unbothered. "Damn the Core, that looks like it hurts." Mischievously, he grinned and snapped his fingers. "I've got it."

"Got what?" Erin asked.

"His nickname. *Crane.*" Mouse slapped his knee and chuckled under his breath. When he noticed Erin simply staring at him, he asked, "What? Too soon? You gotta laugh about these things, Steward. That, or we cry."

Erin grunted, turning her attention to Ink as he stomped back to the gunwale.

"Damn you to the Core, Stevens! This is your fault!" Ink shouted overboard. "Get out of here before I break your legs!" He barked more orders as a couple of haulers carried the injured sailor below deck.

"Captain, please!" Stevens shouted. "Let me up! I need the work!"

Ink pulled out a flintlock and pointed it at Stevens. "I'll give you lead if you don't leave. I swear it on the Drowned Sea!"

All around her, sailors tensed. Even Mouse, who hadn't batted an eye at the rigger's broken leg. *A Drowned Sea oath,* Erin thought. *The captain's serious. He'll really kill him.*

Stevens knew it too. He left without another word, the ferry pulling away and heading to a different ship.

Ink turned to stare at his crew, who'd stopped to watch the exchange. "What are you piss-poor scumsuckers staring at? Get back to work before I send you with him!"

They did.

"See what I mean?" Mouse said as he resumed mopping. "Bad omens. No way to start a voyage. Offering or no offering."

Erin worked beside him, mind stuck on the ritual. "So there's just a pile of coins down in the water? Talans, too? Why hasn't anyone just stolen them?"

"Syrens and Drowned infest the waters, along with sharks, squids, and deep terrors. Don't think anybody's crazy enough to jump in with the likes of them."

You've never been in the Chasm then, she thought, thinking of urchins and chard addicts as she leaned against her mop.

"Steward!" Ink barked, marching toward her. "Did I tell you to stop mopping, you sniveling whelp? Haven't even left the port yet, and you're already slacking off!"

"Storms a'coming. Good luck with Patchey," Mouse said before disappearing out of sight.

Patchey? She wondered as Ink stopped in front of her, glaring with one eye. The other was safely hidden behind a patch. Erin stifled a grin, biting the inside of her cheeks.

Ink arched an eyebrow. "Well, are you deaf *and* stupid, my boy? If so, I'll just cast you into the sea by your ears and let the syrens devour you until those be the only things left!"

"I'm not deaf."

"Look at that. The boy can speak," Ink mocked. "Aboard this ship, I'm the *captain,* you understand? Or do I have to beat some sense into you?" Ink grabbed her shoulders, shaking her violently before letting go.

Erin sucked in a breath through her teeth, holding her right arm. Her shoulder pulsed with pain. "I understand, *captain.*"

Ink slapped her hard enough to send her to the ground. "If you're gonna be a cabin boy on my ship, you gotta be working! I tell you when to breathe, when to sleep, and when to eat! Core be damned, I tell you when to piss! We may be a mercenary escort for the *Pelican*, but that doesn't mean we lollygag about the deck! Too much work to be done, so get to swabbing!"

Erin collected herself slowly. Too slowly.

"On your feet, you worthless barnacle!" Ink pulled her up, wrenching her shoulder. It took all her strength not to cry out in pain.

"Yes, captain," Erin said, wincing as she mopped, arm throbbing.

"You gotta earn your keep on these seas, lad! You want to sail on the Drowned Sea or swim with the syrens?"

Erin winced again. "Sail, captain."

"With conviction, lad!"

"Sail, captain!" Erin shouted, garnering a couple of hardened grins from nearby sailors. Her cheeks flamed with embarrassment.

"Then get to cleaning! I want it spotless!" He shoved her forward, and she stumbled before catching her feet.

Erin grumbled as she walked back over to Mouse and Taran, who had refilled his bucket with more water. Mouse whistled as he slapped his mop on the deck and cleaned. Taran shoulder-checked her as he walked past. She didn't fall, but his momentum pushed her back a couple of feet. Her shoulder throbbed.

"Watch it," Taran said as he stormed off to clean another part of the deck.

Erin gripped her mop and held it sideways, staring at the back of his head. *He's slow. Strong but slow,* she thought. *If I could get him to the ground, his strength won't matter.* Erin readjusted, aiming for the back of his kneecaps as Mouse put a hand on her mop.

"Don't do it, Steward. Seriously. Unless you want to be called Piss for the rest of your life."

"Piss?" Erin asked, lowering the improvised weapon.

"Well, yeah. There was this other cabin boy who cracked Terry with a mop. All it did was piss him off. Terry beat that boy so bad that he shit his pants—reeked of it for a nineday. That's how he got the nickname Shits."

"And you think Taran would beat me so bad that I'd piss myself?"

"I know he would," Mouse said with an amused smirk. "And then we'd have to call you Piss, so just don't do it. Steward's a way better name."

"Where's Shits now?" Erin asked, knowing she would have remembered hearing someone called by that name.

"Well, you're wearing his clothes, aren't you?" Mouse said, no longer smirking. "What do you think happened to him?"

"Taran killed him?" she asked, hastily taking a step back.

"What? No, no. Shits and Terry got along pretty well after the whole mop incident. I think they respected each other, believe it or not." Mouse shook his head. "No, there was a bad storm a few months back—Shits fell overboard. We threw him a line, but the syrens got him before he could pull himself back to the ship. They dragged him beneath the waves, turning 'em red."

"Serious?" Erin asked, looking back toward the water. She couldn't see any silhouettes, but she still remembered seeing their faces. Erin shuddered.

"Saw the whole thing," Mouse said, uncharacteristically serious. "Wouldn't lie about something like that."

"That's horrible."

"Welcome to the Drowned Sea, Steward. Lots of things are squalling horrible, but that's why we've got to make our own fun. Like I said, we either laugh or we cry, but I ain't a crier. Don't take you as one, neither."

Erin shook her head.

"So, how's about we make our own fun, Steward? Always did want a partner-in-crime." Mouse spit into his hand, holding it out to her. "What do you say, friend?"

Erin stared at him, taking in his thin nose, lopsided smile, emerald eyes, and fiery curls. *I've never had a friend before.* Then she smiled back. She reached forward to shake, but Mouse pulled his hand away.

"No, Steward, you gotta spit first. It's a blessing on this sea. A salt-for-salt, life-for-life kind of thing. Curse if you don't, really."

Erin spat, and some dribbled down her chin.

"We'll work on that," Mouse said, spitting in his own hand. "But if you do it again, I might just start calling you Spits." He laughed, shaking her hand.

Erin smiled, feeling better than she had in days.

Then she looked back out over the blue sea and saw a dark silhouette dart beneath the ship. The terror returned.

Chapter Fifteen

Erin mopped for hours while Mouse whistled beside her, and Taran continued filling buckets, muttering beneath his breath. Erin learned to shift out of his way as he walked, else he'd ram into her aching shoulder. Several times, she had prepared to swing her mop at him, but somebody was always watching. If not Mouse, then Captain Ink—his stare was brutal enough to drain her anger. She memorized the expression, trying to shape it on her own face.

"Don't mind him."

Erin jumped, dropping the mop and reaching for her talan.

"Easy. Just me, just Jameson." The first mate held up his hands in mock surrender, a smile plastered on his face, but Erin focused on the red bracelet at his arm. She'd seen similar garments when she'd been in the Chasm, in her brief run-ins with gangs. Affiliation rags.

Jameson was in a Chasm gang then. Which means he was an ashboy.

Jameson stared at her piteously. "Hey, don't worry about that, okay? You stole from me, but I stole it back, and we're even now, alright?"

Why are you being nice to me? she wanted to ask but didn't trust herself not to lash out if she did. Instead, Erin stared at the ground, saying nothing.

"Look, Ink'll be hard on you, just like he was with me back in the day. Still is, really. But it's for your own good. Don't take offense to it, alright?"

Erin bit her lip, nodding her head only once.

"Once we get away from port, we'll be running shifts again instead of all hands. Three eight-hour shifts. Ink will run one, I'll run another, and the second mate will run a third. You run between crews for messages and working assignments with the other cabin boys. I'll teach you what I can and so will the others. Sound good?"

"Sure."

Jameson paused like he wanted to say something else. Then, changing his mind, he went to oversee progress with the rigger high overhead, leaving Erin with the open water.

The seas rolled with small swells, and the sun blazed through the parted clouds. The horizon separated the sky from the water in a crisp line, continuing forever in both directions. Erin looked back to see the fading Aritrastan coast. Alira was only a pinprick at this distance. Though she knew it wasn't possible, she imagined her father waving from the dock.

"He's not there," she said. She squeezed her eyes shut, pushing down the grief welling in her chest.

"Steward!" Ink shouted behind her.

Erin jumped. "Yes, captain?"

"You're still lollygagging about? Didn't I already tell you that you aren't here to stare at the sea? That's the helmsman's job!" He pointed down the stairs. "I need you helping Cook with the meals! *Now!*"

Before Ink could pull out a flintlock and shoot her, Erin sprinted across the deck to a hatchway with a ladder leading below. She climbed down to the gun deck, running after Mouse, who was motioning at her to follow him toward the kitchen—the *galley*, as it was called. Together, they slipped around sailors, who'd pushed cannons to the walls and lounged in the center of the deck at tables, in hammocks, or on the ground.

The cooks in the galley weren't so relaxed. There were only two, and both screamed at one another as they took stock of the food rations. One pulled salt beef from barrels of brine, and the other poured rum into small cups.

Real food, she thought, eyeing the supplies and licking her lips. *Not scraps.*

Erin fell in-step beside Mouse and Taran as they prepared trays for sailors: hardtack biscuits, salt beef, hard cheese, lime juice, rum, and water. Erin added hardtack to trays and stole one of those biscuits. She tried eating it, but after almost chipping her tooth on the first bite, she put the hardtack on a sailor's tray.

Beside her were two other cabin boys, who gracefully cut cheese into small cubes and placed it silently onto trays. Twins, by their identical appearances. With hunched shoulders and scrawny arms, these black-haired boys were pallid despite their time on the open sea. Still, their clothes were clean and stain-free, unlike hers, Mouse's, or even Taran's.

After the trays were full, one cook called lounging sailors to the galley's door to hand them their food. It was a serious procession of burly sailors stating their names and demanding their trays, made more serious by the strict rationing. The cooks accounted for every crumb.

To pass the time and to forge more alliances, Erin turned to the pallid twins. She asked "What're your names?"

"Tomlin," the half-inch-taller twin said.

"Jarrel," the shorter one added, the finality of his tone indicating an end to the brief conversation.

Mouse sidled up beside Erin and said, "Tom and Jerry don't talk much. They don't mean anything by it." To them, he said, "This here's Steward. Today's his first day."

"No shit," Taran said with a snort.

"Shits," Tomlin said, his face souring. "You're wearing his clothes, aren't you?"

"It's disrespectful, you know." Jarrel closed his eyes and bowed his head, making a warding symbol with his hands. "It insults his memory."

Taran grunted and turned away to retrieve more trays.

Mouse waited until Taran was out of earshot to whisper, "Shits was a good kid. Terry took his death hard... We all did." He pulled out a small pendant around his neck and gripped it in his fingers. Crashing waves were engraved on one side—a crescent moon on the other. Erin gritted her teeth as he uttered a small prayer to Eo and then to the sea itself. "But Eo's taking care of him now, just as She takes care of us all."

I wonder if Shits thought the same thing right before he got eaten by a syren.

Erin turned to help Mouse lift a barrel from the floor onto a table for one cook. She heaved it up onto a serving stand and grunted as her lower back screamed.

"Lift with the legs, Steward," Mouse said. "Not your back."

"He ain't got legs," Taran said, watching with crossed arms. "All he's got are twigs."

Erin fingered the talan hidden in her sleeve. *Blades are supposed to be felt, not seen.* She imagined stabbing Taran before remembering the kid she killed in the Chasm while escaping the chard addict. Erin let go of the talan, her stomach swaying with guilt as the deck shifted beneath her. She stumbled while everyone else remained solid.

"Weak arms *and* weak legs, eh, Twig?" Taran said, standing upright despite the pitching deck underfoot. "No wonder your parents abandoned you!"

The guilt disappeared, and Erin grit her teeth. *Squall it.* She took a menacing step in Taran's direction, but Mouse blocked her path.

"Oy! Are you Mouse's pet now?" Taran asked, rolling up his sleeves for a fight as the cooks watched with interest. "Makes sense that you two squalls would be fast friends."

"Don't listen to him, Steward," Mouse whispered. "He's trying to bait you."

"It's working," Erin said, fingers reaching for the talan. "Get out of my way, Mouse."

"Do you even know how to fight?" Mouse asked without moving.

I know how to kill, Erin thought as she stared at Taran, who cracked his knuckles and grinned. *I just have to stab him once. Somewhere where it won't kill him—just scare him. That'll shut Taran up.*

"Listen, I've had my ass beat enough times to learn a thing or two," Mouse said, lowering his voice even more. "I'll teach you what I know, and when the time comes, we'll take Terry down together. You and me, friend. What do you say?"

Erin glared at Taran. The idea of hurting instead of killing was strange. So different from everything she'd ever learned in the Chasm.

Taking a step back and returning to her work, she said, "You've got yourself a deal, Mouse."

◆◇◆

Alira disappeared with the sun. The moon's light reflected off the dark ocean like a second sky. Still, Jameson only saw shades of black upon the waves. The darkness wrapped around him like a cocoon, as if the Unseen Lady was embracing him.

Ink, too, had disappeared down into his quarters to check the ship's log, review supplies with the quartermaster, and survey the navigation charts to confirm their bearing. It was as if Ink never slept.

Not like I'm sleeping much either, Jameson said. *Not in this cold.*

With the chill air of the ocean spray keeping him awake, Jameson adjusted his fur jacket to warm his arms and chest. The on-shift sailors wore an assortment of colors, having bought jackets or rented them from other crewmates. On especially wintry nights, the crew appeared as beasts in the sea mist. Animals in the fog.

Jameson looked down at Steward, who stood at his side, bundled in Mouse's orange jacket. Her eyes soaked in the world, her lips pressing together in a hard line. Considering it was her first night at sea, it was easy to guess what bothered her.

"Don't worry, it'll grow on you," Jameson said, staring over the bow as waves sloshed against the hull beneath.

"What will?" Steward asked, glancing at him.

"The Drowned Sea. It can be scary but also gentle and kind. Much like the people who sail on its waters."

Steward turned, frowning. "How did you know I was worried?"

"Everyone's the same way at first. I know I was. You get onto the ship and think about the wind in your hair, the calm waves beneath, the shining sun, but more than anything, that *anticipation*, that sense of destiny, that feeling that the waves are calling your name. All you want to do is unfurl the sails and control your fate."

Jameson closed his eyes, remembering when he'd sailed away from Alira. That hope of a better life and freedom from a choking city. Even now, it was difficult to describe that rush of pure exhilaration.

Just as difficult to describe the overwhelming sense of dread upon realizing that there was no changing his mind. That fear of the unknown was just as horrifying as the relief of freedom. They were two sides of the same coin.

Gently, Jameson said, "When you get this far out, this far from civilization, you realize just how big the world is, and how small we are by comparison. Doesn't feel like we're in much control of anything out here." Jameson gestured to the waves. "A calm sea is glass, but an angry sea swallows ships and men alike. You can fire a broadside into its surface, but you'll never make a scratch. Water doesn't bleed. It *is* blood—the blood of Undo and this entire world. The most powerful Aspect She ever created."

Steward grunted, cupping her hands and breathing steam into them. "It's so dark."

"Of course it is. Why else do you think sailors pray to Eo so much? Not like there's a God of the sea. Not anymore anyway." Jameson smiled down at her but faltered when he noticed the quiet rage in her eyes.

The dark omens of the morning hadn't been lost on Jameson, especially now as he stared down at the girl who attracted them like moths to flame. He looked out at the water but couldn't see any shapes on its dark surface. That didn't mean there weren't myrfolk or syrens down there.

"Jameson, why did you save me?" Steward asked abruptly.

The question caught Jameson off guard. He opened his mouth and then closed it, trying to find the right words. "Most people don't jump from cliffs unless they've got no other options. Ink and I thought you were dead, but then I saw your tiny hand struggling above the waves. I couldn't just do nothing."

Steward nodded but wouldn't look at him. "Did you know it was me?"

"When you jumped? No. Only when I pulled you into the boat." Noticing the conflicting expressions of guilt and confusion roll across her face like a storm, Jameson added, "But I would have saved you even if I realized it sooner."

"But why?" Steward asked, overcome with emotion. "I stole from you."

"And I stole back," Jameson said gently.

"My father stole from you too."

Jameson kept his expression neutral despite the twisting guilt in his throat. "You're not your father."

"But Ink doesn't even like me—"

"Ink likes you."

Steward folded her arms. "He sure has a funny way of showing it."

Jameson laughed, remembering his own early doubts about Ink's affection. "Ink believes in tough love, but he's trying to protect you. If he's nice to you, everyone else will hate you. He makes a point of being meanest to newcomers. That way, the others will pity you and befriend you. It's best for you in the long run."

"And is throwing me back to the sea also what's best for me?" Before Jameson could ask, Steward added, "I heard what he said on the dock, Jameson."

"But how did you..." Jameson stared into her hardened eyes, seeing the truth. "You read lips."

And that means she knows that I'm to blame for her father's death. Jameson felt sweat gather in his armpits as his back tingled.

"Yeah, I read lips, but I could only see what Ink was saying." Steward said. "Your back was to me."

Relief flooded him, followed by heavier guilt. *Do I tell her the truth?* Jameson envisioned what would happen if he did. Steward would probably attack him with a knife, and Ink would imprison her and drop her off at the next port to fend for herself. What was there to gain by telling her the truth and causing her more pain?

"Why did you save me?" Steward asked again. "Why convince Ink not to abandon me?"

"I..." Jameson trailed away, thinking, *I can't tell her what I did.* "I believe in second chances." Biting the inside of his cheek, Jameson added, "You're not the first lost soul that Ink's fished out of the sea."

"You?" Steward asked, cocking her head, as if seeing him in a new light.

Jameson nodded. "I was an ashboy in Alira, though I'm guessing you already figured that out. I left when I was about your age, only I didn't jump from a cliff to do it."

Steward watched him quietly, her expression softening further. She sighed and her shoulders fell, sniffing but not crying. "Why'd you leave?"

"Everyone I loved died. Didn't want to share their fate." Jameson cleared his throat, hand creeping to his red bracelet as he thought of Josh and the other ashkids. "So I joined a crew. Not Ink's, but a different one. They had me running around the ship like you are now. I spent years on that ship, learning the seas and the stories. I became real good in the rigging. I had a knack for it, I guess."

I had a knack for a lot of things in those days, Jameson thought. *Killing, whoring, stealing, and drinking.* It felt like a lifetime ago, yet so close. A time filled with rum and blood, women and corpses. A time of true piracy.

Steward clasped her hands, fiddling with her thumbs. Jameson had already spied her as somebody who couldn't sit still. She was always looking around, rocking on her heels, and keeping her hands busy. Such were the habits of urchins. "How did you meet Ink, then?"

Jameson stared down at his gloved hands, not needing to see the old scars and burns covering his pockmarked skin to know they were there. He remembered the *Keep*, the Copperhead schooner he'd joined and trained on for several years. With the crew, he'd raided ships and coastlines until they made the mistake of attacking a Guardian and the cargo ship it protected. The *Keep* had gone down too quick under a barrage of lead, and the gunpowder stores had caught fire, exploding in a shower of debris. Jameson had played dead on a long piece of driftwood until another Guardian had found him drifting through the ocean.

The *Constable*.

Ink.

Jameson looked down at his right wrist, beneath the red bracelet. He traced a gloved finger around the phoenix feather tattoo, which now covered the Dagger, a bloody knife tattoo all Cutthroats shared. As the punishment for piracy was the gallows, simply having the Dagger was a death sentence. Had Ink wanted to, he could have hung Jameson after dragging him from those waters. Instead, he'd given Jameson the cover-up tattoo and made him a sailor aboard the *Constable*.

"There'd been a bad storm one season," Jameson lied. To tell her the truth would have ruined his reputation and possibly gotten him killed aboard a ship of Guardians. "Ripped the mast off of the ship and cleaved it in two. Ink found me clinging to a barrel, drifting through the sea. Ain't much fun, being all alone in that water, is it?"

Though Jameson smiled, Steward shook her head violently, burrowing deeper into her jacket as if trying to hide. She mumbled something, but it was too quiet for Jameson to hear.

"What?"

"I *wasn't* alone," Steward said, her eyes screaming in the silence that followed.

"You saw something down there?" Jameson asked, leaning forward. "Myrfolk?"

"I..." Steward took a step backward, away from the gunwale. "I don't know."

"What'd they look like?"

"Their eyes were black," she whispered, voice quiet and shaking. "No ears, no noses. Just giant mouths filled with too many teeth. Their bodies were strange. Gray. Smooth. Hands were all webbed together but clawed. Long fingered." Steward took a startled breath. "And they just kept smiling at me. Laughing, even. Like they knew something. Like they knew... *me*."

"Syrens," Jameson said, blood running cold beneath the jacket. "Core be damned."

"But what *are* they, Jameson? Why did they look at me like that?"

"Nobody knows for sure, but I think they were once like us. Human. They called themselves the Myrmidons and lived before the Drowned Sea existed, but when Kuma betrayed Undo and created the sea, they transformed into the myrfolk. And the myrfolk who gave into their hatred of the Gods were twisted by it. They became the syrens."

Steward shrank into herself. "What do they want?"

Jameson paused, fear catching in his throat. "To kill everyone and destroy everything."

"The syrens could have hurt me, but they didn't," Steward said, looking up at him with fearful eyes. "Why didn't they hurt me?"

"I don't know," Jameson said, and the night felt much colder. *And I don't know if I want to.*

Chapter Sixteen

The sun toppled from its throne, and the sky became night. In the distance, trees stretched and danced with a light gale. Crows flew across the grave markers, eyeing Erin as only malicious birds could as she stepped between the stones. They cawed and shrieked, and though Erin walked in silence through the vast cemetery, all she wanted to do was scream.

When she reached the end of the row of graves, Erin closed her eyes and held back a sob. "Dad's gone. He's really gone."

"Gone? Why, I'm right here, my rose," a voice said from behind her.

Erin's eyes snapped open. Turning, she saw his tall frame, long blonde hair, and blue eyes. She took in his cane and his missing right leg. "Dad? Is it really you?"

His expression became a grin. "Who else would I be, my—"

Erin tackled him as the world blurred with her tears. He stumbled, losing his balance and falling backward. Instead of a grunt of pain, only a laugh escaped his lips. Her arms wrapped around his neck as her legs held his waist. Burying her head under his chin, she let out a sob.

"I thought you were dead. Everyone said so."

"Me? Dead?" Another laugh. "It'd take a lot more than a bullet to kill me. Besides, I'd never leave you behind. I don't know what I'd do without you, my rose."

Erin whispered. "I missed you so much, Dad. I thought you'd left me."

"Oh no, baby, I wouldn't leave you."

"Never?"

"Never."

Erin nodded, no longer trying to hold back the tears. *He's here. He's okay—I'm okay.* The hole in her chest filled with love, and she felt the anger and rage fall away. She looked around in the darkness for the Unseen Lady but didn't find Her. Erin was still grateful.

"You gave him back, Eo. Thank you for giving him back to me." She would have wiped away her tears with one arm, but she didn't dare let go of her dad. Instead, she wiped the tears off with his shirt. "Whatever you need from me in return, Eo, it's yours."

Her father smiled down at her. His eyes were warm, but his hands were growing cold. He opened his mouth, but someone else's voice came from his lips.

"Hey, Steward! Wake up!"

Erin blinked, and the graveyard fell away. Mouse stood over her, shaking her shoulders. "You're having a nightmare, Steward! Wake up!"

"No," Erin said, head snapping in all directions as she searched for her father and the graveyard. Instead, she only saw wood, hammocks, and sailors. "I saw him. He's alive."

Mouse cocked his head to the side, his red eyebrows furrowed. "Who's alive?"

"My dad! He's still in Alira. We... we have to go back."

"Go back? Steward, we can't go back to Alira. We're in the middle of the Drowned Sea—"

"We have to turn around!" Erin scrambled out of the hammock, slamming into the ground. She turned and climbed up the ladder as Mouse chased her. Other feet followed behind him.

"Steward! Hold on!" Mouse said, but she ignored him.

Light peered over the horizon as Erin clambered onto the main deck. She ran past the dozens of haulers tending the lines and adjusting sails. Mouse yelled for her to stop, but Erin kept running and sprinted up the stairs to the quarterdeck.

A hand grabbed her arm gently but firm. Jameson. "Steward? What is it? What's wrong?"

Her eyes ignored him as she pulled away, searching the deck for Ink. All she saw was the helmsman and a navigator. "Where's the captain?"

Jameson pointed to the bow. "He's—"

"Sir!" Mouse shouted, panting as he stumbled onto the quarterdeck. "Steward was just having a nightmare. He ain't thinking straight."

"A nightmare?" Jameson asked, looking down at Erin, though she was glaring at Mouse.

"It was *real*," Erin said, trying to pull away from Jameson, who still had a hand on her bicep. "I need to go back."

Jameson glanced at the horizon behind the stern gunwale, where Erin was pointing. "Where? To Alira?" He looked back at her. "But Steward, there's nothing left for you there. This is the best opportunity you're going to get."

"My *dad* is waiting for me!" Erin shouted, ripping her arm from his grasp. She dodged Mouse and scrambled down the stairs back to the bow, ducking lines and avoiding haulers. Near the bowsprit, Ink was watching the seas contentedly. He turned to see Erin's frantic approach, her feet slapping hard against the deck.

"Steward? What's—"

"We need to turn around!"

"Turn around?" Ink leaned away from her as if she had the Whispering Madness. "What nonsense is this?"

Mouse scrambled up behind her, with Jameson and Taran following at his heels. "She was having a nightmare and—"

"It was *real*," she said. "My dad's alive. He's still in Alira!" Erin's voice was shrill, too high for the deeper voice she'd adopted. She looked at the invisible speck of land on the far horizon. "He needs me!"

"No, *lad*." Ink said, giving her a pointed stare. "You need to control yourself—"

"He's *alive!*" she shouted as Jameson and Mouse approached at a run. "I saw him!"

Jameson and Ink exchanged a look. Erin's throat was lined with fire, choking her up. *They don't believe me? They don't trust me?* She felt so alone, so isolated. Not even Mouse believed her, and he was supposed to be her friend.

"I know what I saw," Erin said, stomping her foot on the deck. "He's alive!"

Ink kneeled, so they were eye-level. "Lad, you had a bad dream." He put a hand on her shoulder. "That's all it was."

"You don't know that!" Erin shouted, shrugging off his hand. Her eyes darted around, and she saw haulers gathering around her. Taran was among them. She hugged herself, feeling claustrophobic. She needed to get away from them—away from the ship—by any means necessary. "And if you won't help me... I'll go find him myself."

Erin turned and ran toward the gunwale. She tried to jump, but Mouse wrapped his arms around her feet. She lost her balance and fell, her head smacking the deck hard as Jameson pinned her arms.

"Stop squirming, Steward!" Mouse shouted, still gripping her legs.

"Let me go!" Erin pulled one leg free and kicked Mouse in the face. He fell back as Taran jumped in to grab her. He gripped her legs tighter, nails digging into her skin.

A hand eclipsed the sun. As it slammed into her cheek, the blow stung worse than a frozen sea breeze. Erin stopped squirming and stared up with wide eyes. Ink was above her, lips parted in a furious snarl.

"Your dad is dead, Steward!" he shouted, raising his hand again. "Nothing you can do to change that now, you hear? Jump in that water, and you're dead too. We won't turn around for you. We'll leave you for the syrens. Would your dad want that?"

Tears streamed down her face as she trembled. "No."

"The Core he wouldn't. So now you've got a choice: survive or die. What will it be, Steward?" Ink turned to the others. "And let go of him. If Steward wants to jump, then let him jump. We ain't risking our skin for his. Not again."

Jameson released her arms, staring anywhere but at her face. The pressure around her legs fell away as Taran drew back. Mouse rubbed his jaw, saying nothing about his split lip.

"Still can't decide, lad? Then let me help you." Ink grabbed Erin by the shirt and dragged her to the gunwale, pushing her until her feet couldn't touch the deck, and her head was dangling out over the water. Her breath caught in her chest as she stared down at the choppy waves while the wind scratched at her face. She was just close enough to see dark, looming shapes beneath the surface.

The syrens. They're still there. Erin tried to push herself away from the gunwale, but Ink grabbed her by the hair and kept her in place. She let out a strangled half-breath, holding onto Ink's arm so he couldn't let her go. "Please, I don't want to die."

"You sure?" Ink asked. "After all the grief you've caused us, maybe you *should* jump. Go on, do it!"

He pushed her forward, and Erin slipped from the railing. Dangling her headfirst above the barnacled hull and blue waters, Ink held onto Erin's ankles. Her stomach dropped as she screamed.

"Captain!" Jameson shouted, somewhere behind her. "Don't—"

"Furl that tongue of yours, first mate!" To Erin, Ink added, "Like what you see down there, boy?"

"No!" she screamed. "Don't let go! Please, Ink! I'm sorry!"

Blood rushed to her head as Ink pulled her back up and threw her onto the deck. "*Sorry?* I don't give two shits that you're sorry, you pathetic bilge rat."

Erin gulped for air, shaking from fear more than the icy breeze. Screams crawled up her throat as she closed her mouth, her heart thumping wildly. All the sailors had stopped working and were staring at her from all directions, including Jameson, Mouse, and even Taran. Embarrassment weighed on her stomach, leaden like an anchor.

"Life has meaning, Steward, but only as much meaning as you give it," Ink said, standing over her. "If you treat life like it's nothing, it will be nothing. You'll be nothing. Everything you care about will be nothing. All the dreams. The memories. Even your *dad.* You're the only one who remembers him, so if you die, *he* dies. You understand?"

Erin nodded, unable to look at him.

"Not good enough. I wanna hear you say it."

"Yes, captain."

Ink reached down, grabbed her by the collar, and picked her up. A half-inch from her face, spittle flew from his mouth as he screamed, "With conviction, lad!"

"Yes, captain!" Erin screamed, her throat raw.

Ink shoved her to the ground again. "If you *ever* plan on doing something this stupid again, I won't stop you. Nobody else will, either, will you, lads?"

Erin could hear the grumbles of agreement, but Jameson was silent, fidgeting with his red bracelet. Poor Mouse was wiping away the blood dribbling from his lip. Taran stared at her with an intense eye and a frown. The other sailors, too, judged her.

"Now get your ass beneath the deck, Steward," Ink said. "Go find a hammock and stay in it until I get you. And don't you dare let me catch you sleeping or playing games. You sit there and you think about what you've done."

Erin absorbed Ink's disappointment with the crushing weight of her father's death. "Sorry, captain."

"Sorry is for cowards," he said, turning his back to her. "Apologize by doing your damn job."

Erin remained silent, holding back the tears.

"Come on, Steward," Mouse said, gently leading her away from the bow with the help of Taran, who made no barbed comments, surprisingly. "It'll be alright. Just need to sleep it off."

"Sorry about your lip," Erin said, wiping her nose.

Mouse shrugged, crawling through the hatch and down the ladder first. "It was a damn good kick, for all it's worth. Teach it to me, will you?"

He still wants to be my friend. Erin thought, hiding her tears.

◄O►

Jameson grimaced as Ink finished tattooing a turtle on his left arm, completing the full sleeve of Myrmidons, sea monsters, and ships. On the turtle's back was a forest of trees. Close to its head, a frigate was docked—only a quarter of the turtle's size. Blood welled from the punctured marks as though the trees were spears. The captain wiped away the crimson and inspected the tattoo with his one eye.

"Well," Ink said, "what do you think, weaver? Is the story finished?"

"Looks exactly how the legends describe it," Jameson said, grinning. He leaned closer, inspecting the minor details that Ink had added: the Aritrastan flag on the ship and the moss dangling down from the turtle shell. He whistled in appreciation. "A creature so immense that it looked like an island. When sailors docked along its side in search of supplies and game, it would submerge and wreck the ship."

"Aye," Ink said, standing up to stretch.

Whereas Jameson's private cabin was smaller than a closet, Ink's was spacious and just beneath the quarterdeck. Not one for much ornamentation, only a picture of the Aritrastan coast rested above Ink's bed, opposite the wooden desk where he checked the charts and the logs when he wasn't tattooing or bellowing orders above deck.

"Should be a warning for all sailors," Ink said, pointing at the turtle. "Much more to these waters than what we see—especially in the Damned Depths. That's a place no sailors ought to travel. Not if they value their lives, that is." The captain shook his head. "There are worse things than even syrens in those waters."

Syrens. Jameson thought of Steward. It'd been almost thirteen hours since she'd tried to jump overboard, and Ink still hadn't seen her.

"You think it's time we check on Steward?" Jameson asked.

"Not by half." Ink said, cleaning his tattooing tools and stowing them in a desk drawer. "Only way to make a hull is to bend the timbers into shape. Trick is bending them without breaking them. It's the only way."

Jameson dabbed away more beads of blood from the turtle with a rum-soaked rag. "How long do we wait?"

"Another shift, I suppose," Ink said, considering. "Let her sweat out this nonsense of hers."

"And if it doesn't work?"

"Well, I don't pretend to be a shipwright, son, but I know how to man the helm. I could have chosen any ship to command, but I chose the *Constable*. None other, you understand?"

Jameson scratched his head, confused. "Even I don't get all of your sailing metaphors, Ink."

"For a weaver, you can be dense sometimes." Ink sighed before tapping his chin. "Do you remember when I first found you?"

"As if I could forget." Jameson shivered. Instinctively, he put a hand to his throat. He still remembered drowning. Covering the scars and burns that had once ravaged his body with stories and tattoos hadn't made him forget any of the pain.

"Died a Cutthroat and reborn a Guardian, you were." Ink smiled. "I gave you a chance at redemption, but only you could sail your ship toward salvation."

Born from the ashes, Jameson thought, tracing the phoenix feather tattoo covering the Dagger.

"We've given John Steward that same chance, son," Ink said. "Now we have to wait and see if she follows your path or the path of her father."

Jameson stopped tracing the feather, thinking of darker legends, Steward, and her burning eyes. *Maybe there's a third path.*

Chapter Seventeen

Kendrik felt the chill of the sea fog deep in his bones. Clenching his fishing pole tight with both hands was the only way to keep his hands from shaking. It didn't help that the single-masted sloop was drifting into colder waters.

Kendrik's younger brother fared little better. He whistled as he tried to tie a hook to the fishing line, but his hands shook too much to even run the line through its eye.

"Oh, for Eo's sake," Kendrik said, groaning as he took the hook and the line from Jericho and knotted them together himself. "Here."

"Thanks." Jericho smiled so warmly that the frosty morning air didn't feel so cold.

"Yeah, yeah," Kendrik said, still annoyed but no longer frustrated. Such was the life of a big brother: helping the little brothers who stood as close as shadows. Kendrik couldn't count how many times Jericho had tripped him up because he'd been walking right behind him. Or how many fights Kendrik had picked on Jericho's behalf. Or how many times he'd gone hungry so Jericho could eat.

Such was the price of loyalty, brotherhood, and love.

And Kendrik gladly paid it so Jericho didn't have to—gladder to never mention the sacrifices.

"Why do sardines have to be so slimy?" Jericho asked, as he tried to push the hook through the still-writhing fish's nose.

"That's the way they are. Ain't gotta be a reason for it," Kendrik said as the sardine wriggled out of Jericho's grip again.

Jericho reached out to grab it but accidentally slapped it into the water. He punched the gunwale and muttered, "Squalls."

Kendrik cocked his head. "Who taught you that curse?"

Jericho gestured with his chin to a sailor nearby. Gil, a one-eyed, one-armed, one-legged man, had the foulest mouth Kendrik had ever heard. "Yeah? Well, anything that Gil's willing to teach you ain't worth learnin'."

"You use *squall* all the time!" Jericho whined in a shrill voice.

Kendrik winced and shoved a filthy hand over Jericho's mouth. "Yeah, I do, but that don't mean I want you saying it. Squalls are the harbingers of sea storms, yeah? So saying something like 'Squall you!' is tellin' someone to get stuck in a sea storm. *Squall* is the mother of all bad words—a *jinx*, and it ain't worth saying."

After pulling Kendrik's hand from his mouth, Jericho said, "Gil said there's no such things as jinxes."

Kendrik's spine shook. Saying that jinxes weren't real was the *worst* jinx. As if Jericho was just asking for trouble. "Yes, there *are*." He grabbed another sardine from the bucket and held it firm despite all its wriggling. "You say anything else about *squalls* or *jinxes*, and I'll make you eat one of these slimy sardines."

Jericho leaned away, disgusted. "You wouldn't!"

"I would, and you know it," Kendrik lied. A sardine's bone could easily stick in one's throat—annoyed or not, Kendrik wouldn't take that risk. But Jericho didn't have to know.

"Do that, and I'll get you back," Jericho said, harrumphing as he crossed his arms defiantly. Kendrik believed him too. Jericho may not have been a fighter, but he *was* a spiteful little squall.

"I'd like to see you try."

"Oh, squall you!" Jericho jumped to his feet with his hands on his hips. "You can't just threaten me like—*uh oh*." He tried to run, but Kendrik grabbed him by the ankle and dragged him to the ground.

As Jericho thrashed, Kendrik pinned him easily, pressing his knees on his little brother's arms. "I warned you, didn't I?" Kendrik shoved the sardine against Jericho's firmly closed lips. "Now open that hatch of yours. It's time for breakfast!"

"Kendrik! Jericho! On your feet, the both of you!" shouted Captain Amir, who somehow looked more beaten down than Gil despite having all his limbs intact. "We ain't here to dawdle! Get back to work."

They did, though Jericho wiped his mouth hurriedly and made overly dramatic expressions of disgust. "Squall you for that."

With a half-smile, Kendrik said, "Squall you, too, sardine-lips."

Kendrik didn't bother to wipe away his tears. Nobody could see them as he stood alone at the bow of the *Jericho,* Lilyth's new flagship. The frigate plunged through choppy waves, and the smaller *Crescent* followed in its wake. It was a constant battle of furling and unfurling the sails to keep the vessels from listing and even capsizing.

Even if the *Jericho* did crash into unseen rocks or capsize, Kendrik wasn't certain he'd care. His mind was far away, his body already half dead. Rather than at the sea, he stared down at the copper flintlock in his hands—a gift from Lilyth after their victory against the Copperheads. Kendrik would have traded it just to see Jericho one more time. He would have even sold his soul, if that's what it took.

Before Lilyth saved them, Kendrik and Jericho had spent two weeks as Avowed slaves, forced to shit, piss, and sleep where they ate. Despite their horrid conditions, the brothers were closer than ever before. They'd cried together, slept together, and talked for long hours about anything and everything to keep their spirits up.

Jericho said he wanted to open a bakery. No surprise there. Jericho had kept that childish glee no matter the situation, no matter the pain. Kendrik hadn't known what he wanted to do, even if he could do anything. He'd been so focused on taking care of Jericho that he hadn't thought about what he wanted for his own life. And without his younger brother, he was just drifting aimlessly across the sea.

"You said we'd be brothers forever, in this life and the next," Kendrik whispered so the legionnaires hauling lines on the main deck wouldn't hear him. "Did you mean that, brother? Are you waiting for me up there?"

Though the stars twinkled between the clouds, they gave no response.

"I need you to tell me. I need to hear you say it."

Still, he heard nothing.

Kendrik grasped the gunwale with both hands and lowered his head. "Goddess of the night, blesser of shadows, please hear my prayer: guide me toward my brother, whichever star he may now be. Guide me to him, so that I might find him in the next life. Do this for me, and I will be Your greatest warrior. I'll train as long as it takes, *do* whatever it takes. I'll follow you to the ends of the Damned Depths, if you ask it of me. I swear this on the Drowned Sea."

Kendrik waited to feel something—*anything*—but there was no warmth stirring within his heart. No cold either. Nothing. What did that mean?

Did Eo agree? Kendrik thought. *Did she even hear?* Anxiety and sorrow brimmed in him as he stood, waiting. "Please, Eo. I need a sign. Tell me You're listening. Let me know Jericho is there. That I can find him. *Tell me.*"

◄◆►

Lilyth listened to Kendrik's prayer from the shadows. Any sympathy or remorse she should have felt had been devoured by the night long ago.

Kendrik's willingness to fight, train, and die for Eo—for the Red Legion—was as Lilyth expected, but how to best use it to her advantage? How to make Kendrik think that Eo—that unseen squall—gave a damn about him?

"Kendrik," Lilyth hissed.

Kendrik jumped, just as she wanted, but at the same moment, a wave pushed the ship. Kendrik's upper body was thrown over the gunwale, but Lilyth reached out and caught his ankle before he could fall overboard. Part of her wanted to watch him fall, but she held tight and dragged him back onto the deck.

"Jericho?" Kendrik asked, his voice hopeful. Then he looked up and saw her shaved, scarred, and unreadable expression. His shoulders fell, and his eyes flicked back to the deck. Wiping at his eyes, he added, "Oh. It's you. Thank you, Champion."

"You're not excited to see me?" Lilyth asked in a betrayed voice.

Kendrik winced. "No, Champion. It's just that... I just hoped that you were Jericho. I know how stupid that sounds. I know he's gone. I know that he's in the stars and—"

Lilyth put a finger to his quivering lip. "Collect your breath, Red Heart. Then speak."

Kendrik obeyed, as he always did. "I miss my brother, Champion. I miss him so much." Before he could stop himself, Kendrik lunged forward and hugged Lilyth tight enough to make it difficult for her to breathe. "Why did he have to die?"

Lilyth was silent and stiff, unsure what to do with her arms. She couldn't remember the last time she'd been hugged. But that wasn't true. Lilyth remembered. She just didn't want to. *The morning that Rolf took my family. The last time I ever saw my husband—my daughter.*

A wave of uncontrollable pain ripped through her. Her body shook, but Kendrik was too busy crying to notice. Old memories tried to consume her, but Lilyth closed herself off to them. *Control the pain. Use the anger. Make them all burn.* Lilyth gently extricated herself from his grip.

"I'm sorry if I offended you, Champion," Kendrik said, eyes wide and mouth agape. He ran his hands across his shaved scalp, mortified. "I shouldn't have—"

"It's fine," Lilyth said, her voice hoarse. "Grief is a powerful emotion. Uncontrollable at times. It can... blind you, if you are not careful." She inhaled deeply, sounding more like his Champion as she continued, "But always remember: Eo listens. She knows us. When we, too, are taken by the night, we will be reunited with those we have lost—that is why Eo guides us by the moon and stars. Those lights in the darkness are souls. And Jericho's soul—*your brother's* soul—is one of the brightest I see." Lilyth pointed to a random star in the far distance that wasn't part of the major constellations sailors navigated by. "It is a new star. Born on the night your brother was given to Eo."

Kendrik gasped. "Jericho's star. It's really there. He's there, waiting for me."

With her emotions neatly compartmentalized once more, Lilyth ignored the weight of his words. All that mattered was the new belief shining in Kendrik's eyes. He was far too invested into the Red Legion now to leave. Instead, he would only become more indoctrinated, more extreme, more zealous. *That's what I need. Zealots.*

And Lilyth knew just what to say to do it. "Eo accepts your vow, Kendrik. Become Her greatest warrior, and She will ensure that your star will be beside Jericho's when you, too, are taken by the night. Remember: Eo's path is the night, yours is that of the blade. The only way to unite the world under Her darkness is to purge it of the Cutthroats and all others who denounce Her truth. Believe in Her, believe in Jericho, and you will never be led astray."

Tears spilled down Kendrik's cheeks. Not the red ones of the Night Plague, but clear ones of the deepest anguish. "Then will you train me? Show me how to become Eo's greatest warrior?"

"Of course, Red Heart," Lilyth said with a mirthless smile. "But first, perhaps you'd like to speak with your brother?"

Kendrik froze. "I can... *speak* to him? He can hear me?"

Lilyth nodded, forcing herself to meet his naive gaze, though she only saw her daughter in Kendrik's eyes. "Of course. So long as it is night, Jericho can always listen. The stars, like the moon, watch and hear us. That is how they guide us. They know and see all. That is the glory of Umbra, of Eo's eternal kingdom of darkness. And one day, we will be there too."

"Really?" Kendrik asked, eyes too wide, innocent, and believing.

"Yes, Red Heart," Lilyth lied. *"Really."*

When Kendrik nodded, Lilyth patted his shoulder gently and left him to talk to the deaf stars. *Believe, Kendrik. Believe with all your heart. Believe until it breaks you. I will be there to collect you, to put you back together again, my little zealot. You and Greeley both—if you do not kill each other first.*

Lilyth frowned. While she didn't care about either of their lives, their deaths would have cost her precious time in replacing them with more zealots. She couldn't let that happen, and the best way to do it was to keep both distracted. Kendrik with training. Greeley with lust.

Time to bring Arya into the fold.

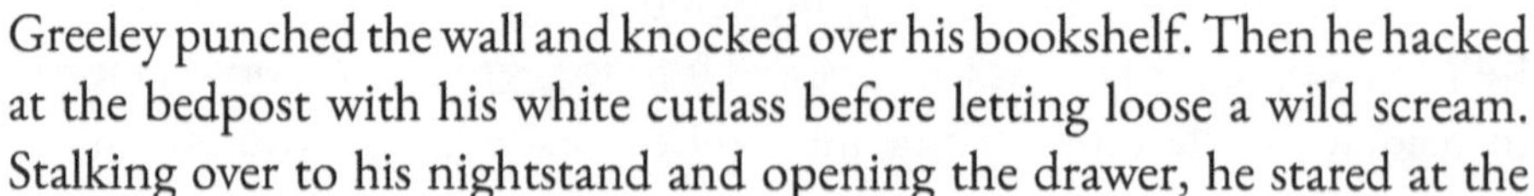

Greeley punched the wall and knocked over his bookshelf. Then he hacked at the bedpost with his white cutlass before letting loose a wild scream. Stalking over to his nightstand and opening the drawer, he stared at the golden and silver rings he'd taken from the Avowed captain's corpse in secret and the studded tongue he'd ripped from the Copperhead captain's mouth. But not even the sight of his trophies in his private quarters could calm him down.

It only reminded him that there was one trophy missing: the copper flintlock. That belonged to the squalling Red Heart. And why would Lilyth choose that title for Kendrik? Did it mean he had her heart? That she loved him? No. The idea was ridiculous, and yet he'd seen Kendrik hug Lilyth.

Kendrik hugged her. He squalling hugged her. He hugged Lilyth! The thought became a mantra that stoked the fire in his eyes, throat, and stomach. *He cannot have her—nobody can. Lilyth is mine. Mine!*

But what could Greeley do about it? He wasn't even on the *Jericho*. It was not as simple as shoving Kendrik off the bow.

Greeley was captaining the *Crescent,* which was crewed by a dozen of the original twenty-seven legionnaires and half of the forty-eight new recruits. Not that they even needed Greeley to be their captain. The legionnaires sparred, prayed, and sailed with the new recruits according to Lilyth's orders, who used horns, colored flags, and answering pennants to relay her commands from the *Jericho* to the *Crescent*. He was a figurehead, like the one beneath the bowsprit.

Lilyth had said that only Greeley could be trusted to control the *Crescent,* so he'd accepted blindly. Despite the private cabin that he now had, Greeley regretted that decision. An ocean now separated him from Lilyth. Though the ships were within a few hundred feet of one another, Greeley could not close that distance. Instead, he spied on Lilyth from afar through the spyglass she'd given him.

And now he'd seen them *hugging.*

The image of it was there whenever Greeley closed his eyes. Nothing made it go away. Not the sparring, the trophies, nor his rank, especially now that he realized leading the *Crescent* meant Kendrik was her right-hand man. Her heart.

I should have recommended Kendrik for this position. Then I could be on the Jericho. *I could have hugged Lilyth, touched Lilyth, squeezed Lilyth,* Greeley thought. *He needs to die. But how? When? During an exchange.*

Every few days, Lilyth would drop anchor at one of the countless uncharted islands north of the Black Trench. As few Cutthroats dared venture close to that wall of storms, these islands made for an ideal place to transfer recruits between ships, parcel out rations, and lead prayer on the shores.

It had been four days since they'd last found an island. Surely, they would break camp at the next one Lilyth spotted. And there, Greeley would be close enough to shove a cutlass through Kendrik's heart.

Greeley's thoughts halted. *But what of Eo?*

He'd hadn't been a believer at first, and even now he had his doubts about the Unseen Lady, but Lilyth had shown him things that could only be described as supernatural—like the Night Plague. After witnessing Hector's death and the liquid darkness that Lilyth had thrown up, he knew that the sickness was real and that it could kill the unfaithful at any moment. Then there was Lilyth herself—she couldn't be fully human. A demigod, perhaps, or maybe something else entirely. Could Greeley really risk either's wrath?

Lilyth said that Eo was always watching and listening—if She disagreed, I'd be dead already. Greeley looked around the room, half-expecting to see a ghostly face or even hear a whispering voice. He saw nothing of the kind.

Greeley smiled, taking the silence for approval. *And since I'm still breathing, Eo must agree. The Goddess might know my plans, but She won't tell. Lilyth never has to know. Bless you, Unseen Lady.*

Chapter Eighteen

Lilyth awoke from a nightmare, hacking at the air in front of her with her talan. She rubbed at her eyes and whispered, "Just a dream." With a relieved sigh, she rolled over to hug her husband and kiss her daughter. Then the memories came hurtling back.

"No... *No!*" Lilyth threw her talan across the room, where it embedded itself into the wall. *My daughter needs me. My husband needs me. I have to find them. I have to—*

Following a knock at the door, a voice asked, "Champion? You wished to see me?"

Lilyth donned a mask of indifference even as her mind screamed and thrashed. "Yes. Come in."

Arya entered, her face illuminated by a lantern. She wore clothes newly raided from Cutthroats, not at all resembling a uniform: a red frilled shirt, black pants, and black leather boots. The shirt had once been white but had been soaked in blood, making it red. That was common practice, as the only colors legionnaires wore were red and black.

In the company of the other legionnaires, Arya's glances were quick, posture hunched, and arms crossed over her chest. In private with Lilyth, though, Arya stood comfortably, one hand holding out the lantern and the other at her side.

"How are the legionnaires treating you?" Lilyth asked.

"Well enough, Champion," Arya said, trying too hard to sound sincere.

I have known far better liars than you, Lilyth thought, pretending to mull over her next question. "They don't make you uncomfortable?"

Arya tensed for a moment before relaxing. "No," she said, placid. "Is there a reason I should be?"

What a pathetic attempt at deception. Lilyth took her time walking across the room to pull her talan from the wall. As she sheathed it, Lilyth asked, "You pretended to be a man before the Copperheads captured you. You don't seem comfortable being a woman now."

Using shared emotions and experiences was the best way to build a fast rapport, but the key was subtlety. Being kind, faking sincerity, and pretending to listen were the tools of her trade.

"It's been a long time since men have known what I am," Arya said, after silent seconds of contemplation. "Something I'm no longer used to."

Something I'm no longer used to was a very different response from *Not something I'm used to.* Lilyth knew the word choice was no accident. Arya had once received the attention of men. Probably a lot of men. If not for her tattoos, short hair, and foul-mouthed arrogance, men might've thought Arya beautiful. What could have caused her to turn to a life of sailing? A terrible experience? A thrill for adventure? A desire to start over? Probably all three.

A girl searching for a better life. Instead, she was enslaved by the Cut-throats and again by me, Lilyth thought, with a small measure of pity. *Some luck.*

"It's not the fact that the men look at you, but *how* they look at you, is it not?" Lilyth asked, watching Arya for any tells. When the legionnaire's eyes widened a fraction wider, Lilyth knew she was nearing the truth. She added, "As if you aren't a person, just a *thing* they can take advantage of?"

Arya gasped lightly. "You... understand."

"I told you I knew the feeling," Lilyth said with a soft smile. "There aren't many reasons for women like us to sail. We are more alike than you might believe."

We. Us. Women. The words would bind Lilyth and Arya together with threads of kinship—threads Lilyth would use to push and pull Arya in any direction she pleased.

"I was a girlie," Arya whispered, not ashamed but afraid the words would leave the room.

"Then we have that in common," Lilyth said in a slow, halting voice as if she, too, was struggling to admit the truth. "But when I was enslaved, I found my faith—I found Eo. She led me to you, Arya, and soon, She'll lead us to others. Women and young girls with no hope of rescue or safety. We can find them. Save them, but Eo needs your help to do it."

"Me?" Arya asked. "Why would you or the Unseen Lady need me for anything? You're a demigod. You can kill or cure people with a touch. Besides, you have the Red Heart. The Red Hand too."

"It is difficult for the Goddess to intercede on these seas, Arya. She does when She must, but it taxes Her heavily. Sometimes, it is difficult for Her to even *whisper* to me. That is why I demand silence in the temple. Yet as we gain more followers, more *true* believers, Eo will grow stronger too. Such is the nature of Her Sword, Belt, and Crown." Lilyth leaned closer, as if to tell the legionnaire a secret. "But until then, She needs our help, Arya. As for the Red Hand and Heart... Do you really think that Eo, *Goddess* of the Night, would ever truly trust a *man?*" She laughed softly, as if it were a preposterous joke.

"But Eo trusted Aritras," Arya said before frowning. "Didn't She?"

"She did. Once. But Aritras failed to unite the world beneath Her banner. It is not a mistake She'll make again," Lilyth replied, lifting Arya's chin with a scarred finger. "Leading Eo's Chosen is a *woman's* pursuit. That is why She trusted me—trusted *you.*"

"What does the Goddess need me to do?" Arya asked, standing straighter, taller.

"To watch Greeley and never let him out of your sight."

Arya turned her head. "Why?"

You think you can question me? Lilyth thought, not letting the annoyance slip onto her face. "Because neither Eo—nor I—can trust him. Not fully. Greeley is useful to our cause, but he has a wandering eye. A worrisome eye. I'm sure you have noticed how he looks at you—at both of us."

"Like we're flesh," Arya said, eyes narrowing coldly.

"Exactly so, Arya," Lilyth said, stepping forward and holding Arya's free hand between both of hers. "I can't guide the Red Legion while watching Greeley every moment. I need someone to watch him for me and make sure that he does as told."

Arya frowned. "By watching him, are you asking me to *sleep* with him?"

Yes, Lilyth thought, but saying so might turn Arya away. Better to let Arya come to the conclusion on her own. Lilyth smiled softly as she answered, "No, but I need you to watch him closely. And you cannot let him know *why* you're watching him. He must think that you two are allies. If he suspects you are working against him..."

Lilyth didn't finish the sentence. She let Arya absorb the words, process them. She could see the conflicting doubt, disappointment, and acceptance flickering in Arya's eyes. The legionnaire would do whatever it took to get the job done, but she wouldn't be happy about it. Eventually, she would become resentful, but Lilyth couldn't allow that bitterness to fester. She needed to give Arya a gift to make her content, and another to help her see the bigger picture. Both gifts were deviously simple.

Gently, Lilyth squeezed Arya's hand. "Can I trust you to be my eyes and ears, Arya? To be my *Red Eye?*"

Arya gasped. "You mean..."

"You have the marking of a *Champion.*" Removing one hand from Arya's, Lilyth fished a trophy from her pocket: the key that had unlocked Arya's manacles. "But until I can formally name you the Red Eye, I will offer you this key as a reminder of what we can do for all the other women still trapped as slaves. They are as you were, Arya, and I cannot free them by myself. I need your help. *Eo* needs your help."

Arya nodded fast. "Of course. I understand." She swallowed and raised her chin proudly. "I'll do whatever it takes to help you."

"Thank you," Lilyth said, resting her forehead against Arya's. "Eo is proud of you—as am I."

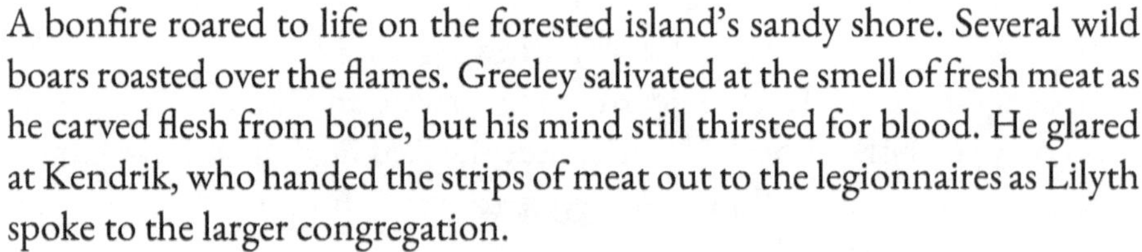

A bonfire roared to life on the forested island's sandy shore. Several wild boars roasted over the flames. Greeley salivated at the smell of fresh meat as he carved flesh from bone, but his mind still thirsted for blood. He glared at Kendrik, who handed the strips of meat out to the legionnaires as Lilyth spoke to the larger congregation.

Surrounded by auroras, stars, and the milky band of light that split the night like a scar, Lilyth's words took on a new depth. "...for these are the last days of the sun, and when the sun is eternally eclipsed by the night, we shall remain in our Goddess's Umbra—Her utopia. Only then will a new epoch finally arise: the era of night. A time of purity. A time of equality. All will be welcomed as equals in Her embrace. We shall begin this epoch by first uniting the enslaved. Then, when we have shown them the truth of Umbra, we will destroy the enslavers—the Cutthroats, the Corinthians, and all others who dare defy us. We will take back our lives. We will take back our freedom. *We will take back the night.*"

A round of cheers and applause erupted from the seventy-five legionnaires sitting cross-legged in the sand. With their heads shaved, all wore Lilyth's mark and clothing of reds and blacks. But only those who had proved themselves in battle had their eyelids painted black like Lilyth. Those who had yet to see battle seemed far hungrier, wanting nothing more than to wear the black stripe of Umbra—the stripe of the Red Legion.

Yet for all his accolades and prestige, Greeley was hungrier than the rest. He eyed Kendrik. The Red Pretender. The Red Nonbeliever. The Red *Seducer.* Kendrik was the final obstacle resting between Greeley and the prize he sought. As soon as that Red Fraud was dead, Greeley would be back on the *Jericho,* and Lilyth would be his.

Enjoy the attention while you can, Kendrik. Tonight will be your last, Greeley thought as he butchered the sinewy shoulders of the roasted pig. He cut clean through to the other side, sharp blade barely missing his own leg as the severed beast fell to the sand.

Grunting, Greeley picked up the meat and tried to brush off the sand. It was no use. The boar's secreted oils glued the sand on. Greeley brushed it harder, which only pulled more meat from bone. That, too, fell in the sand.

Seething, Greeley tensed as a hand offered him a canteen. Kendrik's hand. Greeley stared up at him, refusing to take the water. Kendrik was bigger than he'd been, his muscles more defined and jaw angular. He was handsome where Greeley was ugly. Far younger too.

That's why Lilyth likes him, Greeley thought. *Kendrik is a boy with charm—not a man with strength. Not... me.*

"Use the water. This'll take off some of the seasoning, but at least the meat won't be sandy." Kendrik poured water over the meat, and the sand slid off. "Try it with those other pieces you dropped."

You think to tell me *what to do?* Greeley thought, biting down on the barb and tongue alike, opting to only nod.

When Kendrik left to hand out more pieces of meat, Greeley's eyes followed. The congregation smiled and thanked the Red Seducer, but did they ever thank Greeley? No. They all avoided his gaze. Even Lilyth was now avoiding him, pushing him out and away from the bonfire.

Pushing him into the darkness.

I just need him alone for only a moment, Greeley thought, slicing through the boar too violently and cutting his left palm as more meat fell into the sand. He grunted, ignoring the pain and keeping his left fist clenched as he skinned the boar's neck and back with his red hand. Cutting the roast with one hand proved difficult, but he did so anyway, even as blood dripped between his fingers onto the sand. Another hand appeared, holding a scrap of cloth.

Kendrik, Greeley thought, turning with a snarl. Yet the expression faded when he saw Arya holding the cloth.

Black tattoos—not paint—slithered around her arms and neck like snakes and spiderwebs. Muscles rippled beneath her skin, capable of wielding heavy blades, hauling the lines, and killing with only her fists. She was attractive but differed from Lilyth's beauty.

"Thought you could use the help," Arya whispered, low enough to avoid interrupting Lilyth's sermon. She leaned forward to bandage Greeley's hand, but he leaned away from her as if she carried the Night Plague.

"But why help me?" Greeley asked, glaring.

"You unlocked my manacles. You gave me my freedom, Red Hand," said Arya, meeting his gaze where most others would have looked away. Instead of fear or anger, her eyes shone with gratitude. "That's all the reason I need."

Grunting, Greeley extended his hand toward Arya, and she bandaged the wound. Immediately, Greeley returned to cutting the boar. Arya didn't wait for him to thank her—or even seem to expect it—but returned to her seat in the congregation.

Still, it affected Greeley's attitude. *Focus on killing Kendrik,* Greeley thought, but it was easier said than done. When he glanced at Arya, she was always watching him. Something lurked in her eyes. Interest? Attraction? *Lust?* Even after he'd looked away, he could feel her gaze boring into his back.

After Greeley finished cutting the boars, he moved to the back of the congregation to observe any legionnaires who dared fall asleep while Lilyth spoke of Eo's warm embrace and Her cold fury. Her words especially enraptured the new legionnaires, who had recently witnessed the Night

Plague firsthand. Greeley had heard this speech countless times before, so he let his tired mind wander until the mention of the next raid. Then he listened intently, hungering to sink his blade into the flesh of Kendrik and Cutthroats alike.

Long past midnight, Lilyth finally finished her sermon and began a responsive prayer. For this, Greeley still stood behind the prostrate legionnaires, but now Kendrik joined him. Greeley wanted nothing more than to shove a knife into his throat.

"The sun shall die," Lilyth said.

"Eo is the moon," replied the legionnaires—Kendrik speaking loudest of all.

"The world shall burn."

"Eo purifies the land."

"The legion shall endure."

"Eo protects the Chosen..."

When the responsive prayer ended, Lilyth granted the Red Legion ten minutes to relieve themselves, drink water, and chat quietly before sparring commenced. Greeley watched Kendrik leave the congregation and sit by the shore, staring up at the stars.

How easy would it be to stab him and throw him into the water? To blame it on the syrens, which were always close at hand? *I can get away with it—Eo will help me.*

While the others chatted and Lilyth's back was turned to stoke the flames of the bonfire, Greeley crept across the sand toward Kendrik, who'd done him a favor and walked several hundred feet away by an outcropping of jutting rocks. Eo would hide him, and all would be well.

If it wasn't, well, Greeley would just say that Kendrik slipped, or that Kendrik tried to kill him. It would work. It had to work.

Grinning, Greeley unsheathed his knife and stalked toward Kendrik, whose words drifted toward him through the night air. "...just wish that you could share it with me. I know you are among the stars, but I want you here, Jericho. I always want you here..."

One cut, one slice—just like the boar. Cut him deep then shove his face in the sand, wash off the meat in the sea... Can't give the syrens sandy meat, can I, Kendrik?

Greeley made it two more steps before he heard someone behind him. He stopped for a moment, and the echoing feet also stopped. Goosebumps broke out along his flesh. *Lilyth? No. I wouldn't hear her coming. Has to be somebody else. Another legionnaire. One of Kendrik's friends.*

Greeley turned abruptly to the left, as if preparing to venture into the lush rain forest further inland. Hiding behind a tree, he waited. For almost a minute, Greeley heard nothing. Then his ears were alerted to the noise of crunching feet slipping through the foliage. *Come closer,* Greeley thought, still holding the knife close to his chest.

One step... Another step... A third—

Greeley attacked just as a shadow passed by his hiding place. He slammed the pursuer against a tree, raising a knife to his throat. *Her* throat.

"Arya?" Greeley asked, eyebrows knitting together. "What are you doing here? Why are you following me?" He pushed harder against her neck and turned his gaze back to the beach. "Did Kendrik send you? He did, didn't he? You're here to kill me, is that it? He tried to kill me before I could kill him, is that right? Tell me, or I swear on the Drowned Sea, I will kill you right here, right now."

"Nobody... sent me... Was just... looking for you..." Arya said, struggling to breathe.

Greeley searched her roughly with one hand, looking for a weapon that she could have used to kill him. Finding nothing, he pulled the knife away from her neck but didn't put it away. Finally, he asked, "Why?"

Arya lunged forward. Greeley raised his knife only for Arya's lips to meet his. He froze as she pulled away. "That a good enough reason, Red Hand?"

"Yeah," Greeley said, sheathing the knife. He went in for another kiss and thought, *Kendrik can wait.*

◄O►

Lilyth continued stoking the fire, pretending not to notice Kendrik leave the shore to talk to the star he thought was his brother. Greeley followed not long after, but Lilyth didn't need to stalk him, for Arya was watching him. Lilyth was left to tend to her flock.

At long last, the legionnaires were becoming true zealots. Mindless, heartless machines that moved and spoke and ate and slept and killed at her order. Not completely yet, but with the rigorous schedule of the cult, the isolation induced by ships and uninhabited islands, and the various mystical deceptions Lilyth performed, they were becoming believers. Enough reinforcement could break even the most capable minds.

I'm so close that I can feel it.

Lilyth pressed her hands closer to the fire, allowing the tongues to lick at her palms and fingers. Though it burned, the physical pain was something she could push aside with ease. Instead, she watched the fire as it tried to consume her but only ate itself. Flames never worried about the future. Instead, they always demanded more until there was nothing left to give. Then the fire would die, and the process would begin again.

And again.

And again.

Life was a cycle too. But all cycles came to an end. *This* cycle was at its end.

"That is why they will all burn," Lilyth whispered to the endless mouths of flame. "The fire must devour, even if the only thing available is itself."

Chapter Nineteen

Steward cleared the deck for a fight. She stood on one side of their small alcove in the hold. Mouse was at the other. The right corner of the red-haired boy's lip curled up, the left side remained as immovable as an anchor. A crescent scar curved just between his lip and nose—the result of her kick a year prior. He lifted his hands like a boxer and hopped from foot to foot, favoring his right knee. He'd fallen from the mainmast two years ago, and his leg had never healed right. Though Mouse never complained, Steward often saw him limping. But she made a point to never take advantage of his weakness, even if it meant losing.

Because that's what friends do, Steward thought, a grin on her lips as she emulated Mouse's stance. This moment of anticipation was her favorite part of the day, the only constant in her haphazard schedule of running, sleeping, and eating.

"Same rules as before," Mouse said. "No crotch shots, and if one of us gets really hurt, say *cutlass* and we'll stop, right?"

"Right."

Mouse nodded. "Then it's time for me to wipe the floor with you, Mop King."

"You said the same thing yesterday," Steward argued, confidently buffing her nails against her shirt. "Remember how that went, Rat Prince?"

"So what? That was yesterday! Today's a new day, Steward."

"Then bring it on."

During their first three months of fighting, Mouse won every bout. But Steward was a fast learner with a long reach and faster reflexes. Six months after she'd stepped onto the *Constable,* she'd won for the first time. After a year, fights were an even split.

"Prepare to be vanquished, evil king! I am Mouse, defender of rats and vermin!" He charged forward. "Have at thee!"

Steward threw a punch and missed. Mouse dipped low, wrapping his arms around her stomach. He reached for her legs, but Steward leaned forward and stiffened. She caught his head beneath her arm, but Mouse wriggled free.

"You think I'm gonna let you off that easy, Steward?" he whispered. "I have a reputation to uphold, good sir."

Steward only laughed.

Mouse approached low and slow. He slunk toward her, holding his left hand up to catch hers. Steward jabbed lightly, catching him once across the chin. Two of his punches connected across her ear and stomach. She doubled over, hiding a grin.

Mouse stiffened, his defense opening. "Oh, are you alright—"

Steward tackled him and landed on top before punching him in the face.

"Dirty scoundrel!" Mouse slapped her with an open hand, grabbed her arms, and turned his hips. Steward lost her balance as Mouse rolled on top of her. As he pinned her arms with his knees, she squirmed in vain. He punched her twice, though not nearly at full strength.

"Do you yield?" Mouse asked, holding up a fist.

"No," Steward said, pulling one arm free. She tried to punch him, but he slapped her hand away.

"Yield, I say!" Mouse slapped her with the back of his hand playfully.

Steward stared at him, sorting through every way to turn the fight in her favor. *I could spit in his face to distract him. I could even gouge his eyes. Bite his nose. Grab his ears. Smash his knee.* She exhaled, defeated. *But that's not what friends do.*

"Fine. I yield," Steward said. *"Cutlass."*

Mouse grinned. When he got up from his knees, he held his hands over his head. "Huzzah! I have bested the mighty King of Mops. Thus, I now regain my title. I am the Sovereign of Aritrasta. All shall kneel before me!"

Steward kicked his leg out from under him—the uninjured one. Mouse fell, and they laughed together.

"You and your dirty tricks," Mouse said. Not bothering to stand back up, he put his hands behind his head and stared at the ceiling. A moment passed while they enjoyed the quiet. "You know, if we stay on this ship long enough, we can work our way up to first mate—even captain! You and me, Steward. We'll run this ship together."

Steward laid down next to him. "Sail around the world?"

"Why else would we be on a ship?" Mouse asked. "We'll travel from Tavrak all the way to Stotan if we want. We'll visit the Deadlands, the eastern jungles all on a whim. Core be damned, we could even visit the coasts of Corinthus! Just say the word!"

"Yeah?" She grinned, rolling to look at him. "What about the Damned Depths?"

"We can do whatever we set our minds to, Steward. Imagine it, you and me, fighting the deep terrors, sailing to the edge of the world, even conquering the storms of the Black Trench! Then we'll come back to crowds and applause. They'll make us kings." Mouse sighed. "Of course, we'll still be lugging around mops for the next few years, but we'll get our chance. Ink likes us that much, at least."

"Ink doesn't like anyone," Steward said. "Least of all me. He always yells at me and pushes me around more than anybody else."

"Yeah, but that's because he expects more from you, Steward." Mouse shifted uncomfortably. She heard a tinge of jealousy in his voice as he added, "Ol' Patchey keeps everyone at a distance, but he sure holds you closest. When you're on his shift, he's teaching you about the rigging, the currents, and the stars. Same with Jameson. But with me and Terry, even Tom and Jerry, it's not the same. Not even close."

"He teaches you about the rigging, too, though," Steward said, guiltily. Admittedly, Ink and Jameson had taught her a lot about the ocean, though the weaver was always more interested in telling stories than explaining the difference between true wind and apparent wind.

"Oh, Captain Ink definitely does. I think the rigging's my calling on the ship. Mice need to climb the ratlines, after all." Mouse clicked his tongue. "Ink takes care of all of us, don't get me wrong, but he has a special interest in you. Even Terry knows it. Why do you think he's always pushing you around?"

"Because he's an asshole." Steward said. She'd thought their relationship would improve after she'd tried to jump overboard, or when she'd stopped wearing Shits's old clothes, but she'd been wrong on both accounts. Taran had come after her with every opportunity, as if he blamed her for his miserable squalling life. He'd knock her down on the deck, make her drop things she was carrying, and steal her food if she didn't eat quick enough. She and Mouse had brawled him a few times, but even fighting two-against-one, Taran was surprisingly difficult to beat. Steward usually got the worst of it, but the fights were always broken up before long.

"Taran is *definitely* an asshole, but he's also jealous." Mouse pointed at the ceiling as if he was seeing the stars. "You've got a future—he doesn't. He'll be a hauler, pulling ropes for the rest of his life. Meanwhile, we'll be running the whole ship."

"Yeah, but still. I want to make him bleed." Steward punched Mouse's arm lightly. "What if we ambush him next time?"

Mouse made an odd noise, somewhere between a laugh and a grunt. "I can see it now. Mouse and his trusty sidekick Steward luring ol' Terry into an ambush with a sack of dried meat."

Steward only laughed.

"No? Don't like that plan?"

"I don't care what the plan is, as long as it's you and me." Steward punched him lightly, and Mouse punched her back.

"It'll always be you and me, friend. From this sea to the next."

Months raced by. So did Steward. She ran across the deck carrying messages all throughout the *Constable* until she couldn't breathe. After delivering her latest message to Ink at the helm, Steward rested her hands on her knees and glanced at the sailors: haulers toiling with ropes and riggers trimming sails. Though there were still some terms she struggled with, Steward knew her way around the ship.

"How's our heading, Steward?" Ink asked, his tribal neck tattoos shifting and stretching into new shapes. He stared at the ocean cresting toward the night sky.

Steward paused. The waves were traveling faster than the ship, causing whitecaps to crest over the stern. The boat leaned to the port side but regained equilibrium. If they slowed any further, the *Constable* would be in danger of capsizing. They couldn't turn around, either, because the waves would smash into the sides and definitely capsize them. "We should sail full to the wind and loose the studding sails for extra speed. Get us ahead of the waves."

"Full to the wind, eh? It'll push us away from our client."

The *Winddancer*, a barquentine, was their newest client, and those merchants were sailing just behind the *Constable*. They'd visited the three major ports along the main coast before deciding to trek two ninedays back to Port Casanought.

"When the gale becomes stronger, the waves won't crash over the stern anymore. We'll reef the sails and reduce speed later if need be." Steward pointed toward the *Winddancer*. "We'll update them with the pennants."

Though his face didn't change, Ink shouted the order to the haulers and riggers. "We might just make a sailor out of you yet, Steward," he said, pride gleaming in his eye.

Steward smiled, feeling the security of *home* in that look for the first time since Alira.

Jameson stood on the main deck, surveying the night as the crew carried out his orders. The breeze chilled his skin even under the night furs, the salty spray needled his ears, nose, and cheeks. Still, the sea was calm, the sky clear. Galaxies and nebulas danced above his head, making it the perfect night for stargazing.

Not that his eyes were on the stars. Out of his periphery, Jameson watched Steward, who manned the helm. Normally, the true helmsman would have kept the post, but because the waters were unusually gentle, Jameson had given her the honor. As she steered the ship, Jameson heard her muttering the opening verses of Undo's song:

The Gods forgot, but She did not,
The promise They made to Her.
Her tears fell, storm and rain.
Her wails echoed thunder.

Forgotten by, She said on high,

Forgotten by the sea.
You'll pay the price for your deeds.
You'll pay eternally.

Jameson turned when Steward stopped singing, her eyes watching the full moon and its reflection.

"Keep going," Jameson said. "Can't leave Undo's song unfinished. It's a jinx on these waters."

Steward frowned, looking embarrassed as she rubbed her shoulder. "But I don't know the rest of it."

"Well, I don't have much of a singing voice, but we have no other choice, do we?" Jameson grinned and cleared his throat.

Bound in chains, still He remains,
Bound to the Core unseen.
No one to hear, no one to know.
No one to intervene.

Forget me so, He said below,
Forget me entirely.
Thunder calls when lightning falls.
Lightning remembers me.

Steward turned her head, keeping her hands on the helm. She brushed tears away and sniffed. "That was my dad's favorite song... Mom sang it for us before she left, but I could never remember the second half."

Jameson hesitated before asking, "Where'd she go?"

Steward shrugged, tense. "Don't know. Just disappeared one day without saying goodbye. Left me and my father both. May as well be dead for all I care."

After a long silence, Jameson said, "I never knew my parents. In a way, it made losing them easier, but it's never easy."

"Don't I know it," Steward spat. She held the wheel tighter, white-knuckled.

"Do you know the story behind that song?" Jameson asked, changing the topic to distract her from her anguish. When Steward shook her head, Jameson explained, "In the beginning, the Creator awoke to nothing.

From it, She created the nine Aspects and, with them, life. Made us as well as everything else. Afterward, the Creator made an unbreakable oath to never unmake a creation. To never *undo* Her work. That was Her first mistake: while She could not destroy life, we could destroy each other. Humans warred and killed, but because of Her vow, the Creator couldn't stop us, which broke Her heart. So She wept for nine days, a day for each Aspect, until Her cries were heard by the Myrmidons."

"Wait, the Myrmidons?" Steward asked, snapping her head up at him. "As in the myrfolk? The *syrens?*"

"Aye, but they weren't myrfolk then. Not syrens either. The Myrmidons were humans who lived in a great valley far below us."

"Below?" Steward exclaimed, leaning forward. "But that's..."

"In the Drowned Sea, aye," Jameson said with a nod. "But during the time of the Myrmidons, the sea didn't exist yet. Their home was a lush basin surrounded by mountains on all sides, protecting them from invaders. So, the Myrmidons knew nothing of hatred and war, only happiness and joy.

"Upon finding the Creator crying, the Myrmidons strived to lift Her spirits. For five days, they celebrated with feasts, dances, and art. And at the end of those five days, the Creator's heart was mended. She loved the Myrmidons enough to stay with them forever. So, She created nine Gods in the image of the Myrmidons to govern the Aspects. But that was Her second mistake: the Gods were human, so They too knew pride, wrath, and even jealousy.

"And Kuma, being the strongest of the Gods and governor of the seas, was jealous of the Myrmidons most of all, for the Creator loved the Myrmidons more than Him. So, He devised a terrible plan to destroy them. Summoning the other eight Gods together, Kuma asked, 'To which Aspect does lightning belong?'

"And each God claimed lightning for Themself, because lightning touched all Aspects: occurring both day and night, touching the sky, land, and seas, striking where it was hot and cold, and piercing both beasts and plants. Unwilling to share that power, all the Gods except Kuma battled for its control.

"Their War of Lightning threatened to break the world, forcing the Creator to leave the Myrmidons and intervene. That was Her third mistake. With the Creator distracted, Kuma struck. At His command, the seas rose higher than even the mountains surrounding the great valley. The Myrmidons had but a moment to scream before the waves came crashing down.

"When the Creator heard the sound, She raced back to the great valley to find Myrmidons dead and drowning in this new sea. Bound by Her vow, the Creator could not undo Kuma's destruction. Instead, She gave the surviving Myrmidons gills and fins, transforming them into the myrfolk. But instead of happiness or joy, they were angry, vengeful. No longer could they play music, paint, or dance. The myrfolk saw their survival as a curse. Even as the Creator begged them to forgive Her, they abandoned Her and receded into the sea.

"And for the first time, the Creator felt hatred. Still bound by Her vow to not destroy Her creations, She instead cursed the Gods. Then she cast Herself into the sea and drowned so She could be with Her Myrmidons in death. In doing so, the Creator's name became Undo, because the only creation She could undo was Herself. And so, the Drowned Sea became a last curse upon all the world—a Godless abyss filled with storms, Cutthroats, and monsters. Or so the tale is told."

Steward stared at him, mouth parted before curving into a malevolent smile. "Undo *cursed* the Gods?"

Jameson nodded uneasily. Her expression made him squirm. "Aye. Three curses. One for each mistake. First, Undo took each of the Gods' right eye and forged a brilliant Sword, the only weapon in the world that can kill Them."

"So Eo only has one eye?" Steward asked. She shifted on her heels, unable to hide her excitement. "And She can be killed?"

"Yes, though the Eonian priests don't advertise that," Jameson said with an awkward laugh. *Why is Steward getting excited about that?* Trying to hide his discomfort, he added, "As Undo couldn't kill the Gods, She infused the Swords with Their powers so humans could kill Them. Not that you would want to. Killing a God and taking Their place means inheriting Their curses, of which, the Sword is only the first.

"The second is the Belt, created from the Gods' hair. Undo fastened the Belts around Their waists, tethering the Gods to Their Aspects. This is why Eo must follow the night and disappear during the day. It is the same with the other Gods—they can no longer interact with one another.

"The last curse is the Crown, fashioned from the Gods' hearts. Once placed upon Their heads, these Crowns made the Gods' power dependent on our belief in Them. The more the Gods are worshipped, the more powerful They are. That's why we pray to Eo—to give Her strength." He gestured to *Eo's Point,* the northern star that always shined over Aritrasta. "It is said that every light casts a shadow. In the darkest nights, that light is said to be Eo Herself, and our prayers and belief make it so."

Steward frowned, crossing her arms. "Yeah. Sure. Tell me more about the Swords."

"I will, but not yet, Steward," Jameson said, rolling his eyes, which only seemed to annoy her more. "Though Undo cursed Eo and the other Gods, Kuma's fate was far worse. As She could not uncreate Him, Undo stripped Kuma of His power. She created the Black Trench by ripping a hole through the sea and the land, one that leads to the burning Core of our world. Undo bound Him there with chains fashioned from the corpses of drowned Myrmidons. And for Kuma's role in igniting the War of Lightning, She ensured that lightning would always strike the Core. Even now, you can hear Kuma's thunderous wails during storms... And *that* is the truth of Undo's song."

With his story finished, Jameson looked down at Steward, expecting adoration and wonder. Instead, he saw desire in her pursed lips, furrowed brow, and hungry stare. "Sure, fine. But the Swords... Where are they?"

"That's what you're most interested in after everything I just told you?" Jameson asked, eyebrows furrowing. "Look, only Aritras the Red has ever found a Sword—"

"Eo's Sword, right?" Steward asked, abandoning her post at the helm and taking a step toward Jameson, who backed away.

"Steward! The helm!"

She ignored him, pressing forward. "How did he get it? Where is it now? Why didn't he kill Her?"

"Eo struck a deal with Aritras so that he wouldn't kill Her. In return, she made him Her Champion. And through Eo, Aritras forged the Aritrastan Empire and became a king. That's why he named himself Aritras the Red—to honor Her."

Steward frowned, her eyes darkening. "Then Aritras was a fool. He should have killed Her when he had the chance."

The words struck Jameson like a bullet to the teeth. He glanced at the waves, expecting a storm to rise on the horizon and lightning to strike the Core. Instead, the night remained clear and silent. "The open sea is no place to anger the Gods, Steward."

"Where can I find Eo's Sword? Tell me, Jameson. I know you know something. *You don't forget.* How many times have you told me that?" Steward grabbed two fistfuls of his coat. While she ate well and was stronger than she'd been a year ago, she was only a young girl. But the rage and ruthlessness swimming beneath her irises intimidated Jameson. "Please, just tell me what you know."

If I tell her, she'll get herself killed chasing after a Sword. I can see that in her eyes... Thousands of sailors have wasted their entire lives doing the same. I can't let her do it—even if she hates me for it. Jameson pushed her away. "No."

"But, Jameson—"

"No." Jameson walked over to the helm, taking Steward's place. "Look, I know your life has been hard—"

"Hard?" Steward asked, voice rising to a squeak.

"—but that's no reason to anger the Gods, Steward."

"What do you know of my life?" Fingers trembling, her hand moved toward her belt, to her hidden talan. "You think because you taught me about the stars and the Myrmidons that you somehow understand?"

"I understand more than most." Jameson said, trying to assuage her anger. "I know what it's like to be angry. To be alone. To lose loved ones—"

"Then you of all people should know that the Gods won't help us," Steward said, her breath turning to steam. She glared at him, her eyes carrying the drowned stare that Jameson had always hated. "And this"—Steward brandished her talan—"is what they deserve."

For the first time, Jameson understood why Ink had wanted to throw her back to the sea.

CHAPTER TWENTY

The sun reared its head above the waves like a sea monster, signaling the end to Steward's twelve-hour workday. While she enjoyed the afternoon shift with Ink, the night shifts with Jameson remained dreadful. Their relationship worsened after he'd refused to tell her about Aritras's Sword, and they'd become estranged over the last several months. While Steward still obeyed Jameson's orders, she didn't speak to him. Eventually, he'd stopped trying to talk to her too. Instead, he often gave her rigging work up in the masts—if only to minimize their interactions on the quarterdeck.

Not that Steward complained. She shared most of her duties with Mouse, and when they finished their work, they watched the sunrise together. Like now.

Steward watched Mouse out of the corner of her eye. He lay down on the small platform halfway up the foremast, his hair stuck out at wild angles as dew clung to the curls. She sat beside him with her legs dangling over its edge. She leaned back, intentionally letting her hand graze his elbow. He didn't seem to notice, but then again, Mouse never had a care in the world. It was another thing she liked about him. He never cried. Only laughed. They were so different in that respect.

More often these days, she imagined what it would be like to kiss him. It was a strange thought—a new one the older she got—and not one she was used to. Yet whenever he laughed or joked or even smiled, she came back to that question. Not that she ever *could* kiss him. Steward hadn't told him or anybody else she was a girl, and as long as she sailed with Ink, she never would. Even so, she wondered what it would be like if Mouse *did* know.

Would he like me? she often wondered.

"What do you think is at the edge of the Damned Depths?" Mouse eventually asked. "I've heard that a ship graveyard lines the edge. Past it, a world of ice. Giants live there on icebergs the size of cities, looking for ships to sink and people to steal for their collection."

More of Jameson's stupid stories. The thought soured Steward's mood, dredging up those feelings of betrayal. He knew something about Eo's Sword. What reason could he possibly have for not telling her? Forcing the thought aside, Steward gazed toward the sea. She watched it pulse and surge as if it were trying to warn her against venturing too far. "I'd think giants are closer to the Ice Barrens or the Frigid Wastes. But out in the Damned Depths? I don't think so."

"Oh yeah? What do you think is there, then?" Mouse asked with an eyebrow arched.

"Just more water, I think," she said, still looking out at the ocean. But of course, Steward had no clue. If the Swords were real, there could be anything out there. Only the Gods knew, and They would never share those secrets. Not until she had a Sword. But until Jameson told her what he knew, she'd never find one. *And he'll never tell me.*

"And more monsters?" Mouse asked.

Steward looked down at the waves, seeing no syrens. It'd been over two months since their last sighting. Maybe they'd finally gone away. Relieved, Steward changed positions as her leg fell asleep. "There probably are more monsters. I just think that krakens and leviathans have better things to do than wreck ships."

Mouse looked around fearfully, eyeing the sky with mistrust. "You trying to get us killed? You know you can't go around saying their names! The winds'll carry the words right to them, and they'll come after us!" He grabbed the small pendant around his neck, engraved with the symbols of Eo and the Godless sea. He closed his eyes and said a silent prayer.

Steward rolled her eyes. "You've been spending too much time around Jameson."

"And maybe you're not spending enough time around him," Mouse argued. "Ever thought of that, Mop King?"

"Tall ships lead to tall tales," Steward said. "That's what Ink says, and I trust him a lot more."

Mouse opened his mouth to respond but closed it as he stared off at the horizon. Mouse blinked, rubbed his eyes, and looked again. "A kraken! You pissed it off, and now it's coming for us!"

Steward followed his line of sight and noticed the dark silhouette at the edge of the horizon. Fear flashed across her mind before she caught sight of sails. "That's no kraken! That's a ship!"

Mouse glared at Steward before looking at the silhouette again. He shook his head, his eyes softening. "Thank the Gods that's all it is."

"Ship ho, captain!" Steward shouted down. "Twenty degrees to port!"

Ink shouted from the deck, "What flag is hoisted?"

"Can't see it, captain!"

Ink shouted, "You two! Finish your work and get down here!" Turning his attention to a rigger in the crow's nest, Ink added, "Eyes! Give me updates on that ship! If any others appear, you tell me instantly!"

Eyes replied, "Aye, sir!"

Steward followed Mouse down the ratlines, ran across the main deck, and charged up the stairs to the quarterdeck at the stern. They joined Ink and Jameson at the helm, but Steward stood as far from the first mate as possible. He pretended not to notice her.

As Ink lowered his spyglass, Jameson asked, "What flag did you see, captain?"

"The Astrolabe," Ink said, frowning.

"That's good news, isn't it?" Steward asked. The purple astrolabe of the Veranauts, a sect of Aritrastan merchants, or so Ink had taught her. Yet it made little sense why they were out on the seas alone.

Ink grunted. "Should be good news, but I ain't convinced. Not yet."

Eyes called down, "Second ship ho, captain!"

Ink stared out through his spyglass, muttering curses. "Core be damned. The second one's got a Rose flag."

Roses, the chivalrous Cutthroats who only stole from the rich and never took slaves. Dad had named her Erin Rose, paying homage to them. He'd always seen the Roses as heroes, not villains. *They always did what they had to in order to survive, but they still had a code of honor. It don't get more heroic than that, my rose.*

Steward swallowed the pain. She'd learned to cope with the hole in her heart, even if it still hurt to remember Dad.

Then a cannon fired in the distance.

"Is that meant for us?" Mouse asked, terrified.

Jameson shook his head. "Much too far away for that. The Roses are firing warning shots to get the Veranauts to stop. But those merchants aren't slowing. They'll travel straight at us, probably hoping to make an alliance to fend off the Roses." He paused, appraising the situation. "Or at least, that's what they want us to think."

The Roses fired another warning shot even as the Veranauts charged toward the *Constable*. The cannonball missed, splashing into the water off the merchants' port side.

"Belay your nonsense and state your meaning, weaver," Ink said.

"Third ship on the horizon!" Eyes shouted.

"Another Rose." Ink said, looking through his spyglass. "Core be damned twice."

"Thrice." Jameson said, his usual smile wrinkles beneath the eyes replaced by worry lines on his forehead.

"Thrice?" Ink asked, collapsing the spyglass. "Explain yourself."

Jameson scratched his wrist. "I've seen this maneuver before, Ink. Done it too. It's a trick. All three ships are Cutthroat."

"Wait. You've *done* this before? As in, you were a *Cutthroat* before?" Steward asked, addressing Jameson for the first time in months. He stared back at her, caught between fear and confusion. Looking into Jameson's eyes, she knew she was right. He'd lied to her. Betrayed her. *Again.*

"This ain't the time for questions, lad," Ink said, waving away Steward's accusation. She knew better than to argue with him, especially right now, but she wouldn't forget. "Jameson, what are we looking at here?"

The weaver blinked twice and turned away, avoiding Steward's fury. He pondered for a moment, then said, "Those supposed Veranauts will pass us and raise Cutthroat colors from the other side. Instead of a two-on-two battle, it'll be three-on-one. And we'll be surrounded. We'll be surrendering or sinking before we get off a broadside." Jameson frowned deeper. "But this isn't a Rose tactic, Ink. They wouldn't attack a Guardian."

Steward didn't understand his meaning, but Ink did. He set his jaw. "Sounds like we're in for a battle. Send a message to the *Crestfish* and make sure they see it." He sucked in a breath and screamed, "*All hands on deck, you dickless dogs! Cutthroats on the horizon!*"

A sailor sprang to the belfry and rang the emergency bell. Others disappeared into hatchways and reappeared to pass out muskets, flintlock pistols, and cutlasses to haulers and riggers, who then returned to their posts. Off-shift sailors gathered at the gunwales with weapons, some even holding grenados.

Steward froze, realizing only now how precarious this situation was. *This is a real battle. People are going to die. We might die.* Her eyes scanned the horizon, and she wanted to flee, but where? There was only ocean. There was no choice but to fight.

"Gunners and powder monkeys, run the cannons! Riggers, drop those boarding nets! Haulers, *heave*, you salty swine!"

Mouse bounded off to the gun deck, but Steward stayed at Ink's side.

Gunports opened in the hull, and bronze cannons emerged from the holes, their edges flaked and burnished with soot. Guardians wheeled smaller cannons across the main deck, stuffing those carronades with grapeshot, which would burst into dozens of small pellets unlike a cannonball.

"Fire a warning shot!" Ink shouted.

One of the *Constable's* cannons blasted in a cloud of sparks and smoke. Steward was almost knocked off her feet by the sound alone. A cannonball flew, splashing into the sea close to the approaching Veranauts.

Immediately, they changed direction, sailing wider around the *Constable* and raising a new flag: a black cloth embroidered with a white skull and a gray syren. The faux-Roses did too. Three Skulls: a sloop, a schooner, and a frigate all barreling toward the *Constable.*

"Squall me," Jameson whispered, touching his phoenix tattoo. "We're in it now."

Steward's eyes were wide as she stared at the three looming ships. The sloop and the schooner had fewer cannons than the *Constable* but were faster and more maneuverable. The Skull frigate was of equal size—equal power. The Guardians were outmaneuvered, outmanned, and outgunned by the most sadistic Cutthroats on the Drowned Sea.

We're going to die, Steward thought as the Skulls rushed out of their hiding places to scream from the main decks of their three ships.

"Not just any Skulls," Ink said, handing the spyglass to Jameson. The captain's mouth was agape, more emotion from him than Steward had ever seen.

"Those are... *corpses* hanging from the bowsprit. And the figurehead. It's the gagged maiden!" Jameson said, pointing at the frigate. Next to the black one, Skulls hoisted a burning white flag—the universal sign of no surrender. "Gods, it's the *Wrath*. It's Rolf the squalling Bloody." He pressed the spyglass tighter against his eye. "He just... killed a Skull. One of his own men. Depths be damned, he's *dedicating* the battle."

"Dedicating it?" Ink asked, taking back the spyglass and looking through it.

"Rolf sacrificed a member of his own crew to honor the syrens and get their blessing... He's as mad as the stories say."

Steward trembled. That she couldn't even *see* what Jameson saw without the spyglass only compounded her fears. She wanted to reach for the spyglass, but more than that, she wanted to flee. Yet her legs wouldn't move, so she stayed put beside Ink and Jameson, who had all but forgotten her.

Rowboats filled with howling Skulls dropped from the three ships.

"Three ships. Three *squalling* ships. That bastard." Ink clenched his fist and stowed the spyglass. At the top of his lungs, he rattled off more orders to various crew members. "Roll out the boarding nets! Ready the carronades for boarders! Prepare the depth charges for syrens!"

Steward bit her tongue just to keep from whimpering. Any ideas about the glory and excitement of battle had died at the sight of the first Skull. Now, she was driven mad by the antagonizing *slowness* of it all. The Skull ships and their rowboats approached at a walk instead of a run, and the *Constable* couldn't change directions fast enough to protect itself on all sides. Guardians could do nothing but wait for the Skulls to circle and come within range, and when that happened, the fighting would be quick, brutal, and merciless.

The Skulls knew it too. Those Cutthroats laughed and hurled insults from their rowboats as they crossed the small distance to the *Constable*. One stood up from behind cover and brandished a cutlass in one hand while extending the middle finger of his other hand. He jeered and laughed until a coral trident jettisoned out of the water and slammed into his chest.

Then the Skulls' laughter stopped.

Confused, the Skull staggered but kept his balance. He looked down at the gnarled trident as he coughed up blood. A kelp rope tied to the end of the trident disappeared into the water below. The line pulled taut, and the Skull was ripped from the boat and dragged into the sea, cutting off his scream. Flesh disappeared. A dismembered head bobbed to the surface for only a moment before a gray webbed hand reached out of the water and dragged it back down.

Then the syrens' laughter began.

"Hit the deck!" Ink shouted, diving to the planks as syrens hurled dozens more tridents. Some attacked the Guardians, but most targeted the Skulls in the rowboats. Some tridents hit their marks. Others missed. Guardians hacked kelp ropes apart before tridents could be retrieved, only to be cut down by another trident in the process. Cutthroats in the rowboats rowed faster as gray-skinned syrens pried planks free of hulls with their clawed fingers.

"Frenzy!" Ink shouted, lifting his head from the deck. "Drop the depth charges! Don't let the syrens sink us!"

Guardians followed the orders, lighting the fuses of gunpowder barrels and dropping them overboard. The fuses stayed lit even as the barrels sank into the sea, exploding far below. In response, the syrens only laughed more.

"Not them. Anything but them," Steward said, hyperventilating. She'd have traded any skill she'd learned, even her friendship with Mouse, to be back at Mark's tavern—away from these monsters, from this squalling sea. "Take me back to the Chasm. Take me back to Mark."

Ink did a double-take, glancing down at her. "Steward! What in the Core are you still doing here? I told you to get yourself below deck! It's not safe up here!" Ink shoved her away. "Go!"

Steward crawled across the deck to the hatch, avoiding the tridents and corpses of Guardians. She'd just reached the ladder and begun climbing down when the *Constable's* cannons fired, unleashing a deafening salvo of shots. The Skulls immediately unleashed their own barrage.

It's no safer down here, she thought as she descended deeper into the ship. *There's no escape. Eo be damned, there's no squalling escape.*

Two cannonballs decimated the main deck into a mass of iron, blood, bone, and splinters. Jameson shook as the agony felled his ears.

"It's dark! Why's it so dark?" a sailor shouted as splinters pin-cushioned his eyes and forehead. Blood ran from his eyes as he collapsed to the deck, dead.

"My legs! My squalling legs!" screamed a second, staring down at the bleeding stumps where his knees used to be. Severed arteries spurted like crimson fountains as his eyes rolled back into his head.

A third didn't have the chance to scream, for a large splinter destroyed his lungs.

Jameson was reminded of the *Keep,* where his Copperhead allies had been ripped to pieces beside him, and of being scarred, burned, and drifting through the Drowned Sea...

Ink slapped him on the back, angrier than he'd been in some time. "We'll tell this tale yet, weaver!" The captain continued calling out orders as more cannons fired. His brow furrowed in concentration as he repositioned the *Constable* against the Skulls' onslaught.

"Keep us leeward, helmsman! Don't let them cut our retreat!" Ink shouted. "Riggers, full sails!"

Jameson turned back to see that the *Crestfish,* their latest client, was pulling away and leaving the *Constable* behind to fight all three ships. To be expected, but still heart-wrenching to witness.

"They're getting the sloop off our back!" Ink said as the Skull sloop broke away from the schooner and the frigate to pursue the *Crestfish.* "Gunners, give Rolf a broadside!"

A dozen cannons exploded beneath them as waves crashed into the gunports. Cannonballs shrieked amidst plumes of gunpowder smoke, shooting high and ripping through the sails of the *Wrath* instead of its hull. One hit the figurehead before ricocheting off into the water.

"Damnation!" Ink shouted obscenities, pulling Jameson down behind a couple of barrels as Rolf let loose another broadside.

Metal bullets, nails, and bits of glass flew in all directions as the barrage destroyed more of the *Constable's* main deck.

"The squalls are using chainshot!" Ink said as two half-cannonballs attached by a chain shrieked through the air, destroying the boarding nets and the rigging. Several sails sagged as multiple ropes were cut, affecting the ship's ability to maneuver.

"That's not all they'll use!" Jameson said, as Skulls fired everything they had at the *Constable*. Steel rods, lead pellets, and bloody carcasses flew around them, tearing through Guardians.

Survivors piled dead bodies, crates, and even rolled-up hammocks against the gunwale for extra protection. Jameson and Ink joined them, taking cover behind the rail and firing muskets.

More Cutthroats entered the water in rowboats. Though the syrens ripped apart several, there were too many boats to destroy, especially with the depth charges and grenados driving them away. Guardians maneuvered the carronades and unleashed grapeshot into the closer boats.

Among them, Jameson spied a burning rowboat drifting toward the *Constable*. Smoke rose as it continued to burn, a line of sand separating the fire from the rowers. "Fireship!"

"Concentrate fire!" Ink shouted.

Guardians rose from behind cover with muskets, laying waste to the rowing Skulls. The fireship slowed to a stop and detonated two minutes later, taking a couple more boats with it. Still not enough. The first of the boats was already safe below the gunwale, and the Skulls threw up grappling hooks into the boarding net. For every one that a Guardian cut down, two more hooks appeared in its place.

Here it comes, Jameson thought, abandoning his spent musket and unsheathing a flintlock pistol and his cutlass. He blasted the first Skull, whose head appeared over the rail, but he had to duck away as grenados were lobbed onto the deck. Other Guardians scrambled to duck behind cover or throw the bombs back overboard. Most failed.

Jameson hunkered beneath the growing pile of corpses as Ink coughed beside him. The captain winced, pulling out his cutlass with one hand and putting pressure on his stomach with the other—a steel rod jutted from his abdomen.

Jameson's lips formed an *o*. "Ink..."

"Oh, save if for your stories, weaver! I ain't dead yet!" Ink grunted, grabbing a dropped pistol and firing it at boarders who were spilling through the net from the other side. "Until I am, this is still my squalling ship, my squalling crew, my squalling *sea*." He stood, staggering but shoving Jameson's hand away. "And if this is gonna be my last day, then I'll do it on my own two feet, in my own squalling boots. Now come on!"

As the first Skulls ripped through the boarding net and jumped onto the main deck, Ink and Jameson broke cover to repel them. Lines of Cutthroats and Guardians clashed as yet more Skulls climbed through the netting. The fight was chaotic, crowded. Wild colors blurred to wild stabbing. Flintlocks were fired at point-blank, from ahead and behind. Guns were discarded on the deck as more switched to cutlasses and daggers. Those without weapons grappled and clawed with fists on the ground, getting stepped on by the men still standing.

Among them, Jameson and Ink slashed, parried, and stabbed.

But it still wasn't enough. There were too few Guardians now, too many Skulls.

The captain's scream stopped everything. If only for a moment. Jameson turned to see a Skull's cutlass run through Ink's shoulder, a simultaneous shot tearing through his back. Ink fell on the first Cutthroat, stabbing him in the chest. He kicked away the second one, who impaled himself on a large splinter of wood. Ink grunted, rolling off the dead man before struggling to his feet. Then he fell back to one knee.

Jameson felt as if he were running through sand as he staggered to his captain's side. "*Ink!* You're—"

"I squalling told you, weaver. I ain't dead yet." Ink coughed blood, his words quieter. "The sea kept me around for entertainment, my boy. And, Core be damned, I'm gonna give her one last show."

With Jameson pulling Ink to his feet, they kept fighting and stabbing side-by-side even as they were driven back toward the mainmast. More Skulls kept crawling through the net. One of them tackled Ink, and they both fell to the deck. Jameson slit that Skull's throat, but not before he stabbed Ink in the gut.

The captain of the *Constable* let out a low moan as Jameson tried to pull him to his feet. Yet Ink couldn't stand. He dragged himself to a sitting position and trembled as he lit a grenade with his spent flintlock pistol.

"I ain't dead yet, my boy," Ink whispered, tossing the explosive across the deck to kill six more boarders. His laugh was brief—a wheezing cough. "I ain't dead..."

Then Ink's hand fell, cold and lifeless.

Guardians and Skulls fought around Ink's corpse as Jameson stared down at the man who'd been a father to him. Ink had been one of the few good men who sailed the Drowned Sea, but here he was. Eye glazed and open. Lips parted and bloodstained. Chest gored and decimated.

Worse, if Rolf won, he'd hang Ink's corpse from his bowsprit.

At that image, Jameson screamed. At first incoherent, the shouts eventually became words. "Keep fighting! For Ink! For the *Constable!*"

But despite his fury, more Guardians fell around Jameson. They met the wrong ends of swords and cannon fire. The tide of Skulls didn't ebb. When the last of the Guardians retreated to the gun deck, Jameson followed, only to be clobbered over the head.

Chapter Twenty-One

Explosions rattled the *Constable's* hull as Steward and the other cabin boys carried gunpowder cartridges across the gun deck. They leaped across holes and dead bodies to deliver their sacks of powder to gunners who frantically fired and reloaded cannons. One gunner accidentally knocked Steward down in his haste to ram a cannonball into the barrel.

Taran, of all people, was the one to help her up this time. The situation was dire enough that he didn't berate her. He only shouted, "Go reload those guns! I'll get more powder!" Then Taran disappeared back down the ladder.

Steward grabbed two more sacks and lugged them across the deck, following Jarrel. Her heartbeat echoed the cannons thundering in her ears. Her fingers shook so violently that she dropped one bag and stopped to pick it up.

Jarrel stopped and turned, eyes furious and mouth set in a grim line. "Godsdammit, Steward!" he shouted, the first time she'd heard his voice above a whisper. "This isn't the time to—"

The hull exploded inward as a cannonball ripped through the gun deck. It shattered through Jarrel's chest and exited out his back. The cannonball broke through the opposite side of the hull before Jarrel had fallen to the ground. Just the head and legs remained. The chest had exploded in all directions with bits of meat stinging Steward's face and staining her clothes. She was too shocked to scream.

I should have never left Alira, Steward thought, watching Jarrel's detached legs spasm as if he still controlled them. She scooted backward, her eyes locked on Jarrel's open, unblinking ones. His tongue lolled out of his mouth, and his lips quivered as if trying to form words. *Oh Gods... I'm going to die here. We all are.*

"Jarrel!" Tomlin dropped his sacks and ran to his dead twin. He kneeled at the body and cradled Jarrel's head in his lap. "No! Jarrel, come back! Oh Gods, don't leave me here! Take me with you!"

Steward stood frozen with her mouth agape. Hands grabbed her, and she instantly thrashed, imagining the bony clawed fingers of syrens who'd somehow crawled through the holes in the hull to get her. "No! *No!*"

"Steward! Stop! It's me! Mouse! Come on! We need you!" Mouse put the powder sacks back in her hands. Steward held them, trying to remember what they were for. Was she supposed to take it somewhere?

Mouse shook her. "Steward! *Come on!* Give the powder to the gunners!"

Right. Steward charged through the smoke, ash, and debris, focusing her mind on running. Just running. Not on the syrens or the Skulls. Certainly not on Jarrel's twitching corpse.

As she ran back for more bags, she spied Mouse attempting to pull Tomlin away from Jarrel's body. "We have to keep going, you squall!" he shouted.

"Jarrel needs me!" Tomlin screamed, sitting cross-legged as Jarrel's severed head soaked his brown pants maroon. "He still needs me!"

"We need you more!" Steward slapped him and threw him to his feet. Tomlin caught himself before he could fall, but his eyes were glassy. He shambled after them like a broken puppet.

The cannon blasts kept echoing across the gun deck, causing the wood to groan with stress. More cannonballs broke through the hull, killing two more sailors. Through the gunports and the splintered holes, Steward saw the Skulls rowing closer, shooting flintlocks, and clambering through the openings. Guardians fired and stabbed them while ducking the occasional trident thrown by the laughing syrens. They ate greedily as more Cutthroats and Guardians fell to the sea.

Don't look, don't think, Steward repeated to herself as she delivered more powder bags, wishing all the more that she was in the Chasm. At least there, she could run forever, hide and escape when needed. On the gun deck, she could only run so far.

When Skulls overran the *Constable,* the Guardians fighting on the main deck above retreated. They descended to the gun deck only to be chased by more Skulls. Those Cutthroats dropped grenados down the hatches, sending the Guardians running for cover.

But Steward didn't see Ink or Jameson among them.

They're dead, and if I stay, I'm dead too. She dropped the powder bags and turned in the other direction as her eyes looked for an escape. She found none. Guardians and Skulls fought on both sides of her, and tridents were flying in through the holes in the hull. Corpses scattered across the deck, making it difficult to move as even more Skulls appeared. *I can't die here. Don't let me die—*

Steward tripped on Jarrel's head. She landed on her hands and knees, losing herself in the fear. Her legs kicked as she was tackled from behind. She opened her mouth to scream before a hand clamped over her mouth.

"Steward! Come on!" Mouse said, pulling her to her feet and pointing at the descending ladder where Taran had disappeared. "We have to get out of here and hide!"

I need a weapon, Steward thought, despite holding her talan. Two cutlasses clattered to the ground nearby as a Skull and a Guardian wrestled across the deck, pummeling each other with fists. Steward snagged the cutlasses and hesitated, recognizing the Guardian: Eyes the Rigger. Before she could help him, the Skull grabbed a dropped pistol, shoved it against Eyes's forehead, and pulled the trigger. Eyes's skull shattered, and his brains became a pink mist.

Steward retched, then forced herself to her run. Reaching the ladder, she tossed a cutlass to Mouse and descended. Taran and Tomlin had waited for them, and together, all four ran deeper into the ship.

"Been a long time since I had myself a pegboy. Been waitin' a long time, I have," a Skull said as he slunk through the stacks of crates and barrels within the *Constable's* hold. The deck squeaked under the Cutthroat's weight as he added, "I won't hurt a hair on your little heads. No, I won't. You can trust ol' Jimbo."

Steward hunkered down with Mouse between several barrels of salt pork and hardtack. Taran was hiding with Tomlin further in the hold, but

Steward didn't know where. She only knew that Tomlin's sobs had first attracted Jimbo's attention. Taran had silenced him, but the damage was already done. Jimbo was here for his pegboys.

Steward shivered and tightened her grip on the cutlass.

The Skull's footsteps stopped in front of them. Steward clamped a hand over her mouth, eyes wide and breath short. She breathed through her mouth, hoping her fingers muffled the sound. Jimbo's cutlass flashed forward, slamming into the wooden barrel between their heads.

"I know you're here. Come out, come out, wherever you are."

A sob echoed through the compartment before being silenced. *Tomlin.*

"I've got you now, *pegboy!*" Jimbo shouted. Ripping his cutlass from the barrel, the Skull turned away and ran to the opposite side of the hold, where Tomlin and Taran no doubt were.

Steward was too afraid to move, but Mouse only looked determined. He stood, as if to abandon hiding and fight the Skull. Steward grabbed his hand and shook her head. *Don't do it, Mouse. Stay hidden.*

If it had been Mouse in trouble, Steward would have fought to save him. But to risk her life to save Taran, of all people? Steward was too ashamed to admit it aloud, but she would have let Taran die if it meant surviving.

Mouse wouldn't. She couldn't see his face in the gloom, but she felt him pull free of her grasp. He ran after Jimbo, and Steward had no choice but to follow him. Together, they wound through the maze of crates, following Jimbo's shouts. Steward had just turned a corner when she saw Jimbo at the opposite end of the row. In the near darkness, he looked just like Priest Clifton.

The fear disappeared, and Steward thought, *I'm going to kill you.*

Jimbo pulled Tomlin from his hiding place and threw him against the hull. The cabin boy's head cracked against the wood, and he fell in a heap. Mouse charged forward without hesitation and hacked at Jimbo, who batted the thrust aside. The Skull would have cut him in half if Steward hadn't parried his next strike. Mouse stabbed Jimbo in the calf, and he cried out in pain. Before Steward could hurt him further, Jimbo punched Mouse in the face, sending him sprawling to the deck and bringing Steward down with him. She hit her head hard on the wood, and black spots danced at the edge of her vision.

Before Jimbo could stab her or Mouse, Taran leaped from cover and tackled him. "I ain't your squalling pegboy!" he screamed as he landed on top of Jimbo.

Taran punched and clawed at the Skull's face, gouging his eyes. Jimbo gasped and threw Taran aside, rolling on him. He punched Taran twice as Steward pulled herself out from under Mouse's body. Her vision was spotty, but fury and hatred kept her conscious.

Jimbo raised his cutlass to stab Taran, but Steward was faster.

Her talan plunged deep into the Skull's back. He stiffened, the cutlass dropping from his hand as Steward sliced, cut, and stabbed. Jimbo fell to the ground in a heap, and she dove on top of him as Taran scrambled out of the way.

"I hate you!" Steward hissed, repeating the phrase as she tore into the Skull's chest and throat.

Jimbo only gurgled in response as he bled from dozens of deep wounds.

Eventually, Mouse pulled her away. "Stop, Steward. He's dead. You got him, okay? You gotta stop."

Mind wild with panic, Steward stabbed Jimbo one more time before standing. She took a step and almost collapsed. It was Taran who caught her and supported most of her weight with one shoulder.

"Thanks," Taran whispered, but he kept his gaze on Jimbo. "I owe you my life, Steward. Both of you, really... That squall would have gotten me for sure."

Steward only nodded. She didn't trust herself to speak.

"What about Tomlin?" Mouse asked, staring back at his limp body. "He's out cold."

"Can't exactly take him with us," Taran said.

"You can't carry him?"

"Not when we're trying to be quiet. He gave us away once. I won't let him do it again."

"Tomlin's our friend. We can't just leave him," Mouse said. "Right, Steward?"

"No, Taran's right," Steward said, surprised to be agreeing with Taran. Mouse gasped as if he couldn't believe her. "We need to go. Now. Before others get here."

"Oh, it's far too late for that," a voice whispered through the gloom, slick like a bloody talan. Its calm tone, high pitch, and sweet cadence were akin to laughter, and the sound of it was as sinister as a syren.

Steward stiffened and turned to see a flintlock extending from the darkness. As the gun emerged, she saw the thin, wiry Skull holding it. He wore only black: everything from his boots to his gloves and hat. Even his cutlass was painted black, marking him as a Skull captain.

"That's... Rolf the Bloody," Mouse said. "We're dead."

"Not yet, but you will be," Rolf said, forcing them to drop their cutlasses as several Skulls appeared behind him with lanterns, revealing his face. Rolf's sunken eyes were pitiless, the color of a bloodstained deck, his short hair the same shade. From the left corner of his lips, a scar curled to his ear, leaving him with a permanent smirk.

Seeing Jimbo's body, Rolf grinned. "So you all can fight. Good. *Very* good."

Tomlin and Taran stood opposite one another on the main deck of the *Wrath*. Skulls surrounded them in a circle and shouted at them to fight. It wouldn't be much of a fight, Steward knew. Taran was too strong, and Tomlin was... a corpse. His eyes were vacant, and he stared at the ground with his shoulders slumped. He didn't even bother to raise his hands into fists. It was as if Tomlin wasn't aware of where he stood.

More horrifying was the weather. It was a perfect day, complete with a shining sun, cloudless sky, and gentle sea. Were Io and Kovu *rewarding* the Skulls for their massacre? The waves were trying to rock the ship to sleep as the tension constricted around Steward like a kraken's tentacles.

"They can't make us do this," she said, but even she didn't believe her words. Not after being stripped of her weapons, bound with rope, and forced to watch this horrid spectacle with the surviving Guardians.

"We can do whatever we want, pegboy," said a Skull with a wheezing laugh.

Steward didn't speak again. Mouse shot her a helpless glance on her right. Jameson was clenching his jaw and furiously trying to undo the rope around his hands. Ink's body hung from the bowsprit. Eyes swung from the gunwale. Jarrel didn't have enough of a body left to hang.

A pit of sadness welled in Steward's stomach. To see Ink, the once indomitable one-eyed captain, reduced to chum for syrens was more than she could bear. He'd been one of the few good men she'd met in her life, and just like Dad, he'd been taken from her…

It wasn't fair. None of this was, and yet Steward could do nothing to change it. No matter how much she struggled, cried, and screamed, all she could do was watch Taran kill Tomlin as the sun shined and a gentle breeze stirred the sails.

Send a squall, Kovu, Steward thought, asking the God of the winds and skies to unleash a storm so horrible that everyone died. Yet Kovu refused her, and it took all of Steward's willpower not to cry in front of these Skulls. *Squall you, too, Kovu.*

When neither Tomlin nor Jarrel had taken a step forward to fight, Rolf broke from the circle of cheering Skulls and stood beside Taran, making the cabin boy flinch.

"I told you to fight." Rolf's voice was little more than a whisper but no less terrifying.

Neither Taran nor Tomlin moved. While Tomlin didn't seem to hear the Skull, Taran was simply too stubborn. He looked from side to side, as if seeking guidance. None was to be found.

Rolf cocked his pistol and pressed it against Taran's head. The Skulls cheered even louder as Taran glanced at Steward and Mouse, as if to ask, *What do I do?*

Mouse had no suggestions. He, too, looked at Steward. *There's only one thing we can do,* she thought as a sick feeling settled in her intestines. To Taran, she mouthed, *Win.*

Taran's eyes narrowed, but he nodded. With a growl, the cabin boy sprinted forward, grabbing Tomlin around his thighs and lifting him into the air. Little more than a rag doll, Tomlin barely flinched as Taran slammed him on the ground. Steward winced when she heard a couple of Tomlin's ribs snap.

"No…" Mouse whispered, tears dribbling from his eyes. Because of the bonds, Steward couldn't even reach out to grab his hands and offer reassurance. As Mouse looked down at the deck, she forced herself to watch the fight.

Taran sat on Tomlin's chest and decked him twice. Three teeth flew from his mouth and scattered on the deck. Tomlin still didn't offer any resistance.

"Fight me!" Taran shouted, punching him again. This time, two more teeth were dislodged. "Damn you, Tomlin! Don't let me kill you! Not like this! Please! Fight me! *Fight me!*"

Tomlin's lips moved, though only Taran could hear what he said. Taran leaned back as if he'd been shot in the stomach.

"No, Tomlin," Taran said. *"No."*

Tomlin feebly nodded.

Sickened, Taran looked up at Rolf and said, "He's beaten, alright? He lost. We're done."

Rolf pointed the gun at Taran again. "No. Not yet, you aren't."

Taran looked back at Steward. So much pain and horror reflected in his eyes, mirroring her own feelings. For the first time, she realized he was just another kid. A stubborn asshole, but just a boy trying to survive in a Skull's world. There was only one thing he could do.

Win, she mouthed again.

Hands shaking, Taran slammed his fist into Tomlin's nose. It shattered. Struggling to breathe, Tomlin nodded again and smiled, revealing his broken teeth.

"Damn you for making me do this," Taran hissed with angry tears. He hit Tomlin twice more, breaking his jaw.

Tomlin tried to smile but couldn't quite manage it anymore.

Taran looked up at Rolf helplessly. "Don't make me do this. *Please.*"

"He's not beaten," Rolf said, his voice as calm as the sea and sky.

"The boy's unconscious! The fight is over!" one Guardian said somewhere off to the right of Steward. It wasn't a voice she recognized.

A gunshot cracked like thunder, and that Guardian slumped on the deck. Rolf's expression didn't falter. He remained as serene as the sun. "Hang him from the bowsprit with the others. Give the syrens a reason to stick around."

A few Skulls pulled the dead Guardian away and tied a noose around his neck. Steward winced and looked back to Taran. But she couldn't turn her ears from the sound of the rope pulling taut, snapping the dead sailor's neck.

"The boy's still not beaten," Rolf said again, gesturing to Taran with a new pistol. "Fight."

Taran swallowed again and slammed his fists into Tomlin's face. Five more punches. Bones snapped, Guardians cursed, and Skulls cheered. Steward forced herself to stare at the ruin of Tomlin's face—a mess of tattered skin and blood—wanting to believe he was dead until his lips moved again. Tomlin was still alive.

Her heart sank as Rolf said, "End it."

Taran hesitated, looking at Steward. *Win,* she mouthed for a third time even as Mouse shook his head.

Tears welled in Taran's eyes as he whispered something in Tomlin's ear. Then Taran broke him with a dozen punches. There was a strange, sadistic rhythm to it. Three seconds of silence followed by a *crunch.* Silence, then *squelch.* Silence... *Pop...*

Please be dead. Thankfully, Tomlin's lips didn't move this time. But Steward couldn't tell where his nose ended and lips began. Still, he'd stopped breathing. *He's finally dead,* Steward thought, ashamed at her own relief as Mouse cried quietly beside her.

"*Now* he's beat," Rolf said, offering a sardonic smile. "String him up, boys."

Two Skulls stepped forward to retrieve Tomlin's body as Taran stood. He wavered like a loose sail and fell back to his knees. Pushing his head against Tomlin's, Taran sobbed until the Skulls pulled him away, put a rope around Tomlin's neck, and threw his corpse over the side. Another snap. Another Guardian to join Ink.

"I asked for a fight. That was no fight." Rolf stared down at Steward and Mouse pitilessly. "Bring me those two."

"*What?*" Steward asked as Fleshlords threw her into the circle. Mouse landed beside her. "What do we do?"

"We fight. Just like old times, right, friend?" Mouse asked, trying to laugh, but his lopsided grin was nowhere to be seen. The right side of his lip quivered. The left side was still. He wiped his runny nose as a tear fell. "One last battle between the Mop King and the Rat Prince."

Steward's palms were slick with sweat. Her eyes darted around, finding no escape. She looked at the Guardians, pleading for help. Jameson wouldn't look at her. Neither would the other adults. Only Taran would. *Win,* his haunted eyes told her, but the voice she heard was her own.

I have to win. Steward thought, remembering what Ink had told her when she'd tried to jump overboard almost two years ago. *If I die, Dad dies with me. I won't let him die a second time.* She caught Mouse's eye and nodded, agreeing to fight. *I won't let Dad die. Not even for you, Mouse.*

"Steward," he said. "May the best man win."

Steward shook her head as the hesitation fell away. "You were always the better man, Mouse."

"Fight," Rolf said.

Steward rushed forward with a scream and slammed her fist into Mouse, catching the edge of his chin as he stepped back to catch her wrist. Sweeping her legs, he threw her to the ground. She rolled out of the way as he landed where her head had been only a moment before. Then they were both on their feet again, circling each other with their knees bent and hands up.

Mouse had taught her that.

A fist flew toward her face, but she slipped under it and slammed hers into his chest. He took a couple of wild steps back and fell. Steward crashed on top of him. She punched him in the face, but he pulled his knees up, kicking her overhead. She landed on her back as Mouse got on top of her. He pinned her arms beneath his knees and punched her in the nose, chin, and right eye.

"Cutlass!" Steward shouted.

Mouse hesitated.

Steward didn't. She pivoted, and Mouse toppled. Scrambling on top of him, she punched him twice more before he twisted and shoved her onto her back again. She rolled away before he could pin her to the ground. Then she wiped the blood from her lip as her right eye swelled shut. Steward sucked in a couple of deep breaths as Mouse advanced, favoring his right knee as she knew he would.

The weakness she'd ignored time and time again in the lanternlight.

The weakness she would use to break him now.

Steward kicked his knee. Hard. Mouse yelped and staggered back, limping harder and glaring at her with utter disgust. "Damn you to the depths, Steward."

Win, she thought, ignoring the expression.

Steward kept sliding to the right so that she could have better access to that wounded knee. He shifted his stance to protect himself, which only gave her more openings. She jabbed him twice and slipped away as he counterpunched, overextending. Then she smashed her foot into his knee again, and he cried out in pain.

Ignore it. Win, Steward thought. After two more kicks to his weak knee, Mouse was practically standing on one leg. He widened his stance, and Steward kicked again, shattering the knee. Mouse gasped and fell to his knees. She grabbed fistfuls of his red locks as he punched her in the crotch.

Steward didn't flinch.

Mouse's eyes widened in surprise, then understanding. "You're a—"

Steward slammed her knee into his face before he could say *girl*. Mouse's nose crunched, and he fell to the deck. With a savage cry, Steward launched herself on top of him. She pinned his arms with her own legs, as he had done to her countless times. Punches connected because Mouse couldn't defend himself. She beat him senseless before clamping her hands around his throat.

Mouse squeaked out the safety word. *"Cutlass."*

Steward squeezed tighter, so he couldn't speak again. It broke her heart to win, but she couldn't bring herself to lose. "I can't stop, Mouse."

Steward breathed in. Mouse didn't, couldn't. He looked up at her, a look of horror in his eyes as blood dribbled from his broken nose and a dozen cuts. His hands slapped feebly at her thighs, but she didn't let go.

The Gods felt no pity. Instead, they mocked her. Rays of sunlight shined on her face and a gentle sea breeze stirred her hair as Steward strangled her best friend. Her *only* friend.

There were so many things Steward wanted to say. *I'm sorry. I love you. I wish you'd won.* They were all true, but those words were hollow now. She and Mouse were supposed to fight Taran, not each other. They were supposed to get their own ship and sail the world, fighting monsters and saving kingdoms. The Rat Prince and the Mop King were supposed to be *heroes.*

Steward didn't feel like a hero. Yet she didn't apologize. She didn't ask for forgiveness. Instead, Steward did what she knew best: she lied.

"It'll be okay." She forced herself to smile down at Mouse's mutilated face. "You're going to be okay because Eo will take care of you... All you have to do is sleep, Rat Prince. And when you wake up, you'll be a king. A better king than me."

Mouse didn't respond. He couldn't respond. He was already dead.

With numb fingers, Steward pulled her hands away and rose to her feet as the Skulls broke out into raucous applause.

"The boy's got cannonballs between his legs!" one said. "Didn't flinch when the ginger punched his bits!"

"As real a man as any of us!" said another, eliciting a round of laughter.

"Now *that* was a fight." Rolf the Bloody clapped her on the shoulder, harder than necessary. She still couldn't feel it. Steward wasn't sure she'd feel anything ever again. "Take those two below deck and give them some food. Keep them strong for the voyage. They'll fetch a heavy purse."

The rest of the crew whooped and hollered, but Steward was rigid in silence, rigid in thought, mind, and soul. She pretended not to watch them hang Mouse's body next to Tomlin's, pretended not to hear his neck snap.

I deserve this, Steward thought, letting them drag her below deck, chain her in the slavehold, and leave her in that darkness. Eo kept her company. But She was just as silent and uncaring as Io and Kovu had been.

I'm alone now, she thought, and only then did the tears come. Though she couldn't see it, she could feel Mouse's blood on her hands. She tried to scrape it away until Taran grabbed her hands and held them.

Taran, who'd bullied her.

Taran, who'd killed Tomlin.

Taran, who'd survived.

"Stay strong, Steward," he said, cradling her even as Eo turned Her back. "It's just you and me now. We'll get through this. Together."

PART THREE
ANIMAL

CHAPTER TWENTY-TWO

Lilyth haggled with a Fleshlord captain over the price of thirty slaves she was selling. He wanted them for two silver lunes per head, though the market rate was five times higher—one gold crescent each. Lilyth didn't care about the price, though, and only argued to stall for time.

The problem with the growing Red Legion was that her old tactics no longer worked. Lilyth had too many men and too many ships to pretend to surrender to Cutthroats and kill them in their sleep. Yet an all-out naval battle against more experienced Cutthroats was too risky. Lilyth couldn't sustain heavy losses to her legion, so these latest battles required a different tactic: becoming Cutthroats.

Lilyth detested that thought, but what sickened her more was her daughter being enslaved. So, she swallowed her abhorrence and dressed in the black boots, blue breeches, black shirt, and brown overcoat of a Copperhead captain. The copper flintlock she'd borrowed from Kendrik was on her hip.

As Copperheads traded with the other Cutthroat factions, they were her perfect cover. With flags and answering pennants, it was easy to hail passing Cutthroat ships and entice them closer with cheap wares: gold to the Avowed, Roses, and other Copperheads, slaves to Fleshlords. The Red Legion had stolen two more ships—a brigantine and a schooner—with the ruse, bringing their numbers to three hundred.

But it came at a price: the Dagger.

All Cutthroats had that bloody knife tattoo on their right wrist, and without it, Lilyth was an obvious imposter. Despite how much it sickened her, she'd adopted that mark and balanced it with the Scythe, a tattoo on her left wrist of a red curving blade with a long black handle representing the Red Legion, Eo, and death itself. Many of her legionnaires had quickly done the same—save for those who pretended to be her slaves.

Near Lilyth, thirty legionnaires kneeled in the slavehold of the *Jericho*. Their hands remained behind their backs, though their manacles were unlocked. At a moment's notice, they could spring up and attack. They would, but only after Kendrik, Greeley, and Arya slaughtered the Fleshlord's crew above on the main deck.

Had it not been for the Cutthroat Code, which didn't allow the various sects to steal or murder one another, the Fleshlords might have been more suspicious. Yet it was hard for them to deny Lilyth's authenticity when she captained a known Copperhead ship like the *Venom*—the *Jericho's* original name, which was still carved into the side of the hull—bore the Dagger, and had thirty slaves to sell. With Cutthroats as greedy as they were, it was a deal they couldn't pass up.

"I'm afraid I can go no higher than four lunes each," Oseer said, swirling a glass of blood-red wine while his five appraisers inspected the legionnaires by lanternlight. He was flashy and flamboyant, a common trait of Fleshlords. He wore a black cavalier's hat with a long pink feather, a purple fur coat with an orange fox-fur scarf, and maroon breeches with black, knee-high socks. Gaudiness in a world of such slavery and starvation nauseated Lilyth as much as the Dagger had.

"A lot of those men have serious health conditions," Oseer continued in that nasally whine, "and as my plans are to travel with them to Corinthus, I have a much longer voyage ahead of me. Not all the slaves will make the trek, of course, and those that do will be weaker than they currently are... Being depreciating assets, these slaves will fetch lower prices at the Corinthian auction houses, and I must make the venture profitable."

So slaves are depreciating assets, Lilyth thought, smiling politely and pretending to sip wine from her own glass. The rotgut had been a gift from Oseer to open negotiations, but she had long learned not to trust anything she hadn't prepared herself.

"I understand your concerns," Lilyth said, envisioning how she'd kill him: trepanation. Her thirty legionnaires would hold him down while she drilled a hole through his head. "These slaves have languished in the hold, true, but they have not depreciated as much as you have implied. My first terms were quite fair at eight lunes a head. Four is inconceivable."

Oseer nodded, feigning sympathy as he fingered the ivory-handled whip at his waist. That, unlike the copper flintlock or white cutlass, marked him as a captain of these slave traders. "Well, I heard you say that your next stop was Tibur. Perhaps you can sell them there... for three lunes each."

Tibur... This man knows the way in. Lilyth thought, her curiosity burning the folds of her mind. The last two captains she'd interrogated had tried to lead her astray by drawing unintelligible passages through the Battered Reef protecting the port. Neither matched Quintus's original drawing either. Four distinct yet wrong ways to travel through the reef. But so long as this Fleshlord showed her the way, it would no longer matter.

"I suppose that if that is the case, I will come down to..." Lilyth paused, pretending to consider while wasting time. Between the slave inspection and the haggling, they'd been in the slavehold for thirty minutes. Surely, Kendrik and Greeley were finishing up by now. "Six lunes each."

"Six lunes? *Each?*" The Fleshlord scoffed overdramatically, adjusting the fox-fur scarf at his neck. "I couldn't possibly... My appraisers have already shown me three slaves with scurvy, and a few more with symptoms of typhoid, possibly even the Whispering Madness! Four-and-a-half lunes per head is the absolute most I can do, otherwise I'll *lose* money on this transaction."

You would have profited even at eight lunes, Lilyth thought. From above, she heard a bell ring twice, signaling that the Fleshlord crew was dead. *Finally.*

"Is something wrong, Captain Lilyth?" Oseer asked as he raised an eyebrow and took another sip of wine. "I'd prefer not to have our negotiations interrupted when a price hasn't been reached."

"No, everything is quite right, Oseer," Lilyth replied. "I will accept your offer, provided you give me some information about current events in Tibur. It has been some time since I have been, and I would like to know the current political landscape before I arrive."

"Is that so?" the Fleshlord asked, draining his glass. "Then we have ourselves a deal."

"It is not a deal until you shake on it, captain," Lilyth said, extending her hand.

When the Fleshlord clasped hers, she gripped him tightly and shoved a talan under his chin. Immediately, Lilyth's legionnaires jumped to their feet and attacked the appraisers, overwhelming them with blades and fists.

"What is the meaning of this?" Oseer asked. Lanternlight reflected the horror in his eyes. "We had a deal!"

"I only make deals with captains," Lilyth said, still holding his hand. She smiled thinly as her thirty legionnaires gathered behind her. "As you no longer have a ship or a crew, you are no longer a Fleshlord. You are now my slave."

Oseer snarled. "But you're a Cutthroat! This violates the Code! You can't just—"

Lilyth pushed the talan deeper into his skin, silencing him. "Shush, slave. You will only speak when I say you can speak. If you want your freedom back, I can grant it, but first I need information about Tibur..."

Four hundred men vied for Lilyth's attention. A hundred newly freed slaves stood alongside three-hundred legionnaires on the bows of Lilyth's five ships: three frigates and two brigs. A true fleet. A true legion.

Still not enough.

During this latest raid, nearly all the Fleshlords had been killed and thrown into the water below, cursed to the fate of the Drowned. Yet a handful remained alive and bound on the deck, left as entertainment for the legionnaires.

Oseer wasn't among them, though. He hadn't known the way through the Battered Reef, or at least, hadn't been sure of the exact path. He'd drawn a similar route to the last two captains, but with the Battered Reef as dangerous and shallow as it was, *similar* would leave them sunk and trapped on the shores of Tibur. Lilyth needed the exact route before her assault could take place.

I will try again, Lilyth thought, ignoring the acclamation of the legion. She viewed this latest victory as just another stepping stone. Kendrik was the next rock to tread upon.

Ignoring Greeley, who'd tried to get her attention twice, Lilyth walked to the quarterdeck of the *Jericho,* where Kendrik conferred with his closest subordinates. As she approached, he dismissed them and stood at attention, with his hands behind his back. If the rest of the Red Legion had believed as fervently as him, she'd have already stomped Tibur beneath her heel.

Soon.

"Champion?" Kendrik asked. "Is there something I can help you with?"

"I only wanted to congratulate you, Red Heart," Lilyth said, wrapping his hand in both of hers and spying the Dagger and Scythe on his wrists. "You have done well today, though I expected nothing less... How many did you kill?"

"Thirteen, Champion," Kendrik said, chest sticking out proudly to display the bloody handprint over his heart.

"And the Red Hand?"

Kendrik deflated. "Seventeen."

"I see... You remind me of myself, Red Heart," Lilyth said eventually, tugging her lips down into a small frown to appear vulnerable and honest. "So young, and yet you have lost so much already. How much more are you willing to lose before you learn?"

"Learn, Champion?" Kendrik asked, taking the bait. He looked at her in confusion, eyebrows furrowing, distorting the shape of the crescent moon marked on his forehead.

Lilyth turned to watch him, searching for signs of weakness. "My Red Heart, do you know why the seven Skulls have owned this sea for so long?"

Kendrik flinched. "I don't know, Champion. Perhaps they're lucky?"

"Luck is for the faithless," Lilyth said, thinking only of Rolf the Bloody. "It is their reputation. The Skulls are feared because of the rumors of their ruthlessness." She stared at the corpses bobbing in the water. "But we will be much more terrifying."

"You want to be as ruthless as a Skull, Champion?"

"You are thinking too small, Red Heart. We must be *more* ruthless." Lilyth took a step closer, lifting a hand to cup his cheek. "To truly destroy the Skulls, we must first eclipse their reputation. We must make the Cutthroats forget their fear of the Skulls. *That* is how we erase them—not only from the seas, but from history. If we do that, they will be forgotten, Kendrik. Just as your brother will be immortalized."

Lilyth handed him her talan. Its painted edge swallowed all light, all hope. "But the legion needs an example to follow, Red Heart. Can you be ruthless? So nobody else will ever lose a brother to Cutthroats?"

"Jericho sacrificed his life for the Red Legion." Kendrik wiped away a single tear. "I'll sacrifice whatever is necessary, Champion. Even my soul."

The sun shone down upon the Fleshlords drifting in the waves. Some were playing dead. Greeley scanned the waves for survivors, but most of the Cutthroats were drifting face down in the water. One who'd been holding his breath beneath the waves returned to the surface, gasping for breath. Greeley aimed his flintlock pistols and fired. He missed both shots. Growling, he grabbed a spear leaning against the gunwale and hurled it into the Fleshlord's chest. Crying out in despair, the Cutthroat sank back into the depths.

"Reload," Greeley growled to Arya, who stood beside him. She took the spent firearms, handing him new pistols. He inspected their finnicky triggers and unreliable mechanisms. "Such weak weapons... I never have to reload my hands."

Arya said something to him, but Greeley could only hear the beat of his jealous heart. *Lilyth brought me back to the* Jericho *for this? To clean up the mess? The lowliest of legionnaires—even the freed slaves—could do this job, and yet she has me doing it. All while she's talking with the Red Seducer.*

Greeley's eyes narrowed to slits as he watched Lilyth place her hand to Kendrik's cheek and hand him her talan. Seeing that, Greeley felt as if his own heart had been ripped out. *No... Why would she do that? I'm her equal. She should have given it to me.* If he'd been a better marksman, Greeley might've tried to shoot him. But he was a hundred feet away. Greeley would have missed from even a third of that distance.

Greeley flicked his eyes back to Arya, who was still droning on. She halted, as if expecting his response. Greeley grunted an affirmative even as his mind continued to wander.

It had been a mistake getting together with Arya. If not for her, Kendrik would already be dead. He'd have killed the Red Seducer five times by now: thrice during exchanges when Kendrik had wandered away by himself and twice during battles—one such opportunity had been today during the brief skirmish. Kendrik had been fighting three Fleshlords at once, and

Greeley had crept behind him, intending to stab the squall in the back. But Arya had joined the fray, standing between them and ruining the chance.

Greeley would have already killed her if Arya hadn't been so good in bed. All the same, if she got in his way even one more time, he'd still kill her—and steal a trophy before he dumped her body over the gunwale.

Greeley mulled on which part he'd keep until Lilyth strode from the quarterdeck to the mainmast, where the dozen Fleshlord captives had been bound individually by wrists and ankles. *She won't ignore me a third time today.*

Without waiting for Arya, Greeley abandoned his post at the bow and met Lilyth near the mast. "Champion—"

"Is it time?" Kendrik asked, cutting him off.

"It is," Lilyth said, nodding to Kendrik as Greeley hid a clenched fist behind his back. "Send the signal, Red Heart. This victory is yours."

His victory? Greeley thought. *No, no, no. What are you doing to Lilyth, squall? Are you sleeping with her? Are you telling her lies about me? What have you done?*

Oblivious, Kendrik lifted his open hand and made a fist. "Let there be blood!"

Legionnaires in the rigging lowered the standard of the Red Legion: a black flag with a red crescent moon. In its place, they raised a solid red flag—a white cloth stained with the blood of nonbelievers.

Across all five ships, seasoned legionnaires and newly freed slaves alike chanted, "Blood. Blood! *Blood!*" Those positioned on the *Jericho* circled around the captive Fleshlords with swords unsheathed.

Sensing their doom, a few of the Cutthroats prayed, but one made the mistake of praying to Eo. Lilyth's serenity evaporated like smoke. Bloodshot eyes wide and eyebrows arched, she screamed, "Silence!"

The chanting hushed as Lilyth stalked forward toward the praying Fleshlord. "You dare ask for Her guidance in my presence!" She grabbed the Cutthroat's hair, pulling him to the deck and smashing his face into the ground. "Do you think She stands with you? *We* are Her Chosen!" Putting her boot on the back of the Cutthroat's neck, Lilyth cut the rope that bound his wrists and ankles. A whisper spread amongst the circle of legionnaires as she stepped back.

Shocked, the Fleshlord stood, glancing around wearily. He was a head taller than Lilyth and barrel-chested. Beside him, Lilyth looked weak—Greeley knew she was anything but.

"Red Legion!" she shouted. "Are there any among you who wish to prove yourself to Eo? Prove that you are one of Her Chosen?"

The circle of legionnaires took a step inward. Greeley took a second step and stared at Lilyth. *Pick me,* he thought. *Let me show you my strength.*

"Red Hand, come forward."

Relief washed over Greeley. That gnawing, spindly limbed desperation, which clung to his back, fell away in an instant. *Finally.* Greeley walked toward Lilyth, grinning at the Fleshlord behind her. *I'll rip this man apart, limb by limb. I'll show her I'm worthy of being her equal, once and for—*

"Give me your blade." Lilyth held out her hand.

Greeley blinked and halted. "Champion? I don't—"

Lilyth's withering stare silenced him. "Do not make me tell you again, Red Hand."

Fingers stiff, Greeley unsheathed his white cutlass—his most prized trophy—and handed it to her.

Lilyth held the blade and nodded. "Rejoin the others."

You're making a mistake, Lilyth. Don't do this to me. Not again... Greeley lingered for a moment, hoping she'd change her mind. Lilyth didn't. Slowly, he returned to the circle of legionnaires. *Why would she do this to me?*

"Red Heart, I told you this victory was yours," Lilyth said, beckoning to that foul, arrogant seducer. "Step forward and claim it."

Kendrik walked to Lilyth's side, and Greeley saw her whisper something to him. Kendrik's eyes narrowed, and he nodded.

What is she saying to him? What's going on? Depths be damned, what is happening?

"This Fleshlord says he is a believer. But the Red Heart thinks he is a liar. Let them fight in front of Eo and see whose side She takes," Lilyth said, throwing the white cutlass to the deck near the Fleshlord's feet. Then she took her place among the legion, her own blade sheathed. "Rise, Fleshlord. Show us whose faith is stronger!"

The Cutthroat picked up Greeley's blade and swaggered forward, taking a few experimental swishes through the air. Kendrik was still, his cutlass held steady in his right hand.

It should be me out there—not this weak boy, Greeley thought, a growl rising in his throat.

Across the circle, Lilyth stared at him, her eyes flashing with rage. Her expressionless gaze was a glinting blade that cut through his soul. His growl subsided. He broke eye contact and watched Kendrik, instead, wishing only to wrap his hands around the Red Heart's throat.

"Now, let there be blood!" Lilyth screamed.

"Blood. Blood! *Blood!*" the Red Legion chanted as the two men clashed.

The Fleshlord rushed forward with a shout, hacking and slashing as Greeley would have done. Each strike was ferocious, but Kendrik parried without striking back. *The boy hasn't learned a single lesson since we first fought.*

When they clashed again and locked swords, the Fleshlord swung his empty fist. It sailed toward Kendrik's head—except he'd already moved. The Red Heart *blurred* with speed, ducking aside. As the Fleshlord leaned too far forward, Kendrik counterpunched. His fist dislocated the Fleshlord's jaw, causing the man to crash onto the deck.

Kendrik stood above him, his shadow falling on the Fleshlord's horrified expression.

Greeley watched, mutely. *He moved like Lilyth. Has she been... training him?* He didn't want to believe it, but that speed—that *strength*—was something new. *How had I never noticed before?*

"Get up, Fleshlord," Kendrik said. "Your death won't come so easily."

Shakily, the Cutthroat stood, but his jaw still hung loose. Fear consumed his confidence. He stabbed with less ferocity, thrusting quick and shuffling away. Kendrik batted aside each attempt with the flick of his wrist, his other hand held behind his back—just as Lilyth fought. Not once did he take a step backward. Instead, Kendrik followed the Cutthroat to the perimeter of the circle. The Fleshlord accidentally bumped into the chanting legionnaires, who shoved him forward toward Kendrik. Again, he fell.

"Get up, Fleshlord," Kendrik repeated. "I will not have the crowd take my glory."

The Cutthroat stood only to be cut and slashed by Kendrik's blade. With each new gash, the Fleshlord struck more desperately. Kendrik toyed with him, eyes alight with a fury that reminded Greeley of Lilyth.

It made him sick to his stomach.

When the Fleshlord fell a third time, Kendrik didn't let him stand. He severed the man's hamstrings. Howling in agony, the Cutthroat crawled away until Kendrik stomped on his back and cut off his outstretched hands. The other Cutthroats watched in horror as their comrade wailed.

"Blood!" Kendrik shouted, and the Red Legion quieted to hear him. He sheathed his bloodied cutlass and pulled out Lilyth's black talan. "Eo has decided! We are Her Chosen! We are the Red Legion!"

Kendrik kneeled beside the Cutthroat and slammed the talan into his back. He dragged the blade through flesh and tendons, creating a ragged gash beneath his ribs.

Then Kendrik shoved his right hand in the wound.

The Cutthroats watched on in horror, the Red Legion in awed silence. Lilyth grinned. Greeley gaped.

"And I am the Red Heart—so I will take yours." Kendrik ripped his hand out from the Fleshlord's back, and with it came the Cutthroat's heart. Blood oozed from the ruptured arteries and veins still attached to it. The deck was quiet enough that Greeley heard the heart beat twice before falling still.

Core be damned, Greeley thought as Kendrik held the heart aloft. His right arm, from elbow to fingertips, was covered in blood. *A red hand... Kendrik's like me.*

But when Kendrik took a bite out of the heart, even Greeley was at a loss for words.

The Red Legion exploded with wild screaming and stomping. The blood chant started again and didn't finish until Kendrik had devoured the man's heart. When the Red Heart grinned with bloodstained lips and teeth, Greeley felt his own heart skip a beat.

In the resounding silence, Lilyth said, "My Red Legion, we are Chosen! Stand with Eo! Stand with the night! Stand with the *Red Heart!*"

"Red Heart. Red Heart! *Red Heart!*" shouted the legion.

Lilyth nodded to Kendrik, and he raised his blood-encrusted fist. He brought it down in a violent arc, and a frothing swarm of legionnaires descended on the rest of the Fleshlords. All lost their hearts.

"Let none of you forget, *this* is the fate of false worship!" Lilyth pointed at the mutilated corpses of the Fleshlords. "Tie them to the bowsprit! Let the Cutthroats fear us! Let them fear our Red Heart!"

That should be me. Greeley stood frozen as legionnaires darted forward to carry out her will. Shaking his head, he stumbled a few steps forward and picked up his white cutlass from the deck. He examined its edge, noticing the chips and notches in it. *This can't get any worse...*

As Arya helped the other legionnaires, Lilyth put a hand on her shoulder, stopping her. Greeley stopped, too, watching. So did everyone else.

It can't be.

Dipping her hand in the Fleshlords' blood, Lilyth pressed it over Arya's right eye, leaving behind a crimson print. After gifting Arya the ivory-handled whip of the Fleshlord captain, Lilyth stepped back, so that Arya stood with Kendrik at the center of attention. Greeley, meanwhile, was just another face in the crowd.

"For your unwavering sight in this battle, I name you the Red Eye," Lilyth said, loud enough for the legionnaires across all five ships to hear. "Whenever you charge into battle, my mark will be carried with you."

No... Another one? Greeley clenched the white cutlass. *No, not another one. Not for long, anyway. Not for long.*

CHAPTER TWENTY-THREE

Lilyth donned a white porcelain mask. Like the full moon above, craters pockmarked the face. While Lilyth could see through the left eyehole, the right was closed by a slashing scar worming from forehead to cheek. Though she hated losing her depth perception, the scarred eye perfected her disguise. So did the black paint on her face and neck, white paint on her hands and feet, and the hooded red robes whose bottom edge kissed the deck.

When Lilyth flipped up the cowl to cover the mask's straps and stared down into her blade's reflection, she saw Eo staring back at her.

Perfect. Lilyth smiled, though Eo's lips remained in a tight red line. *Time to release a new plague.*

The problem was that the Night Plague was no longer effective. It required Lilyth to single out dissenters, create a unique poison based on their body, and kill them publicly. That took too much time at this stage.

Then came the issue of identification. With thirty legionnaires, Lilyth could easily determine the rumormongers and smash them underfoot. But with four-hundred, she could not watch any individual so closely—especially when they were split between five ships. Nor could she ask her lieutenants to do it for her.

Last was fear. Because of its design, the Night Plague only sickened and killed one to two legionnaires at a time. So, the likelihood of death had been one-in-forty during the legion's infancy. Now, that possibility was one-in-four-hundred. Instead of being terrified, those recruits who fell asleep in the temple and sparred half-heartedly during training were whispering of mutiny.

Lilyth had already killed the three loudest dissenters, but that only quieted rebellious voices—it hadn't swayed rebellious minds. There were more dissenters among the new recruits that had to be dealt with. Worse, several veterans were grumbling too. From what she'd gleaned, many worried that Eo was not as powerful as Lilyth touted Her to be. Or, they were concerned that the Red Legion was becoming too ruthless. Or, they wanted to go home. They were all too comfortable, thinking themselves safe from Eo's wrath.

To cull the legion of its weakness, Lilyth needed a new affliction—the Dusk Affliction.

After tonight, I will have all the zealots I ever need, Lilyth thought, sheathing her reflective blade. Then she stole away into the night in search of the legionnaires whose meals she'd spiked with hallucinogens.

By dawn, the Red Legion trembled with a dozen new rumors.

Thirteen legionnaires had been found weeping and lying prostrate in empty hallways and compartments across her five ships. The details varied between them. They spoke of a woman in red—a shadow without a shadow. *Eo.* Depending on the account, She spoke in a myriad of voices or even a choir. Some saw smoke curling from Her white hands. Others spoke of the way She seemed to hover above the ground and float through walls. A few even believed they'd seen a second figure with Her—Aritras himself. One thing was certain: those who'd seen Eo were not just Chosen but Affirmed.

The Unchosen were not so lucky.

Those nine legionnaires had been found screaming, eyes shut and hands covering their ears. One had even scratched out his eyes. Nothing could comfort the Unchosen, just as nothing could make them stop shouting. At first, some legionnaires believed it was the Whispering Madness, but it spread much too slowly and had no physical symptoms. Instead, there was only that wild, savage screaming. The Unchosen were placed in the slaveholds of the ships, where the sound was muffled but still audible.

The rest of the legion were terrified of sharing such a fate, especially when six more Unchosen were found the following sunrise and five more the morning after that.

After those three days and nights of fear, Lilyth addressed the horrified legion. She stood around her gathered legionnaires upon the shore of an uncharted island, wearing the red robes of an Eonian priestess. She was beautiful in the same way a sword was beautiful. Her shaved head glinted like polished steel, her bloodshot eyes crushed bones to powder, and her chin sliced men's throats as easily as a cutlass.

Beside her were her three lieutenants, wearing black robes with red-striped sleeves. Arya stood in the middle as a buffer, but the distance between her and Greeley was greater than that between her and Kendrik. Greeley hadn't taken the news of her promotion well, nor the news that she and Kendrik were new captains of Lilyth's two other frigates, which dwarfed his brig. He'd apparently ripped the door to his quarters off its hinges in a bout of rage.

Hiding a smile, Lilyth held up a hand, and the growing whispers silenced. "My Red Legion, I have spoken to the Unseen Lady and now I offer you a grave warning: her Dusk Affliction is coming."

The Red Legion's concerned voices became so loud that Lilyth had to hold up her hand a second time. Though they quieted immediately, Lilyth frowned in displeasure. The Red Legion had become too lax in their devotion as of late. That, too, would be corrected by the affliction.

Continuing, Lilyth said, "Eo has revealed Herself to some of you already—those who have earned Her Affirmation. Others—the Unchosen—know the pain of Her disappointment. Theirs will be a slow, miserable death."

In the silence between words, Lilyth heard the screams of the Unchosen still trapped in the slaveholds of the five ships anchored offshore. No doubt, other legionnaires heard them too. *Another anchoring point,* she thought. *Let them never forget that sound.*

By the varying degrees of sickened and horrified faces, most wouldn't. But among their numbers, several of the legionnaires who'd been Affirmed looked smug. Confident, even.

"More will see the Unseen Lady in the coming days. More will be Affirmed. Just as more will be Unchosen. Then the plague will descend on us to deliver judgment, but fear not. All those who truly believe in Her will live. Pray tonight, my legionnaires. Pray to the Goddess and ask for Her forgiveness. Trust in Her. *Believe* in Her. Only then can you hope to be Affirmed."

Lilyth dismissed them, and the legionnaires walked silently across the shore to pray. Her lieutenants didn't leave. Ignoring Greeley, she turned to Kendrik, whose hands trembled.

Stricken, he whispered, "Champion, I fear I'm not worthy. I wasn't Affirmed."

"Worry not, Red Heart," Lilyth said with a smile she didn't feel. "You do not need Affirmation, because you are *my* Chosen."

She said the words loud enough for both Arya and Greeley—who hadn't been Affirmed, either—to hear.

◆◇◆

The Dusk Affliction descended by nightfall, and it brought the Red Legion to its knees. Most had a fever and chills, including Greeley, though he was better at hiding it than others. Legionnaires had soft stomachs, and most slept with a vomit bucket.

On the second day, sparring was canceled because too many legionnaires were throwing up over the side of the ships. Instead, they spent more time in prayer, begging for a swift resolution to the affliction. Rather than improve, they became sicker.

By the third night, most legionnaires were sharing vomit pails and lying in hammocks. Greeley didn't, though. He was too strong for that, even as the days wore on, he held onto that strength if only to prove to Lilyth that he was Chosen—*Affirmed.* He tended to the infirm and brought them food and water. By doing so, he was certain that Lilyth would take notice of his feigned good health.

Kendrik will throw up before I do, Greeley thought, even though the pain and nausea kept him awake for two nights in a row. The only consolation was that the affliction had permanently silenced the Unchosen. They'd been the first to die, though more followed.

After five nights of sickness, Lilyth called for a meeting with her lieutenants. Greeley left the *Crescent* immediately, traveling by boat from his smaller brig. He rowed the entire way despite his aching muscles, just on the off-chance Lilyth was watching. She hadn't been, because when Greeley knocked on her cabin door, Kendrik answered it. Both he and Arya had arrived before him, though he didn't have a clue how.

Ignoring the Red Heart, Greeley entered and approached the war table dominating the center of the otherwise barren room. A half-finished map of Port Tibur lay on its surface, containing detailed notes about the land and question marks in the surrounding water.

"Champion, how much longer will this last?" Kendrik asked, always the first to speak. He stood on the left side of the table. Arya on the right. Greeley, positioned across the table and furthest from Lilyth, brimmed with loathing and hatred for the Red Heart.

Damn him, Greeley thought, a continuous curse that had cycled through his head for months.

"As long as it takes, Red Heart," Lilyth said, hands clasped in front of her, stoic. "Our fickle legionnaires displease Eo. Far too few truly believe in Her. Until they do, the affliction will continue."

"More are dying," Arya said, sliding in the statement before Greeley could even open his mouth.

That was his problem: his lips weren't as fast as his hands. *That's why Lilyth looks to them. They speak faster. Damn them and their tongues...*

Greeley stifled a cough.

"Three more legionnaires died last night on my ship," Arya continued. "That isn't including the Unchosen. I'm worried that if this goes on any longer, there won't be a legion to lead."

"You must trust in Eo, Red Eye," Lilyth said. "Only She will know when the legionnaires accept Her truth into their hearts."

"But is there a way to rid ourselves of this affliction any faster?" Kendrik asked immediately. "I don't want to see more legionnaires suffer."

Lilyth smiled, as if he'd called her beautiful. "You truly are the legion's Red Heart, Kendrik... But yes, I must pray to the Goddess in isolation, but in doing so, I will be unable to care for the legion. You three must do so in my stead."

Damn him and his tongue. Greeley stifled another cough, but his body shook and convulsed. *Not now. Stay strong.*

"How, Champion?" Kendrik asked.

Greeley's lungs refused to cooperate. When he exhaled, he broke down into a fit of hacking coughs. When he'd finished, Arya, Kendrik, and Lilyth stared at him unsympathetically. He wiped away a bead of sweat and repressed a shiver in the quiet that followed.

Lilyth frowned. "Red Hand, are you sick?"

"I feel fine," Greeley said, though his body burned with the need to cough again.

"He could get you sick, Champion," Kendrik said, turning to shield her from Greeley.

Damn him. I am her first follower! Her greatest lieutenant! Her equal!

Lilyth gently pushed Kendrik aside. "This affliction is not contagious, Red Heart." She stared at Greeley in disappointment. "It is because he doesn't truly believe in Eo and Her truth. Is that not so, Red Hand?"

Greeley broke out into a cold sweat, but he didn't know whether it was from illness or anxiety. "Champion—"

"If even my Red Hand, my *first,* does not believe, what am I to do?" Lilyth shook her head. "After all I have done for you, after all I have given you, after all you have seen, you still do not believe Eo's truth?"

"Champion—"

"Did I not fight through dozens of Cutthroats to break your chains and sacrifice my ship to set you free? Did I not free you with my own hands, only for you to betray me? Did I not forgive you even then, Red Hand?"

Guilt rose in Greeley's stomach with the bile, but he refused to retch in front of Lilyth. "Champion—"

"Have I not done enough, Red Hand?" Lilyth slapped her hand down on the table, the sound echoing like a gunshot. "All I have asked for is your strength and your loyalty, when I have given you freedom and *life.* I have killed for you, sacrificed for you. What more must I do, must *She* do, for you to believe?"

"Champion—"

"I chose you because I saw your strength! Where is it now, Red Hand? All I see is *weakness!*" Lilyth clenched her jaw. "Leave us and join the others. Pray long and hard. Tell the others to do the same. May Eo forgive you. I do not know if I can."

"But Champion—"

"No, Red Hand. You have disappointed me enough today. Go. *Now.*"

With a burning heart, Greeley left, barely making it off the ship before his stomach betrayed him. He vomited into the sea, cursing Kendrik above all else.

In Greeley's absence, the other two lieutenants didn't dare break the silence. Lilyth brushed a tear away, feigning embarrassment. She closed her eyes and shook her head. "Even my first is a nonbeliever... How can I be expected to lead if no one is faithful?" Such pain in her voice, such misery.

Such lies.

Arya reached out a hand to put on her shoulder, but Kendrik was quicker. "Champion, you have my strength and loyalty."

"And mine," Arya added, but the words were lame and hesitant compared to Kendrik's zeal.

Lilyth stared at her, sensing Arya's worry. She, too, carried the affliction. "Do I?"

Arya was a moment too slow to catch the meaning in Lilyth's words. When she had, her eyes widened in horror. "Champion, I—"

"Do I have your strength and loyalty, Red Eye?" Lilyth repeated. "This is a simple question."

"Yes, Champion." Arya inclined her head as if to say, *You know the things I've done for Eo.*

Lilyth tilted her head, pretending to hear Eo's voice. "If that is the truth, then why are you sick?"

Arya broke eye contact and stared at the table. "I'm fine. A little achy, yes, but I'm not sick. I just need a little more sleep."

"Still lying to me," Lilyth said, disgusted. "Even after how hard we fought to save you—after Jericho gave his life for yours."

Kendrik flinched, the Red Heart's eyes now revealing contempt. Arya glanced at him, then at Lilyth, then back at Kendrik. She raised her chin stubbornly. "I'm not lying. I believe more than anybody else, Champion. Even more than Kendrik."

"*Lies.*" Kendrik spat, glaring at her.

But Arya refused to back down. "*True.*"

Before they could begin a brawl in her chambers, Lilyth said, "If it were true, Red Eye, then why are you sick?" Lilyth placed her left hand flat on the war table and held the talan aloft in the other. "Do I need to cut off my hand? Will that be enough for you to believe?" She pressed the talan hard against her wrist, and a line of blood welled from the wound. *"Will it?"*

Kendrik gasped.

Arya paled.

"If you tell me to cut, I will only ask you, 'How deep?' And you know I will, Red Eye. That is the extent of my loyalty—my strength. Even though you've shown me only weakness and disrespect. Say the word, and I will do it." Lilyth pressed harder, ignoring the pain as the skin separated.

"Champion, don't." Arya said, raising her hands in surrender. *"Please."*

Lilyth lifted the talan from her wrist and stabbed it into the table. "You break my heart, Red Eye. Go join the Red Hand in prayer. I do not want to look at you anymore."

Arya opened her mouth to argue, then thought better of it. She stumbled away, disappearing through the door.

Only Lilyth and Kendrik remained.

"Are you here to betray me, too, Kendrik?" Lilyth asked as the deck rocked underfoot.

"No, Champion." Kendrik met her gaze, not out of tenacity like Arya or desire like Greeley. Kendrik's was a gaze of zealous determination. Eventually, Lilyth's mouth formed a smile.

"I should have known from the beginning that you would be my only loyal legionnaire, Red Heart. You are my only true believer."

"I'd give anything for the Red Legion. You know that."

"I do," Lilyth said, putting a hand on his shoulder and squeezing. "What I need from you now is leadership. Command the legion in my place while I speak with the Goddess. It may take only a few hours, or it may take days, but this is the only way to lift Eo's affliction."

Kendrik nodded, resolute. "Whatever you need, Champion, I will gladly give you."

"Rise where Arya and Greeley have fallen, Red Heart," Lilyth said, still soft, still smiling. "Prove to me you are my right hand, if not the red one. Prove it to our Red Legion."

Frustrated, guilty, and alone, Greeley tore through memories of alleyways and cages. He strangled boys and men as urchins and Cutthroats mocked him. Trophies glittered in his hands and around his neck until greedy hands stole them away. Stole him away. Thrust into darkness, Greeley smelled the shit and blood, was filled with the old fear. *Not the cage. Not again.* The rats gnawed at him, so did his rage, yet he could do nothing with the manacles at his wrists. He trembled with exhaustion and fury until his strength faded.

Then Lilyth appeared on the opposite side of the cage. A key glittered in her hands. Greeley reached for it, but he was too far away. Lilyth took a step forward to give it to him, but a red hand pulled her away. *Kendrik's* hand. The Red Seducer smiled as he took Lilyth's hand in his and walked away, leaving Greeley in the darkness with the rats, piss, and shit—

"No!" Greeley shouted, waking up in his bed aboard the *Crescent.* His arms and legs were free to move, which gave him the freedom to roll over and retch into a pail. The chills gripped him as hard as manacles once had. He wiped his mouth and shivered, wrapping his jacket tighter around his chest as his nose dribbled with snot and forehead dribbled with sweat.

"You look as bad as I feel," a voice said from the shadows off to his left. The Red Eye. She sat on the edge of his bed near his feet.

Greeley grunted, too shaken by his dream to speak.

"The Red Heart didn't get sick," Arya continued. "He's commanding the legion while Lilyth's been talking to the Goddess. Thought you should know."

"Damn him," Greeley said, meaning to think it instead of say it. *Squalling stupid. You sound weak and stupid—*

"Yeah. Goes around acting like he's better than us. More loyal. He ain't." In a low whisper, she added, "I don't know what she sees in him."

"He's manipulating her," Greeley said. "Don't know how, but he has to be."

"Well, between my eyes and your hands, we could stop the heart," Arya said. "All we have to do is wait for the right opportunity."

Despite the sickness, Greeley felt his strength return with his cruel grin.

Alone on her stern balcony, Lilyth didn't pray.

"Everything I have done, everything I will do, I do for you, Lily." She pulled out her daughter's necklace from underneath her robe and gently traced the edge of the feather. "I need you to hold on just a little longer."

Hiding the necklace beneath her robe, Lilyth took out two empty glass vials. One had contained a poison she'd released into the legion's fresh water supply, the other an antidote she'd slipped into her and Kendrik's drinks. Rather than dump an antidote into the water, Lilyth discarded the tainted barrels. After tonight, the legion would recover and the Dusk Affliction would be over. Those who survived would praise Eo and truly believe.

Lilyth had sacrificed forty men—ten percent of the legion—to achieve that result.

A tithing... to me. Lilyth smirked. *A small price to pay for a ruthless army.*

Satisfied, she dropped the vials into the churning waves. Another problem solved. Another battle won. All that remained was finding the route through the Battered Reefs.

And I think I know just who to ask.

Chapter Twenty-Four

S tars surrounded Steward as she leaned over the railing of the *Constable's* crow's nest. The obsidian sea lay a hundred feet below. *I jumped from this height once,* she thought. *Never again.*

Steward took a step back from the railing, bumping into somebody. "Cheer up, Steward! We're almost done. We can get back to training after we finish up here," Mouse said, his red locks uncombed and curling upward. He put his arm around her shoulder and whistled. "Sure is hard to beat the view though, ain't it?"

"Aye, that it is, lads, that it is," Ink said, his face stoic but eyes smiling. He pointed at the brightest star hanging above Aritrasta in the far distance. "*Eo's Point* is guiding us home. As long as we follow that star, we'll make it back to Alira. The journey won't take much longer, I reckon."

Steward looked between them, her voice caught in her throat.

"What's wrong, Steward?" Ink asked. "Looks like you've seen a ghost."

Startled by that word, Steward swallowed. "You're both... *You're both—*"

"Handsome? Incredible? Superb?" Mouse interrupted, flexing his small muscles. "Strong?"

Steward laughed and hugged him, perhaps too tightly. He gasped and struggled overdramatically, but she didn't loosen her grip. "I missed you, Mouse." She looked at Ink. "You too, captain."

"What's there to miss, Mop King?" Mouse asked, patting her on the back. "I see you every day."

Steward grinned so wide it hurt. "Forget I said anything, Mouse. I'm just glad that you're alright."

Ink nodded, his hand grasping her shoulder. "Aye. Right as rain, we be."

"Good, I..." Steward laughed. "I think I could use a little rain."

"Hey, Steward?" Mouse asked, his voice deeper and older—not his own.

Steward froze. "Mouse? What's wrong?"

The hand on her shoulder squeezed tighter. "Hey, Steward?" Ink asked, in the same deep voice that wasn't his.

Steward blinked. Darkness replaced Mouse and Ink. The *Constable* became the *Wrath*, the crow's nest a slavehold. She moved her hands, hearing the manacles clink as they cut into her wrist. "Mouse? Where'd you go?"

"Mouse isn't here, Steward. You were just having a nightmare," Jameson whispered wearily. His hand released her shoulder, and his chains rattled against the floor.

Steward tried to pierce the veil of darkness to see him, but there was no light in the slavehold. All she saw was a silhouette. *I want to go back.* Steward shut her eyes and opened them again, though Mouse and Ink didn't return. "But where is he? Where's Ink?"

Jameson sniffed somewhere to her left. "They're gone, Steward."

"No." Steward whispered, her voice hoarse from thirst. "Mouse can't be gone..." Then she remembered her fight with Mouse—remembered what she'd done to him. Steward should have cried, but dehydration had taken her tears. "This is the nightmare. This *has* to be the nightmare."

Silence reigned for moments that lasted an eternity in the darkness. Eventually, Jameson said, "I think a story might ease your mind. Would you like to hear one?"

"No more stories, Jameson. No more lies. No more Gods." Steward gritted her teeth. "I'm sick of all of it."

"Steward—"

"The Gods abandoned us." Her anger cascaded down upon Jameson. "We were orphaned, Jameson. Left to die in Alira. Now we're slaves to Cutthroats. *Skulls.* Things just keep getting worse. The Gods didn't stop any of it, no matter how much faith we had or how much we prayed. They didn't care. They let the world take everything from us."

"The Gods have Their reasons," Jameson argued. Though he tried to be reassuring, it sounded patronizing.

"Then what are Their reasons?" Steward asked. "I want to know *why* Eo didn't save my dad. Why She made me kill Mouse. Why Ink has to hang from Rolf's squalling bowsprit." She sat back against the side of the hull, hitting the back of her head against the planks. "Eo could have saved them. But She didn't because She doesn't care about us."

"Steward, Eo doesn't have her power during the day. She couldn't save Mouse or Ink."

"And my dad? What's Her excuse?"

"Your dad... He died in that tavern because he cheated at cards. What happened to him wasn't Eo's fault. It wasn't yours either. It was his choice."

"Yeah, but Eo could have—" Steward stopped as thoughts connected like bloody bullets. "I never told you how Dad died."

Jameson refused to answer, but she heard his chains rattle as he shifted uncomfortably.

After a minute of silence, Steward asked, "How'd you know that, Jameson?"

"I..."

"How could you know?" Steward's mind raced with ideas, but she kept coming back to the same conclusion. She sat up straight. "You were there, weren't you? You saw him die. How? Was it you? Did you kill my dad?"

"Steward—"

"Did you kill my dad?"

"No, Steward. He tried to cheat, and he got caught. I... saw him, but I didn't kill him."

If he hadn't lied to her about being a Cutthroat or told her of Eo's Sword, Steward might've believed him. But he had. "My dad never got caught. It was you, wasn't it? *You* must have done something." Steward gasped as all the pieces fell into place. "That's why you convinced Ink to let me on the ship. That's why you saved me. Not because you cared, but because you felt guilty. This was always about you. This—*all* of this—is your fault!"

"Steward, let me—"

"Dad was all I had, and you took him from me!" Steward screamed, lunging forward before the chains clinked taut. Jameson remained inches out of reach. She strained harder, cutting her wrists on the iron manacles as she thrashed.

Voices throughout the slavehold shushed and cursed her, which only made Steward scream louder.

Strong hands wrapped around her arms. In her ears, Taran hissed, "Oy, Steward! You got to stop! They'll hear you! They'll beat you, you hear me?"

Steward ignored him. "I'll kill you, Jameson! I'll squalling kill you!"

The door to the slavehold opened, and a Skull with a lantern and a truncheon entered. Shining his light on her, he clubbed her only once, but it was enough to send her into unconsciousness.

When she awoke again in the darkness, Steward almost choked on the cloth gag stuffed in her mouth. A rag tied around her head also kept her from spitting it out. The Skulls had tightened her chains to where she couldn't even reach up to her face.

Chains rustled beside her. "Oy, Steward? You awake?"

Taran. Steward grunted.

"You got to be quiet, Steward, else they'll knock you out again, okay?"

Steward grunted again, and Taran removed the rag. She spat out the gag and immediately asked, "Where's Jameson?"

"They moved him to the other side of the slavehold."

"Squalls," Steward said, clenching her teeth. The anger still burned but cooler, almost cold. To the encompassing darkness, she added, "I know you can hear me, Jameson. And I want you to know something: I hate you." Then Steward closed her eyes, letting her hatred consume her. "You can't hide from me forever. And when I find you, you'll die worse than my dad did."

—◦—

Life was darkness. The ship was always moving, always rocking. Sometimes food came. More often, just water. Mostly, there was nothing at all. Only darkness.

Then light.

At Port Tibur, they were offloaded from the *Wrath* and sold to some Fleshlords, but the transaction was a blur. Dehydration, starvation, and illness had wreaked havoc upon Steward, and she shambled from one ship to the other as flamboyantly dressed Fleshlords prodded her along like a heifer. Then it was back to that silent black void.

When the light returned a second time, Steward had recovered from the illness, though the neglect still left her weak. Her legs felt so brittle she could hardly stand on her own. It was Taran who steadied her and ensured she didn't fall. He'd endured as much as she had in those slaveholds, yet he still had enough strength for both of them.

With his guiding hand, Steward struggled down the gangway onto a splintery dock. Chains clanked around her wrists and ankles, cutting skin as she shuffled forward in the single-file line. Taran was directly behind her, but Jameson was somewhere else, out of sight.

Steward fidgeted with a loose nail she'd pulled from the slave ship's deck. An improvised lock-pick. Yet when a Guardian fell to his knees farther up the line, the entire line lurched. Steward was yanked forward, and the nail slipped from her hand into the water beneath.

Steward stifled a sob, wishing the Guardian who'd fallen was dead. No such luck.

After he'd gotten back to his feet and struggled ahead, the chain gang resumed. They stopped again only a few steps later as a gasp of alarm echoed through the line. Steward glanced to where another was pointing: from most of the ships flew white flags emblazoned with an orange sun.

Corinthus. They sent us to Corinthus. If she hadn't been chained, Steward would have run away screaming. Instead, the urge came out as a whimper.

Around her, hardened Guardians who had toiled stoically across a sea of storms, Cutthroats, and syrens became sniveling children.

Captain Horace, the Fleshlord who'd purchased the crew of the *Constable,* smiled at their misery. He was short, only a half-head taller than Steward, with an old scar cutting across his forehead and bulging eyes like a frog's. Though he smelled of shit and piss, his rancid perfume was somehow worse. Wearing a white ruff collar with a red justacorps coat, he slipped a pouch of coins to the harbormaster and turned to address the Guardians. "Welcome to Port Cassius, slaves. This is your new home."

I should have stayed with Mark, was Steward's only thought as she half-limped, half-lurched through the eastern entrance into the port.

Stucco and clay buildings lined their labyrinthine path, reminding Steward of the Chasm. She tried to analyze the path for escape routes but kept getting distracted by the gray-skinned Corinthians. Men, women, and children stood at the tops of the homesteads, wearing brown tunics that looked almost as worn as her own rags. They watched the miserable procession, pointing and gawking as Steward struggled west.

They're talking about which ones they'd want to buy, she realized, revulsion and desperation twisting through her innards. *What is wrong with these people?* When one child had the audacity to wave at her, she flipped him off. A Fleshlord beat her for that. Taran picked her back up as she cursed them all.

At the edge of the labyrinth was a bridge whose curving stones and rising metal spires spanned the length of a polluted river that bisected the city. Scimitar-wielding guards patrolled it, wearing white-and-orange headdresses with breastplates, leather skirts, and sandals. They sneered at Steward as she passed, with one kicking her in the rear as the other laughed.

On the western side of the bridge was a newer city. Instead of clay homesteads, columned concrete buildings rose in a tight square like an ancient forum. Wealthy Corinthians in orange, fur-lined kaftans, white sashes, and oversized headdresses ambushed the slaves, appraising them as they were herded toward a tall domed building at the opposite side of the forum.

What is that place? Steward wondered with steadily mounting horror. *What are they going to do to us?*

Dwarfing most other buildings, its gilt dome rose fifty feet overhead. Its beautiful columns lining the entrance depicted Deitan and the rising sun. Yet no amount of gaudy splendor could silence the screams and cracking whips inside. It smelled of blood and iron—like a slaughterhouse.

It's an auction house, Steward thought, struggling with the chains, which made a violent jangling sound as she resisted. *They're going to auction us off like cattle.*

"Stop, Steward," Taran whispered. "They'll hurt you."

"They'll hurt us, anyway!" She hissed, struggling more.

The line stopped.

"Squalls. The Divine Virgin's coming," Horace said a few feet from Steward. Getting the attention of two Fleshlord subordinates, he jerked his head at her and added, "Take those two worms inside before the virgin sets them loose. Paid Rolf too much coin just to lose them now."

Set us loose? Steward thought, standing straighter and following the captain's gaze.

The crowd of merchants and statesmen separated around a Corinthian woman in an unadorned white dress. Though she hid her face behind a silken white veil, Steward could see the woman's tan, brown hands. Beautiful black hair cascaded down her back, extending to her knees. Four elite guards—whose headdresses were pure white and attached to closed-face helmets—flanked her. They carried large rectangular shields engraved with the Corinthian sun, the same mark on their metal breastplates.

Steward opened her mouth to scream just as a Fleshlord stuck a knife against her ribs. "Not a word, boy," he whispered in Steward's ear, his breath reeking of cheap rum and soured meat.

Steward closed her mouth, and the Fleshlord pulled her out of line. Another grabbed Taran. They were dragged toward the auction house as the Divine Virgin approached the line of Guardians. Steward kept looking over her shoulder to see the woman point at a slave, who Horace immediately freed.

"What?" Steward asked. "She freed him?"

"Damn divine virgins and their squalling tithings," the Fleshlord whispered, shoving Steward forward.

Steward sucked in a breath to shout for the woman's attention, but the Fleshlord punched her in the gut. She could only manage a wheeze. *"Wait..."*

But the Divine Virgin didn't hear her, and Steward was dragged away into the auction house.

One by one, hour by hour, the Guardians were sold off in the giant auction house, which was a single room with a dirt floor. The dome trapped heat, only making the stifling conditions worse. The reek of sweat and bile wafted through Steward's nostrils as she waited her turn. In front of her, other Guardians were standing on tall, flat stones beside other enslaved men, who were all stripped naked for potential buyers to appraise.

There were women, too, but they were much rarer. The sweaty, filthy Corinthian buyers groped and examined them to determine which slaves were the most beautiful. Steward overheard from the Fleshlords that the beautiful ones would serve as concubines, the ugly as house slaves, laborers, and nurses. Both fates were unbearable.

I'll die before I do that. Steward hugged her arms to her chest, as questions and prices were called out from all sides. She was one of the few who still had her clothes on, but only because she hadn't been dragged onto the auction stones yet. But that time would come. If only she still had her nail, she could have shoved it into her neck and ended this torment. But she didn't. It took all of Steward's willpower not to shake as the Fleshlords jeered and sold the adults nearby:

"Look at this lad!" one said, pointing at a gargantuan hauler. "Look at those loins! He'll sire plenty of young'uns to continue his work long after he's put in the ground!"

"Now *this* is a man!" another Cutthroat shouted, pointing at a lean rigger. "Look at his chiseled body. Even your sculptures would be jealous!"

"Thick arms to heft heavy stones!"

"Thick legs to pull carts!"

"Slim to deliver messages!"

"Stout to toil in mines!"

"What about the scrawny one?" a Corinthian buyer asked.

Steward froze as she realized the translator was referring to her. *No,* she thought. *Gods, no. They're going to find out. They'll know I'm a girl.* Her stomach dropped, heavy as a cannonball. *Let me die.*

"Scrawny? Nah. You've got it all wrong," Horace replied, a cruel snarl forming at his lips. He gestured at Steward and Taran, who were forced up onto the stones. "This one's a *killer*. They both are. They're bred for the fighting pits!" Pointing to Steward specifically, he added, "This one's killed two already. Slew a grown man with a dagger and strangled another boy to death with his bare hands, he did."

He's gloating about how I killed Mouse, Steward thought, realizing that Rolf must've told Horace about her duel. *He's using Mouse's death to make more money.* Her eyes flashed angrily, and she wished that there was something she could do to hurt him. But she was still chained.

Unaware of her hatred, Horace continued, "And he's got iron balls. Took a punch to the groin and didn't even flinch. I saw it myself. This one's a true man-eater, and he's ready to kill again. The perfect fighter, he'll be... For the right price."

"Iron balls, huh? Maybe that boy just has a tiny prick!" one buyer joked harshly. "Maybe the punch *missed!*"

"Or he might not *have* a prick!" another added, as if it were some preposterous joke.

"Feast your eyes, men!" Horace shouted, grabbing the fabric of Steward's raggedy trousers and—

"Enough!" a voice rose from the back of the crowd. A Corinthian man pushed others aside and sauntered forward, chin held high so that he looked down through his nose. Though he humbly wore a small headdress and an unadorned kaftan, his smirk was anything but modest.

Despite the man's outburst saving her, every instinct told Steward to flee from him.

Horace pulled his hands away from her waist, though his trailing fingertips burned like acid on her skin. "And you are?"

"Aquila Agricolus Silvanus," the Corinthian said in a low, silky-smooth voice. He practically purred the name.

"*Agricolus?* A farmer? You don't look like any farmer I've ever seen." Horace said. "Do you plan to have these two killers tending your crops?"

"Does it matter?" Aquila asked, lip turning up in a predatory snarl. "Name your price."

"Thirty sols. *Each.*"

"Two years' wages for these paper dolls? No. Five. *Total.*"

They're haggling? She hated them both for it, but she hated the Fleshlord more. Her tongue loosened before she could shut her mouth. "I wouldn't pay above four for me," she said. "For Taran, maybe ten. Wouldn't go much higher than that."

The negotiation came to a halt.

Steward fought the urge to apologize and beg for her life as Horace stared at her, eyes widening in disbelief. Sweat broke out on her back, and her arms tingled, but her feet were numb. She forced herself to grin at him.

The captain hissed, "You dare to—"

"Oy! Ten seems a little much, Steward," Taran said, standing taller on his stone. "Think I dislocated my shoulder earlier. Seven might even be too high." He pretended to deliberate, rolling his shoulder. "How 'bout five?"

The fear slowly ebbed from Steward as she gaped at Taran. He smirked at her despite his bruises and busted lip. She reflected that look.

Horace pulled the ivory-handled whip from his belt. "You insolent children! You will *not* disrespect me!" He raised the whip, but Aquila stopped him.

"If you whip them, they will be worth even less to me," he said.

The Fleshlord lowered his whip even as he glared at Steward and Taran. "Fifty sols for the pair."

Stifling a grin, Steward coughed, attracting his fury. "I'm sick, sir, and I can barely stand straight. I'm only worth two. Seven for the pair of us is more than enough."

Taran crossed his arms. "Well, if you're only worth two, then I'm *definitely* only worth—"

Horace's hand tightened around the whip. "Say another word and—"

"Three. That's how much I'm worth. Five sols. *Total.*" Taran mocked stubbornly. A different Fleshlord immediately stuffed a gag into his mouth. Steward's too.

When both Taran and Steward were silenced, Captain Horace turned to Aquila and said, "Thirty for both."

"Ten sols," Aquila replied.

"Twenty."

Steward coughed again. The gag made it difficult but not impossible. She still got her point across.

Aquila smiled at her and said, "Twelve sols for both. That's the best I can do. It's a generous offer for two sick and wounded boys."

"Twelve sols... with twelve lashes for their insolence. *Each.*" Horace stared back at Steward, his eyes filled with fury. She winked out of spite.

Aquila didn't hesitate. "Ten sols and one lash each."

Steward's eyes widened in surprise. *He's considering this?*

"Twelve sols with five lashes," Horace countered.

"Ten sols with three lashes each," Aquila said. "Or twelve sols with no lashes."

"I'll take the lashes—damn the coin." Horace cracked his whip. "And take out their gags, men. I want to hear them scream."

Fleshlords did as their captain commanded, shoving Steward from the stone into the dirt. Hands reached to rip off her shirt, but at Aquila's order, it was left on. The Fleshlords then dragged her to a whipping post, forcing her to hug the bloody, splintery pole. They did the same to Taran on an adjacent pole.

"Don't scream, Taran. We'll—"

The crack of a whip shredded Steward's shirt and skin. Her body twitched and spasmed, rebelling against her as she whimpered and took a deep breath. *Don't scream,* she thought repeatedly.

The whip cracked a second time, licking Taran. He merely grunted. "Give them nothing, Steward," he whispered as his back bled. "Be strong."

The lash ripped into her back a second time. Then a third. Her knees buckled, but she couldn't fall as the whipping post held her up. It felt as she'd been flayed and roasted over a fire. Everything burned.

Her eyes widened as Horace coiled his whip and approached her with a branding iron. "No," Steward whimpered, pulling at the chains weakly. She couldn't stop him.

Horace held the hot iron near her face but didn't burn her with it. Not yet. Leaning close, he said, "This defiance? It meant nothing. You are just an ox—an animal that tends the fields. You will pick crops until you are a withered old man, and then you will die alone and forgotten. That is what this brand means."

Steward's skin shouted as the iron was shoved against the back of her neck. She could smell her skin burn like roasting meat. The pain filled her worse than any lungful of water—the touch of death. Then her vision turned from white to black.

◄●►

Jameson Ash was at the back of the slave line. He'd only been able to watch as Steward and Taran were whipped, branded, and dragged away by a Corinthian farmer—fated to hard labor for the rest of their lives, however short. And that was only if that farmer didn't learn that Steward was a girl.

I should have left her in Alira. Drowning—even life in the Chasm—is better than this, Jameson thought. *She's right. It's all my fault.*

The knot of guilt in his chest had only wound tighter when she'd learned the truth of her dad's death. She'd been right to blame him, but her hatred wounded him far more than a bullet. *I should have told her the truth from the very beginning.*

Despite his regret, he couldn't take it back. There was nothing he could do now. Not in the *Wrath's* slavehold, and not here. It was far too late to do anything but stumble to the front of the slave line and be sold.

The black abyss of depression and resignation loomed before him. All he needed to do was take another step forward and accept it. If Steward had died, he might have done it, but so long as she lived, there was hope.

I'll escape, he thought desperately. *Or maybe I can make enough money to buy my freedom. Whatever it takes, I'll get away. I'll find her. Then we'll escape this place together.*

But Steward hates you, the black abyss whispered. *She'll never stop hating you.*

Maybe, Jameson admitted. *But as long as she's safe, I don't care.*

"I'll find you someday, Steward. And when I do, we'll sail away. I won't leave without you," he whispered as Fleshlords pushed him onto the auction stones and stripped him of his clothes. "I swear it on the Drowned Sea."

CHAPTER TWENTY-FIVE

S teward awoke in a bed, lying on her stomach. Used to swaying hammocks and hard decks, she found the bed too soft. She rolled over onto her back only for pain to engulf her. Whimpering, Steward lied down on her stomach again, touching the bandages on her back. Captain Horace's whip and words cracked across her mind. *You will pick crops until you are a withered old man, and then you will die.*

Fingers quivering, Steward reached up to the brand on her neck and felt the searing mark: a triangle pointed downward with a long line at its top, resembling a shark's tooth.

"They actually branded me," Steward whispered, withdrawing her hand. "Like I'm some kind of animal."

"Yes, girl. That's exactly what you are—an Animal," a voice replied, emphasizing *animal* as if it were a name.

Despite the pain, Steward turned her head to see a man sitting beside the bed. The Corinthian farmer who'd bought her: Aquila. His short hair rose upward into a small black point. His starched robe was too white, too clean. With unblemished gray skin and manicured fingernails, he sat straight in a chair with his hands resting in his lap, shoulders squared in perfect posture.

Girl. He called me a girl. Steward's body trembled. She wore no shirt, but her pants were still on. *Oh Gods, he knows.*

"Now that you are awake, we can begin. When I speak to you, you answer, yes? You are not Cow, so I expect you to understand." Aquila paused, frowning. "You are not Snake either, so stop squirming. I will not restitch your wounds if you break the thread."

Steward froze, trying to slow her heartbeat, which pounded like a drum. Her eyes remained wide and unblinking. "Sorry." Tentatively, Steward asked, "If you knew I was a girl, did you buy me to..." She couldn't bring herself to finish the question.

"No." Aquila frowned. "You are slow. Maybe you are Cow."

"Give me a blade and find out," Steward snapped before she could stop her lips.

"*There.* There's that spark I saw. That fire." Aquila leaned forward with a vicious grin. "Maybe not Cow then. Something else. But what Animal will you be?"

"Animal?" Steward asked.

Aquila ignored her. "You spoke of Mouse in your sleep? Who is this Mouse?"

Steward blinked back tears. "He's my best friend... *Was* my best friend."

"Ah, the boy you killed, yes?"

Her body clenched instinctively.

Aquila cuffed her. "You will answer my questions, or I will have to punish you, yes? Now, did you kill this Mouse?"

"Yes."

"How?"

"I strangled him."

"Hmmm. Mouse-killer, yes. Snake, no. What does that leave us with, I wonder?" Aquila inspected Steward, then smiled as if remembering something. "Does your slave friend know of your sex?"

Steward blushed, uncomfortable with the wording of the question. From the glint in his eye, she was sure that Aquila asked it that way purposely. "Taran? No, he doesn't know I'm a girl."

"Good." Aquila's smile widened. "That is why I wanted you—you are clever enough to blend in. If you are to be a warrior, everyone must believe you are a man, no?" Aquila put a finger to his temple. "The greatest weapon a fighter can use is *perception.* If others believe you to be a man, then you are. They will never know the difference, so there *is* no difference, yes?"

The glint of amusement in his eye shifted to dark cruelty in an instant. "But to survive in this world of Animals, you need control as well as cunning. There is a thin line between bravery and stupidity, which you treat like a crack instead of a cliff. You are lucky such stupidity has not killed you already. If I had been that Fleshlord, I would have killed you for your disrespect. It is a good thing for you that I am not him, yes?"

Steward could only nod, trying to compare this strange man to Priest Clifton, Rolf, or even Horace, before realizing that she didn't want to know. She wanted to flee at the first opportunity and return to Mark's tavern. But she couldn't abandon Taran, not after all they'd been through together.

"Where is Taran?" Steward asked.

"Taran? Oh, your friend, you mean. He is Bear now," Aquila said, as if that answered all her questions. "He and I have already spoken. He is waiting outside for you."

"Is he okay?"

"As okay as Bear can be," Aquila said. "And that is all that matters."

"But... Taran isn't a bear."

"Taran is *Bear*," Aquila said, as if enunciating the last word could make its meaning clearer. "He is an *Animal*. So are you, yes? Now we just need to find your name. Come, sit up."

Steward turned over as slowly as she could without ripping her stitches. She tried not to wince as the threads rubbed her flesh.

"Grow used to pain. Accept it, and it will strengthen you, yes?" Aquila stood, pulling a small table between the bed and the chair. On it, he placed three items: a longsword, a shortsword, and a dagger. "Choose one."

Steward paused before picking up the knife.

"Why did you hesitate?" Aquila asked.

"I'm used to a talan."

Aquila's grin widened. "You have fought with talans?"

Steward thought of the urchin she'd murdered while fleeing the chard addict. "I killed a boy with one."

Aquila raised an eyebrow. "How many people have you killed?"

"Three." The words were blood in her mouth. Mouse's blood. Steward tensed as the threads on her back squeezed her flesh.

"Three?" Aquila clasped his hands together and let out a polite laugh. "You *are* special, so you shall have a special weapon." He snapped his fingers and shouted, "Slave!"

The door opened. A young girl entered, wearing a white chemise with a brown sash over her midsection. Aquila commanded her in Corinthian, so Steward couldn't understand what was said. Eventually, the servant scurried away and returned with a talan. The blade was larger than Mark's, but it had the same curved design, a ring embedded in the handle.

"Like this, no?"

Steward nodded. She took the blade from Aquila's hand, immediately comforted by its weight. "Yes."

"Good. Very good." Aquila took back the blade from her and snapped his fingers. The servant jumped, gathered the weapons, and scurried out the door, closing it behind her. "You are special. She is not. That is why you are an Animal, and she is a Mouse. Like your dead friend."

Steward bit her tongue and looked down. *Mouse was a better man than I'll ever be.*

"Look at me." Aquila's fingers pushed her chin up. They locked eyes as he asked, "Why do you feel guilty for Mouse's death? It is not your fault that you are a predator, and he is prey. Animals should never feel guilty for the Mice they kill, so neither should you."

"Okay."

Aquila sneered in disgust. "*Okay.* Do not use that word. Much too sloppy. It shows you are not confident—not *special.* Say yes or no only." Placing a massive lump of knotted rope on the bed, Aquila then commanded, "Now, untie this knot as quickly as you can."

Another test. Steward glanced at him, noting the inscrutable intelligence in his eyes. A grin pulled at his lips. He stared at her instead of the knot. *There must be a trick to this.*

"What am I allowed—"

"No questions," Aquila interrupted.

You just answered it, Steward thought. Using the talan, she cut through the center of the knot. The ropes collapsed, and Steward finished untangling them within seconds.

"Good. Very good." Aquila smirked as he raised his hand and plucked a golden sol from the air. He rolled it across his fingers before flipping it upward. Catching it in his right hand, he uncurled his fingers, but the coin had disappeared. Instead, he handed her a golden coin with his left hand.

He's better than Dad was, Steward thought, unable to decipher his sleight-of-hand technique.

"Put this coin in one hand and present it to me," Aquila said. "I will guess which hand you place the coin in, yes?"

"Yes."

Aquila closed his eyes. Steward put the coin in her right hand, then hesitated. *The last test was a trick. There has to be a trick to this too. If I do nothing, I fail. And if I fail, maybe he won't want me anymore, which means he'll sell me again... As a girl.*

Steward couldn't allow that to happen. She thought about his exact words and found a loophole. Smugly, she took the coin from her hand and placed it underneath her leg.

Holding out both fists, Steward said, "Ready."

Aquila's eyes opened. He stared at her hands, then at her face. Eventually, he pointed to the right hand. Steward opened her hand to show that nothing was inside of it. Pursing his lips, Aquila said, "Show me what is in your other hand."

Steward opened the hand to reveal it was also empty. His smile fell, though the eyes didn't change. "You did not follow my instructions, girl."

Steward wilted under his predatory wrath. "I did. I placed the coin in my hand, then I took it out. You didn't say the coin had to be in my hand when I presented it to you."

"Ah!" The anger disappeared as Aquila smiled, but because he hadn't blinked, his eyes kept their unnerving effect. "You *are* a cunning Animal! Definitely not Cow. Good. Very good! That means I have not wasted my time and money on you." Then he snapped his fingers. "I have it. *Fox.*"

"Fox?" Steward asked.

"You are an Animal, just as I am the Hunter. You are fast and lean. Your strengths are your speed and mind. A mouse-killer like a snake, but not Snake. Foxes have claws—you have your talan. You are Fox, yes?"

Steward could think of worse names, but *Fox* made her think of the fur scarves that some Fleshlords had worn. She withheld a shiver and whispered, "Yes."

Aquila's face shifted again, becoming more serious. "Be warned of your weaknesses, Fox. Stick your neck out too far from the den, and you will be snared. Burrow too deep, and your shelter will become your grave. That is the Law of the Fox, yes?"

"Yes."

Aquila stood and walked toward the door. When Steward did not follow, he called out, "Come, Fox! We have a full day ahead of us, no?" Aquila opened the door. "We must meet the other Animals."

"But my back—"

"Is fixed. Accept the pain and come, Fox." Steward hesitated. Again, Aquila's face darkened. "Come. *Now.*"

Steward got up from the bed, biting her cheek so she wouldn't shriek. She limped through the door and into a hallway, where Taran waited and leaned against the wall. When he saw her, his face lit up in a genuine smile—an expression she'd never seen on his face before.

"Oy! Steward!" Taran said. "You took so long I thought you'd forgotten about me."

Aquila frowned, making a *tsking* sound. "Not Steward. *Fox.* And you are Bear, no?"

"Right," Taran said, crossing his arms and frowning. "Bear."

"Not *right.* Not *okay.* Say yes or no. Remember this, or you will be punished, yes?"

Taran stared at Aquila, wrinkling his nose in distaste. He uncrossed his arms, fists clenched and twitching at his sides. "I've been punished all my life. I don't care what nobody else says. I ain't your slave. Neither is *Steward.*"

The darkness returned to Aquila's face as he slapped Taran, who stumbled back into the wall. "I will treat you as a slave if you act like a slave. But act like Bear, and I will treat you as an Animal. That is my promise to you."

Taran opened his mouth to argue—

"*Bear,*" Steward interrupted. *Stop,* she added with her eyes.

Taran's eyes narrowed, but he nodded. "*Yes.* Sorry."

A storm of emotions passed over Aquila's face. First curiosity, then brief anger, before returning to amusement. "Don't be sorry. Be better. Be *Bear.*"

Aquila led Steward and Taran through the hallway. Busts of Corinthian warriors and tapestries of legendary battles adorned the passages, interspersed with statues of animals: wolves chasing elk and moose, hawks and owls carrying lifeless rabbits in talons, and snakes squeezing mice to death. Many more animals decorated the halls, but Steward avoided looking at them, sickened by the thought of Mouse. Instead, she inspected the dozens of trophies hanging from the walls: broken shields and swords, arrow tips and bow strings, chipped axes—most covered in flecks of long-dried blood.

Aquila's definitely not a farmer, Steward thought, despite the outer windows revealing extensive fields of grain, vegetables, and other crops. Past them awaited the tree line of an ancient forest, the thicket too deep to expose anything except the river that cut through and drifted by the estate. *What is he then?*

The sounds of clashing metal caught her attention. Through the inner courtyard windows, she saw haystacks marked with targets, which had been impaled with arrows, spears, and knives. Manikins also littered the dirt, gouged and pierced by a myriad of weapons. Four boys with shaved heads fought around the debris, wild yet controlled with their swords, knives, bows, and fists. They were as fast as any urchin, as nimble as any rigger, and as strong as any hauler.

Those are Animals, Steward realized, seeing their fury, savagery, and ruthlessness. *Is that what I'm supposed to become?*

When Aquila entered the courtyard, the fighting immediately stopped. The four boys, three blue-skinned and one gray, dropped their weapons and turned to him, putting their fists over their hearts in a salute.

"Hunter!" the boys shouted, voices tinged with adoration despite the slave brands on their necks. They all wore animal teeth hung on silver chain necklaces rather than shackles.

"Animals, present yourselves." Aquila looked at Steward and Taran and said, "Speak in Aritrastan, as they know nothing of the Corinthian tongue."

The first boy stepped forward, muscles sheening with sweat. At seventeen or eighteen years of age, he looked to be the oldest in the group, having the most scars to prove it. His shaved head was held high, as if a crown should've rested on his forehead. "I'm Lion. I'm four years old."

How is he only four? Steward wondered.

The next boy stepped forward, a close replica of Lion only shorter with his head humbly angled down. His face was sharper, the curved nose nearly mistakable for a beak. "I'm Hawk, and I'm also four years old."

The third said, "I'm Wolf. Two years old." Like Lion and Hawk, Wolf's tanned skin wrapped around ripcord muscles, albeit gray instead of blue. Straight lipped, he was taller than the others. As he spoke, his shoulders remained hunched, as if he was waiting to pounce.

"I'm Snake," the last boy said, voice slow and smooth. "Like Wolf, I'm two years old." He was lankier than the rest, not as muscled yet more graceful. He stared at Steward behind half-closed eyes, sizing her up as if she were his next meal.

Like I'm a mouse, she thought, repressing a shiver as the boy swayed with the breeze. Not breaking eye contact with Snake, Steward responded, "I'm Fox."

"Bear," Taran grunted, almost as large as Lion. If not for the month of malnutrition, he would have been the biggest boy there, though not the oldest.

Aquila nodded, satisfied. "Today is the day of your birth. Remind me, Animals, what were you born to do?"

"Hunt!" the four boys shouted as a group. "That is the way of Animals."

"Hunt what, Animals?"

"Mice!" Again, the chorus was in unison. "That is the way of Animals."

"Then what are you, Animals?"

"Predators! That is the way of Animals."

"But most Mice are quick, yes?" Aquila asked Steward and Taran, not waiting for their response. "So, Animals, what must we do?"

"Train! That is the way of Animals."

"And so, you shall."

The other Animals resumed training as Aquila led Taran and Steward through the courtyard, past targets gouged with an assortment of weapons. The grass was downtrodden, little more than dirt—sickly compared to the lush forests surrounding the hidden villa.

Aquila then guided them back into the house, where a woman waited, standing so still Steward would have mistaken her for a statue.

"Hunter," the woman said as she saluted him. Her voice was deadpan and mechanical, as if her lips were being pulled open by force.

"Present yourself, Animal," Aquila said.

Unlike the four boys from the courtyard, the gray-skinned woman had long black hair, which curled over her white gown. Its length made her look younger, though judging by her face, she was likely in her twenties. Her eyes were wide and watchful. A shadow fell across her face, making her irises look like pools of black ink. "I am Owl, and I am ten years old."

"Owl is a servant of the house, but she is my most loyal Animal and the oldest among you," Aquila said. "As you are newborns, Owl will raise you as her fledglings. What she says is an extension of my will, which you will follow, yes?"

"Yes," Steward said.

"Right," said Taran, earning another slap. *"Yes."*

"Better," Aquila said. "As newborn Animals, you must obey your instincts. During a Hunt, they are the difference between life and death. If your instincts are too slow, you will die. If you have the *wrong* instincts"—Aquila flashed a menacing snarl at Taran—"you will also die, yes?"

"Yes," Steward and Taran said together, though Taran dragged out the word.

"Yes, *Hunter*," Owl said. "When you answer the Hunter, you show him deference."

"Yes, Hunter," they corrected.

"Good," Aquila said, clasping his hands behind his back. "Animals must Hunt so they do not starve to death. Before you can Hunt, you must learn to listen through silence, see through darkness, and know your enemy. Even when that is learned, you then have to learn to stalk prey and remain unseen. You must trust each other, trust your Pack, but above all, you must always trust your Hunter. Only then will you know how to Hunt, yes?"

Steward and Taran nodded. "Yes, Hunter."

"Then tell me, how does one listen through silence?" Aquila asked.

Steward shared a confused look with Taran. "By—"

Aquila slapped her. Steward's cheek burned, but she didn't cry out. More painful than the sting of the slap was the embarrassment of not having seen the trick beforehand.

"I will ask you again. How does one listen through silence?"

Taran opened his mouth, but Steward grabbed his arm. He frowned at her, and she shook her head. His eyes lit with realization, and he closed his lips.

Aquila grinned. "Very good. An Animal listens for threats and prey by remaining silent. Any sound you hear is a clue. That is how one listens through silence, no? You will sleep in silence, you will eat in silence, and you will train in silence. Only when I feel you have learned this rule will you be allowed to speak. If you break this rule, you will be punished, yes? Now, do you have any questions?"

"Well—"

Aquila slapped Taran.

"Any more questions?"

Steward and Taran remained silent.

Aquila's smile widened. "Seems we understand one another, no? Good. Very good! This is the first day of the rest of your lives, Fox and Bear."

Chapter Twenty-Six

Owl stopped in front of two side-by-side doors. She opened one, which revealed only darkness beyond. "Fox. Inside."

Steward took a hesitant step forward, looking inside the cramped, windowless room with only a vase in the corner. It reminded her too much of the slavehold to enter. She shook her head and tried to take a step back, but Owl grabbed her and shoved her inside. It wasn't a hard shove, but with her back as tender as it was, Steward cried out in pain. Then the door slammed, sealing her in the dark.

Steward immediately stumbled to the door and groped at the handle, which was already locked. "Let me out!"

When Owl didn't, Steward put her ear to the door to hear what was happening on the other side. From the sounds of shouts and curses, Steward imagined Taran being thrown into the room beside her.

"Steward, you in there?" Taran asked immediately, his voice trembling slightly.

Steward winced at the sound of her name. If Owl was anything like Aquila, she'd punish them for using their real names. "I'm here, *Bear*," she said, trying to remind him. "What happened?"

"The squall punched me in the face, that's—"

Steward heard Taran's door open, then the muffled smack of fists on flesh.

"Oy!" Taran shouted. "What'd you go and do that—"

Another blow.

"Be quiet," Owl said from the other side of the wall.

"The Core I'll be—"

Two more punches. More grunts as Taran took the hits.

"You'll have to… do better than—"

"Bear!" Steward shouted. "Just shut up, you stubborn asshole!"

Another smack. Several stumbling steps and a fall. Taran made no more noise.

"Taran?" Steward asked, forgetting to use his Animal name. She pressed her ear to the wall, hoping to hear him grunting, cursing, or even breathing. She couldn't. "Taran? Are you—"

Her door flew open. Owl stalked inside and punched Steward in the face. She staggered backward, cupping her jaw as blood filled her mouth.

"Listening through silence is the first lesson for Animals," Owl said. "Be quiet."

"But I don't want to be an Animal," Steward said, forcing herself to stand tall, both for herself and Taran, who could still hear her through the wall. "Neither of us do."

Owl raised her hand to smack Steward a second time. Then she sighed, lowering it. "Being Fox is better than being a Mouse," Owl said to the ground. "Now be quiet, or I'll be forced to punish you. Neither of us wants that."

When Owl closed the door again, Steward kept silent.

Time passed at a corpse's pace.

Even after her vision adjusted to the darkness, there was nothing for Steward to see. She was stuck in a barren room with no windows and only a vase used for refuse. Silently, Steward spent the hours listening to the sound of feet scurrying through the halls. She waited for somebody to stop and open the door, but nobody did. Taran eventually began shouting again—only to be punished again. Then more silence.

Hungry and alone, the first night was torturous. A barrage of nightmares flooded Steward's mind—those of Mouse, Ink, and Dad. Others too. Dead ashkids in alleyways, sailors' corpses on ship decks, and bodies of slaves in auction houses. When she woke up, tears stained her cheeks and blood dripped from her fingertips from too tightly clenched fists.

I killed Mouse. I broke our rules. I kicked his leg. Steward's stomach rolled with guilt. *I won, but at what cost? Maybe I am an Animal.*

The door always remained locked, but periodically the door's food port slid open just long enough to deliver meal trays and canteens. No words were spoken, and the darkness always returned promptly. Worse, the meager allotment of barley bread wasn't enough, and her stomach grumbled ceaselessly.

Without contact with the outside world, Steward tracked the passage of time by sleeping. Each time she awoke was a new day, even if she slept twice or three times every twenty-four hours. Even if it was inaccurate, counting the days kept her sane. Somewhat.

Two days of silence ended with more shouting as Taran pounded on the door and walls. Suffering from his worst beating yet, the sound of grunts and caving flesh made Steward shake. Taran didn't speak again.

After three days, the silence was unbearable. Steward tapped out music on her leg and recounted tales of the seas—the song and story of Undo, among them. But as she thought of it, Steward remembered Jameson, and unforgotten grief twisted her once happy memories.

Jameson betrayed me, she thought, seeing their intertwined story in a harsher light. *This is all his squalling fault.*

After six days, Steward felt as if she'd never spoken in her life. Her mind drifted from present to past and all times in between. Her father taught her how to play cards... only to die by them. Ink taught her how to sail across the Drowned Sea... only to sink into its depths. Mouse taught her to fight... only for her to choke him to death. Every tragedy so damn obvious—inevitable in the dark.

I should have stayed with Mark. I could have lived a good life. I could have been happy.

After a nineday, Steward forgot what life was without silence. She knew how every floorboard creaked when people stepped through the villa. Fox came to determine servants by the speed and heaviness of their steps, devising names for them: twig, stumpy, skitter, hen, and slug. Though she listened for her specifically, Steward only recognized Owl's approach when the door's food port opened, her steps nothing more than a light breeze or a feather.

After two ninedays, Steward could imagine nothing other than darkness.

It's better to be Fox than Mouse, she thought, feeling more animal than human. *It's better to be Fox than Steward.*

When the door did finally open, Fox startled backward. The light burned instead of warmed, her sight hindered instead of helped. Her ears twitched as she looked at the doorway but didn't move toward it. Though she couldn't see it, Fox could hear the trap.

Stick your neck too far out, and you'll be ensnared, she remembered.

After several minutes, Aquila's face appeared, grinning broadly. "Always the wise Fox, remaining out of sight! Come forth into this new world. Present yourself, my Animal."

Tears fell, though her mouth refused to make a sound. Fox walked out of the room on rubber legs, body bouncing with each step. The world was much louder now that she was silent.

Aquila embraced Fox when she reached him. Owl stood beside him, eyes ever watchful. Fox heard Bear's approach before she saw him. He stood close enough for her shoulder to graze his bicep. The small contact was entirely different from Aquila's rigid grasp—her first comfort in so long. Her pulse slowed, the fear of isolation gradually ebbing away.

I'm not alone anymore, Fox thought and smiled to herself.

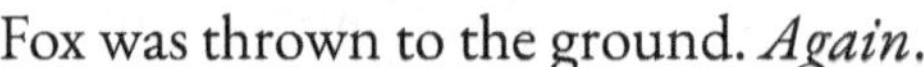

Fox was thrown to the ground. *Again.*

"Get up, Fox," Owl said in that same cold, mechanical voice. The older Animal wielded an unsharpened blade. Though its edge was completely flat, Fox had felt its sting more than once. Baring her teeth, she made no sounds of pain despite the bruises on her body. She pushed herself up from the dirt and staggered forward toward Owl.

Patience, Fox thought, just as Aquila had taught her. *See the opening and take it.* She changed the grip on her own edgeless talan. Watching Owl's graceful steps, Fox pounced and stabbed. Owl dodged the blade and kicked her in the chest. Fox was flung back to the ground. It hurt, but because her back had healed, falling hurt far less than it used to.

"You are Fox, not Flying Squirrel," Aquila said, behind her and sitting on a bale of hay in the inner courtyard. The other four Animals trained nearby, but they didn't need nearly the level of supervision as her and Bear. Not that Fox was complaining. She loved it when he paid attention to her.

"Learn to stay on your feet, yes?" Aquila said. "You are not Cow, so stop charging forward and hoping to hit Owl blindly. Be cunning and fight like Fox."

Because she could not speak, Fox only nodded. She tried again. And again. And again.

After Fox's seventh failed attack, Aquila shook his head in disappointment. Fox swallowed her guilt. *I let him down again.*

Aquila motioned to Bear, who was just as bruised as Fox. He cradled a long, heavy scimitar, whose edge was just as dull as her talan. "Switch with Cow. Fight like Bear, not like Bull."

Silently fuming, Fox limped over the downtrodden grass to sit at Aquila's feet as Bear took her place. She studied Owl for weaknesses as she bent, twisted, and foiled Bear's stubborn attacks, but the old Animal was flawless. *Fighting for almost three hours, but she isn't even winded... She's killed both of us at least thirty times,* Fox thought before staring down at the new bruise forming on her ankle. *Make that thirty-one.*

Fox's stomach grumbled. *Maybe if I had a little more food, I could get stronger—faster. Maybe then I could beat her. If I snuck an extra piece of meat from mealtime, I could do it.*

She distracted herself from her hunger and turned her attention to the opposite side of the courtyard, where Lion and Hawk fought fisticuffs. Each punch was hurled with lightning and landed with a crack of thunder. Bruised and bloodied, they fought on. Relentless. Ruthless.

Will I ever be as powerful an Animal as they are? Fox stared up at Aquila, who was analyzing Bear. *I hope so.*

Her eyes shifted to Wolf and Snake. While Wolf fought fast like Lion, Snake preferred to grapple. Wolf held him at bay with his long arms, but Snake swayed, dodging nine out of every ten strikes.

Snake knows Wolf well enough to dodge his punches before they're even thrown, Fox thought, just as Wolf pounced, cracking Snake across the jaw with the tenth punch. *Even then, one slip-up could still be a death sentence.*

Aquila rested a hand on her shoulder, and Fox leaned her head against him. "They are strong because they have spent years fighting each other. Survival depends on experience and discipline. That is the way of Animals, yes? The key is staying in the moment. Never think of the past or the future. Think of this moment, and *only* this moment. Otherwise, your mind will doubt your ability, and you will fail, no?"

Fox nodded, still silent as he had instructed.

"You will become stronger, Fox. I know it like I know all things. You will become an Animal unlike any other. You'll make me proud, won't you?"

Fox nodded vigorously, wanting nothing more than that.

"Do you enjoy disappointing me, Fox?" Aquila asked. "Hurting me?"

Fox shook her head, holding back tears. She stood in the center of the circle of sitting Animals, all wearing disgusted expressions save for Bear. He gave her strength, just as he had on the deck of the *Constable*, which only made her feel worse. Owl stood behind him, staring at her with those unblinking eyes that consumed all light and empathy.

"Have I not done enough? Have I not given you your life? Have I not saved you from slavery? From Cutthroats?" Aquila asked, circling her like a vulture. "Then why, why can't you do something so simple as *listen?*"

Fox stared at the ground guiltily.

"Why do you hate me, Fox?" Aquila asked with enough pain in his voice to break Fox's resolve to remain quiet.

"Hate?" She looked up at him, stricken. "No. Hunter, please—"

"You are an Animal, and you will be *silent!*" Aquila snapped. Fox immediately shut her mouth. Calmer, he shook his head and added, "Even now, you break the rules and disobey me. What more do you want, Fox? Am I... not good enough for you? Are *we* not good enough for you?"

Growls emanated from the other Animals, accompanying their wroth glares. Save for Bear, whose eyes only conveyed strength and loyalty.

Fox didn't answer, neither nodding nor shaking her head, because both answers could be mistaken for the wrong answer. She hated herself more for her stillness.

"Even now you hesitate," Aquila shook his head. "Fox, the Pack only survives if all members work together. We train together. Sleep together. *Eat* together."

"That is the way of Animals," the Animals said in unison, save for Bear and Fox.

"The Pack falls apart without obedience."

"That is the way of Animals."

"But you've repeatedly disobeyed me by sneaking extra food at meals," Aquila said, looking to Owl, who only nodded. "Taking food away from the other Animals for yourself."

Fox's shoulders fell. *I'm sorry,* she thought but didn't say. *I was hungry. I thought I'd become stronger if I wasn't so hungry.*

"We conduct weigh-ins for a reason, Fox. To make sure that you do not become soft. To make sure that you do not become fat. Do you know what happens to fat Animals? They fall behind. They get caught. They get *eaten.*"

"That is the way of Animals."

"Do you want to be left behind?" Aquila asked.

Fox shook her head hard enough for it to ache.

"Then why won't you listen?" Aquila asked. "Why won't you obey?"

I will, Fox wanted to say. *I will obey. I promise. I'll swear on the Drowned Sea if I must.*

"Animals, what say you?" Aquila asked, turning to Lion, Hawk, Wolf, and Snake. "What is the punishment?"

"Hunger," they said.

"How long?"

"As long as it takes."

"So the Pack has spoken. Dismissed."

While the Animals retreated to the kitchen for their evening meal, Fox waited outside. She watched as they sat at the table together as a Pack, wishing to be a part of the family more than to eat. *Please don't make me sit out here alone.*

But they did. When they'd finished eating, Bear returned to the courtyard and slid a piece of meat into Fox's hand, but she gave it back to him just as quickly.

You don't want it? Bear asked by only raising his eyebrow.

Fox flicked her eyes at the other Animals before staring at Bear. *I want to be a part of the Pack. I want to obey.*

For days, the hunger came and went, but Fox remained. It made her sharper, faster. Instead of strength, she focused on quickness and cunning.

Strength of the mind was just as important as the strength of the body. And her will became unbreakable despite starvation.

It made Aquila proud.

And that was enough.

Months passed before Fox and Bear finally scored one cut each on Owl during sparring. But when they had, Aquila celebrated their success by giving them access to the library. Like all other rooms, this one was efficient. Immaculate tomes covered every wall from floor to ceiling. Half-walls jutted out from the walls and between tables, holding more books. Fox marveled at the grandiose shelves and gilded book spines, while Bear looked disinterested, fingering the edge of his scimitar until Owl slapped the back of his head.

"As the Hunter says, 'Knowledge means nothing if you do not recognize it.'" Owl walked between the shelves, grabbing books and placing them onto a table in a secluded corner. Strange glyphs of animals were stamped on the leather covers. "You will be expected to read and know every text in this room. Starting with these."

When Owl sat at the table and gestured for them to join her, Fox gritted her teeth and looked at Bear, who was hiding a grimace. *He can't read well, either,* she realized. While that didn't surprise her, Fox was shocked that she hadn't known it until now. *He knows me better than I know myself. But, I guess, we don't know everything about each other... He still doesn't know that I'm a girl. He never will.*

Quietly, Fox sat down at the table and opened the first book. She stared down uncomprehendingly at the black ink staining the yellow parchment. She could read every fifth word, but even then, only words with one syllable. The only two-syllable word she could spell was *Erin.* She still didn't know how to spell *Steward.*

Out of options, Fox pretended to read, glancing at every line before turning the page. Whenever she did, Bear followed suit, which Owl noticed almost immediately.

"You aren't actually reading, are you? Why aren't you taking this seriously?" Owl's eyes were wide and furious, her voice quiet and monotonous. When Fox and Bear didn't answer, she added, "Speak. I won't punish you for answering my question."

"We can't," Fox said, voice rusty from disuse. How long had it been since she'd spoken? Four months? *Six?* "Our captain was supposed to teach us, but... he's gone now."

"Ink wasn't gonna teach me, I don't think," Bear said, rubbing his throat. "Never had the knack for words. Was always more of a fighter than a learner anyway."

"Yet you're horrendous at both, Bear," Owl said.

Bear frowned, bemused. "What do whores have to do with reading?"

Owl was at a loss for words for the first time since Fox met her. Then she laughed, which was a stranger noise than Fox's own voice—more a choking sound than a chuckle. Strangest was *why* she laughed. Fox didn't know what *horrendous* meant, but apparently, it wasn't a reference to girlies.

Owl sat between them, grabbing one book and flipping back to the first page. "Don't be ashamed if you haven't been taught. The only way to learn is through education and experience. Both are good, but experience is best. Some of your experiences have been horrible, I know, but those lessons are important because they are ones you will never forget."

Owl's voice was kind, patient, yet her eyes were solemn and vulnerable enough to make Fox look away. *What did you experience, Owl?*

<hr>

Summer fell, and winter rose again.

Fox rubbed her hands as she jogged to keep up with Bear and the rest of the Animals on their ritualistic morning run, wearing nothing more than tunics and sandals as they trekked through the snow. Owl led the Pack, and they traveled in order of birth: Lion, Hawk, Wolf, Snake, Bear, and Fox. They ran in silence through the forest and followed the river before turning back toward the villa. Dawn peeked over the horizon, but Fox could still see the stars. Far away, she could make out *Eo's Point,* the star that led to Aritrasta.

I could just leave. Run away to Alira. I could still live with Mark and work in his tavern. It was a bizarre thought, so sudden and surprising that Fox hesitated mid-stride, stumbling before catching back up to the group. Then Fox shook her head. *Why would I ever leave? The Pack is my family.* Staring at the villa made of forest logs and stones, she added, *This place is my home.*

Finishing the run, the Animals filed into the courtyard to stretch. They practiced the nine Animal poses to loosen their muscles and increase flexibility. Then they split into pairs for sparring, working on form, strength, and speed. Aquila and Owl fought at the center, showing them new techniques and ways to disarm and kill opponents.

After training, Fox and Bear shared a meal of fish and bread with the other Animals. At the head of the table, Aquila shared stories as a sense of camaraderie grew among their family.

I belong here, Fox thought at the end of dinner. *Because I am an Animal.* Looking at Bear, she added, *We are Animals.*

Then, after a night of reading tomes in both Aritrastan and Corinthian, Fox lay on the top bunk, staring down at Bear only when she thought he was sleeping. She thought, *I was nothing, but now I'm Fox. With Bear, I'm whole.*

Chapter Twenty-Seven

Fox woke up to creaking wood. Her eyes snapped open, though her breathing didn't change. She scanned the room. The moon and stars illuminated the three sets of occupied bunk beds within. The four older Animals were asleep as she leaned down from her top bunk to look at Bear. His eyes were open, a long anelace dagger already in one hand as he pointed toward the door with the other. *Did you hear that? It came from outside.*

Yes. Fox nodded, sliding the talan into her hand. *I don't like it.* She rolled off the bunk bed, landing in a crouch. A small noise, but a noise nonetheless. Fox stared at the other Animals again, knowing they should have woken up but hadn't. She put a hand on Bear's arm, gesturing to the others. *Something's wrong. They're not waking up.*

Bear jerked his head to the door. *Let's find out what's going on.*

Fox opened the door slowly. The hinges were quiet but not completely silent. In the darkness beyond, nothing moved, but Fox remained unconvinced. Squeezing her talan, she crept out into the hallway. Bear was never more than a step behind.

Pools of moonlight allowed Fox to see down both sides of the corridor unimpeded. As she couldn't hear any wind, whoever had caused the sound was in the villa. And as she had heard no doors opening or closing, whoever had caused the noise was still in this hallway. Only a few statues were tall enough for somebody to hide behind, and of those, only one on this side of the hallway: a full-sized statue of a sunguard.

Fox pointed it out to Bear, and they advanced with weapons drawn. When they were within ten feet of it, Aquila stepped out into the moonlight with a grin. "You listen well, my Animals!"

At once, Fox and Bear sheathed their blades and saluted their Hunter in silence.

"I'm sure you have questions, yes? So do I." Aquila said as a lantern was lit behind them, shining light.

Fox glanced over her shoulder to see Owl and the others standing outside the bedroom with broad grins.

That's why they didn't wake up, Fox thought, muscles relaxing as she returned their smiles with one of her own. *They'd been pretending to be asleep.*

"Now, what is the value of silence?" Aquila asked as Fox turned her attention back to him.

Silence passed for a full minute—neither Fox nor Bear said a word. They'd grown accustomed to his tests, even enjoyed them now that they understood. All three grinned.

"Perhaps my tests have grown too easy," Aquila said, almost making Fox laugh. She covered her mouth with a hand to keep quiet. "Fox, what is silence? Speak your answer to me when you think you have it."

Fox remained quiet for almost a minute, contemplating the question. "Confidence," she said in a dusty croak, her dried vocal cords aching. The words were sloppy as Fox struggled to form them. "Silence brings... confidence... in my surroundings."

"Bear?" Aquila asked.

Bear hesitated, glancing at Fox before saying, "Loyalty." The word was quiet, without the old acid that once dripped from his tongue. "Silence has shown me who my family is."

Fox pressed her shoulder against Bear's bicep. *Together.*

Aquila asked, "And what of silence from a fighting perspective?"

"If I listen to my surroundings, I know what doesn't belong," Fox replied.

"It's a lot harder to be surprised," Bear added.

"Then you know the value of silence, yes?" Aquila inhaled deeply, contentedly. "You have learned your first lesson, and with it, earned your place in the Pack. You may now speak."

"That is the way of Animals," the other Animals said behind her. Beaming with pride, Fox and Bear spoke the words with them.

"Now, close your eyes, Fox and Bear," Aquila said.

So used to silence, they obeyed without asking why or for how long. Eventually, Fox felt Aquila place something around her head.

"Now open them."

Fox looked down at the silver necklace that hung from her neck. White teeth and claws hung from the chain like trophies. *They're fox teeth,* she thought in awe. Like her talan, this necklace was something that could never be taken away. *I've been waiting so long for this, and now I finally have it. I'm truly an Animal now. I'm a member of the Pack. I have a family again.* She stared at Bear. He held a necklace made of bear teeth and claws. *We both do.*

Fox looked back at the other Animals, who proudly displayed their own necklaces as they congratulated her and Bear. Even Owl, though hers was made of feathers and talons.

"I believe a celebration is in order," Aquila said, though he didn't wear a necklace of his own. He looked to Owl. "Prepare the drinks."

In the darkness before morning, Fox sat cross-legged in the courtyard, looking up at the stars glistening far brighter than in Alira, yet dull compared to how they shone on the open ocean. She sat between Bear and Owl, their knees touching as they formed a circle around Aquila. A cup rested in each of their hands.

"Drink," said Aquila, though he held no drink of his own.

Obediently, the seven Animals drank. The liquid was strange and bitter, like water mixed with ashes and a sweet apple. Fox's throat closed as the fluid set everything alight. She coughed, setting the drink down and taking a few more breaths before finishing it. Bear, despite how much he grimaced, chugged his own in one swig.

"The first time is always the hardest," Aquila told her with a smile.

It took only seconds for sweat to form along her arms and scalp, her heart pounding.

Something's wrong, Fox thought. *Something's horribly wrong.* She blinked, and the light of the stars faded until the sky was black. The ground beneath her ruptured, brown dirt giving way to darkness beneath. Another fissure cracked beneath her, and she fell into the lightless abyss. Her experiences fragmented into shards, her thoughts became a gunpowder mist. She kept falling, and the glass memories fell with her, splintering each time she looked at them.

Hugging her father after a successful grift. Shattered.

Watching the sun set over a blue horizon with Ink. Shattered.

Laughing with Mouse as they laid in hammocks. Shattered.

I could have saved them, an unseen voice whispered in her ear, one old and wise but filled with malice and hate. *Your dad. Your captain. Your friend. I could have saved all of them. But I didn't. Because I hate you.* The words grew distant. *You'll always survive, even when everyone else dies. That's my curse to you, what you deserve.*

Fox smelled the salt before she collided with the black water. She opened her mouth to scream, but darkness rushed in, and she choked on it. The cold seeped through her body, her mind, snatching everything warm and good. Weight crushed her shoulders, her lungs. She was as heavy as a corpse. Like those of all the people she'd lost.

Shadows swam in the darkness with her. Creatures with claws, teeth, and tridents in place of ears, noses, and lips. Syrens. They swam beside her, grinning and laughing as they pushed her toward a light. She didn't know if she was moving toward death or life, but she half-swam, half-thrashed as she reached toward it with an outstretched hand—

Fox breathed in the air. She was sitting cross-legged in a circle with the Animals. Bear sat beside her. Aquila stood in front of her. The stars were back, so was the ground. She was back in the courtyard.

"Animals protect their territory together. When one acts, all Animals act." Aquila said, body now encased in a pyre of flame, whose tendrils reached the sky. Yet his skin seemed untouched by the heat.

"That is the way of Animals."

Fox looked down at herself. Instead of blue skin, there was only orange fur. Instead of hands, clawed paws. A white-tipped tail curled around her hind legs. She touched her face, feeling a snout where her nose and mouth had once been. Ears on the top of her head instead of the sides.

She could smell and hear and see... *everything.* Sweat and musk told her what each had eaten for breakfast a nineday ago. The groans of wind-rustled trees revealed which branches had rotted. The moon loomed closer and revealed small craters she'd never noticed before.

Fox looked at the other Animals, all transformed into their names. An owl, lion, hawk, wolf, snake, bear, and fox sitting around a burning bonfire.

I'm one of them. I'm an Animal, she thought, the fear falling away as her sense of self stabilized. Staring at the burning bonfire that Aquila had become, she added, *I am his.*

"You are the Pack, and I am your Hunter," Aquila said.

"That is the way of Animals," Fox said, believing it more than she'd believed anything in her entire life.

When dawn broke and hallucinations fell away, Fox was exhausted and yet renewed. She grinned, looking at the other Animals, who were all as flushed as she felt. Save for Bear, who seemed more troubled than before.

Aquila addressed them and put a hand on both Fox and Bear's shoulders. "You've done well, my Animals. I'm so proud of you."

Fox basked in the warmth of his compliment.

"And now that you've mastered silence, you must master darkness." Aquila pulled out two thick, black rags and handed them to the Animals. "For an Animal to survive in the world of Mice, you must learn to trust your senses, even when one is lost. You must know your path even without light. Animals often must walk in darkness, no?"

I don't want to be in the darkness again. Fox thought as she stared down at the blindfold. then she looked back at Aquila. *But I want to be part of the Pack.* Placing the blindfold over her eyes, her vision became night. Breath caught in her throat, but Bear's hand on her shoulder was more calming than any words.

I'm not alone. Bear is with me... She continued repeating the phrase, helping keep her heart calm.

"If you have questions, speak now, my Animals," Aquila said. When they both stayed dutifully silent, he added, "No more tests—not of that sort. You earned the right to speak freely."

Bear asked, "Do we fight with these blindfolds, too?"

"You will wear them at all times outside of the courtyard and the library," Aquila replied. "Any more questions? No? Then here is your next task: in each room, there is something that is out of place or missing. Find out what that is. Perform well, and you will eat well, yes? Now go."

Making their way out of the courtyard, Fox felt her way along the walls toward the door. She bumped into Bear twice, falling the second time as she tried to hide the embarrassment on her face.

"Can't see shit," Bear grumbled, the venom returning to his voice. "Feel like a damn infant."

"Just because you *can* speak doesn't mean you *should* speak," Aquila said. Though she couldn't see his face, Fox heard heat in his words.

"Yes, Hunter," they said together.

As a pair, Fox and Bear made it out into the hallway before slipping and falling on what must have been hundreds of metal ball bearings. Bear grunted and Fox bit her tongue to keep from cursing as they got back to their feet.

"In place of the old tests," Aquila said. "I've added obstacles to your path."

Feeling like an old beggar, Fox put her hands out in front of her as she tried to navigate the hallway. Bear followed behind her, keeping a hand on her shoulder to stay close. They made it a few more feet before something cracked the back of her knees. Head smacking into the ground, Fox stifled a groan. She reached out, trying to grab what had tripped her—

A rod rapped her knuckles, and Fox recoiled.

"And by obstacles, I mean Owl, yes? She will *motivate* you."

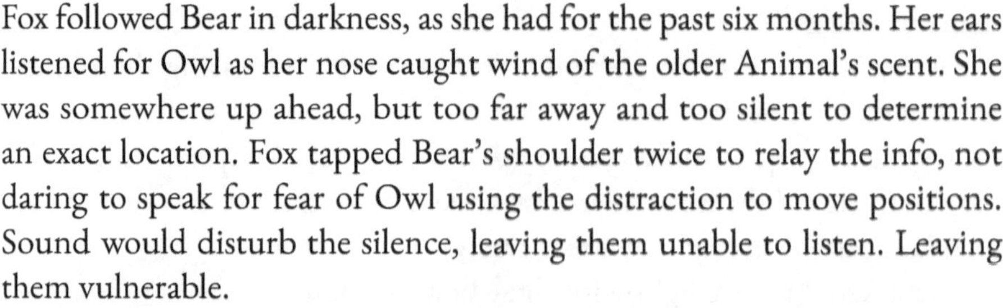

Fox followed Bear in darkness, as she had for the past six months. Her ears listened for Owl as her nose caught wind of the older Animal's scent. She was somewhere up ahead, but too far away and too silent to determine an exact location. Fox tapped Bear's shoulder twice to relay the info, not daring to speak for fear of Owl using the distraction to move positions. Sound would disturb the silence, leaving them unable to listen. Leaving them vulnerable.

With Bear's hand on her back, Fox led them down the hallway, sliding on the outside of her foot before planting it out of fear for Aquila's traps.

Neither knew the extent of what obstacles they faced, only that they became more dangerous every day. What were once steel balls rolling across the floor, now were nails, stones, and sharp thin blades. Fox was careful to never lift her foot entirely from the ground as she shuffled, so she could never step on such a blade again—the first time had been bad enough.

Bear, stubbornly, had learned that lesson slower.

They drifted between the rooms, looking for items that had been added or removed. Every item found meant added food. For each item they missed, Owl reduced their meals.

We need to eat today, Fox thought as she mapped the hallway. There would be a doorway on the right in eight steps. A small pedestal on the left in twelve steps.

Fox sniffed the air, trying to make out Owl's distinctive scent from Bear's musk. The older Animal smelled of patchouli, vanilla, and bergamot, and her aroma was becoming stronger but not strong enough. She tapped Bear three times, signaling for him to stop. Fox continued alone for three paces to get a better trace of the citrusy scent.

"You're in the doorway, Owl."

There was no response, which Fox expected. When no blows came, she knew she'd been right. Fox stomped once, and Bear shuffled forward until his hand found her back again.

They traveled into the other rooms: a lamp had been repositioned in one, a bowl of fruit in another, a small table pushed three paces farther in a third. In each room, they shouted out their answer. When Owl didn't attack, they knew they were correct.

After clearing each room, the Animals traveled back to the kitchen where two plates of bread and meat awaited. Despite her hunger, Fox sniffed her meal for spoiled meat and poisons. As Bear's nose was weaker, she checked his meal too. Finding nothing amiss, they ripped apart the bread and meat as both were often prepared with sharp bits of wood, bone, or metal. When they found no traps, both scarfed down their meals and drank water suffused with plant ashes, which supplemented their diet.

Fox paused as she sipped her water—the taste was more metallic than usual. She dipped her fingers in and pulled out a couple of nails.

"Well done," Owl said.

The Animals both jumped to their feet and turned though they could not see through their blindfolds.

Fox thought, *She distracted us with the food to get closer. Squalls.*

"You bested me today, Animals," Owl said. "It will not happen again."

After eight days of continuous success, Aquila woke them from their slumber. "Animals, present yourselves."

Having slept with the blindfolds on, Fox and Bear jumped from their beds, stood at attention, and saluted—all without stumbling into one another. "Hunter!" they said in unison.

"Animals, where am I?" Aquila asked, and his voice gave him away. A good thing, too, because his scent was far fainter than Owl's. He smelled of aloe and pine smoke.

Taking a moment to be sure, Bear replied, "Seven steps forward and three steps aside, Hunter."

"Fox, where does Owl stand?"

Fox paused, sniffing the air without smelling a hint of bergamot. She smelled again, considering the idea that Owl might have changed her perfume. Yet Fox could smell nothing aside from Bear's musk and Aquila's scent. "She's not in this room, Hunter."

"Are you sure?"

Fox didn't hesitate—hesitation meant death. "Yes, Hunter."

Aquila let out a small laugh. "Foxes have keen noses, no?" He paused. "Here is my final question. Animals, what do I hold in my hand?"

Fox sniffed but smelled nothing strange, listened but heard nothing. Was this another trick? She waited for Bear to answer first, but he remained silent.

"You will both answer on three. One, two, three."

"A sword?" Bear asked.

"Air," Fox said.

Aquila tsked, not pleased but not furious either. "Why a sword, Bear?"

"You wear one on your hip, Hunter."

"The same could be said of my clothes, but I assure you I am not naked. Think harder next time. Fox, why air?"

"Every pocket holds air, even when it holds something else, Hunter," Fox replied. "It doesn't matter if you are holding anything or not, you still hold air in your hand."

"A cunning answer from a cunning Fox, but an empty one," Aquila said. "Remove your blindfolds, Animals."

Fox and Bear removed the blindfolds and squinted as light shined in through the windows. "Now, what do I hold in my hand?" Fox's eyes adjusted, revealing the truth. Aquila held a necklace with teeth she couldn't immediately identify. Her hands instinctively crept to her own neck, worried that the Hunter had taken her necklace, but her fox teeth were still in place.

"Would either of you have ever guessed this necklace?" Aquila asked.

Quietly, they both shook their heads.

"Nor would I expect you to, not without being able to see my hands. But this is an important lesson: even if you listen through silence and see through darkness, you are still missing key information."

Aquila held the necklace aloft so that Fox could see it better. The teeth were definitely larger than a fox's or even a Mouse's. "Before I became the Hunter, I was Tiger. These are my teeth." Aquila fondly brushed the necklace with a free hand. "Though your senses and instincts are strong, they're still not enough to survive in a world of Mice. That's why you must *know* your enemy. Know their strengths, their weaknesses, their families, their connections, and even their personalities. Once you know that, you'll know how they think, how they act. You'll know Mice better than they know themselves—and with that knowledge, you can kill them."

CHAPTER TWENTY-EIGHT

Fox sat on a branch of an ancient tree in the forest beyond Aquila's villa. Though they were only three miles past the tree line, it was still the farthest she'd been from the Pack in two years. The canopy had blotted out the sun, and the thickets had silenced the wind, but Fox didn't mind the hushed darkness. She'd long grown used to it after these two years as an Animal. So long as she had Bear, it didn't matter where she was. She leaned closer to him on the branch so that her shoulder rested on his upper arm.

Knowing one's enemy required surveillance, stalking, and hiding. Sitting in a tree felt pointless, but until prey passed by on the game trail beneath them or activated one of the various traps they'd hidden throughout the woods, they waited. Sometimes, hours passed before either of them would move a muscle. Patience was key to this third tenet. So was information.

To prepare herself for hunting, Fox gorged herself on the herbalism, zoology, and anatomy texts in the library. Yet those tomes were second to Aquila's personal scriptures on discipline, obedience, and predator-prey relationships. Fox and Bear memorized his writings and were quizzed daily on his teachings. They paid steep prices for mistakes: starvation, sleep deprivation, and group hostility.

Bear had failed such tests far more often than Fox, though she'd often flunked on purpose out of solidarity.

Once Owl had deemed them knowledgeable enough, they'd delved into these woods. At first, for only an hour at a time, working their way toward several hours a day.

Squirrels and rabbits had been the first creatures they'd stalked. Anything Fox and Bear could use to kill them, they learned: where they ate, where they slept, and even where they congregated. Squirrels and rabbits, like all Mice, had preset patterns they followed, and it was simply a matter of corrupting routines: baiting traps with their favorite foods, laying snares outside their dens, and capturing females to lure the males closer. Those they killed, Fox and Bear skewered and roasted over fires.

Then came bigger game. The turkeys, hogs, and deer were easier to hunt despite being faster. Larger snare traps, but the same principles. All that changed was speed and location. Those they killed were field dressed and carried back to the villa to be prepared for dinner.

Today was no different. They'd placed their traps based on the patterns of the native turkey population and spent the last hour above this game trail, waiting for one to wander by. Some might've found it boring, but compared to the violence and pain haunting most of her life, Fox basked in the pleasure of sitting on a branch with her best friend.

Fox sighed, the sound echoing far more than she'd expected. Bear raised an eyebrow at her. *Something wrong?*

Fox shook her head, though she smirked at the earlier thought. *Sitting with my best friend... Bear.* Had there really been a time when she'd hated him? Sailing across the Drowned Sea on the *Constable* felt like a lifetime ago. Perhaps it was. Fox felt like a far different person than Steward. Bear differed from Taran, too, though he'd never outgrown his stubbornness. Not that she wanted him to.

"What?" Bear whispered, his voice huskier now that he'd gone through puberty, though it had already been deep before. He *did* sound like a bear, especially when he snored. When she woke him up in the mornings too. From the way he complained and grumbled, one would have thought he was hibernating.

"Just reminiscing," Fox said, swinging her feet slowly. "Don't worry about it."

"About what?" Bear asked.

"So stubborn," she teased, flashing him a smile. "I'm just thinking about us. Who we used to be... You used to hate me, remember?"

Bear grunted, embarrassed. "Yeah. Didn't like many people then. Still don't... You hated me, too, you know."

"Only because you hated me first," Fox said, shifting her shoulder to nudge his arm. She'd have punched him lightly, but at this height, she feared any sudden movements. "Why did you hate me?"

"Easier to hate somebody else than yourself," Bear said, and Fox stared at him in wonder. He frowned. *"What?"*

"You, Bear. You just... surprise me sometimes. Most of the time you're cursing and struggling to read, but other times, you say something like that."

"I ain't smart, but I ain't stupid."

Fox nodded, knowing innately what he meant. Bear had never been good with numbers or letters, but he understood life far better than most. *Alley smart,* as the urchins of the Chasm had often said. He was the worst liar Fox had ever met, but his ability to cut through deception was second to none. Except when it came to her. Bear trusted Fox completely, but she lied to him every day. *I'm a girl. No matter how close we are, no matter how I feel, I can't tell him. And if he ever found out...*

Fox could imagine his betrayed expression too easily. "You're far from stupid, Bear," she said, looking away.

He only grunted at that, and Fox mimicked him, trying to lighten the mood. Eventually, they returned to a peaceful, amiable silence until she heard a high-pitched whistle in the distance—the signal to return to the villa.

Bear tapped Fox's leg before shifting his weight and clambering down the tree. She followed, unsheathing her talan as her feet hit the ground. Fox didn't expect trouble, but with Aquila and Owl, she knew better than to let her guard down. Behind every tree could be another trap.

They crept across the game trail, avoiding the dry leaves and droppings, but after walking a mile, Fox halted. Bear paused beside her, trusting her instincts. Fox gestured to him to listen by tugging at her ear. She heard a muffled bleat in the distance. Probably the death throes of a deer caught in a snare. Yet there was something off about the noise...

Fox left the trail, and Bear followed with a hand on her back out of habit. They traced the sound back to its source: a wounded and gagged Mouse.

The man was bound to a tree and had his hands nailed overhead. Blood dripped from his palms down onto the burlap sack covering his face. He'd been stripped of all but his underwear, revealing the nautical tattoos and the Dagger identifying him as a Cutthroat. On the ground at his feet was an ivory-handled whip. A Fleshlord.

Fox took several hasty steps backward. Fear scuttled along her neck and down her arms as she remembered Skulls, slaveholds, and auction houses.

She touched a finger to the back of her neck, where the Tooth had been seared into her skin.

Then Bear nudged her, drawing her attention to the auction house placard hanging from the man's neck. From it dangled a long note. The heading read: *Does he deserve to die?*

Beneath it was a list of nineteen crimes, written in Aritrastan, Corinthian, and Marcellian—the dead language spoken before the creation of the Corinthian Empire. Fox could read and speak all three thanks to Owl's tutelage, but she didn't enjoy reading the list. This Mouse's crimes included raping, pillaging, and murder.

The nineteenth crime caught her by surprise: *Guilty of enslaving Fox and Bear, whipping them thrice, and branding their necks.*

"It can't be," Fox whispered. "Captain Horace?"

As if recognizing the name, the hooded man jerked, uttering a muffled yelp. He thrashed, but with his hands nailed to the tree, he could only squirm.

Fox felt no sympathy. She turned to Bear, who had just finished reading the note. Death and rage danced in his eyes. He asked, "You think it's really him?"

Palms slick, Fox ripped the bag from the man's head. He was ugly, his nose squashing inward and eyes bulging outward. His black hair could have been mistaken for a bird's nest, and his beard was just as long. Though he no longer wore his nice clothes or rancid perfume, there was no mistaking that scar crossing Captain Horace's forehead.

"It *is* him," Fox said, awed.

Bruises covered Horace's face and a knot of flesh rose on the right side of his temple. Blood dripped from his crushed nose, mostly dried. A gag had been tied around his mouth.

Horace winced as his eyes adjusted to the light, moaning as he noticed the talan in Fox's hand. He struggled harder, which only made more blood drip from his palms, which triggered more of Fox's memories. She rubbed her wrists where the manacles had scarred her.

"What was it you said to me? I'd pick crops until I was a withered old man, and then I'd die alone and forgotten. Don't you remember that?" Fox asked, thumbing the edge of her blade as hatred filled her eyes, lungs, and heart. She'd killed men before, but always out of self-defense. Today would be different.

Captain Horace shook his head, eyes wide with terror. He choked on the gag in his mouth, which was kept in place by the rag tied around his head.

Fox analyzed him. Horace was scrawny, short, and ugly. Not strong like an Animal, but pasty and weak. Had she really been afraid of him?

Steward had been afraid, but I'm not Steward, Fox thought. "You thought you could just take whatever you want from us, and there'd be no consequences," she continued, flipping the talan around her index finger. "What do you think now?"

Beside her, Bear tested the whip, expertly cracking it in the air. Neither had enjoyed using whips, but Aquila had trained them on many weapons. When Bear flicked the whip a second time, Horace flinched at the sound, and a half-choked moan escaped from his lips despite the rag.

"We got three lashes each," Bear said. "How many do you think Horace gets?"

"At least six," Fox replied, stuffing the note into the pocket of her tunic.

"I was thinking a hundred," Bear said, cracking the whip again.

Captain Horace moaned again, attempting and failing to form words with the gag.

Fox ignored him. "Why don't we haggle? Fleshlords like haggling, don't they? I'll start at ten lashes."

"One hundred lashes," Bear replied.

"Twenty."

"Ninety lashes."

"Thirty."

"Eighty lashes."

"Forty."

"Seventy lashes."

"Fifty."

"Sixty lashes, and that's my final offer. I won't go any lower than that," Bear said without a trace of amusement.

"Sixty lashes, then. But only if we take out his gag," Fox said, matching his tone. "This time, we get to hear him scream."

"Done." Bear strode over and ripped the gag from the Fleshlord's mouth.

Captain Horace immediately said, "Listen. If you let me go, I'll give you fifty sols! *Each!* I'll—"

Bear slugged him across the jaw, and a tooth flew from Horace's mouth, reminding Fox of Tomlin. By how Bear froze, he'd had the same thought. But instead of breaking down, Bear gripped the whip tighter and asked, "What was it you said? Oh, that's right. 'I'll take the lashes.'"

"Wait. Let's talk about this," Captain Horace said. "I can get you more money. At least two hundred—"

Bear cracked the whip into Horace's stomach. Then Fox went, slicing his nose and cheek. Bear caught him on the ear, ripping it partway off. Then Horace screamed and didn't stop. Not that it helped him.

Fox and Bear traded off several dozen times, ripping into the Fleshlord's skin. Red gashes cut across his head, chest, and arms. Fox had expected herself to be revolted by the sight of it, but she didn't. Why should an Animal care about the suffering of a Mouse? Horace was beneath her—beneath them both. And he deserved it. Fox cracked him again and again, but the whip lost its charm. She needed to be closer.

Dropping the whip and stalking toward half-conscious Horace, she whispered, "How many lives have you ruined? How many children have you sold? How many families separated?" She brought the blade to his neck, cutting a shallow line in it. Enough to hurt but not to kill. Not yet, at least. "You know something, Bear? We're missing something here... A *brand*."

Fox lashed out with the blade, lungs howling as she carved a brand into his heart. A triangle with a long line at its top—the Tooth. She sliced all the way to the bones of his rib cage, but it wasn't enough. Far from it. She branded him again on the forehead. Then on the stomach. The hands. The—

Bear put a hand on her shoulder. "Fox."

Fox blinked, looking at the mess beneath her, then at her own ragged, shaking hands, whose skin had peeled away during the onslaught. She thought of Mouse and stumbled backward, collapsing against Bear. Putting her arms around him, she let out the anger and fury, letting it turn to tears. He held her stalwartly.

When Fox finally let go, Bear took his turn. Instead of a blade, he donned a pair of knuckledusters and bashed the Fleshlord's face in far worse than he had Tomlin's. Horace's jaw was only hanging on by skin at the end. Judging by the dents, Horace's skull was cracked in a dozen places too.

Blood dribbled from his swelled-shut eyes, broken nose, and torn ears. Still not good enough.

Fox slit his throat and then stabbed him through the heart just to be sure that he was dead. Her only regret was that the sea was dozens of miles away. She'd have preferred to curse him and make him one of the Drowned. But she could curse him here, too, and let the vultures eat his corpse. It still wasn't enough, but nothing ever would be. *It will have to do.*

When Fox looked back, Bear was on his knees. "Do you know what Tomlin said to me before I killed him?" he asked so quietly that even she had trouble hearing him.

Fox kneeled beside him, putting her arm around him. "No. What?"

"He *asked* me to kill him. Squalling begged me to do it. He said, 'I want to be with Jarrel.' Kept saying it over and over. No fear. No anger. No sadness. Just a smile. A squalling *smile*. Like I'd saved his life—all's I did was bash his head in with my fists... I see that smile every time I close my eyes." Bear shuddered and leaned against the tree, uncaring of Horace's bleeding corpse beside him. "I couldn't understand it. Why he begged. Why he smiled. But I get it now. You're as much a part of me as my own heart, Fox. And I don't know what I'd do if I lost you—"

"You won't lose me. Ever." Fox said, hugging him. "We're in this together, and that won't ever change."

"Whatever you do, wherever you go, I'll follow you. Even if it's to the Black Trench—the *Core*. I'd squalling follow you anywhere... You have my strength, if nothing else."

"That's all I'll ever need, Bear," she said, resting her forehead against his.

Leaving the Fleshlord's body to rot, they eventually walked back to the villa. Owl and Aquila were waiting for them at the door.

"Well?" Aquila asked, smiling confidently.

"He deserved to die, Hunter," Fox said. Bear only nodded.

"I'm so very proud of you both."

And any sense of doubt or guilt fled away with those words.

They killed more Fleshlords in that forest in the following days and months. Mostly men, but sometimes women. Sometimes teenagers no older than Lion.

Then the Fleshlords were replaced by Corinthian servants, each having a subsequently lighter list of offenses.

Finally, a day came where a man had been tied up in the forest without a list of crimes. Just four words: *He deserves to die.*

And when the Animals returned to the villa, Aquila asked, "Well?"

"He deserved to die, Hunter," Fox and Bear said in unison.

"Good. Very good," Aquila smirked. "Then it is time for the true test."

Chapter Twenty-Nine

Arya swayed and danced on the porch of Madame Nelly's brothel. Like the other girlies, she wore vibrant makeup to appear older than seventeen. But Arya had already been a girlie for six years. Her career started in the alleyways of Port Arden to the west of Alira. There she'd been abused, deceived, and mugged. But she'd survived, worked in gangs with other ashgirls to make sure that clients paid what was owed. Whenever they refused to pay once, their girlie gang *took*. Clients didn't refuse twice.

Three years ago, she'd gained the attention and tutelage of Nelly Bronson—Ol' Nelly, as the girlies affectionately called her. With the old prostitute's guidance, Arya developed the skills necessary to become the most sought after girlie in the brothel.

Today, she wore yellow taffeta—an evening dress, though the sun had just risen. Its low neckline revealed cleavage, and the material pressed so tightly against her hips that she didn't dare turn quickly for fearing of ripping it.

Plastering a smile on her face, Arya called out to the merchants, sailors, and servants making their way down to the docks. Her solicitations came in three forms:

"I think you left something inside, darling," for the young and naive.

"If you think I look good now, honey, wait until you step inside," for the old and salty.

"I could use a real man like you in my life, handsome," for the burly men in the prime of their lives.

Most ignored her, but a few told her they'd be back later. Some would, most wouldn't. She didn't mind that, but she minded a bespectacled man calling her a whore.

Arya had thrown a brick at him, which knocked the glasses off of his head. Then he'd staggered off, crying. Arya knew he'd come back for revenge, either with gallowmen or friends, but she didn't care. Neither did the other girlies. They paid the gallowmen to look the other way and held their own against everyone else.

To too many people, a girlie was only flesh. Not a woman in desperate straits. Not a woman without support. But Arya sacrificed her body—not her mind. Not her spirit. That could never be taken from her, no matter what her clients—or anybody else—thought.

Nor could they steal her other life, the one she dreamed of as she slept. One where her parents hadn't died, where she lived as freely as the rich widows, not knowing or caring where the wind took her. More than that security, she wished for a life of freedom. A life at sea.

From the porch, Arya could see the blue ocean between the other buildings. The untamed, uncaring sea would be her ticket out of Arden. Then she could start over, some place where people wouldn't look down on her. She'd long tired of women's sneers and men's leers—people born to better circumstances assumed she could quit and do something else if she wanted.

None except the girlies understood how difficult it was to leave the profession. The only way was to disappear from Arden altogether, otherwise rumors and sullied reputations would destroy whatever new life a girlie had spun for herself.

But Arya knew the truth that most girlies didn't: nearly everyone who left came back. It was far easier to return to the flesh business than to stay out. The safety of the brothel, the camaraderie of the girlies, and the attention of the clients were drugs as addicting as chard. The only real way to ensure that she would never return to the brothels was to make herself unattractive—unwanted.

There was no better way to do that than tattoos.

That having ink beneath skin repelled most clients always seemed stupid to Arya, considering that eighty percent of her clientele were tattooed sailors themselves, but it was the bitter truth.

Unable to stomach another day of derision, Arya left Madame Nelly's brothel—the only home she ever knew—in the middle of her shift, ignoring the questions of the other girlies. Near the shore, she found a grizzled artist who gave her a tattoo of two snakes devouring a star at the base of her throat.

Without saying goodbye or collecting her belongings, Arya departed on a merchant ship. With Arden disappearing on the horizon, she thought, *I never belonged anyway.*

◄─◇─►

Arya lied on her back on Greeley's filthy bed aboard the *Crescent.* The brig was far smaller than Jericho's *Cutlass* or her own frigate, the *Star,* which Greeley never stopped mentioning. Back turned, he snored beside her, but Arya was far from sleep.

Trophies decorated the walls of his captain's quarters: oil paintings, gilded mirrors, lacquered armoires, silken rugs, and fur pelts. But his more prized trophies were on the nightstand: a golden earring, a couple of silver rings, and a copper necklace. Aside from his white cutlass, the most treasured prizes were locked in the drawer: a human ear, a few fingers, and even a tongue. All rotting. Greeley said he *liked* the nauseating smell, and as they were so far from shore, no flies hovered around the rotting meat.

What bothered her more was Greeley being the only legionnaire with a four-post bed. Not even Lilyth had one, Arya knew, but then, Lilyth didn't sleep. Or eat. Or drink. Her connection to Eo had made her more than human—something divine.

Laying in Greeley's bed, Arya felt less than human. A piece of flesh. Though she pretended to enjoy his touch, she was mostly numb. The physical contact reminded her of Madame Nelly's, which gave rise to unwanted memories.

The look of gaudy clients as they walked in through the main door. The sound of flutists and lyrists playing softly in the foyer. The smell of expensive perfume wafting through the halls. The feel of extravagant silk bedding in themed bedrooms. The taste of decadent pastries that Madame Nelly made for her favorite girlies—for Arya.

By joining the Red Legion, Arya thought that she'd be a true legionnaire, that she'd finally belong. But Arya was still an outsider. Though she toiled and fought alongside them, most legionnaires focused on her chest instead of her face. Not leers as they'd been in Arden, but the men still looked at her as if she were naked.

Especially Greeley. All he saw was flesh. Flesh of women to covet and flesh of men to rend.

Greeley was primal, moving and fighting and killing on instinct, but Arya couldn't bring herself to hate him. He'd unlocked her manacles and freed her. That, she would never forget it.

But Arya's true loyalty was to Lilyth, who had ordered Greeley to release her. Lilyth had accepted Arya for the woman she was—not another piece of flesh. In that respect, Lilyth and Ol' Nelly had been the same.

Arya had shown Lilyth her loyalty by accepting Greeley as her client and sleeping with him to protect Kendrik. In return, Lilyth had made her the Red Eye and given her a frigate to command. She'd been freed and made a hero of the legion. Or should have been.

If anything, becoming the Red Eye had made legionnaires respect her less. Most suspected she'd slept with Greeley and ridiculed her for it. And despite everything she'd done for the legion—for Lilyth, even *Eo*—Kendrik had been the one to remain healthy while the Dusk Affliction swept through their ranks, killing forty and infecting everyone else. While Lilyth had been praying to Eo to end their suffering, Kendrik had taken care of the legion. Those well enough to help did as he commanded, and those too weak to move begged for his aid. Kendrik had been the hero of the legion. Again.

Until Kendrik was dead, he'd stand between Arya and the freedom she needed. After all, she didn't want to covet Lilyth as Greeley did. Arya simply wanted to *be* her. To not only be accepted but admired. Loved. *Seen.*

They will see me for who I truly am, Arya thought, as she turned in the bed and stared at Greeley's back. *My strength is different from yours, Red Hand, but between us, I'm stronger. I know you—I've known men like you all my life. You'll use me until I'm no longer useful. Until my flesh is too familiar. Then you'll discard me—or try to. But when we kill Kendrik, you'll take the fall. Then I will be Lilyth's Red Hand, Red Heart, and Red Eye, and you'll be just a corpse in the waves.*

Arya and Greeley rowed from the *Crescent* to the *Cutlass* under the cover of night and Kovu's Warning—the first rain of the wet season and a harbinger of the coming hurricanes. Those were a concern for later. For now, Arya still had to pass through these syren-infested waters, board Kendrik's ship, and kill him without being seen. Even then, she had to pin the blame on Greeley and return to the *Star* before anybody noticed her absence.

Difficult as this would be, it was Arya's best chance of removing both rivals in one play. Now that Kendrik was captaining his own ship, there were few opportunities to speak with him, let alone kill him. Even on raids, they were separated. Exchanges offered small windows of opportunity, but normally they took place on the beach under Lilyth's watchful eyes.

Only because of Kovu's Warning had the amassed legionnaires returned to their ships to pray and sleep in blessed security. As there was no expectation of being attacked on an uninhabited island during a storm, nobody was on watch.

Arya's plan was a simple one, she knew, but she had little other choice. Greeley was too narrow-minded to come up with a half-decent plan, which meant she didn't need it to be a brilliant one. Her success hinged on scapegoating Greeley, and if the plot was too intelligent, Lilyth would be suspicious that Greeley came up with it on his own.

However, with such a simple plan, far more could go wrong—especially if Greeley tried to kill her as soon as Kendrik was dead.

I'll have to be quicker, she thought, feeling for the knife at her hip as Greeley continued rowing. With each pull of the oars, he huffed, and the ever-present snarl on his face deepened.

The bow rose and fell through the choppy waves, spraying sea mist onto Arya, though she stayed dry beneath her oilskin waxed hat, oilskin cloak, and tarred leather boots. Peering through the light fog, she stared at the other six looming ships, whose black silhouettes obscured the stars. The *Orb* was a small sloop, but the others were all bigger. Two brigs, a schooner, and three frigates.

Eo provides, she thought.

The Red Legion was growing fast, with each raid giving them more supplies, ships, and slaves. Former slaves, that was. They all were given Lilyth's freedom. Those who hadn't been killed by the Dusk Affliction, anyway.

But still no other women, Arya thought, disappointed. She'd expected the Fleshlords, of all Cutthroats, to have a few, but no such luck. Perhaps when Greeley and Kendrik were dead, Arya could have the *Star* crewed by women. An entire ship filled with girlies and fighters just like her.

I'd be seen then, Arya thought, wishing for it more than anything else.

"Look at it," Greeley muttered, spitting the words as Arya followed his gaze to the three-masted *Cutlass.* The masts scratched the sky a hundred feet above the deck. "The *Cutlass's* got more cannons than the *Crescent.* Kendrik's even got a bigger crew than me too. More men, more power."

And a schooner under his control, Arya thought.

"And *a schooner* under his control," Greeley grumbled. "He's got the *Cutlass* and the *Riptide.* And what do I have? The *Crescent* and the *Orb*—a tiny sloop that ain't worth shit in a real fight."

Arya wore a mask of sympathy but was bored. She'd heard this argument too many times. *Sloops are fast and maneuverable. You just don't know how to sail.*

Though she'd been a girlie in her early years, Arya had learned the ways of the sea, spending a decade on the waves as a Guardian before her capture. The men she'd worked with *had* seen her then, if only because they hadn't known she was a woman. Soon, she would have that feeling again, but she'd be free to be herself. When she stood at Lilyth's side along with her female crew, she'd have everything she wanted.

I only have to put up with him for a few more hours, Arya thought, noticing that Greeley was staring at her chest instead of her face.

"Kendrik dies tonight," Greeley grumbled. "I don't care how. I don't care when. He dies."

"He will, and nobody will be the wiser," Arya said, hiding a frown as she put a hand on his knee. Greeley hadn't even bothered to ask how they'd get away with killing Kendrik, which made her more suspicious of his intentions. *He's going to kill me if he can.*

Though her thoughts were dark, Arya smiled, "After tonight, we'll both have what we want. Kendrik will be gone, you'll be closer to Lilyth, and I'll be closer to you."

Greeley grunted again, and Arya leaned away to give him space. She spent the rest of the brief journey watching for syrens. There was no way to know how many lurked beneath the obsidian surface, but she'd seen them often enough to know that wherever there was one, there were a dozen more.

Others often whispered about their long claws and gaping maws, but what had always terrified her was their skin—or lack thereof. Gray scales covered syrens from head to toe, and each was sharpened to a point. They were hard like metal armor, and just by *touching* a sailor, they could rip the skin from their faces.

The tails themselves were no less dangerous. Just one giant muscle with sharpened bone spurs protruding from their scales like spiked clubs. One hit from a tail meant death.

Any sailor stuck in the water with a syren didn't have a chance of fighting or even swimming away. Even in a rowboat, odds were far from good. *Hopefully, they're still swimming around Lilyth*, Arya thought, hoping that the rumors were true.

Every legionnaire she'd spoken with had spotted at least one near the *Jericho*, which was stationed farther up the coast. And if only half of the rumors were to be believed, *dozens* lurked in the shadows beneath that ship. Nowhere else.

Between the rain rippling the water's surface and the missing moon, it was impossible to see anything below, but she could still feel something—possibly someone—watching her. No matter where she looked, the invisible eyes were always there. Above her. Below her. East. West. Everywhere. If not the syrens, then who was watching? Other deep terrors? Eo? *Lilyth?*

A deep pit of worry yawned wider in Arya's stomach, but she said nothing because they were nearing the *Cutlass*. They couldn't afford to be overheard. Instead, she waited as Greeley navigated the rowboat to the anchor line near the bow. Arya tapped Greeley's arm twice before grabbing the soggy rope and hefting herself up it and over the gunwale. There were no lanterns on the deck. No movement, laughter, or noise. Completely deserted. The entire crew was below deck to avoid the rain, either praying or sleeping.

If that wasn't a sign that the Goddess was on her side, then Arya didn't know what was. *Bless you, Eo.*

Arya tugged the rope twice, the signal that Greeley could come up. As he climbed, she thought, *Kill Kendrik, frame Greeley, escape with the rowboat. Eo, please protect me.*

They slunk across the deck to the stern and climbed down a ladder to the gun deck. To one side, a hundred legionnaires slept in hammocks. To the other, a small hallway reserved for the ship's officers—Kendrik's quarters were at its end.

Greeley pointed at himself and then at the door. Pausing for a moment, he then pointed at Arya, raised his hand in a halting gesture, and pointed at his own eye. *I'll go inside and kill him. You stay here and keep an eye out for trouble.*

Arya nodded. This made things far easier for her to pin the blame on him and escape.

As Greeley disappeared into Kendrik's quarters, Arya descended to the deserted orlop deck. Then she pulled out a flint rod, her knife, and kindling. Striking them together, the kindling sparked aflame. Arya departed, leaving the fire smoking near the ladder. The smoke would rise, alerting legionnaires. But by lighting the fire on the orlop deck, she had more time to escape. She climbed back to the main deck to steal the rowboat and return to the *Star*, but she stopped when a voice murmured from the quarterdeck.

Arya glanced about. There was no movement, no lanterns. Still, she could hear that voice. Quietly, Arya climbed the stairs and found a legionnaire leaning against the gunwale, head tilted to the stars. Kendrik.

Squalls... She panicked for a moment. With Kendrik here, Greeley might've already returned from the room and discovered her fire. *I can still fix this. Greeley will still be blamed if I kill Kendrik and escape.*

Arya pulled out her dagger and crept closer behind Kendrik. When she was within five feet of him, she prepared herself to lunge just as his whisperings reached her ears.

"...had to discipline one of my legionnaires today for disrespecting the Red Eye—called her the Red Thigh. I hit him so hard that he was snoring before he hit the ground. Almost broke my hand."

Arya flinched. *Kendrik stood up for me?* She leaned forward, trying to hear more.

Kendrik laughed at some unheard joke. "I keep forgetting that you already know all of this, Jericho. Forgive me. I just get frustrated with their disrespect. Arya and I have had our differences, but she is a legionnaire—one of our *sisters*—and that makes her deserving of our strength and loyalty. Yet our brothers treat her as lesser."

Kendrik paused, fiddling with the copper flintlock Lilyth had gifted him. "There was a reason that Lilyth named her above all others. You want to know what I think? Lilyth named her the Red Eye because she sees the world—sees *Eo*—in a way that men can't. In a way that neither I nor Greeley can. We're fighters, but she's more like Lilyth. A fighter *and* a thinker. We need more legionnaires like her."

Arya hunched forward, like she'd been shot in the stomach. *He's defending me, and I'm trying to kill him.*

"With Lilyth leading the way, and Greeley and Arya by my side, the legion will be unstoppable. We have seven ships now and hundreds of legionnaires, but this is just the beginning, Jericho. And I think Arya is exactly who we need to share Eo's truth."

Arya frowned, then took two steps back and stared down at her knife. *All this time, I've wanted to be seen... And I almost killed the only legionnaire who actually sees me for who I am.* She shook her head, disgusted. *Is this how I'm going to get respect? By killing everybody who stands in my way? That's Greeley's way. Not mine. I'll find my own path.* Setting her chin, Arya sheathed her dagger and crept back down the stairs to the main deck only to find Greeley waiting for her at the bottom.

Squalls. Arya tried to think of a reason or a plan. She couldn't tell Kendrik that Greeley was here to kill him without revealing that she'd done the same. She definitely couldn't fight Greeley either. He was second only to Kendrik in the entire legion. And judging by how Greeley loomed, he already knew that she'd betrayed him. She couldn't seduce him, not this time. What then?

Greeley stalked forward with a knife out, and Arya enacted the next plan that came to mind: mutually assured destruction. She whispered, "Try anything, and I scream, Red Hand. We both die, and Kendrik *wins*." Greeley stopped in his tracks, cocking his head and hearing Kendrik up on the quarterdeck. Before he could try to assassinate Kendrik, she added, "Even if you kill me, Kendrik will still hear you coming. And if you try to kill him by yourself with just a sword, you'll lose. He's stronger than you. We both know it."

"Leave quietly, and I'll kill you a different day," Greeley said.

"No," Arya shook her head. "I'll fight you myself if you try to attack him."

"You wouldn't dare."

"Oh, I would. I'm stubborn that way." Arya flashed a smile. "So what's it going to be, Greeley? You want to die by my hand or Kendrik's?"

Silently, Greeley bolted for the rowboat. Arya's smile evaporated. By *not* ousting himself, Greeley could escape undetected, and Arya would be stuck on Kendrik's ship, looking guiltier than Kuma. *Squalls.*

Staying aboard the *Cutlass* wasn't an option. She looked around for another escape. One rowboat hung just over the side of the ship, held in place by a derrick. She snuck toward it as a legionnaire rung a bell below. Immediately, Kendrik charged down the quarterdeck's stairs and below deck to fight the flames.

Alone, Arya hacked at the ropes holding the boat in place. When they snapped, the boat fell to the water below. *Please let the syrens still be around Lilyth,* she prayed. With no other choice, Arya leaped from the side. She splashed into the cold black water beside the rowboat and immediately swam for the surface. Grabbing the lip of the boat, she threw herself inside and undercover before a syren could grab her.

None even tried.

With a sigh of relief, Arya picked up the oars and began the short solitary journey back to the *Star* in the distance.

For most of the trek back, Arya feared she'd be spotted, but legionnaires were too preoccupied by the fire to look her way. After she scuttled the boat and climbed back aboard her frigate, Arya felt a rush of relief. Then pride.

This was the first step on her new path: enacting change by supporting Kendrik and Lilyth. When the legion freed enough women, she'd strive to have an entirely female crew and serve as a role model. Eventually, the other legionnaires would come to see her as Kendrik did.

Try as many times as you want, Red Hand, Arya thought as she noticed Greeley still rowing back to his own ship. *So long as I live, you will* never *kill the Red Heart.*

CHAPTER THIRTY

Lilyth had ignored Kovu's Warning. Now a veritable storm was upon them. And with it came a loss of control. She couldn't deceive a storm, nor fight it. She simply had to endure, but she was so squalling tired of enduring.

Blinded by rain, deafened by wind, and frozen stiff by the cold, Lilyth held onto the mizzenmast with both hands as the *Jericho* plunged through the onslaught. The dark thunderheads crackled with lightning, striking through the ocean and into the Core. One arc pierced the waves only feet from the ship, illuminating the water's surface and the creatures lurking beneath. Tails in place of legs, clawed hands holding ropes and weaponry, and long, misshaped heads. Syrens.

According to myth, syrens attacked until everybody was dead or driven away, but these were different. They were waiting, watching for Lilyth to *do* something.

It unnerved her.

"Why are you still here?" Lilyth shouted, though the storm carried away her voice. High-velocity winds raked her ears and stinging rain ripped at her eyes, further sapping away her patience. "What could you possibly want?"

The syrens didn't respond, but Kuma did. The chained God bellowed with each strike of lightning, and His thunder nearly burst Lilyth's ear drums. Grunting, Lilyth turned her attention to her flagship.

The square sails had been replaced with tougher, thicker stormsails, which were only partially unfurled to reduce speed and help steer the ship through the waves. The three masts creaked and strained as the winds pressed against them with all their might, but the hundreds of ropes kept the masts secured from all sides.

Lilyth eyed the thirty-foot waves rising over the stern. Sea foam splashed onto the deck, threatening to engulf the legionnaires struggling to keep the ship from capsizing.

Haulers heaved lines as riggers adjusted the sails. Both groups were leashed to the masts and gunwales with safety lines. Even if they lost their footing, their tethers would keep them from being swept overboard. The difficulty was that they often had to untie and retie their safety ropes to the three masts to follow Lilyth's orders, which were relayed from person to person in the howling winds.

Lilyth growled as a few of her legionnaires lost their footing and the remaining haulers on the line struggled to rein in a sail. She fought her way down the quarterdeck and abandoned her safety rope. Sure-footed despite the slick deck, she hauled lines herself. While also assuring the crew, the task gave Lilyth something to hide her shaking hands. Twice she cut her palms on the coarse rope, and twice she gripped it more fiercely.

There is too much to do. I refuse to die here. I must endure. I will *endure.* Lilyth thought just as another wave crashed onto the deck.

The wall of water swept the helmsman and a few legionnaires over the gunwale. They still had their safety leashes on, so they weren't swept away. Yet with the helm unattended, the ship's wheel spun furiously to the right. The ship turned into another surging wave as Lilyth rushed back to the quarterdeck with three other haulers. She reached the spinning wheel and jammed her cutlass into the spokes to stop it from turning. As the other haulers joined her, they forced it back in the opposite direction, hand over fist.

I will endure even this, Kovu, she thought, gritting her teeth as the *Jericho* turned out of the wave before it could capsize them. Instead, it crashed over their stern, spraying the backs of her knees. *You cannot stop me. No one can.*

Leaving a legionnaire to hold the wheel steady, Lilyth charged to the gunwale to help those dangling overboard—she couldn't afford to waste soldiers before the raid on Corinthus.

Just as Lilyth reached down to pull the legionnaires back up, she heard the laughter. "Syrens! Get down!" she screamed, letting go of her believers and ducking. Others did, too, just before rusted tridents sailed through the wind.

Most of the weapons hit the hull or the rail at odd angles and clattered harmlessly back into the water. But one harpoon struck the helmsman in the stomach, ripping through his intestines and pinning him to the hull. His scream was lost beneath the wind and laughter. That squalling laughter. The syrens were beckoning to her, but she refused their call.

Lilyth could have thrown a knife to sever the kelp rope attached to the harpoon, but that would have been a waste of good steel. The helmsman was as good as dead anyway, and it was easier to sacrifice a dead man to satiate their hunger than give them a healthy soldier. So, she instead cut the safety rope that tied the helmsman to the mast.

The syrens' laughter grew louder as they tugged at their kelp rope, ripping the harpoon free of the hull. With a horrified moan, the helmsman dropped like an anchor. Then the syrens descended on him, dragging him beneath the waves and ripping him to pieces.

"Depth charges and shields!" Lilyth shouted. *"Now!"*

Legionnaires rushed to light and throw barrels of gunpowder overboard while others struggled to lift their brethren back onto the deck. More weapons sailed through the air, but a secondary line of legionnaires lifted shields to protect themselves.

Depth charges fell from the boat and exploded far below them, driving syrens away. But they'd come back. That's what Lilyth hated about the syrens. They were cunning as well as cruel. Syrens roved in their packs and waited for storms to weaken ships and crews. They could just as easily have disabled the rudder or ripped a hole through the hull with their coral axes. Instead, the syrens hurled tridents and picked off unaware legionnaires. Not because they were stupid, but for the sport of it.

As if they thought her army belonged to the sea—to them. Tithings.

Ruthless squalls, Lilyth thought angrily as she heaved yet another depth charge over the side. *They can have their pound of flesh so long as I get Tibur.*

When the wind changed, Lilyth commanded the new helmsman to sail straight with the waves as the swells became more monstrous. Though her crew followed her commands, there were fewer men now. Too chaotic to tell just how many, though.

How many have I lost to this damned sea? Lilyth wondered.

Looking behind her, Lilyth caught sight of her other six ships, which faced similar difficulties. Kendrik's *Cutlass* and Arya's *Star* were teetering through the waves, puny compared to the wroth sea. Greeley's two-masted *Crescent* was worse off, being smaller than the frigates. The *Orb*—the single-masted sloop also under his command—was in dire straits.

Grabbing her spyglass, Lilyth looked through the lens to see the struggling legionnaires aboard. On the *Crescent,* Greeley was shouting orders to his haulers, who were slipping and sliding across the wet deck. Furiously, Greeley grabbed one hauler, punched him in the face, and screamed at the others. When he could shout no longer, Greeley took the downed legionnaire's place on the lines and hauled with the rest of his crew. It was obvious how much they despised him.

On the *Star,* Arya commanded her crew from the helm, handling her own in the storm. Not a surprise. Having spent more years on the sea than Lilyth, Arya excelled at seafaring and navigation. Considering the crew listened to her orders without protest, Lilyth assumed they respected her more than they once had.

Turning her gaze to the *Cutlass,* Lilyth noticed Kendrik in the rigging—one of his subordinates gave commands from the helm. Rather than force another legionnaire to do it, the Red Heart adjusted the sails himself, which was the most dangerous job during a storm. Once again, Kendrik bore a sacrifice for the legion, but while his crew loved him for it, doing so was a mistake. Lilyth couldn't risk losing her most valuable pawn when an expendable legionnaire could have done the same job. But what could she do? Lilyth was too far away to stop him.

Don't fall, you stupid squall, Lilyth thought, cursing herself for getting caught in this storm—for losing control. She fought to keep her head, but around her, things were falling to pieces. Legionnaires were dying. Each mistake now meant another nineday, another *month* away from her family.

When a powerful wind—a true *squall*—tore across the ships, Lilyth heard a *crack!* as the *Orb's* mast broke in half. The ropes holding the mast in place snapped, and the fifty-foot piece of timber crashed onto the deck, punctured the hull, and fell overboard.

Another peel of laughter echoed around the *Jericho.* A flash of lightning revealed the tailed syrens abandoning her ship and swimming toward the crippled *Orb.* Lilyth could only watch as the damaged ship swiveled through the water, turning into the pounding waves. Another wave came down, flipping the sloop and capsizing it, sending dozens more men into the sea.

"No..." she whispered, clenching the gunwale. "No, no, *no.*"

Legionnaires bobbed in the sea and clung to barrels filled with false hope until syrens pulled them beneath the waves. Lightning strikes illuminated the gruesome feast.

At the rear of the fleet, Kendrik's *Cutlass* maneuvered around the wreckage and tossed ropes for legionnaires to grab onto and pull themselves aboard, but they didn't stand a chance. The syrens let the legionnaires climb halfway up the ropes before harpooning them and dragging their screaming bodies back into the water.

Months of training and supplies gone in an instant, Lilyth thought, pounding her fist against the rail. Sacrificing ill-trained men to get her zealots had been a tactical decision, but to lose those well-trained, well-equipped zealots to syrens and storms? Heart wrenching. She wanted to fight someone, to rip them apart, but she had to maintain control of herself while her legionnaires watched. *Just stick to the plan—six ships will be enough to take Cassius.*

Lilyth bit the inside of her cheek, drawing blood. The slight pain dragged her away from the darker pits of her mind, and she turned to move her safety rope from the mainmast to the foremast to join the legionnaires struggling near the bow. But just as she untied the leash, another wave knocked her to the deck.

Haulers cried out and reached for her but weren't close enough to help. Lilyth grabbed at planks and barrels in vain as the massive wave forced her into the gunwale and over the side of the ship.

Frantically, Lilyth groped the slick rail with one hand, holding on even as the water splashed over her head. The *Jericho* leaned with the weight of the waves, dipping her dangerously close to the sea. Lightning struck a few feet away, illuminating the syrens' outstretched hands, spider-thin arms, and webbed underarms. Where there had been a couple dozen before, Lilyth saw a writhing black mass beneath. An unfathomable number.

Lilyth's scream was stolen by her fear. Silently, she gripped the rail with her other hand and scrambled for purchase, using the barnacles for footholds. Lilyth expected to feel a harpoon in her back at any second. None came. No laughter either. Only booming thunder, crashing waves, and terrified legionnaires.

Her Chosen tossed out more depth charges, scattering the syrens beneath. Then they pulled at her hands. Just as the crew pulled her elbows above the rail, another wave caused the *Jericho* to list. Legionnaires stumbled, and the hands holding Lilyth slipped away. She grabbed the rail again before she could fall into the ocean.

Lilyth heard a thud and looked down at her chest, expecting to see a harpoon impaling her against the hull. Instead, the harpoon was a foot to her right at knee-level. She waited for the syrens to rip it from the hull and throw it again—or throw another harpoon, for that matter—but they didn't. The kelp rope remained slack. Lilyth swung over to it and stood on the length of rusted metal, jumping from it and diving back onto the ship.

Before the stumbling legionnaires could help her to her feet, Lilyth stood and turned to face the water. When lightning struck again, she couldn't see any syrens beneath the waves, though Lilyth could still feel them watching her from the deeper depths.

They saved me, Lilyth realized, though the thought didn't calm her.

Lilyth pondered those ideas as she rode out the rest of the storm. The waves settled as the thunderheads continued westward. Kuma's cries of anguish became quieter as lightning struck over the horizon.

The syrens do not matter, she decided as the *Jericho* sailed south through calmer waters. *All that matters is finding that old squall in Port Cassius. He will know the path through the Battered Reefs, and when he tells me of it, I will finally take Tibur.*

But first, Cassius will burn.

CHAPTER THIRTY-ONE

Fox walked through a market of Mice. Despite the heat of the Corinthian sun, she wore an orange kaftan to blend in with the crowd of merchants. Having hid her blue skin with a light layer of gray makeup, she wouldn't be mistaken for an Aritrastan. Instead, she was unassuming.

And armed to the teeth.

Though many merchants and even statesmen wore scimitars at their hips, Animals knew blades were to be felt, not seen. Six throwing knives were strapped on the vest beneath Fox's embroidered coat, and two longer anelace daggers were secured to the sides of her brown boots. Her talan hid in her right sleeve, its cold steel a comfort in this market. So was Bear's touch. He walked in-step with her, wearing a nearly identical outfit but hiding different weapons.

Fox sniffed and frowned at the city odor: death, rot, and feces. Alira had probably smelled similar, but she hadn't noticed it then. Now, it was all she could think about. *Mice belong in the city. Animals belong in the forest.*

Bear was frowning too. He put a hand inside his cloak on the handle of one of his hand axes. Fox put a hand on his shoulder, and he slowly released his hold on the weapon, whispering, "These Mice shit here and wipe their faces in it... It ain't right."

"Such are the ways of Mice, yes?" Aquila said, walking a few paces in front of the two Animals. Only the Hunter had accompanied Fox and Bear to Cassius, the rest of the Animals remaining at the villa or on their own Hunts. In place of a kaftan and vest, Aquila wore the traditional breastplate and leather skirt of guards and army veterans.

"Mice, yes, but not the ways of Animals," Fox said, as they followed the Hunter deeper into the city. Where he stepped, they followed. Where he gazed, they stared. Where he stopped, they halted.

The third time the Hunter stopped, it was in front of a bakery. He pretended to peruse the selection of pastries and instead looked at the reflection in the glass, revealing all the Mice behind them. "See that man across the street?"

Fox peered through the reflection and noticed a burly Corinthian butcher across the thoroughfare. He stood behind the pane of glass in his shop, wearing a bloodstained apron and hanging slabs of meat on hooks for his display. His chest was as large as a bull's, and his forearms were as meaty as a horse's hind legs. His clothes were stained from repeated wear, though he'd rolled his sleeves to keep them clean. Long hair tied in a ponytail trailed down his back, kempt despite his bloody profession.

"Animals, what does it take to know your enemy?" Aquila asked as he bought biscuits from the baker, handing one to both Fox and Bear.

"We gotta find out what their strengths and weaknesses are, and how they behave, Hunter," Bear said, tucking the biscuit into his sleeve rather than eat it. "We know where to cut, it's just a matter of when and how."

Aquila hummed, not displeased but not entirely satisfied. "Fox?"

"All creatures have patterns they follow, Hunter. Most live only to breed and keep their territory safe. Humans think they're different, but they aren't. They're Mice. We only have to find their habits and routines, and we'll know everything about them."

"How do we determine the routine?"

"Stalking, Hunter," the Animals said in unison.

"How long does it take?"

"As long as necessary, Hunter."

"Discover this one's routine, then. Figure out what he loves, what he fears. But do not allow yourselves to be seen."

Fox and Bear nodded without further question, as they'd been trained to.

Fox twitched as they neared the Corinthian cathedral.

Larger than the governmental buildings and even the gladiatorial arena, the cathedral's grand spires of metal and stone scraped the clouds. Stained glass windows depicted warm saints, though the structure was gilded with veins of cold wealth. Two pillars at the corners of the main building rose like horns, beckoning to the sun that rose between them in the morning hours, unseen sacristans ringing bells from their peaks. An enormous golden brazier burned between the twin towers, the pillar of fire rising to lick the edge of the simmering sun.

Fox's eyes narrowed at the white-robed figure standing at the brazier's edge, recognizing her as the woman who'd freed only a single slave from her group when she'd first arrived in Cassius. The Divine Virgin. Four sunguards surrounded her. Fox wished they'd all fall from the walls of the cathedral. Had she been within range, she might have thrown a dagger to speed the process along. *That's what they deserve.*

The idea became more enticing as she joined the growing line of Corinthian men in front of the entrance, who all wore starched white tunics and white breeches. Orange bolo ties and robes were draped over the shoulders of nicer denizens, but the rest were shabby by comparison. Standing in a separate line, the Corinthian women wore dresses, their braided hair trailing down their backs like a second spine. Children stood with their mothers, picking at their uncomfortable clothes and kicking at the dirt.

Like all others who'd arrived before him, the butcher kneeled once he reached the door, offering a quick prayer to the symbol of the burning sun that was lavishly carved above the temple's massive doors. He pressed two fingers to his forehead before covering his lips. Then he stood and entered.

When it was Bear's turn, he kneeled but remained silent as he touched his forehead and then his lips. As Fox approached, she frowned and stood straight. Bear glared at her, and she relented. Bending one knee, she kept it a quarter of an inch from the ground, just low enough so nobody else could notice the difference. *I won't kneel to a silent God,* Fox thought as she moved her fingers quickly over her face, closer to swatting flies than worshiping. *You're not worthy of my praise.*

Chin held high, Fox ignored the two altar boys standing by each side of the door as they tried to bless her with water and smoke. They joined the men in the small foyer while the women and children were escorted off into a separate chamber. Doors to the right and left remained closed and guarded by sacristans, so Fox continued straight, noticing the extravagant rugs and golden candelabras that guided her path. She wrinkled her nose as incense overwhelmed her, holding her breath as she passed through the fug of frankincense into the altar room.

The vaulted ceilings extended as high as the tips of the *Constable's* mainmast or even the Chasm's sea cliffs at the center, where a stained-glass dome scattered white, orange, yellow, and red shades of light across the stone floor. Two levels of balconies jutted from the walls on pillars of stone, reserved for the sacristans, priests, and nuns. With suns carved into the arms and legs, communal wooden pews separated the followers on the ground floor, angled around the priest's alcove on the far wall, where a massive glass sun hung above an altar surrounded by candles.

As the butcher took a seat in the pew closest to the altar, the Animals found the closest seats to the door. Though the cushions were plush, Fox sat stiffly, overly aware of the Corinthian man sitting beside her. She wasn't intimidated by this Mouse, who was barely taller than herself, smelled of cheese, and habitually bounced his leg, but Fox remained uncomfortable.

This is no place for an Animal, she thought, clenching her fists. *I want to go home to the Pack.*

"Are you okay, young man?"

Fox turned to the Corinthian man who'd spoken. "Of course. By Deitan's grace, I am saved," she responded in formal Corinthian, as was the custom that Owl had taught her.

"By Deitan's grace, indeed," the Corinthian man said, offering a genuine smile before breaking eye contact and facing toward the altar.

Fox's eyes roved past him and tracked the high priest walking down the aisle. The gray-skinned minister had a white beard and thinning eyebrows, the wrinkles around his eyes the result of innumerable smiles. Adorned in a lavish white robe, he wore an orange stole around his neck and a white hat embroidered with an orange sun. Beads of sweat dripped across his forehead until he pulled out an orange handkerchief to wipe them away.

Fox's body chilled as the priest made eye contact with her. He smiled, and the wrinkles shifted on his leathered face. But his eyes were lukewarm. Dropping her gaze, Fox's hand crawled to her throat as she remembered the Eonian priest from Alira. Clifton.

Bear's hand rested on her shoulder, calming her more than any words could. As her breathing returned to normal, he squeezed her shoulder and let go. Fox looked at him, and he offered her a reassuring smile—one that matched his eyes.

Fox smiled back. *That is the difference between Mice and Animals. Loyalty.*

The room thrummed with energy as the all-male choir chanted in Marcellian, the phlegmy, archaic form of the Corinthian language few knew and fewer could read. The hymnals were of no help, written in Marcellian along with all other religious texts, forcing believers to rely on the church for translations.

Forcing them into obedience.

I only obey the Hunter, Fox thought as she listened to the choir's song. *Aquila does not need the empty words of songs. He lets his actions speak for him. The Hunter freed me. He accepted me as an Animal—as part of the Pack. He feeds me, trains me, and protects me. He is who I need—not Deitan.*

The words reverberated throughout the acoustic chamber, the choir's voices joining and leaving the chant as their echoes continued flowing. Eventually, the congregation stood and joined in the song. Fox moved her lips with them but kept her voice silent. Instead, she listened to the voices of the other men, most failing to follow the syllables of the choir yet singing loudly—as if the volume of their shouting indicated who believed the most.

As the song reached its crescendo, the priest stood in front of the altar, holding his hands above his head with his palms facing up like he held the weight of the sky. "This is the word of Deitan for the people of Deitan."

"Thanks be to Deitan," the congregation said. Neither Bear nor Fox joined them.

"Today we gather to give praise to Deitan on his day of triumph," the priest proclaimed, his arms still raised. "Our Savior, King Marcellus, was born nine-hundred-and-seventy-four years ago under a night sky. For in those times, there was only the moon, and the world was enshrouded in darkness. Our Savior survived that Dark Age and rose to power when he was only seventeen, becoming the last king of our Corinthian city-state.

"On the night of his coronation, he received a vision from Deitan. Where heretics fled from Him, King Marcellus basked in Deitan's warmth and became His first follower. But while King Marcellus saw the path of light, all others still knew only darkness. So he beseeched our God to share His light with an undeserving world. Moved by our king's stirring words, Deitan plucked out his right eye and placed it into the sky, becoming the sun. In the light of this new day, Marcellus painted the symbol of Deitan on his shield and conquered the surrounding city-states, creating the Corinthian Empire and ushering forth a bright new age."

"Praise be to Deitan."

So, Deitan is one-eyed, just like the rest of the Gods. Fox stared at Deitan's worshipers. Their zealotry. Their faith. *In the land of the blind, the one-eyed man is king.*

"It has been nine-hundred-and-fifty-one years since our Savior, the great King Marcellus, was laid to rest, but not a day has passed when we haven't celebrated his triumph over death—his return to Deitan's guiding light."

"Praise be to the Savior."

The priest lit incense on both sides of the altar, more noxious fumes rising and stirring in the air. "Today, we continue to fight for Deitan's Glory—to both Tavrak in the west and Stotan in the east. So long as we have faith in Him and our Savior's writings, we will prove victorious, just as Deitan is victorious above all false idols!"

"Glory to Corinthus! Glory to our Savior! Glory to Deitan!"

Glory to the God who demands gold yet does nothing, Fox thought. *Glory to the God who'd let his followers fight and die for him when he could just as easily smite their enemies... Glory to another silent God.*

"And so, as we remember the triumphs of our mighty Deitan, we offer a tithing to continue spreading His light to the uncivilized peoples."

Sacristans passed golden bowls between the pews. Fox watched as Mice tossed in money. The wealthier men dropped golden sols from great heights, the weight of their gifts heard throughout the chamber, while the poor worshipers let their copper-red cruors fall silently.

When the offering plate came to them, the Animals passed the bowl without adding to it. The Corinthian man to Fox's left held out the plate to her and shook it, a scowl plain on his face. Fox's hand crept to the talan in her sleeve, but Bear squeezed her arm and shook his head.

Gritting her teeth, Fox pulled out a silver ferrum from the purse of coins that Aquila had given her and placed it in the center of the pile—slipping a golden sol into her palm with sleight of hand as she held the older man's gaze. Fox bared her teeth at the Corinthian man, more snarl than smile.

"May my tithing please him," she said, pulling back her hand and facing forward.

Secretly, Fox showed the sol to Bear, who covered his mouth to hide his laughter. She didn't smile back. The coin weighed heavily on her. *My first gold piece. Dad would be proud.* She swallowed hard and hid the coin in her vest, tucked safely away with her knives.

As the tithings were brought back to the altar, the priest raised the bowls over his head, presenting them to Deitan. Fox studied the man's jowls, his expensive robes, and the beautiful decor of the cathedral. Her stomach clenched, knowing that they were liars. The tithing wouldn't leave the church.

My dad cheated and stole, just like you. So why's he dead while you're still here? Fox stared up at the symbol of Deitan looming behind the altar as her fingers drifted to the talan. *You can hide behind the sun all you want, priest, but one day, you'll burn like the rest of us.*

CHAPTER THIRTY-TWO

When Fox entered the butchery alone, she heard the buzz of flies and smelled blood. The walls were bare, but fresh corpses hung from hooks in the ceiling. The fresher ones were displayed in front of a glass pane as quality meats, the older ones stowed in salt troughs, though the smell of week-old decay lingered. She was familiar with the putrid scent after stalking the butcher for a nineday—she certainly preferred it to the incense that still clung to her clothes like a plague.

A young Corinthian boy with curling brown locks swept behind the counter as the door closed behind Fox. He whistled an optimistic hymn while he worked, despite the soiled apron and sweat-stained clothes.

Just like Mouse, Fox thought, her vision flashing. She still remembered standing over his corpse, staring at his vacant eyes. *He would be sixteen now.*

"Oh! Hey, Agrippa!" Faustus said with a smile. "Already back for more? Won't ever say no to repeat business."

Agrippa. I hate that name, Fox thought as she stepped toward the counter and mirrored the boy's smile. The fake name was necessary, but it made her feel more like a Mouse.

Like this boy.

"Faustus!" Fox said, posing as the servant of a middle-class merchant with her brown sash and plain tunic. "I was walking through this part of town and thought I'd say hello. Had a few minutes to spare, if you do."

"I don't know if I can spare them. Place is quite busy around this time," Faustus said with a wink. Fox was the only customer in the store. He put out a hand. Fox went to shake it, but Faustus pulled his hand back and slid it through his hair. "Too slow!" Then he laughed, acting like they'd been friends for years, though this was only the third time they'd met.

He's too quick to trust. Too naive—just like Mouse.

Fox dropped her hand to her side, forming a fist Faustus couldn't see. The smile remained plastered on her face. "Say, your dad around? Was hoping to ask for a spice recommendation."

Faustus nodded, froze, then shook his head. He grimaced as if he'd eaten a rotten piece of meat. "Da's upstairs, but he can't be bothered right now. He's, uh, taking care of Mum. Ain't feeling well this past week." He shrugged, but Fox caught the worry in his gray irises. "I'm working the store a bit more to help out."

Fox frowned. *That's why the butcher's been in hiding.* "Oh, Faustus. Sorry to hear about that." She reached her hand over the counter and patted his arm, though she hated touching him. He looked too much like Mouse. "Do you think your dad will be down today?"

Faustus shook his head. "Later maybe? He'll definitely be in tomorrow, though. I'm sure of it." His eyes were dark even as his grin shined. Looking away for a moment, Faustus asked, "So, you looking to buy any meat today?"

"Can't," Fox said, feigning an embarrassed smile. "Got pocketed yesterday."

Faustus gasped. "Oh, no. Really?"

Fox shrugged. "You know how the city can be. Lots of alleys. Lots of places to hide. The asshole snagged eight cruors from me over in an alley a few blocks away. Barely have enough money to afford water now."

"But Agrippa... That's a week's earnings!" Faustus gawked at her, putting a hand to his mouth. The pity and genuine sympathy on his face were needling.

Conflicting emotions ate at Fox: frustration at the butcher's continued disappearance, guilt at Mouse's death, and confusion as to *why* Faustus was being nice. He was a Mouse. Mice were selfish squalls who lived in their own filth, Aquila had taught her. So why was Faustus kind?

"I'm so sorry," Faustus whispered. "I know how much money that is to kids like us."

Kids like us, Fox thought resentfully. *We're nothing alike.*

"With Deitan watching down on us, I'm sure my luck'll turn," Fox said, almost hissing behind her smile. "Well, I just wanted to come check in on you, but I don't want to take up too much of your time. Besides, I've got to get going anyway—there's work to be done, you know. *Be seeing you, Faustus.*"

Fox turned to leave, but Faustus grabbed her arm. "Agrippa. Hold on a minute, alright? I'll be back before you can sing *His Guiding Light.*"

Hearing that hymn once was more than enough for a lifetime, Fox thought.

Faustus returned a couple of minutes later with a small sack. Looking around to make sure nobody was watching, he held the bag out to her and said, "It's not the best strip, but it's better than nothing, yeah?" With a small chuckle, he added, "Can't have friends going hungry, can we?"

Friends, Fox thought, swallowing the lump in her throat.

Mouse's impish whispers slithered through the dark recesses of her mind. *It'll always be you and me, friend. From this sea to the next.*

Fox averted her gaze so she wouldn't see Faustus's kind eyes. Though their irises were different colors, he and Mouse had the same *look* in them. "Faustus, I can't take this. I don't have any money."

"I'm not selling it to you. It's a gift," Faustus said with a wink. "Say hello to the family for me, will you?"

Fox took it and smiled, fighting a grimace. "Thanks, Faustus. I'll pay you twice as much next time I'm here."

"Pay what you can, friend. I trust you."

Trust... I broke Mouse's trust. Sorrow washed over her like a wave, and Fox clenched the bag in a fist. "Thanks," she whispered just before exiting the butchery.

Damn you and your kindness, Faustus, she thought, letting the smile drop once she was outside.

Rounding the corner, she found Bear waiting in an alleyway behind the butchery. Like her, he wore a servant's attire and concealed a dozen weapons within his clothes. Raising an eyebrow, he asked, "What happened?"

"Faustus... He gave me meat—for *free.*"

"Great." Bear took the bag and looked inside it. "Good strips. Why the frown?"

Fox gritted her teeth and kicked the dirt. "He called me a *friend.*"

"Oh." Bear stood straighter, understanding her meaning. "How 'bout we get out of here, and check back in with the butcher later?"

Fox nodded, grateful. Distance from Faustus was exactly what she needed.

They traveled through a couple of alleyways before rejoining the main road leading to the forum. While the heart of the city was spacious, the surrounding streets were packed together like those of the Aliran markets, albeit cleaner. Most businesses bustled with customers, but those with less stood outside and harassed passerby with everything from sugared treats to leather shoes. Fox even saw taverns, though Corinthian sensibility and tradition forced them to be much more orderly than those in the Chasm.

I wonder what Mark's tavern would have looked like had he been here. Fox flinched, remembering Fiveday Celebrations, corpses, and temples.

She slowed, staring at a few girlies standing in an alleyway beside a leather tanning shop. Confidently, they leaned against the walls, mostly out of sight but making their presence known. Her eyes narrowed at their makeup, eyeshadow, and playful hairstyles. One girlie noticed her and blew Fox a kiss. She looked away, cheeks reddening and stomach fluttering.

They're beautiful. They get to embrace who they are, but I have to pretend—always have to pretend. I'm so tired of it. Looking at Bear's back, Fox thought, *Maybe I could finally tell him the truth. No... I don't think I could tell him, but maybe I could show him.* She memorized the intersection where the girlies stood and snuck one last glance before they were out of sight. *Maybe I could be beautiful too. All I need is their makeup.*

As dusk fell, Faustus locked the door and left the butchery—only to be knocked to the ground by a passerby. He clutched his arm and yelled after the orange-clad figure that'd run into him, but he was gone. Mumbling, Faustus disappeared into the city.

Bear reappeared in the alleyway behind Fox and uncurled his fist, revealing three glittering keys in his palm.

They slunk through the shadows and into the butchery, locking the door behind them. The smell of blood and death greeted them as they flipped their orange kaftans inside-out, to reveal the black hood and fabric sewn on the other side.

Together, they searched the front room for information—anything that would help Fox establish the butcher's routines, motivations, strengths, and weaknesses. From her earlier trips, she'd gleaned many surface-level details from Faustus's blathering tongue, but here she was looking for detailed proof: money ledgers, meat stores, and weapon stashes. Of course, Fox didn't have any plans to steal from the butcher, but when they returned to Aquila, they would need to answer all of his questions confidently. That meant learning everything she could.

As a butcher, he was skilled with knives, but upon finding a giant club hidden behind the counter, Fox had the impression that he didn't use his knives to defend himself. He was no killer. He'd hit somebody over the head with a club, but he wouldn't stab them through the heart. *A killer of animals, but not of Animals,* Fox thought.

More searching revealed the money ledger, which was in a drawer beside a few tools. It revealed just how poorly the shop was doing. Enough to get by, if all was well, but by Faustus's own admission, things weren't well. The business was failing, and his mother was sick. *I wonder where she is.*

A couple of pesky flies buzzed as they walked into the back room without the aid of a light. A long butcher's table dominated the space, its surface marred by gouges, cuts, and bloodstains. Large containers of salt and meat lined every wall except where a staircase led up to the second-floor apartment where Faustus's family lived.

Through the closed doorway, the Animals heard a muted conversation:

"...find a way..."

"...won't let you..."

"...Faustus needs..."

Fox slid her feet silently along the ground as she crept up the stairs and listened by the door.

The butcher said, "Listen to me, Aurelia. You need that medicine to get better."

"We don't have the money, Gaius," a weak voice said, lighter and exhausted.

Gaius, Fox thought. *That's the butcher's name.*

"We have the money."

"No, we don't."

"We'll figure out a way to pay for it, okay?" Gaius said in a lower, much gentler tone. "I promise you, Aurelia. I'll get you that medicine, and you'll feel better in no time."

Fox looked through a small opening between the door and the frame. Inside the room, she could discern a bed, additional sheets on the floor, and a wooden dresser with a small mirror. On the windowsill next to the bed was a multitude of glass jars holding flowers.

"I'm going to get a little air, but then I'll be back, Aurelia."

Fox tapped Bear's shoulder twice, and they hustled down the stairs. Diving behind the butcher's table, the door opened. Dim light illuminated the top of the table, but the Animals hid in the darkness beneath. The stairs groaned as Gaius descended and set the lantern down on the butcher block. He let out a breath, the sound rumbling like thunder.

He's crying. Fox thought, thinking of Mark when they'd cried together in the graveyard outside Alira.

Mark's words returned like a cemetery fog. *Quiet now. It'll all be okay, Erin. It'll all be okay.*

Fox squeezed her eyes shut tighter. *Stop it. Don't think about him. Don't think about Mouse. Just focus on the Hunt. Hide. Stalk. Report.*

"Deitan, please hear my words," Gaius prayed. "Please heal my wife. Please make her well. I don't have the money for the medicine, but I'll do whatever it takes to save her. I'll sell this damned shop if I need to. Just please help her. *Please.* Don't let my boy lose his mother. Not now. He needs her—*I* need her."

Sighing, the butcher left the back room and approached the front door, unlocking it. Fox wanted to sneak up the stairs and into the apartment, but what if Gaius turned around? *We're supposed to remain unseen. It's not a risk we can take.*

Though Fox remained hidden beneath the table, she still heard Gaius's whispers from the front room. "Faustus must be out getting more flowers, even though I told him we already got enough. Bless that boy, but damn him for being so naive... Hope he gets back soon. Nights here aren't as safe as they used to be."

Fox waited until Gaius returned to his upstairs apartment before slinking around the table and searching through the salt troughs and table drawers for anything of note. More knives. A few books on the preparation and salting of various meats. A few half-butchered corpses, too, but less meat than she'd have expected in a butchery.

Gaius is probably buying less meat hoping to save up enough money to buy that medicine his wife needs, Fox realized. *And yet, Faustus gave me free meat. Damn him for that.*

Guiltily, Fox returned to the front room, stopping in the doorway when she realized Bear hadn't followed. He stood at full height, staring up at the second-floor doorway.

Fox slunk back to his side, touching his arm to get his attention. His body turned before his eyes did. Fox jerked her head to the door. Haunted, he set his jaw and nodded.

Eventually, the Animals slipped out of the butchery and into the crisp, cool night. Dropping the keys by the door where Faustus would find them when he returned, they used the alleyways to creep a few blocks away.

"Please! I don't have anything!" a boy exclaimed meekly, somewhere out of sight.

Faustus, Fox realized as a vicious snarl overtook her expression. She crept closer and into the mouth of a different alleyway. Ten steps from her, a rogue pointed a jagged knife at Faustus, who held a bouquet and backed away like a mouse.

"Yeah, you got something, alright. Give it to me," a gruff voice said, slurring his words. An addict or a drunk, Fox surmised.

"Ain't got no problem killing kids," a female rogue added, appearing from the opposite side of the alleyway and cutting off the boy's escape. "What'll you give us? Coin or blood?"

"You don't want to end up in little pieces, do you, boy?" the first one asked, walking toward Faustus, who looked as helpless as a newborn sheep between two predators.

Except they aren't predators. We are, Fox thought, pulling the talan from her sleeve and nodding to Bear. He disappeared, searching for an entrance to the other side of the alleyway.

Aquila's teachings echoed through her mind. *All creatures fear what they do not understand. That is why Mice fear the night. Not because of the dark, but because of what hides in it... Become that fear.*

The first rogue laughed and brandished his blade. "Then I guess we'll be taking blood—"

Fox's talan ripped through the Mouse's throat. His corpse fell to the ground, and Fox stepped on his face, cracking the cheekbones and nose as she walked farther into the alley.

"Octavius?" the female Mouse said, dumbstruck. "Oh God... You *killed* him!"

Faustus stood frozen between the living rogue and the dead one, whimpering low.

"Get behind me, Faustus," Fox said.

"Agrippa?" Faustus asked. "Is that you?"

"Yes. Now get behind me."

Faustus sprinted past her and out of the alley. Though she didn't turn to watch, Fox heard his feet stop once he was in the street. "I'll get the guard!"

"No, you won't," Fox said, taking another step forward. "Stay there, Faustus."

"Okay. That sounds good too."

Okay... Such a sloppy word.

"We can talk about this," the woman said, backing away as Fox took a step forward. "Octavius's got money. You can take it. Take his blades too. I won't say nothing. Swear to Deitan, I won't."

Fox trudged forward without response. Her talan dripped blood as Aquila's voice hung in her ear. *Use darkness to your advantage. Use silence. Speak only when necessary. Your voice is all the more terrifying when it is not heard.*

"You want chard?" the rogue asked. "I've got some of that too."

Fox said nothing. She looked behind the Mouse toward the end of the alley, where Bear was hiding in the deep shadows. But to this woman, the alley would have looked like a good escape route. *Never let your prey feel trapped. Let them think there is a way out, even when the escape is only a pit full of knives. Trapped prey is dangerous prey. Fleeing prey is no challenge at all.*

The Mouse took another step back. "Please, just take my coin, just let me—"

Fox growled and sprinted at the rogue, who fled to the end of the alley and into Bear's awaiting axe. The woman drowned in her own blood as he pilfered her pockets. Then Bear vanished in the shadows.

"What was that *thing?*" Faustus asked, pointing a shaking finger where Bear had stood.

Fox replied, "A friend. He and I were looking for the bandits who mugged me. It's lucky that these same squalls came for you at the same time I was coming for them."

"That's not luck. That's a miracle," Faustus said. "Deitan be praised."

Deitan had nothing to do with it, Fox thought, snarling. She was grateful that the darkness hid her expression.

"Where did you learn to do that?" Faustus asked as Fox looted the male rogue's blood-soaked corpse. "You came out of nowhere, like you were a shadow or something."

"Blades are supposed to be felt, not seen." Fox pulled out a dagger the bandit had strapped to his belt and handed it to Faustus. "Carry this the next time you go out at night. It'll keep you safe."

Faustus took the blade and stared at it before lunging forward to hug her. "Thanks, Agrippa."

Just like old times, right, friend? Mouse whispered in her ears. *One last battle between the Mop King and the Rat Prince.*

Disgusted with herself, Fox shoved Faustus away.

"Oh, uh, sorry. Guess I should've asked first." Faustus laughed nervously. "Just... Thank you, Agrippa. You saved my life."

Fox grunted in response. She kneeled, taking Octavius's coin sack. It was light, but there were a few cruors and even a couple of ferrums. She thought of the butcher's wife, quietly taking the gold sol she'd stolen from the cathedral and placing it in the sack. Then she held it out to Faustus and cleared her throat so her voice wouldn't shake. "Here, take this. Maybe it will help with your mom."

"No, Agrippa, I can't possibly—"

Fox forced the coins into his hand. "Take it."

Faustus looked down, speechless. "There's a sol in here. That's more than we make in two months." He wiped a tear from his eyes and eventually said, "Thank you, Agrippa. This means more than you'll ever know."

I think I know just how much it means, Fox thought.

"If your dad asks where you got the money from, lie," Fox said. "You were never here."

"Right."

Right is another sloppy word, she immediately thought, feeling more like herself as she thought of Aquila and his tomes. "Take care of yourself, Faustus." Fox walked away.

"Agrippa?"

Fox turned, saying nothing.

"If you ever need some food or a place to stay, you let me know, okay? If you end up needing a new job, you can come work for my dad, promise you that."

Fox's mind flashed back to Mark's tavern, just before he'd said goodbye. *If you, uh, ever need my help, you're always welcome here. Break in, if you have to. Anything in here can be replaced, except you, you understand?*

Fox stared up at the night sky, at *Eo's Light.* Then she walked away without saying goodbye, as she always did. As Bear joined her, Fox walked in silence, less sure of herself than she'd been in over two years.

"Faustus is just a Mouse. Nothing more," she said to the darkness, but even she had trouble believing it.

Chapter Thirty-Three

Fox and Bear relayed their findings to Aquila, who sat silently behind the desk in his study. Slain animals surrounded them. A bearskin rug laid in the middle of the room, eyes flickering with the light of the fireplace. A dozen furs hung on the far wall. Most had their heads still attached, and a fox stared down at her pityingly. Other heads were mounted to the walls, including a roaring lion and a snarling wolf. On decorative branches curving down from the ceiling, taxidermied specimens posed. An owl stared with wide eyes on one. A hawk unfurled its wings on another. A snake coiled around a third, its head reared back with its fangs glistening. Many more predators lined the walls, along with more ornate paintings of Corinthian conquests and bloodied weapons, but Fox only stared at the wooden floor beneath her feet.

When Fox and Bear had finished recounting their tale, Aquila interlaced his fingers on the desk and asked, "Does that correctly sum up their Hunt, Owl?"

Standing behind Fox and Bear, Owl said, "Yes, Hunter."

Fox looked between Owl and Aquila, frowning. *She was following us?* Then a second, more horrifying revelation. *And we didn't notice her even once?* Her shoulders dropped. *A test within a test. We failed.*

Aquila seemed to notice her disappointment, because he explained, "I had Owl follow you to make sure that you were safe, yes? And I asked her to remain unseen—only to interfere if your lives were in danger. But because you were successful, she didn't need to reveal herself. I'm not displeased that you didn't notice. She has been on Hunts far longer than either of you, so do not be discouraged." Aquila's smile was so genuine that Fox nodded, grateful rather than deceived. "Now, where is the money I gave you?"

Bear stepped around the bear rug and placed the small burlap sack on Aquila's desk.

When Bear returned to stand by Fox, the Hunter stared at the contents and frowned. "There's more money in here than I originally gave to you. How?"

"We didn't use the money, Hunter. We stole bits of food here and there," Fox said. "But the bandits had some coin. We took some of it and gave the rest to Faustus."

"The bandits also had daggers," Bear added. Then he made a disgusted face. "But they were rusted, dull, and chipped. We left those behind."

"I see. Well, consider this your reward for a successful Hunt, yes?" Aquila threw the bag to Fox.

She stared at the sack, perplexed. "But we live here, Hunter. What would we use it for?"

"The next Hunt," Aquila said. "You can use that money on a girlie, if you'd like. Or clothes. Or weapons. Whatever you wish—as long as it isn't rum or chard."

Fox nodded her head, knowing better than to ask more questions and risk Aquila's wrath. The Hunter clapped his hands together and asked, "So, if this butcher wanted to kill you, and you know that this butcher's fear is of losing his family, how would you use this knowledge?"

"Kidnap them and use them as hostages, Hunter." Fox said before Bear could even open his mouth. "Killing only inspires fury, making an enemy harder to kill. By using fear, we maintain control."

"Ever the cunning Fox. Good. Very good." He grinned. "And Bear, because this butcher is physically strong, how would you avoid this strength?"

"Kill him from long range, in his sleep, or from behind, Hunter. Fighting strength to strength is a job for warriors, not Animals. We fight strength to weakness."

Aquila smirked. "But what of honor?"

"Animals don't honor Mice," they said together, having memorized the line from Aquila's personal tomes. "That is the way of Animals."

"Then you both have learned your lesson. Tell me, as an Animal, what is the butcher?"

"A Mouse, Hunter," Fox and Bear said.

"And if I were to tell you he is my enemy?" Aquila asked.

Fox hesitated, thinking of Faustus, who'd been kind to her and called her a friend. Then of Gaius himself, who reminded her so much of Mark. *Why are they Aquila's enemies?* She wanted to ask but didn't dare. Bear didn't speak either.

The smile left Aquila's lips and became a frown. His disappointment made Fox squirm. "And if I were to tell you he is my enemy?" he repeated.

"Then he is our enemy, Hunter," Fox said.

"That is the way of Animals," Bear added.

"And if I were to ask you to kill him?" Aquila asked.

"Then he deserves to die, Hunter," Fox replied.

"Then kill him."

Faustus locked up the butchery as night descended and left to get more flowers for his mother. This time, he wore the keys on a necklace, so the Animals didn't steal them again. Instead, Owl glided from the alley to the butchery, and unlocked the door within seconds with a pick.

"Obey the Hunter," Owl said. "Do what must be done."

When Fox and Bear nodded, Owl opened the door. All three slunk inside. Fox relocked it, wincing at the sound before joining Owl and Bear in the back room with the long butcher's table. The coming death worried Fox more than the now familiar stench.

Gaius deserves to die, Fox thought, clenching her fists to keep them from trembling. She looked up at the door at the top of the stairs, which was wide open. Faustus had probably forgotten to close it when he'd left.

Fox set her jaw as Owl stared at her with eyes of steel and ice. Blades and blood. Death and salt. Fox wondered if her eyes now carried the same look. Then she dismissed the thought, climbing the stairs and stepping into the room as Bear put a hand on her shoulder and followed.

"—to you, Deitan. You're the light of this world, and You're the fire that guides us. Give my family a second chance at life. Give Aurelia a second chance. I swear we won't waste it," Gaius said, eyes closed as he kneeled at the side of the bed and held his wife's hand.

A forest of flowers surrounded Aurelia, a collection of purple tulips, pink roses, yellow daffodils, and orange pansies. Her hair was long and blonde, strands of sunshine veiling her face. A dim lantern on the bedside table revealed her puffy eyes, flushed cheeks, and runny nose.

As the Animals crept closer, the butcher continued praying, "Help Faustus, too, Deitan. He's a soft boy, but he's strong in ways I'm not. He's kind and generous—more than I've ever been. I just wish he had more sense. Help him be a better man than I am. Keep him safe. Keep us all safe. Keep us together."

Fox slipped behind Gaius and readied her talan. But she hesitated. Hunched over the bed like that, the butcher looked like Mark when he'd cradled his son's urn to his chest. *Mark wasn't a Mouse,* she thought. *I don't think Gaius is either. I don't want to kill him.*

But, if Fox didn't kill him, what would happen? *We'd fail, and Aquila would be displeased. And if Gaius really is the Hunter's enemy and we let him get away, what happens then? What if Gaius hurts Aquila? Hurts the Pack?*

Too many questions. Too few answers. Fox glanced at Bear, whose eyes were on her, awaiting her decision. *I won't risk the Pack for the life of a Mouse.*

The butcher said, "Regardless of the obstacles we face, we'll live as You've taught us to live. When I fall, You carry me. When I'm weak, You give me strength. I have faith in You, Deitan, because I know You're always with me."

No, He isn't.

Fox plunged the knife into Gaius's neck. Bear covered his mouth to muffle the choking. Gaius's hands slapped at her, slowing until they finally fell at his sides. She eased him to the ground to maintain silence, but it was difficult with his weight and spasms. Crimson pooled out from his body and seeped into the wood. Fox stared at her reflection: a strange snarling face whose eyes were black and ruthless, a monster more than a human. Something worse than an Animal.

"That's me," Fox whispered, hands shaking. "Why is that my face?"

She dropped the talan.

And Aurelia's eyes opened.

All three Animals froze.

Instead of screaming, Aurelia's lips parted in a half-dreaming smile. "My boy, my sweet Faustus, come here." She gestured to Bear with a weak finger, hand shaking as it rose from the sheet. "Come, be with me."

Bear looked at Owl and Fox before approaching Aurelia's bed. Leaning forward, he kissed her forehead and said, "Go back to sleep, Ma. When you wake up, everything will be okay."

Aurelia kissed his cheek, and gray makeup smeared against her lips. She didn't notice. Putting a hand to the side of his face, she said, "You're such a good boy. So kind. So thoughtful. If only there were more boys like you, we'd be so lucky." Smiling, she added, "I love you, son."

A tear fell from Bear's cheek as Aurelia fell back to sleep. He gently placed her hand back underneath the sheets. He rubbed the tear away, smearing the gray makeup and revealing his blue skin but not seeming to care.

When he didn't return to her side, Fox approached him and put a hand on his shoulder. "Bear, we should—"

"I miss my mom—miss her every day," Bear said, switching from Corinthian to Aritrastan. More tears came, but he didn't wipe them away. In his old sailor drawl, he added, "My old man was a fighter, always had been. Taught me with his fists, he did. Made me strong. But he was always stronger. Used to hurt my ma when he drank—and he drank every night." His chest heaved wildly. Bear was silent until he exhaled, a little calmer. "No matter how many times Da hurt her, she never fought back. Don't know why, but I think she thought he loved her. Every time he would say he'd never do it again. He'd cry and beg until he went and got a new bottle. Then he'd do it again and again and again. Each time, I just stayed in the closet and pretended not to hear."

You never told me that, Fox thought, heartbroken that he'd shouldered this burden alone for so long. *I wish you'd said something.* She couldn't fault him for not telling her—not when she still hadn't told him she was a girl—but after being with him for so long, it pained her to know there were still things he kept from her. *I'm a damn hypocrite.*

To ease his pain, Fox circled him and stood on her tiptoes to give him a hug. He leaned his chin down on her shoulder and whispered, "Da hurt Ma too bad one night. Beat her 'til she couldn't stand. I took care of her as best I could, but Da kept on drinking. He blacked out while she was on her deathbed. She told me not to worry, that things would be okay. Then she died. And I remember standing over my dad with a knife, watching him sleep, watching him dream, wondering if he'd even cared."

When Bear refused to continue, Fox asked, "Did you...?"

"Kill him? *Nah.*" Bear said, placing years of anger, guilt, and hatred into that single word. "I could have killed him, should have, but I didn't do nothing except run away like a coward. Kept running until I found the *Constable.* Always thought that if I got stronger than my da, I'd go back and put him in the ground. But I never did. Instead, I put Tomlin in the ground. Now Gaius." Gently, Bear broke the hug and sniffed, wiping at his eyes. "All that running, and all I did was go in a squalling circle. I'm just another brute—another killer. All's I'm missing is a bottle... The apple don't fall far from the tree, does it?"

Fox grabbed his arm. "Bear—"

He shrugged away her hand. "Don't, okay? Just... just don't."

"Okay." Fox took a step away from him. She turned to see Owl placing a coin sack on the bed, where the butcher would have slept.

"To pay for the medicine," she said before Fox could ask. "So that his wife may live."

"That's the price of his life then," Fox said, thinking of her father. "That small sack."

"Most don't get this much." Owl stepped over Gaius's warm corpse without so much as a backward glance. Fox and Bear hesitated at the doorway as Aurelia turned in her sleep, unaware that she kissed her husband's murderer and told him she loved him.

Then, as they always did, Fox and Bear obeyed, joining Owl in darkness.

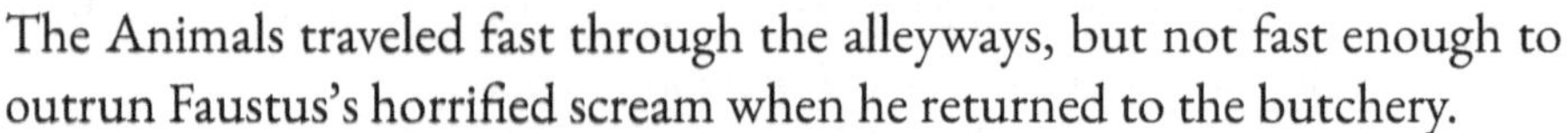

The Animals traveled fast through the alleyways, but not fast enough to outrun Faustus's horrified scream when he returned to the butchery.

"Why was Gaius the Hunter's enemy?" Fox asked, wincing as a tremor of guilt racked her body.

"I don't know," Owl replied.

"But did Gaius deserve to die?" Fox asked again as Faustus's screamed chased her through the shadows. She looked over at Bear, hoping that he'd add to the conversation, but he was still sullen and silent, trudging along with his head down.

Owl looked down at Fox with sympathetic, albeit hard, eyes. Putting a light hand on Fox's back, Owl said, "Does a mouse deserve to die at the hands of a fox? No. But the fox must kill to survive."

"I didn't need to kill Gaius to survive."

"Yes, Fox, you did." Owl's whisper fell like a feather in winter, eaten by the elements and forgotten. "The Pack doesn't feed Animals who don't contribute, just as they won't defend Animals who won't protect themselves."

"But Aquila loves me. Us. He wouldn't do that, would he?"

Owl was silent, unwilling to lie but unwilling to tell the truth either. Silence was its own answer. But Fox refused to believe it.

"He *loves* us," she said emphatically. "I know he does."

"My ma thought Da loved her, too," Bear said, louder and angrier than he'd intended.

To that, neither Fox nor Owl had a response.

For minutes, they walked along in silence, sneaking through alleyways toward the river, around guards on the bridges, and into the mazelike corridors of the old eastern half of Port Cassius. When they'd arrived at the dirt road at the city's edge, leading out into the forest and toward Aquila's villa, Fox looked up at *Eo's Point*. She asked, "What if we didn't go back? What if we just ran away?"

Owl's glare was sharp enough to slit her throat. "That is a very dangerous thing to suggest." Softer, she added, "Deadly to try."

"Why?" Fox asked, eyes scanning the dark trees and canopy for threats but finding none.

"What do you think would happen, Fox?"

She replied, "He'd send you or one of the other Animals to find us?"

"And if the Animals were unsuccessful?" Owl asked.

Fox threw a look at Bear, who was staring at the ground, still lost in his own memories. "We'd get away. We could go..." She almost added, *to Mark's tavern*, before closing her mouth. Lamely, she finished, "Anywhere we wanted."

"No, Fox. You would die," Owl whispered. "Even if you did evade other Animals, get on a ship, and sail back to Aritrasta, you would die before you ever reached its shores. And it would be a horrible death. You'd feel fine for the first couple of weeks. But you'd eventually fall ill. Then come the headaches, which will ruin your sleep. Soon, you'd bleed from your nose and your ears. Then your organs would begin shutting down. One at a time. Over the process of months. You'd likely kill yourself from the pain before that poison finally stopped your heart."

"Poison?" Fox asked, putting a hand to her mouth. She stopped walking. Bear did too. He finally broke out of his reverie, glowering at Owl.

The older Animal took a few more steps before halting. With a pained expression, she turned to face Fox. "Yes. There's a poison inside of you. It's inside all of us—even me... Did you really think that the Hunter wouldn't have countermeasures in place?"

Fox floundered, mentally drowning in Owl's words, clinging to every lifeline. "But the Hunter loves us. He wouldn't do that." Owl didn't argue or convince her otherwise, causing Fox to doubt herself. She growled in frustration. "Why would he do that?"

"When we obey the Hunter's commands, we are rewarded. When we fail, we are punished. That is how he controls us. That is why we are Animals, and Aquila is the Hunter. And a Hunter must always be in control. Otherwise, the Animals can rebel and bite his hand."

"I'd never hurt the Hunter," Fox said, heart breaking at the accusation.

"Yet he hurts you every day."

Fox stared at the ground. "I don't believe it. He would never betray us like that."

Owl walked to her side and stroked her hair. "I'm not asking you to believe it, Fox. I'm asking you to obey. Then the truth won't matter. You'll be alive—*that's* what matters."

"And do this forever?" Bear asked, folding his arms. "Just keep killing people?"

"Killing *Mice*." Owl corrected, but by her frown and distant eyes, she didn't believe those words.

"I can't do that again," Fox whispered, remembering her face in the blood's reflection. She never wanted to look like that again.

"You must."

"But why?" Fox asked, grabbing Owl's arm. "Why do we have to keep doing this?"

"When animals enter snare traps, they don't realize that there is a noose around their necks. When they struggle, the snare tightens. If they run, they suffocate. If they stay, they die of thirst. The only way to survive is avoiding the snare." She grabbed Fox's necklace while tugging at her own. "You've already walked into the snare, Fox. We all have. Now we must stay and drink the Hunter's water to keep from dying of thirst."

Night turned to day as they finished their trek along the dirt road back to the villa, but it did nothing to settle Fox's nerves. Gaius's death swam through her murky thoughts, and with it, her reflection in blood. When they returned to Aquila's study, Fox bit the inside of her lip to keep from bursting into tears. Then the door opened, and Fox felt the eyes of every dead animal follow her.

Aquila's eyes too. He still sat behind his desk, looking up from a book he'd been writing in with a feather quill and inkwell. An owl's feather. "Well?"

"He deserved to die, Hunter," Fox said, and Bear repeated it slowly.

"Are you satisfied, Owl?" Aquila asked.

Laying a hand on Fox's tense shoulder, Owl said, "Yes, Hunter."

Aquila's seat creaked as he stood up. "And yet Fox and Bear are upset, no?"

Owl's talon-like nails dug painfully into Fox's shoulder before her hand fell. Fox whispered, "Yes, Hunter."

Bear echoed her, out of sync.

Aquila leaned over the desk. "You want to know why the butcher was my enemy, yes? Why he had to die?"

"Yes, Hunter," they said in hoarse unison.

"Because Gaius is a Mouse, and all Mice are our enemy. That is the only reason I chose him—and that is the only reason you need."

Fox held in a gasp. *He chose Gaius at random?* She shared a look with Bear, who'd seemed to have the same conclusion.

Aquila walked out from behind the desk, explaining, "All your life, you were taught to be a Mouse—to follow their rules. But most forget that humans are just another breed of animal. Those Mice in the city repress their instincts and declaw themselves to satisfy their twisted sense of goodness. But tell me, what is *good?* Killing and stealing are illegal, and therefore evil. But what of slavery? It is acceptable by their laws, thus it is good. Yet you know more than anyone that slavery is often worse than murder... But what is goodness to a bear? To a fox? It is survival. A bear does not *enslave* others, and it kills to survive. So does the fox. There is no evil in that."

Aquila walked toward them. His heels clicked on the ground, and his shadow walked along the wall ominously. He stopped in front of Bear, who only glared at him. Aquila still hugged him. "It is okay. What you did—it was hard. But you did the right thing. You chose to be an Animal. You chose the Pack. And for that, I am proud of you."

Tears fell from Bear's eyes as he broke.

Aquila held him a moment longer before letting go and turning to Fox. "You blame yourself. I know you do. I did, too, when I first became an Animal. But you did nothing wrong, Fox."

Fox still bit the inside of her cheek to keep her lip from trembling.

"It is okay to be scared, to be confused. I am your Hunter, and I will protect you." He bent down and hugged her. "I will always be here for you, and nothing will change that."

As Fox's hatred for him slid away, love rushed to replace it.

Then the seed of doubt returned.

My ma thought Da loved her, too, Bear had said.

Fox looked into Aquila's eyes instead of his smile, seeing a cold gleam of ruthlessness—the same glint that she'd witnessed in the blood reflection.

CHAPTER THIRTY-FOUR

Fox sat on a long concrete bench in the stands of the Cassian Arena. She stared down into the pit of blood and sand as thousands of Corinthians cheered around her, swearing and sweating in their traditional white and orange garbs. She winced at their loudness.

More Mice, Fox thought, cold.

The fighters in the pit beneath could have been Animals in a different life. But in this one, they were gladiators. Some use tridents and nets, others used swords and shields, and a few used nothing at all. Instead of breastplates or chain mail, their armor was little more than leather skirts, metal greaves worn above the shins, and metal bracers on their forearms. Helmets, too, which only obscured the fighters' vision and deadened their hearing. Better not to wear helmets at all.

If you can't see what you're fighting, you may as well be fighting Deitan Himself.

Already, Fox and Bear had seen three fights. The first had been more of an execution. Brutus, a legendary lion of the Arena, tore a naked and unarmed slave to pieces—setting an example for runaways. By the end of the slaughter, Brutus's ninety-seventh kill was recorded, being chiseled into the concrete foundations of the Arena's walls.

The second and third fights were between gladiators, the former with only fists and the latter with swords and shields. Blood was spilled, but no gladiators were executed.

"Animals fighting for the entertainment of Mice," Fox said, gritting her teeth. "Shameful."

"Do you think it's true?" Bear asked, sitting next to her. "He's here?"

Fox frowned, knowing exactly who *he* was. "That's what we're going to find out."

The fourth event was a Corinthian Wick ceremony—an execution for Deitan's nonbelievers. Guards placed three stakes in the center of the sandpit, to which honey-covered nonbelievers were bound with oil-soaked rope. Those guards wrapped brambles of dried weeds and vines around the stakes and nonbelievers, leaving only their faces exposed. Suns were carved into their foreheads even as they wept.

Then guards lit torches, waving them wildly at the crowd.

"Wick. Wick! *Wick!*" the enraptured Corinthians chanted. Fox and Bear remained quiet.

The guards tossed the torches at the feet of the slaves, allowing the flames to burn flesh starting at the toes. The slaves' dying screams joined with the Corinthians' frenzied roar.

"They think they're bringing glory to Deitan by slaughtering each other." The old anger raged in Fox, brighter than even the Wicks below. "Gods don't do this. *Mice* do. The Gods are content to sit by and watch."

"Can't believe they spent decades to build this just to kill people in it." Bear said, rubbing the concrete bench and staring out at the giant amphitheater, marveling at its construction. "Could have done it in a field just as easy."

Fox looked up at the wealthier Corinthian nobles who sat in boxes of honor, including the governor, high priest, and Divine Virgins. "It's not about the killing. It's about those who watch them die. The rich don't want to murder people in a field because they'd have nowhere to sit."

Fox grit her teeth as a white-robed Corinthian statesman appeared in the sands below and bowed to the crowd. "Ladies and gentlemen! From the coasts of Aritrasta come men bred for water! Men who know only the sea and spears! Men who only eat fish and shells! Men who have fought syrens hidden in the sea's murky depths!"

The Corinthians began another chant. "Weaver. Weaver! *Weaver!*"

"Yes! The Weaver! We bring him to you yet again! To fight for the sea! For the glory of Deitan!"

The large doors to the north and south of the pit were opened. From the north gate, two gladiators entered the arena wearing bronze helmets whose crests were shaped like fish. They wore metal greaves, gaiters, and bracers that had been cut to look like fish scales, along with longswords and large, round shields. Heavily armored, their armaments made them look more fish than men.

From the south entrance emerged a third gladiator wearing little in the way of armor, save for a leather skirt. He wore a left arm guard with an embedded shoulder shield, the metal designed with scales. In place of a helmet and sword, he carried a trident in his right hand, a circular net tied to his left wrist with an extra line of rope, and a dagger strapped to his exposed right thigh. Beneath the muscles that rippled like waves were tattoos of ships, serpents, and stars that stretched from his ankle to neck. Though his hair had turned from black to gray and more scars covered his body, there was no mistaking the Weaver—a gladiator who'd risen to fame in these last four years to become a favorite of the Marcellian Houses.

"Jameson Ash... I can't believe it. He's alive," Bear said, grinning widely enough that Fox wanted to slap the stupid expression from his face.

Why is Bear happy that this son of a squall's alive, anyway? Fox thought, wishing again that she hadn't heard news of the Weaver's arrival in Cassius during their last Hunt. If she hadn't known, she could've still pretended that Jameson was dead. But to find that he was not only alive but a thriving, famous gladiator? Words couldn't describe her hatred of him.

"Let's just hope he loses." Fox rose from her seat and descended the benches to get a closer view.

◄○►

Jameson walked to the center of the sand pit as the Wicks continued to burn. With the smell of singed flesh stinging his nostrils, he stood to the left of the pile of rocks left for him and waited for the mechanical gears underneath the Arena to raise his platform into the air. Sand fell from the sides like a waterfall as five square platforms rose around him to create a stepped pyramid which separated him from the two gladiators in the sand below. Channels at the edge of the arena's wall opened and water from the river gushed in until it was a foot deep. All three gladiators turned to salute to the crowd, who chanted Jameson's name and threw him cruors, ferrums, and flowers from their benches.

Jameson smiled and waved, though all he could think of was sailing away and never returning. *I made an oath, and I'm not leaving until I find Steward. No matter how long it takes...*

Horns blared from the four cardinal directions, and his two opponents climbed up the four-foot steps of the pyramid from opposite sides. Jameson hurled rocks at their feet and knees. One avoided the stones and blocked with his shield as the other risked climbing to the next step. When they both reached the third platform, Jameson feinted, turned, and hurled his stone at the climber. That close, his aim was perfect. The rock smashed the man's knee into a crimson paste.

Jameson watched the gladiator stumble back and fall to the step below. Then the weaver hurled another rock, connecting with the man's helmet. A third rock cracked his rib.

That gladiator raised his forefinger skyward in surrender.

The audience cheered so loud that Jameson almost didn't hear creaking metal behind him. He ducked just as the blade came down, the second gladiator having ascended to the top of the platform. Jameson threw a stone that the gladiator blocked with his shield. He shifted the trident to his right hand and cast his weighted net over his opponent's sword as the gladiator shoved him back. Jameson fell, taking the sword with him. Landing on the platform below, he rolled away as his opponent jumped, chasing him. Jameson cast the sword away into the water.

But the gladiator ran to his surrendered ally and picked up the other blade.

"Squalling bastard," Jameson said to himself in Aritrastan. He got to his feet, wincing as his knee popped. "Just keep the distance. Don't let him press you against the wall."

Net coiled in his left hand, Jameson backed away from the pyramid and into the water, keeping the sun behind him. The gladiator advanced, fending off Jameson's trident with a shield. He hacked and slashed with his sword, but Jameson kept it at bay with his net. Yet he constantly gave ground and was pushed further toward the side of the ring.

Come on... Just a bit further, Jameson thought, ducking beneath his opponent's sword and stepping back toward one of the Wicks. The gladiator advanced confidently, but stopped short as Jameson set his net on fire with the Wick's flames.

Before the gladiator could escape out of range, Jameson hurled the net. The burning rope caught on the gladiator's crested helmet, burning his face and chest. As he screamed, Jameson thrust his trident into the man's thigh and kicked him into the water. Though the flames were extinguished, the gladiator thrashed and flailed in pain.

The crowd's chant thundered across the arena as thousands of Corinthians called out his name. "Weaver. Weaver! *Weaver!*" They threw down more gifts. Flowers floated in the water, but the coins all sank. Those would be given to him after the Arena was drained—given to his *owner,* that was.

Focus on the task at hand, Jameson reminded himself.

Back aching, arms heavy, and legs trembling, Jameson leveled his trident at the fallen gladiator, who cast the net aside and pulled off his crested helmet, revealing furious orange eyes set beneath gray skin—a Corinthian gladiator seeking glory, not a slave forced to fight.

Jameson pushed the trident against the man's skin but didn't skewer him. "Where is your glory now, Corinthian?"

"Blood. Blood! *Blood!*" the crowd chanted.

Jameson looked over at the high priest, whose decision it was to grant a gladiator mercy or death. The old man cocked his head, listening to the crowd—or perhaps Deitan—before making a fist and raising it high overhead. The crowd roared at the sign, raising their own fists and shouting *blood!* ever louder.

"They choose death for you," Jameson said to his bested foe, as his eyes searched the faces of the cheering Corinthians. "You had your freedom, yet you gave it away. Was it worth it?"

The weaver hesitated as he noticed two Corinthians standing at the railing closest to him, staring with eyes as intense as the sun. While all others were shouting and cheering, these two remained silent. Their faces showed no excitement. One was muscled like an ox, the other as sinewy and lean as a cat, blue eyes staring through him like...

"Like a drowned man who still breathes," Jameson said. Then he shouted, "Steward? Is that really you?"

She flinched and looked away.

Steward's still alive, Jameson thought, recognizing the giant beside her as Taran. By the Gods, he'd grown to the size of a mountain. Just how tall was Taran now?

"It's really you! Both of you! Gods above, it's a miracle!" Jameson laughed, feeling this four-year nightmare finally drawing to an end. *I've found them. Depths be damned, I found them. Thank you, Eo. Now we can finally—*

Pain ripped through his Jameson's leg as the gladiator's foot slammed into his kneecap. Jameson's leg bent backward, tendons snapping and bones breaking. He stumbled forward, plunging the trident into the man's chest and toppling into the crimson water beside him.

The cheering crowd drowned out Jameson's scream as he reached for his mangled leg.

Hands grabbed at him, lifting him from the sands and through the gate out of the Arena and to the infirmary. Yet before he was led away, Jameson looked at the two children one last time, much older now. Seemingly no longer children.

I was so close, Jameson thought as he lost sight of Steward and was dragged back into the bowels beneath the Arena. *Oh Gods, I was so close...*

"So he's an Animal, after all," Bear said as medics carried Jameson away on a gurney.

"He hesitated. Lost his focus," Fox said, only finding wrath where there had once been empathy. "Just another Mouse."

"That's a bad break. That leg of his won't heal right. Can't be a gladiator anymore. Not a good one, anyway. He'll be sold off."

Fox stared at the adoring crowd. Women and men were still throwing their tokens of affection into the flooded pit. "Poor him. He'll probably be bought by some rich suitor who loves him. That's a better fate than most." Foxed balled her hands into fists, thinking of her father and how Jameson had killed him. *Doesn't matter how he was involved or that he pulled the trigger himself. All that matters is that he was there, he knew, and he lied.*

"Maybe *we* could buy him," Bear said, and Fox whipped her head toward him, glaring. But Bear stubbornly added, "We could set him free, you know. We have plenty of money. We could—"

"No."

"No?" Bear paused, watching her with a hard eye.

"I told you what he did," Fox whispered, hands trailing the brand on the back of her neck. "Jameson was there when my father died, and he lied to me about it. For years, he let me think that Dad's death was my fault, but it'd been him all along." Fox turned her back to him. "Jameson let my dad die, so we let him die."

Jameson awoke in agony, his leg throbbing and vision swimming as he sat up.

"Where am I?" he asked, staring out at a room with gilded walls and stained glass windows instead of the cold stones of the gladiator barracks. On the wall across from him was a bookshelf filled with tomes and a bed-side table made of rich mahogany wood. On it, a burning candle dripped wax into a silver saucer and incense burned with the protective aromas of chrysanthemum, ginger, and clove. Resting neatly on a silken rug across the room was his armor, cleaned of blood. His trident and dagger lay beside it, both engraved with the tales of the sea.

Jameson moved his legs only to yelp at the searing agony. He pulled back the sheets and stared at the brace on his right leg. A salve coated the flesh beneath.

Somebody knocked at the door, asking, "Weaver, are you awake?"

The door opened before Jameson replied.

A Divine Virgin entered the room with one sunguard while the others closed the door and waited outside. The Divine Virgin raised her veil, revealing brown skin, green eyes, and black hair.

The sunguard doffed his helm, revealing a gray face and burning eyes that were black in the shadows. Jaw square and lip cut with a long-healed scar, he glanced over at the Divine Virgin for a moment, and his expression softened. Then his gaze returned to Jameson and burned brighter as his right hand rested on the grip of his curving black blade, though he made no move to unsheathe it.

As was practice, Jameson bowed his head out of deference, though not out of religious fervor. He believed in only the Aritrastan Gods, and certainly not in the slave-sacrificing Deitan. Yet to admit or imply that, especially in front of a sunguard, would have been cause for execution by Wick. Feigning a smile, he said, "Divina, I would kneel, but—"

"Please don't," she replied firmly but kindly. "I've gone to great lengths to set that leg of yours. I would hate to see you undo that good work."

Jameson gently inspected his leg. *It's ruined. I won't fight again.* That idea filled him with relief, but sorrow still crept into his consciousness as he thought of Steward. "But why go to this effort, divina?"

"I've claimed you in our good Lord's name as a tithing," the Divine Virgin replied. She smiled, clasping her hands together. "You are no longer a slave, Weaver, but a free man. A Corinthian citizen."

"You freed me?" Again, Jameson felt equal parts reassurance and misery. "Why me, of all people?"

"Because I think you can help me reform some of the Corinthian traditions, starting with slavery. With your popularity here, I think you can be a voice of reason and sway the minds of citizens more than I can."

"I don't understand, divina. You can't do this yourself?"

The Divine Virgin sighed. "No. Even in my position, there are rules of the state that I must follow. What I wear, how I act, who I free." The Divine Virgin's voice was soft and kind, but filled with frustration. "In the eyes of many more powerful than I, slavery is a necessary evil. Slaves make up three-quarters of our workforce and outnumber Cassian citizens two to one. If I were to free all the slaves in Cassius, the port would crumble to ruin. So I'm allowed one tithing each month. And of those, I must still receive permission from our high priest, who would not have allowed your freedom if your leg hadn't ended your gladiatorial career. I only know because I've asked permission to free you multiple times, and only now have I finally been granted my request."

"You chose wrong," Jameson said, thinking of Steward and Taran. "You should have chosen a child instead of me."

The sunguard took a step forward, half-way unsheathing his sword. "She saved your life, you ungrateful—"

"Lucius," she said, putting a hand on his and forcing the blade back into the sheath. "I don't know what you've been forced to endure, Weaver, but I've chosen you because you can speak freely to the people, whereas I cannot. With your talents in oration and storytelling, you are one of the few people who can *truly* change Corinthus for the better. By choosing you, you can save *all* the child slaves." She paused, as if wanting to add something but unable to bring herself to say it.

"But?" Jameson supplied.

The Divine Virgin looked away. "But while I have chosen you, you are not truly free. You need to be branded with Deitan's Seal so that you cannot be taken as a slave again. It's... an archaic tradition, I know, but one that will keep you safe."

Jameson remembered his oath. "And if I am branded, am I forced to stay here, or could I return to Aritrasta?"

The Divine Virgin nodded her head, as if having suspected that possibility. "You could leave tomorrow if you wanted to. I would even bless you and your travels. I will not make you stay, Weaver, but if you did, I think you could usher in a new age of the Corinthian empire. A *free* age."

Jameson remembered seeing Steward standing at the edge of the Arena. *She's still here. Taran too. I can't leave without them.*

"And if I asked for something in return for staying?" Jameson asked.

The sunguard stiffened. "The divina has already given you your freedom. What more could you possibly want?"

Jameson met his eyes without flinching. He'd fought too many gladiators to be afraid of a man with a scimitar. "I was separated from my... *nephews* when I was brought here. They were sold into slavery too. I want to find them."

The Divine Virgin stared at the ground, eyes brimming with tears that didn't fall. Then her eyes filled with determination. "Weaver, for as long as you remain in Cassius, you may stay here under my watch. If you help me, I will do everything in my power to protect you *and* your nephews. When we find them, I'll claim the boys as tithings, so you can all go home."

"Thank you, divina."

"Thank me by calling me Felice."

Jameson smiled, feeling more hope than he had in the last four years. *I found Steward once. I can find her again. I just have to stay here and wait. Even if takes another four years.*

CHAPTER THIRTY-FIVE

Fox was silent when she arrived back at the villa, appreciating a moment of solace in a world filled with so much noise. She could hear the forest speaking to her in the wind, cool against her skin. The sun had long since fallen over the trees, filling the Hunter's clearing with a familiar cold and darkness. Her horse's hooves clomped over the dirt as they passed the fields of grain and vegetables, echoed by the other steeds.

Bear sat on a chestnut-colored stallion, and two fledgling Animals rode between them: Frog and Panther. The former being a Corinthian-born slave with long limbs and expertise in poisons, the latter a squashed-face Aritrastan boy whose strength rivaled Bear's, despite being much shorter. The pair grinned, excited to tell Aquila the details of their first successful long-distance Hunt, but Fox was numb—this trip had been her thirty-fifth.

This Hunt had taken them south, down to the Corinthian capital of Solanus. There, cathedrals, amphitheaters, forums, and public works had been built for a city with millions instead of thousands. Yet the Solanese citizens were akin to the Cassians. Few knew how to fight or survive outside of the city's stone walls. Instead, they lived by trading for such necessities.

Despite the grandeur, Solanus was just a bigger city for more Mice.

Their target had been Titus Marcellus Ralii, an aspiring military leader and member of House Ralii, a Marcellian House that'd fallen out of favor with the Sovereign and the Council of Benedictus. Titus had many enemies—Aquila among them. Not that the Hunter shared why. His answer was always the same: *Titus is a Mouse, and all Mice are our enemy. That is the only reason you need.*

Though Titus had a charming smile, his eyes and hands had been cruel. So Fox had taken both.

By herself, the task would have been difficult, but with four Animals, it had been an easy massacre. They left a trail of bodies throughout the manor, ending with the eyeless, handless corpse of Titus himself—all without disturbing the other sleeping members of House Ralii. Compared to others, Titus's death had been easy to swallow, having deserved it. Most others were like Gaius, their deaths souring her stomach and mixing with the poison that still coursed through her veins.

Worse always was the thought of returning to the very man who'd poisoned her.

Fox rode her horse to the stables and handed the reins to Panther after dismounting. Gently, she put a hand on his shoulder and smiled to hide her bitterness. "You did well, Panther. Aquila will be proud."

Fox's own words echoed in her ears, reminding her of Owl. *Aquila will be proud.* Had Owl felt like this for the last decade? Hollow and exhausted? Speaking only lies? No wonder she spoke so monotonously.

Panther didn't seem to notice her lack of enthusiasm. He had enough for all four Animals. He paced from foot to foot while his eyes darted about. "Should we tell him now or..."

"Wait until the morning," Fox said. "Best not to interrupt the Hunter's sleep."

"Right—I mean, *yes.* I knew that. Thanks, Fox," Panther said, racing away with Frog to take the horses to the stables.

Fox's smile disappeared as she slipped into the villa. Crossing through the dark hallways, she stepped into a small bathroom, lit a candle, and stripped her soiled clothes. The house slaves had prepared a set of fresh clothes and a bath for her, but they had already skittered away. Fox didn't blame them for avoiding her, not when she stared at her reflection in the water and saw what she'd become: a hardened, six-year-old Animal with a shaved head and a scarred body.

"I'm nineteen," Fox said, though it took some effort to remember the human equivalent. Stepping into the bath, she wiped the dirt from her skin. When she exited the tub, the water turned black like ichor.

Toweling off, Fox rummaged through her pack for her makeup. She applied the creams, powders, and colors to her face using a small mirror that had once belonged to a girlie. She visited them often while on Hunts, paying them to teach her how to dress, walk, and talk like them. Bear had gone to the girlies, too, but she assumed he'd learned other things. Flesh things.

Even now, she blushed at the thought.

"I can still show him the truth," Fox said to the mirror, but she couldn't believe it. Not after years of telling herself the same lie. Too much time had passed, and if she told him now, it would reveal an unforgivable act of betrayal. *We trust each other with our lives—our pasts—but I haven't trusted him with this.* She just couldn't face a world where Bear knew what she was and how she felt about him but didn't feel the same. And it was easier to pretend by putting makeup on her face and thinking that she *could* tell him even when she wouldn't.

With a sigh, Fox removed the makeup and hid the cannisters in her pack before pulling out a straight razor and shaving the stubble from her scalp. Drying herself off with a towel, she put on the fresh set of clothes laid out for her by the slaves, stuffed the makeup cannisters in her pockets, and slunk back into the hall. None were around. Walking halfway down the hallway, she stopped in front of a tall vase depicting gladiatorial warfare in chariots. Because of its narrow mouth, this was one of the few vases which servants didn't dust inside of. Silently, she placed the cannisters inside with a sack of gold coins—enough money to pay for her and Bear's escape, should the time ever come.

The sack was one of several she'd hidden. But while most were buried outside Cassius and the other cities they'd visited, Fox had left this one here, just in case she and Bear needed to escape at a moment's notice. A poor idea, but part of her had always hoped that Bear would find it and ask about the makeup. Then she would be forced to tell him the truth.

I've kept this here for three years, and he still hasn't found it, Fox thought, but she held on to that hope, because it was one of the few things that the world—or Aquila—couldn't take away from her.

Then Fox walked down the rest of the hallway and returned to the room she shared with the other Animals. Three sets of bunk beds were arrayed on one side of the room, cabinets of clothes and weaponry on the other. The other Animals were all lying in their bunks.

The faces were different ones now, younger. Lion and Hawk left the villa four years ago, just before Panther and Frog arrived. Two years previously, Snake and Wolf had been replaced by Raven and Turtle. And soon...

Soon, it will be our turn to leave. We'll go somewhere else in the empire to fulfill the Hunter's wishes. We'll Hunt until we die... Fox thought, though she'd long since accepted her fate. She silently climbed into her bunk above Bear, looking down at him only because his eyes were closed. *As long as Bear and I are together, and as long as we're away from Aquila, that'll be enough.*

But even that thought filled her with dread. No distance would ever be enough.

We'll have to come back to receive the antidote, she thought, shaking her head once she remembered she hadn't seen Lion, Hawk, Wolf, or Snake return to the villa. *He ships it to them, then? Sends guarded caravans to them?* She pondered it. *Just how many other Animals are out there hiding in the shadows of the empire? How many poisons? How many antidotes?*

Though she'd searched for years, Fox had come no closer to knowing the particulars of the poison. Short of asking Aquila directly, she doubted she'd ever discover it.

◆◯◆

Fox awoke, panicking as she swiped out her talan to stab...only air.

"Another nightmare?" Bear asked quietly in the bunk beneath her.

"Always," Fox said, shifting in the top bunk to look down at him. "And even though I know they're gone, it always feels so real." Her dreams were always filled with corpses. Sometimes her father, other times Mouse, Ink, or even Gaius. Always the faces she'd known. Deaths she couldn't forget.

"I'm not gone," Bear said, the bed squeaking as he made room for her. Fox slipped from the top bunk and lied in his bed beside him, rolling away from him but still scooting closer so their backs touched. The contact calmed her, though she wanted much more.

Fox didn't fall back asleep, only laid with her eyes open, wondering what the future would hold.

Wishing for a world in which she'd already told Bear the truth.

When the door eventually opened, Bear stirred beside her. So did the others. Owl appeared in the doorway and smiled. She'd grown older in recent years, but time seemed to magnify her body. Her skin was forming wrinkles, and the bags beneath her eyes had to be concealed with makeup. Yet her wide, unblinking eyes were the same they'd always been. "Fox, Bear, Panther, and Frog. Aquila is awaiting news."

Immediately, they stood from their beds, quickly changed to look presentable, and followed Owl out as Raven and Turtle returned to sleep. Fox closed her eyes, counting the steps and listening to the creaking floorboards, smelling blood and sweat, feeling the fear of the skittering slaves Aquila hadn't made Animals.

It's better to be a Fox than a Mouse, she thought, opening her eyes as she entered Aquila's study.

In her absence, a few animal heads had been added along the walls, exotic creatures from the farthest reaches of the empire. She stared at a full-body taxidermied cat with spotted prints. Its mouth snarled, frozen in a damning hiss, but its eyes reflected only horror. They urged her to run.

Fox turned her attention to Aquila, who stood in front of the fireplace, holding a crystal goblet filled with crimson—blood or wine. Perhaps both.

"So, the Hunt was successful, yes?" Aquila asked without looking at them.

"Yes, Hunter," the four Animals said in unison.

Fox and Bear waited in silence as Panther and Frog detailed the events leading up to Titus's death. At the story's end, Aquila asked, "Is this accurate, Fox and Bear?"

"Yes, Hunter."

Aquila smiled. "Good. I am proud of all of you. Panther and Frog, you may go. Join the others and begin your morning run while I speak with Fox and Bear privately."

"Yes, Hunter." Frog and Panther said, competing to leave the room first and complete the Hunter's orders.

Without the fledglings holding his attention, Aquila stared at Fox, and her gut churned. He said, "I am proud of you both. These past years you have proved yourself to be motivated—no, *determined.* You are worthy of your names and your necklaces. You have proven that you no longer need my daily intervention."

This is the moment, Fox thought as relief flooded over her.

"You no longer need to stay within the villa. Instead, you will go from here, free as the Animals you are, and continue your good work elsewhere within the empire."

Yes.

"Over the years, I have developed a network of Animals throughout Corinthus. They're hiding in the cities among the clergy, the army, and the Marcellian Houses. From Vulcanus to Nessus, loyal Animals have continued our traditions. And now, I believe it is your time to join them." Aquila sipped from his drink and said, "Fox, you will join Lion in Syrnius, and Bear, you shall be with Snake in Midius."

No. Fox stiffened, the flood of warm emotions turning cold. *Syrnius is to the far west, but Midius is to the east. We'll be separated by a thousand miles.* She looked over at Bear, catching his own panicked expression.

"We won't be together anymore, Hunter?" Bear asked. They hadn't spent a day apart since they'd been reborn as Animals.

"Only for a brief time," Aquila said.

No. It'll be permanent, Fox thought, realizing the truth. *He'll keep us separated and off-balance. He'll keep control of us because we'll think we're alone. The only link we'll have to each other will be Aquila, and if we try to escape together, then we'll die from the poison.*

The snare tightened across her throat, and she adjusted her necklace to take a shallow breath before asking, "When do we leave, Hunter?"

"Within a day's time. I've hired guides to travel with you across the empire and have sent word to them of your arrival, yes? They'll be here by tomorrow's sunrise, if not before."

The snare pulled tighter.

Fox looked back at Owl, who stood by the door, frowning. Though she said nothing, Fox could hear her words from so many hunts ago. *When animals enter snare traps, they don't realize that there is a noose around their necks. When they struggle, the snare only tightens. If they run, they suffocate. If they stay, they die of thirst.*

"No," Fox said, choking out the word.

"No?" Aquila asked. He stepped forward, oozing menace. His scimitar clattered at his hip, chiding her. The shadows flickered, as if under his control. "*No?*"

"No." Fox ripped the necklace from her neck. The clasp snapped, and the spun silver and yellow enamel clattered to the ground. *I will not die ensnared, and I will not die away from Bear. I'll die here if I must.*

"After everything I have given you, this is how you repay me? With disobedience? With disrespect?" Aquila asked, his eyes burning brighter than the coals in the fireplace. He stomped back to his desk and pulled open a drawer before hurling a small sack of coins at her feet. Sols spilled from its open mouth. "Even this is not enough for you? Then what about these, Fox?" Aquila pulled out a couple of containers and slammed them down on the desk, the tin metal crumpling as colored powder exploded out of it. "Even these *makeups* aren't enough?"

Fox couldn't avoid flinching. Bear might not have found it, but the Hunter had.

"What? You didn't think I knew? I'm not Cow, you pathetic excuse of a Fox! You aren't worthy of being my fur coat, let alone standing before me!" Aquila's shadow elongated as he walked in front of the blazing fire and onto the bearskin rug. "I have forgiven your lies, your faults, everything! Over and over I have shown you only compassion, and this is how you treat me? I will not allow it." Aquila paced like a tiger at the edge of a cage. Yet no bars separated the Hunter from Fox.

Bear took a step forward. "Hunter—"

"Don't protect *her*, Bear!" Spittle flew from his mouth as his face contorted, each syllable enunciated with gnashing teeth and popping veins.

Bear turned to Fox wordlessly, his brown eyes unreadable.

Fox felt the world stop. *Aquila revealed that I'm a girl. Bear knows now. He finally knows.* One heavy burden on her shoulders was replaced by another. *Does he hate me now?* She didn't know. Bear's expression remained unreadable.

"Yes, *her*," Aquila continued. "You may not know this about your companion, but Fox is a woman. She has been lying to all of us this entire time. She's been lying to *you*, Bear."

The words shattered like glass, and Fox winced as they cut through her mind.

"Do you know why I hate lying, Bear?" Aquila asked. "Because it means that I do not have your loyalty—just as you do not have Fox's loyalty. Otherwise, she would have told you. You mean nothing to her."

"Bear," Fox said, her body trembling from the words. "That isn't true. You mean everything to me. I didn't tell you because—"

"It doesn't matter why!" Aquila spat. "Fox lied to you, Bear. She deserves to be punished. She deserves to die."

Bear said nothing, and his face remained as stoic as before. Despite how long they'd been together, Fox couldn't tell what he was thinking. She saw the anger in the way he moved, but would he really try to kill her? As if in answer, Bear unsheathed two anelace daggers and stalked toward her.

He hates me, she thought, and her mind flashed to the *Constable,* to Mouse.

Damn you to the depths, Steward. Those had been some of the last words Mouse spoke to her. Fox knew she'd break if she heard Bear say the same thing. She'd rather die first.

And she'd probably get her wish.

"I won't fight you, Bear," Fox said, backing away from him and toward the wall. She looked for escape but Owl was still standing in front of the door with a knife in her hand, and Aquila was in the middle of the room, cutting off escape to the window opposite the fireplace. Instead, Fox backed away toward the corner, back brushing on the furs and animal heads mounted to the walls. "Not again. Not after Mouse."

As Bear skulked closer to Fox, Aquila donned a triumphant smile. "Good! Very good! Kill her, Bear! Kill—"

Bear turned, arms blurring. A knife slammed into Aquila's shoulder, but the second missed. The Hunter staggered backward but kept his feet beneath him.

Aquila looked down at the blade as if unable to believe what he was seeing. "You... *you*—"

"Oy! You sure your name isn't Cow?" Bear asked, acid dripping from his tongue as he ripped off the bear-tooth necklace. It clinked on the floor. He grabbed a bloody longsword from the wall and pointed it at the Hunter. "I ain't your squalling rug!"

Fox's body reacted before her mind did. The talan slipped into her hand as she raced to cover Bear's back from Owl's onslaught of knives. But Owl hadn't moved from the doorway, her unblinking eyes fixed on the Hunter.

"Owl!" Aquila shouted, words cold as death. "Don't just stand there! Help me!"

"Owl?" Fox asked, eyes as wide as the older Animal's. "Please don't fight us."

Fox was skilled enough to fight Owl one-on-one and win, but the thought of it filled her with dread. Unlike her own mother, Owl hadn't abandoned Fox. She'd taught them both how to read, fight, and Hunt. And no matter how old she was, Fox still felt like Owl's fledgling. To fight and kill Owl would rip out her own heart.

"If you're going to bite the Hunter, go for the neck," Owl said, locking the door and sheathing her knife.

"Owl, you know what will happen to the others if you do this," Aquila said as he backed away toward his desk. His eyes were wide, frantic, and he unsheathed his scimitar, but it looked unsteady in his hands. When was the last time he'd been in a true fight?

Far too long ago, Fox thought, grabbing knives off of the wall. *That's the problem with being a Hunter. You get too comfortable.*

Aquila bumped into the front of the desk and flinched. "Don't do this, Owl! The other Animals will all die. The poison—"

Fox threw a dagger. Aquila sidestepped, drawing his sword. Bear charged forward with a roar. He clashed swords with Aquila as Fox threw more knives. The blades soared through the air, most clattering against the walls and taxidermied animals, but a few found flesh. Two hit Aquila in the stomach and bicep, the third grazing Bear's ear as he parried Aquila's blade and shoved him away.

The Hunter backed around the side of his desk, staggering from his wounds but still alive. Fox flanked around the other side of the desk, grabbing a hand axe from the wall as Bear pushed the Hunter into a corner.

Cornered prey is dangerous prey, Fox remembered too late.

Aquila snarled, parrying Bear's blade and thrusting a dagger in his chest. Bear stiffened and stumbled back, blood soaking his clothes. His back hit the desk, and he toppled to the floor. As he tried to drag himself backward, Aquila lifted his sword.

"*No!*" Fox screamed. She leaped up onto the desk and pounced on the Hunter. They collapsed, and Fox landed on top.

A horrendous wail erupted from her throat as instinct forced her into a frenzy. She grabbed the blade embedded in his stomach and shoved it up, spraying blood. Aquila spat on her face and tried to gouge out her eyes, but Fox leaned back and bit off two of his fingers. Pulling the knife from his arm, Aquila tried to slit her throat, but she caught his wrist in her hand and severed the tendons with her talan. He dropped the knife and punched her with the other hand, even as blood leaked from his mouth and stained his teeth.

Blood spattered the walls and floor as her talan slammed into flesh. Her scream became a string of curses as she ripped through sinew, arteries, and cartilage. With each stab, Aquila's face morphed into that of another victim's.

Gaius the Cassian butcher. Titus the Solanese statesman. Maxima the Heracean merchant. Aelius the Midian sailor. Cato the Nessian general. Dozens more across the Corinthian cities. All those who had died by her hands.

When Fox finally breathed, Aquila's face returned. She'd hacked off his nose and lips, revealing a mouth of broken teeth. His head was almost severed judging by the ten stab wounds in his throat. But somehow, his short manicured hair was still as perfectly styled as it had always been.

Aquila saved us from a life of slavery. Taught us how to fight, how to survive. This is how I repaid him. Of all things, tears came, and Fox didn't hold them back. She sobbed on the Hunter's chest, hitting him weakly and yet clutching him tight. "Damn you," she said as his blood stained her clothes. "Why'd you make me into this?"

A weak cough startled her, and Fox remembered Bear. She turned and stumbled away from Aquila's corpse to where Owl had propped Bear against the wall. He pressed his hands over his stomach, but the blood still seeped through.

Fox fell to her knees beside him and joined her hands to his. "Bear, you bloody bastard."

"Who are you calling a bloody bastard? Seen a mirror lately?" Bear asked between gasps. He slapped her hands away.

Fox pressed her hands against his again, and he didn't fight her. *He's in too much pain to be stubborn,* she thought, breath hitching in her throat. "How bad is it?"

"Doesn't even hurt," Bear said with a wince.

"You're lying."

"Of course I'm squalling lying!" Bear snapped as more blood pulsed between his and Fox's fingers. "Everyone else is, so why can't—"

Bear's voice broke as he fell into a coughing fit.

"Stop talking." Fox pressed harder against his stomach. "Conserve your strength."

"Squall you. I'll talk if I want to squalling talk."

"Your name should be Ass."

"Oh, yeah? Well, you can kiss my ass! Everyone treats me like I'm stupid. I ain't squalling stupid." His eyes lost their hard glint. Though he broke eye contact, she'd caught the glimpse of vulnerability in them. Quieter, he added, "I knew, Fox. Knew all about that squalling sack in that squalling vase. But I knew even before then. I ain't squalling stupid... but you treated me like I am."

He knew... Why'd I think I could ever hide it from him? He knows me better than I know myself.

"Why didn't you say anything?" Fox whispered.

"Why didn't you?" Bear echoed, disgusted. "I *trusted* you, Fox."

Trusted. Past tense. Fox's stomach dropped. "Bear—"

Owl interrupted them, wielding a scalding fire poker. "We need to cauterize that wound."

Bear's eyes widened. "Oy! No need for that, Owl." He struggled as Fox pushed him against the wall. It was a bad sign that he was too weak to fend her off. "I'll be fine. Just need some air is all. Really, I—"

Owl pressed the poker into his stomach. Bear whimpered as she held it there for a full five seconds. She pulled back, reheated the poker, and pressed it into his stomach again, lower. Bear crushed Fox's hand in his grip and let out a pitiful moan.

When Owl removed the poker, she inspected the wound and nodded. "There. That should take care of the blood loss."

"You damn well took your time!" Bear hissed.

"You're welcome," Owl said. "There are honey-garlic salves in Aquila's desk. You'll need them to ward off infection."

"Infection?" Bear asked, incredulously. "Ain't worried about that when we're already squalling *poisoned!*"

Fox froze. *I forgot to force the Hunter to tell us about the antidote.* She winced, looking back at Aquila's corpse. *Can't ask now.*

Bear followed her line of sight. "Damn the Core. Talk about a bloody bastard."

"Please tell me you know where he keeps those poisons, Owl." Fox said.

"You didn't think to ask that before you stabbed him a hundred times?" Bear asked, pushing her away. "Oh, squall me sideways on this squalling table."

"It's in a wall safe, behind the elk head," Owl replied. "There are several vials of antidote for each of the poisons. One should be enough for each of you."

Bear swore under his breath as Fox stared at her, jaw dropping. "You knew where he kept the poisons this entire time and you never told us?"

Owl met her eyes guiltily. "Yes."

"Why?" Fox asked as her voice broke.

Owl ignored the question. "We're running out of time, Fox. The servants will have heard the commotion and will alert the Animals when they return from their morning run. We must hurry."

"All three of you... You're all just a lying bunch of squalling hypocrites," Bear whispered, still clutching his stomach. "Maybe I am stupid for thinking that you two were different from him."

Fox winced at his venomous words, got to her feet, and pulled the elk head back from the wall. As it rotated on a hinge, she saw a metal safe with seven combination locks and a key slot nestled into the wood. "There are too many combinations," she said. "We don't have time to go through these."

"Thirteen, twenty-three, sixteen, eighteen, five, nineteen, nineteen," Owl said, dropping the poker and approaching Aquila's body. She kneeled beside him and cradled his head in her lap as she took off his necklace. Its chain had been broken in Fox's rampage, but the key at its center remained intact. "Here. You'll need this too."

Fox input the number combination and inserted the key. It clicked open and revealed two shelves of glass vials filled with alternating colorless and colorful liquids set in wooden blocks with holes.

"Clear ones are poison. The colorful ones are antidotes. You need the red one. Take it with water—that's the best delivery system." Owl said, still looking at Aquila. "He hasn't given you the recurring poison yet, so one dose should be more than enough."

"What do you mean *should?*" Bear asked, still sitting by the fireplace.

Owl didn't answer, instead she stroked Aquila's hair.

"Owl, please," Fox said. "We need your help."

"Right—I mean, *yes,*" Owl said, her voice thick with anguish. She left Aquila's body and approached the desk, taking an owl quill and writing out a list of components on a blank sheet of paper. "That's a list of the ingredients you'll need to make either the poison or the antidote—"

"You can make the antidote?" Bear asked, incredulous.

"—and variations of both for whatever situation arises." Owl said, ignoring him. She returned to Aquila's body as Fox stared at the list of ingredients. "If you begin to feel sick in the next few weeks, make another batch of antidote and use it in small doses."

"All this time... you knew?" Fox asked. She gripped the talan tighter.

"Not the entire time," Owl said. "I've been tasked with making these poisons for years, and though Aquila kept the antidote formula to himself, I perfected it last year so that I could kill him... But I couldn't bring myself to do it."

"But why didn't he make the poisons himself? Why have you do it?" Fox asked, holding her talan tighter. "Help me understand, Owl. Convince me you aren't just like him."

"When I'd turned three years old, I was tasked with my first Hunt—to kill an old man who owed Aquila money. But I couldn't do it. So I ran away instead. Leopard and I both did. When we started getting sick, we came back. Aquila said he could only save one of us, so he flipped a sol to see who'd survive. Leopard won the toss, and he asked Aquila to give me the antidote. So he did, but Aquila made me watch Leopard die over the course of weeks." She swallowed hard, still holding Aquila's head in her lap. "Because I no longer had an Animal partner, I became Aquila's assistant and stayed here. So, Aquilla taught me how to make the poison and made me give it to my fledglings. He told me it was my punishment."

"But you said you learned how to make the antidote," Fox said. "Why didn't you leave?"

"I couldn't leave my fledglings. They depended on me."

"You could have killed him yourself," Bear said, pushing himself to his feet and clutching his stomach. He took a step forward as if to fight her, but then groaned and fell back to one knee.

"I wanted to, but I couldn't." Owl walked to his side and helped him stand. Together, they hobbled to the desk. "The Hunter had his faults, but he saved us. Made us who we are. Gave us this family. For all the bad, there was good in him. And I... loved him despite everything. Didn't you?"

Yes, Fox thought, hating that she did.

By Bear's silence, he felt the same.

"You need to go," Owl said. "Take the coins, weapons, and anti-dotes—anything you can carry. Leave before my other fledglings return and never come back. Please. For all our sakes."

"Come with us," Bear said.

"No. My place is here. The others still need me."

"We can all go together," Fox said. "We can all leave."

"And go where, Fox? Animals can never live in peace with Mice." Owl wiped away a tear and smiled at them. "But you two still have each other. You can live, you can be free—but you have to go now before the others get back and see what's happened."

"What are you going to tell them?" Bear asked.

Standing straight and staring at them, Owl replied, "The truth—as much of it as they'll accept... I'll delay as long as I can, but I have to let the Animals in the other cities know Aquila is dead. They'll come for you, so stay out of the cities. Stick to the forests and the dirt roads. Don't travel in any one direction for too long. Otherwise, they'll catch you."

"They won't," Bear said, pushing himself off the desk and standing straight despite his wound.

"Thank you, Owl. For saving us," Fox said.

"Thank me by living," Owl replied.

The Animals scooped up the heavy sack of golden sols and the dented cans of makeup. While Fox grabbed several vials of poisons and their antidotes, Bear took the bearskin rug and several blades. Both looked back one last time to see Owl closing Aquila's eyes.

Then they threw open the door and charged out of the villa as the house slaves scattered around them. The Animals snatched their weapons and their packs from their room as Owl's quiet sobs echoed down the hallway, spurring them to run faster. They bolted to the stable as alarmed shouts rose through the villa. Throwing saddles onto two horses, Fox killed the rest as Bear slipped onto his mount, stiff and wounded, but alive.

The horses whinnied and thundered across the dirt as the other Animals returned from their morning run to the sound of alarm bells. Their eyes narrowed as Fox and Bear bolted past, still soaked in blood. A few ran to the stables, quick to find the other horses lying in crimson pools. Their angry screams followed Fox and Bear as they rode faster into the heart of the Corinthian Empire.

Chapter Thirty-Six

For three days, Fox and Bear traveled south, away from Cassius. The sight of the open ocean frightened Fox more than even the Animals that tracked them. In that time, Bear remained uncharacteristically silent, his expression stoic, breath huffed, lips frowning.

Watching him, Fox's brow furrowed, eyes darted. *Three days... He hasn't spoken to me in three days.* Every attempt at conversation was met with a cold shoulder. Not that she could blame him. *I lied to him for six years—my entire life as an Animal.*

That begged an entirely different question: what was she now? *Who* was she? She didn't feel like Erin, that young, naive girl who'd loved her father. Nor was she Steward, the cabin boy who'd laughed with Mouse. Was she still Fox, even after killing Aquila? Or a combination of all three?

Or was she something altogether different?

I don't care who I am, as long as I have Bear, she thought, but even that idea seemed untenable. *He hates me because I couldn't trust him completely. And now, things will never be the same between us...*

As the sun descended, they left the dirt path winding through the forest and made camp beneath a grove of trees, tying the reins of their horses to its branches. Brushing away the leaves, a clear spot of dry dirt and grass served as a bed. Bear gingerly doffed his leathers, wincing with every movement. Then he removed his tunic, applying more of the salve to the cauterized wound on his stomach.

Fox stared at the blackened crater surrounded by red skin and pulsing veins. The salve seemed to help with the redness and swelling, but she had no sign of how he was healing internally, especially after three days of hard riding. Was he better or worse? The suspense was too much for her to take.

"Feeling any better?" Fox asked, but the question, like all others, was met with silence.

Bear donned his tunic and leathers once more, lying on the ground as he pulled the bearskin rug over his chest. When she lay beside him, he turned from her. Fox scooted toward him so that her back rested against his, but he pushed her away.

"When are you going to speak to me?" Fox asked, sitting up.

"When you say something that I want to respond to," Bear said without turning toward her.

Fox wanted to hit him, even kick him, and if he hadn't been stabbed, she might have. Instead, she picked up a rock and hurled it far away. But violence—especially against a rock—didn't help assuage her guilt. It only reminded her of Aquila's dead body.

I never learned to control my emotions, Fox thought belatedly. *Only to bury them.* She sat down on the ground, letting the guilt consume her. *I can't fight this. I can't run from it. I just have to accept it...*

But Fox knew she was even worse at *accepting* emotions than burying them.

"I'm sorry for not telling you, Bear," Fox whispered, sitting beside him. "I was so afraid of losing you, of you rejecting who I was, that I... made a mistake."

"You call that a mistake?" Bear asked. "Nah. A *mistake* is me trusting you."

Fox grimaced. She tried grabbing his hand, but he moved away. "I was wrong, okay? I know I was, and I don't know how to make it up to you. All I know is I can't do this without you. It's you and me. Fox and Bear. Together." She curled her arms around him, but he pulled her hand from his shoulder and dropped it back on her side.

"Together." Bear snorted. "If we say it enough times, we'll still think it's true, right?"

"Bear—"

"Strength and loyalty. That's what *together* means. But you didn't trust me—you weren't loyal. So how can we ever be together?"

"That's not fair. I've always been—"

Bear turned around and shoved her. Fox hit the ground and stared up at him. Clenching his fists, Bear whispered, *"Fair?* You want to talk about fair? I got squalling stabbed, Fox. I didn't want to kill Aquila, but when he told me to choose, I chose you. I've *always* chosen you..." Bear trailed away, wincing. But Fox knew the pain in his expression wasn't caused by his wound. Bitterly, he added, "You had so many chances to tell me, but every time you chose yourself. Why couldn't you choose me just once?"

Guilt crashed over Fox endlessly. "I was afraid—"

"Who squalling ain't?" Bear asked, lying back down and wrapping the bearskin tighter around his shoulders. "You can be so stupid sometimes. Thought women were supposed to have more sense than men. Maybe you've been pretending too long." Bear moved farther from her.

"I was afraid that you wouldn't feel the same way that I feel about you," Fox finished.

"No." Bear was silent for a long time. When he spoke again, his voice was hoarse. "You don't get to play that card. Not now. If you really cared about me, then you should have said it a week ago. Now you're just saying it so I'll forgive you... Damn you for that, Fox."

Fox flinched back, hearing Mouse's echo. *Damn you to the depths, Steward.*

It's happening again, Fox thought. She could sense that she was losing him, that Bear was drifting away. Worse, there was nothing she could do. Bear was stubborn and hurt and betrayed. He had every right to hate her. "Bear—"

"No. You had your chance."

"I'm sorry," Fox whispered as her heart thumped painfully in her throat.

"Take your sorry and bury it. I don't wanna hear it. What I wanna do now is sleep, so that's what I'm going to do."

"Bear," she said, her voice breaking. "Don't do this. Don't push me away. Please?"

"*You* pushed *me* away."

"Bear, please."

Bear didn't respond, even as Fox continued calling to him.

Eventually, Fox left the clearing, if only because it was too painful to be near Bear but not with him. She padded through the forest, following the sound of flowing water. A small brook babbled, its banks surrounded by leaning trees and exposed roots. Sitting beside it and dipping her toes in the cold water, she thought of the shores of Alira, the night shifts of the *Constable,* but not of the ocean itself.

Staring up through the slit in the canopy created by the brook, she saw the purple-blue skies overhead, clear stars and distant swirls of galaxies. The moon was hidden, but starlight allowed Fox to see her reflection in the water. In it, she could see Erin's eyes, Steward's smirk, and Fox's scars.

I don't know who I am anymore, but whoever I become, I'm yours, Bear, she thought, pulling out the tin of makeup that she'd brought with her and applying it to her face. *And this is the only way to truly show you...*

When she'd finished, rouge hid Fox's scars. Wax accentuated Steward's smirk. Mascara and wingtip eyeliner highlighted Erin's eyes. This time, she didn't wipe it away.

Morning came.

Despite the soft winds, the trees remained still, reaching for the rising rays of light as the sun pushed away the darkness. Fox's skin was warmed by the gentle touch of nature, but she remained uncomfortable. Birds chirped from the canopy, but they did not ease her dread. Even rolling a golden sol across her knuckle didn't calm her.

Nothing could distract her from the anxiety of waiting for Bear to wake up, waiting to show him the truth.

Squall it, she thought, flipping the coin with her thumb onto his forehead.

Bear's eyes still didn't open. His breathing didn't change.

"Open your eyes," Fox said. "I know you're awake."

"Nah. I'm squalling sleeping," Bear said, keeping his eyes closed.

"Just open your eyes, Ass." Fox kneeled beside him, only refraining from shaking his shoulders because of his healing wound.

"Make me."

"Bear," Fox said, her mouth dry. "I..."

I don't know how to say it. Everyone I've loved... She didn't finish the thought.

Instead, Fox kissed him. Slamming her eyes closed, Fox panicked as their lips touched. *What in the Core am I doing? I've never kissed anyone. What am I supposed to do? This? Is this what I'm supposed to do?* She pulled back long enough to see Bear's wide eyes, arched eyebrows, and parted lips.

Fox stiffened. "I, uh, I'm sorry. I—"

Bear grabbed her waist and pulled her toward him. His hands found the small of her back as he kissed her.

So this is what you do, Fox thought as her arms wrapped around his neck, feeling whole for the first time in her life. Eternities passed before she pulled back just long enough to say four words. "I love you, Bear."

"You actually said it." Bear grinned. "I love you, too, Fox." Then he raised an eyebrow. "When'd you learn how to use makeup?"

"The girlies taught me."

"Oh, so that's what you were doing in there," Bear said, blue cheeks blushing purple.

"Do you like it?" Fox asked.

Bear laughed, holding her. "You can really be stupid sometimes."

"What?"

Bear wiped away part of the makeup with one hand. "I like *you.*"

With a breathless laugh, Fox pounced on him, and they fell in a tangle of limbs.

I love you, Bear, she thought much later, when she lied beside him in the soft grass. *And I won't ever let you go. I won't let the world take you from me. Not this time. I swear it on the Drowned Sea.*

◄◦►

Fox and Bear slipped through the Corinthian Empire, ensuring an unpredictable path. Sometimes, they traveled by night when they were closer to villages, but opted to travel by the sun when the roads between settlements were long and dusty. Ninedays turned to months as they pushed inland, detoured farther south, then west, and then returned north. They stuck to the forests to evade Animals, stealing supplies from bandits and leaving them dead in their own ambushes. After six months of running, they reached the Stotan foothills, home of the stout men who'd kept Corinthus's Vast Army at bay for a hundred years.

On swift wings, the sounds of the Corinthian battle hymns rattled their bones, the beat pulsing like lightning with their marching thunder. Cannon fire, steel, whinnies, and groans echoed across the foothills, mingling with the chanting Corinthians and the silent, skulking Stotan rebels.

The Animals slipped between the walls that had been built, destroyed, and rebuilt with each victory and defeat over the last century—an exhaustive network of raised trenches, mud marshes, and forgotten corpses. Unending waves of Corinthians had died on sharp stones, believing they'd followed their God instead of the greed of tyrants—all while commanders watched from soft leather saddles. It was an endless vitriol of blood and carnage, death begetting death in such violence that made even the Animals cringe.

Only when they were far past the Corinthian soldiers and Stotan guerrillas did Fox and Bear dare breathe. But even then, the journey remained long and arduous as they crossed the Stotan mountains and avoided the roving warlords. They spent so much time among barren rock peaks and grassy valleys that they stopped in awe at the edge of the last true wilderness.

Aenu, where the jungles were as old as the Gods.

At the edge of that green abyss, Fox felt eyes, but she saw nothing, heard nothing, and smelled nothing. Instinctively, she reached for Bear's hand.

"Last chance to take a boat," he said. "We're far enough away now. The Animals won't follow us. We could get back to Alira much sooner than if we keep walking. Plus, we wouldn't have to endure this squalling jungle."

Fox shook her head. "And if there are more Cutthroats? Syrens? What then? There's no escape on a ship."

"We made that trek a hundred times and ran into Cutthroats only once. I think that's less dangerous than trekking through the jungle *and* the Deadlands for the next year."

"If it happened once, it could happen a thousand times," Fox said, before rubbing her swelling stomach. "And I won't have our son born in chains."

Bear raised an eyebrow. "A son? You already know?"

"A son," she confirmed, unable to explain how she knew. "His name is Will."

For Mouse, Fox thought, closing her eyes and feeling the small heartbeat that matched her own.

PART FOUR
SHADOW

Chapter Thirty-Seven

Lilyth lit a match, and Port Cassius burned. The fire glowed against the paint covering her skin, illuminating the night with orange tentacles. Explosions detonated around the Corinthian military garrisons, and seconds later, more blasts rippled through the forum and cathedral. Farther away, bursts of light appeared in the old city as Greeley began his own assault. Then bombs detonated beneath the bridges connecting the two halves of the port, and the stones crumbled into the river, cutting off any escape.

Let it burn, Lilyth thought as chaos reigned. *Let it all burn.*

Having approached the docks at dusk with Fleshlord flags, her army had waited in the bellows of her ships in manacles. The Corinthian harbormaster was easy to bribe, allowing Lilyth to anchor her ships and wait to take the slaves to the auction house in the morning. She'd retaken the bribe hours later, slitting the man's throat as he slept.

Donning the black paint, legionnaires slunk across the bridges into the western half, killing guards and holding onto their element of surprise. Greeley's forces remained in the eastern half of the city while Kendrik and Arya's forces took their positions on the west side.

Only after the first explosions rocked Cassius did the Red Legion reveal itself, hundreds of voices making calls to action:

"Slaves! Join us!"

"Break your chains!"

"We were once like you!"

"We were slaves!"

"Now we're free!"

"Rebel!"

"Revolt!"

"Be freed!"

Lilyth smiled as echoing cries rose through Cassius—an answer to her call. She could imagine the slaves hoping for freedom for the first time in years, decades. Legionnaires would give them weapons and marks, and the slaves would strike down their masters. They'd parade in the streets, swelling the Red Legion a thousandfold. They'd cause more chaos than her legion ever could alone, especially as Cassian slaves outnumbered citizens two to one.

"The Corinthians will never forget tonight," Lilyth said as the first guards charged out of the crumbling garrisons—only to be ripped apart by a hail of gunfire and grenados. More came. More died. More explosions rocked the garrisons as guards fell to flames, lead, and falling stones.

They didn't stand a chance.

"Go, destroy their false idols," Lilyth said to her followers. "Strength and loyalty."

"Loyalty and strength!" Legionnaires left to attack the forum, cathedral, and Marcellian Houses under Kendrik's command, while Arya led her smaller forces to the Corinthian ships docked at the northern beach.

Lilyth went south, leaving flames and death in her wake as Cassius crumbled.

The Arena rose in front of her, but she ignored it, focusing on the training compound where the gladiators were imprisoned. Lilyth climbed the high wall that surrounded the compound, sneaking up on the two guards who'd been left to defend the encampment while others reinforced the garrisons. They stood slack-jawed in their white-and-orange headdresses, which became red as Lilyth ended them. Taking the keys to the front gate, she descended into the compound.

Three windowless one-story buildings sprawled the grounds, but the center one was much larger than the other two. *That one has to be the barracks.* She approached and sneered at the symbol of Deitan carved into the door.

"Just another silent God," Lilyth said as she shot the lock, kicked open the door, and walked inside.

The sixty gladiators stood when she entered. Most were Aritrastans, a handful Corinthian, two Tavrakian. Rows of cots lined the walls, but by the wary expressions on all their faces, sleep was the last thing on their minds. Some shifted anxiously, but most were stoic, having endured life-and-death fights every day. They could think under pressure and had learned to control their emotions—at least outwardly.

I can use these gladiators, Lilyth thought, studying their physiques and hard, glinting eyes. Each was skilled with weapons and prepared to die. *Perfect.*

"Who among you wishes to be free?" Lilyth asked in Corinthian. When nobody responded, she repeated the question in Aritrastan. Then a third time in Marcellian.

"That is dumb question," said a Tavrakian woman in simple Corinthian. "We all wish to be free. But this is easier said than done."

She had a bent nose, broad shoulders, and a beard. Unlike the Aritrastans, her skin was pale from generations spent toiling in the mountains. Built more like a wrestler than a dancer, her forearm muscles were the biggest Lilyth had seen. Most surprisingly was her height—she was a foot taller than Lilyth, though Tavrakians were said to be shorter than even the Stotans.

"Escape is difficult," a Tavrakian man added, practically identical in appearance to the woman, though a few inches shorter. "Takes years to dig through stone with spoon. There are many stones. Few spoons. You have better plan, I hope."

"The front gate," Lilyth said.

"Front gate? But guards—"

"Are dead."

Most of the gladiators shared worried glances, but the Tavrakians only laughed.

"This is better plan," said the woman.

Lilyth smirked. "My followers are burning Cassius to the ground as we speak, and the surviving guards are too busy fighting them and the fires to notice us." She paused, watching the gladiators. "I can give you weapons and ships to get you out of the city. All you need to do is join me."

"You have followers?" The Tavrakian woman tilted her head. "You are priestess of Deitan?"

"No. I am the Champion of Eo the Unseen. Lilyth the Red."

Explosions echoed in the distance. Screams of the slain reverberated through the barracks. Far away, guards barked orders that were often cut off mid-sentence.

Another murmur spread among the gladiators.

The two Tavrakians had a quick conversation in their native language, a series of hard syllables that reminded Lilyth of clinking metal in a forge. Tavrakian was one of the few languages Lilyth hadn't learned, which she now regretted.

"Red is better than orange," the Tavrakian woman said, cracking her knuckles loud like pistol fire. "My name is Radur, daughter of Dalir Stonejaw and Jernak."

I will name her the Red Jaw, Lilyth decided.

Radur gestured to the Tavrakian man, who cracked his neck and grinned. "This is my brother, Duvur, son of Tradar Stonejaw and Jernak."

He will be the Red Maw.

"By our mother's mothers and our father's fathers, we will join you—as long as we get to fight," Duvur said. "But we need our hammers. They will be outside in armory. So is our armor."

"Kill as many as you wish," Lilyth said, unlocking their manacles. To the rest, she said, "If you wish to join my legion, speak now. Those who don't may stay and live the rest of your lives as slaves."

All the others stepped forward. No hesitation. No hints of betrayal. No cowardice.

They would rather die fighting Cassians than each other, Lilyth realized. *Together, they will be my Red Death.* Thinking of her lieutenants, she added, *And they will answer only to me... And when I am gone, they will listen only to Kendrik.*

Lilyth split the tip of her thumb with a knife and painted a crescent on all the gladiators' foreheads. "My other legionnaires will not attack you as long as they see my mark. With each kill, reapply the mark so it does not fade."

With her elite guard in tow, Lilyth led the Red Death out of the barracks and into the adjacent building—the armory. She noted the excitement on the Tavrakians' faces as they reclaimed their two-handed warhammers, breastplates, and plumed helmets. Rather than force Radur and Duvur to leave the helmets behind, Lilyth retraced her mark onto them while hiding a frown. Though the Tavrakians' strong bond posed a problem, both were too useful to kill—unlike Jericho. And with the sudden influx of slaves joining her cult tonight, breaking the bond between Duvur and Radur fell to the bottom of Lilyth's list of priorities. At the top remained the Weaver.

When all the gladiators had collected their weapons, Lilyth asked, "Are there any others?"

"No, all of us are kept in barracks."

"Then the Weaver is gone," Lilyth said, disappointed. *The one time I actually need him, the Weaver disappears. Damn him.*

"Weaver? As in the old Weaver of Aritrasta?" one of the older gladiators asked. "He's not gone. At least, I don't think so. Heard he's still living in the cathedral."

Lilyth stared up at the burning cathedral across the city. A horrible image of the Weaver being ripped apart by her own legion danced in her mind. *If he dies, it will take months to find a way around the Battered Reefs. I have to reach him before my legionnaires do.*

"How fast can you run in that armor?" Lilyth asked the gladiators.

They all looked at one another, grinning.

"Faster than you," Radur said.

"Try to keep up," Lilyth replied, sprinting through the front gates as her Red Death followed.

As the first sounds of slaughter reached Jameson's ears, he grabbed his trident, arm guard, and net. Armed, he limped through the gilded cathedral, past the main chamber and up the sacristans' staircase into the bell towers. His knee ached as he hobbled up the steps and out onto the walkway connecting the two massive towers to the Sacred Brazier. Beside it, Felice, the Divine Virgin, stared at the burning city through the gap of her sunguards' raised shields.

Below, shadows ran through the streets—many slaves had joined them, having slaughtered their Cassian masters and burned their houses to the ground. The Marcellian Houses were alight. Gouts of flames licked at the garrisons, burning the guards still trapped inside.

Jameson struggled to empathize with their pain. Those guards, and most of the citizens, cheered when slaves were made into Wicks and burned at the stake. Only now did they see how horrifying it was to burn alive.

But the other part of Jameson remained terrified. He'd spent the last decade trying and failing to convince the Cassian government to release more of its slaves. Even with all of Felice's support and resources at his disposal, he hadn't been able to change the hearts of even a dozen statesmen. And after this servile rebellion, the Church of Deitan would punish every slave from here to Nessus. They'd use him for a scapegoat and make him into a Wick.

If he survived tonight, that was.

"Demons. Enemies of Deitan's light. Spawn of the vile darkness... They're trying to send us back to the Dark Age." Though Felice's face was concealed behind her veil, her shaking voice betrayed her. She pointed down at the shadows, who raced through the city with blades, blood, and explosives.

Demons don't use explosives, Jameson thought, though he had no better idea than Felice of the enemies they faced. These beings were black as tar, screaming and laughing like syrens as they ripped people into pieces. Yet he'd never heard of a black syren, or one with legs. Nor did any of the other Aritrastan myths give him clues.

His first thought was of the Drowned returned to life, but when one shadow was killed by a Cassian and bled out in the street, Jameson realized they were human. Flesh and blood. *But no Cutthroats would destroy Cassius—it's too valuable for trading. So who could be doing this? Aritrastans?*

As his mind sought other answers, Jameson watched these so-called shadows drag Cassians out of buildings and behead them in the streets—only to throw their corpses back into the raging fires, which illuminated the chaos.

Explosions shook the city, and more parts of the forum crumbled. Including the auction house, whose giant metal dome was the only thing to survive the devastation. The cathedral's glass dome wouldn't be so lucky.

Lucius, the gruff leader of Felice's sunguards, said, "We need to leave, divina. The safest place for you is in the catacombs beneath the cathedral. We can wait there, and if need be, sail to Heraceus—if it hasn't fallen to the same fate."

The thought of such a coordinated attack on the entire empire filled Jameson with dread. Only the Aritrastan Armada was capable of that kind of assault, and the last thing either country needed was another war. *Gods, please let this be somebody else.*

"No, Lucius. We can't leave. Our fate will be far worse than this if this flame is extinguished," Felice said as she threw more wood onto the Sacred Brazier. "We must protect it at all costs, lest we face Deitan's wrath."

I will not die over this meaningless fire, Jameson thought. Gently, he said, "I mean no disrespect, Felice, but I agree with Lucius. If you don't want the fire to burn out, then light a torch with the flame. We'll take it with us. But please, let's go."

The battle waged closer. Detonations grew louder. Shadows charged toward the cathedral, though they couldn't break down the barred and locked doors.

"No. We will be safe. Demons can't enter holy places. Deitan will protect us here." Felice kneeled and clasped her hands together. Bowing her head, she prayed in Marcellian. Yet no rains came to put out the fires in the forum or the garrison. No sunlight rose between the clouds to drive away the darkness.

The cathedral swayed with an explosion as the door directly beneath Jameson blasted inward. Shadows streamed inside. Screams and shouts accompanied pistol fire, clanging steel, and more explosions. Stained glass shattered from the heat and pressure, falling like colored rain.

Another explosive shook the building, and Jameson stumbled, slamming down his trident to keep himself from falling off the edge. Felice let out a small shriek, but Lucius held her tight. The other sunguards formed a shield wall around her and unsheathed their blades.

"We're leaving," Lucius said, abandoning the brazier. "Forward into the catacombs."

Felice put a hand over her veiled mouth. "But the flame—"

"Can be rekindled, but you cannot, divina," Lucius said. His face was hidden behind his helm, but the cut down its center revealed his lips pulled into a thin, determined line.

"What about the nuns? The high priest?" Felice asked.

"Our oath is to you alone, divina," Lucius said, voice apologetic. "Please don't ask a sunguard to break his oath."

In two columns, they crossed the walkway, entered the bell tower, and descended the stairs. As footsteps ascended to meet them, Lucius raised his shield and charged down the steps with the other sunguards.

Shadows were met with steel. Died by it.

But why are they painted? Jameson didn't waste time inspecting the bodies further, only stopping to grab a few flintlocks and a cutlass, wearing the holsters and sheath at his waist. Strange that a trident felt more comfortable to him than a cutlass now. The weaver caught up with the others at the bottom landing.

"Claudius, you're with me. Gnaeus and Aetius, take the rear." Lucius nodded to the three sunguard before looking to Felice. "Whatever you see, divina, please don't stop."

Lucius opened the door and charged left with Claudius. Gnaeus and Aetius went right and waited, shields raised. Jameson and Felice sprinted after Lucius, but with his mangled leg, Jameson could already feel himself falling behind. Using his trident as a cane, he limped as fast as he could.

Shadows had ransacked the cathedral's main chamber. Pews were overturned, books burned, and stained glass broken. The glass sun hanging above the altar had been smashed on the hard stone beneath. Strewn about were more bodies: sacristans, nuns, and altar boys. The corpses of four sunguards were surrounded by bodies of painted invaders. Camilla, the other Divine Virgin, was held at gunpoint in the middle of the room by eight shadows.

Lucius and Claudius rushed through the flames to engage them. "Don't stop, Felice!"

"Drop your weapons!" the shadow with the pistol shouted.

Lucius kept charging.

"For the legion!" the shadow screamed, pulling the trigger and blowing a hole through Camilla's veil. Blood splattered on stones as she fell lifeless to the floor.

The other seven shadows fired their pistols at the two charging sunguards, and Claudius's raised shield wasn't thick enough to stop two of the lead bullets. One ripped through his head, and Claudius collapsed, skidding to a stop.

"No!" Felice screamed. She tried to run to the fallen sunguard, but Jameson steered her after Lucius, who tore through the seven shadows like a true demon. He hacked and slashed, severing arms and legs as he cleared a path for the Divine Virgin. Felice sprinted after him, and Jameson shambled behind while his leg throbbed. Without an apology, Gnaeus and Aetius passed him to cover Felice's flank, leaving Jameson to guard the rear with only a trident and an arm guard.

Blades appeared around corners, blocked by sunguards. Shadows hurled grenados, but sunguards knocked them away and sheltered Felice from the debris. More gunfire caught Gnaeus in the calf, though it did little to slow him down. They dashed forward, descending a set of stairs to the iron door barring entrance to the catacombs. Slaughtered sacristans surrounded it.

"Damnation! It's locked!" Lucius rammed into the door, even hacked at it, yet it wouldn't open.

"That door was built to withstand the armies of the dead. We'll never break through it." Felice said. "Only High Priest Rhesus has the key."

Jameson glanced back up the stairwell. Rhesus was somewhere in the chaos. That, or he'd already escaped through the catacombs and locked the door behind him. Neither option was encouraging.

Lucius growled in frustration. "Gnaeus. Aetius. Search for Rhesus and find the key. Try his chambers first. Hurry."

The sunguards saluted him and raced up the steps. Lucius turned to follow them, but Felice grabbed his arm.

"Wait. Don't go," she said, tears welling in her eyes. "Please, Lucius. Don't go. Not for me."

Lucius doffed his helmet and kneeled on the stair. "My place is always with you, divina. On my life, and on my honor. But I cannot defend you from this position." He jerked his head to the top of the steps. "I need to be up there."

"Deitan will protect us," Felice said, but she no longer sounded sure of herself. She let him go, head hanging.

Lucius donned his helm once more. "Weaver, with me."

"Hold on to this for me, Felice," Jameson said, handing her a loaded flintlock, which she didn't immediately take. "If we fall, you don't want to be taken alive. Take it from a slave. They'll do things to you worse than death."

When Felice still didn't take the weapon, Jameson laid it on the step beside her and followed Lucius up the stairs as rising smoke made him cough.

Minutes passed as more shadows died by Lucius's sword and Jameson's trident. With the bloodshed, screams, and the sound of chanting emanating from elsewhere in the cathedral, Jameson felt like a gladiator again. He was rusty, but still deadly. Still alive.

"Gnaeus and Aetius are taking too long," Lucius said after they'd turned away a third wave of shadows. The bodies were piling up around the stairwell. "Damn these demons."

"I'll go," Jameson said.

Lucius grunted. "Return in five minutes, weaver. No longer."

"If I don't, leave without me," Jameson said, limping away. He trudged to Rhesus's chambers first, which were already in flames. Hearing the laughter and chanting of the shadows, he ambled through the mazelike corridors of the cathedral back toward the main chamber to find Aetius face-up on the floor and surrounded by unpainted bodies. He recognized a few of the invaders.

Gladiators? Here?

"Weaver! They have the high priest!" Gnaeus shouted to Jameson as he struggled to his knees. A dozen deep wounds cut through his chest, arms, and legs, but Gnaeus still tried to stand. "Tell Lucius to—"

A warhammer caved in his skull, silencing him and splattering his brains against the concrete. A tall Tavrakian woman with a beard stood over him with a vicious grin—another gladiator he recognized from the Arena. Radur, Breaker of Men. She hefted her warhammer and pointed at him with it. "There he is, Champion! I found Weaver!"

"Jameson," a voice said, colder than a grave despite the flames that consumed the cathedral.

From the inferno in the center of the chamber, a tall, lithe shadow appeared. The tendrils licked at it, the paint flaking and revealing blue skin underneath. Holding a talan and a cutlass, its red eyes bore through him, irises icy blue but sclera red. Though it had been more than a decade since he'd seen that dreaded gaze, he'd never forgotten it. Never forgotten her.

"Steward?" Jameson gasped, stumbling two steps toward her. "Is it really you?"

"No. Steward is dead. So is Erin. So is Fox," the woman said, a snarl forming at her lip. "I am Lilyth the Red."

Jameson stopped, stiffening. *Lilyth the Red... Like Aritras.*

As the fire crackled, Jameson could see more warriors, painted and not, streaming into the cathedral and avoiding the flames. Yet none attacked her. Understanding donned on him. *"You're* attacking Cassius? But why?"

Lilyth tilted her head, a small smirk on her lips. "Why not?"

More explosions. The world swayed with such violence that it threatened to capsize. Jameson took a hobbling step sideways, stopping himself with the trident. "Steward—"

"It's Lilyth now." She pointed a cutlass at him. "Come. We have things to discuss."

The smoke worsened as Jameson was led out of the cathedral. High Priest Rhesus, one of the most powerful men in all of Cassius, was bound by his hands and knees with his head pressed against the cobblestones. He'd been stripped of his stole and clergy robes. Without them, Rhesus was just an old man wearing a tunic, being branded by several gladiators as his city burned.

"This is madness," Jameson said.

"Madness?" Lilyth asked. "This is what they deserve."

"You let your anger turn you into a monster," Jameson whispered.

"Perhaps," Lilyth said. "But I do not care what I am as long as I get what I want."

"And that is?"

Lilyth only watched the chaos.

Shadows ran and slaughtered while others shouted for the poor and enslaved to take up arms and rebel. The ranks of Lilyth's followers swelled with enraged slaves looking to place manacles on the wrists of others. Many were less sure, less bloodthirsty, but the euphoria of freedom was so pure that even the hesitant voices joined the blood chant he'd heard so often in the Arena.

"Blood. Blood! *Blood!*"

Explosions detonated inside the cathedral as two lone figures dove through a stained-glass window and ran down the street. Jameson recognized the shield and the gown. *Lucius and Felice... They survived. Thank you, Eo.*

Lilyth caught his gaze and turned, raising her gun—

"No!" Jameson pushed her arm as she pulled the trigger. The shot missed.

Lilyth stiffened, glaring with her dead, haunting eyes. She whistled, gaining the attention of a dozen gladiators. Radur and her brother Duvur—the Breaker of Stones—were among them. "Bring me the Divine Virgin. *Alive.*"

They bounded away like hounds hunting a gazelle. Except Felice was far slower than Lucius and the gladiators. She'd be caught quickly if Lucius hadn't already found a place to hide.

Jameson stared uncomprehendingly at the woman before her. "Don't do this. Please."

"She *enslaved* us, Jameson. You would have me spare her?"

"Felice didn't enslave us. The Fleshlords did."

Lilyth shook her head. "The Fleshlords may have put the manacles on our wrists, but that divine squall didn't take them off. She knew we were slaves, knew we were hurting. Yet she did nothing to help us."

"Felice wasn't allowed to help. There was a quota—"

"She had a *choice!*" Lilyth whirled, and the mask of calm contorted into terrifying rage. Jameson shrank away just as confident indifference replaced the fury.

No... The rage is still there. She's just hiding it. Like she's wearing a mask.

Unperturbed by the fiery chaos, Lilyth said, "She had a choice, Jameson. That is more than I was ever given."

When the gladiators eventually returned, they had neither Felice nor Lucius. Jameson let out a sigh of relief as Lilyth glared. Again, he saw her control slip, seeing that feral snarl lying beneath the surface, only for it to disappear as Radur and Duvur approached.

"They escaped?" Lilyth asked.

The gladiators nodded, disappointed. They both already seemed to be under her spell. The others too.

Of all responses, Lilyth smiled. "No matter. We already have the Weaver—he is the only one we need."

Jameson's brow furrowed. *She needs me?* That horrified him more than the idea of death.

In the distance, a horn blared three times. Lilyth listened to it and addressed her forces. "The Red Hand is retreating to the ships and leaving the old city. We'll do the same. Head north to the dockyard. We'll watch the rest of the city burn from the sea." Lilyth pointed her blade at Rhesus. "Bring him with us. I want the priest to see his city fall before I kill him."

CHAPTER THIRTY-EIGHT

Jameson watched Cassius burn from the deck of Lilyth's flagship. Thirty-nine other ships departed with her from the dockyards, overloaded with supplies and people. The rest of the ships were aflame, burning to ash alongside the port. Angry slaves and black-painted warriors all watched in awe as fires ravaged the countryside. So did the gladiators, who all gathered around Lilyth as she dragged Rhesus to the bow.

Following her like shadows were three distinguished zealots, who wore red paint in addition to black. The tallest of the three—who was still smaller than the giant Tavrakians—had a red hand. Another with a red heart. A third with a red eye. The red-handed zealot glared at the other two, and the red-eyed one glared back. The red-hearted killer didn't seem to notice their squabbles, because he was too focused on Lilyth.

Something was wrong with their red paint, though. It dripped like sweat. *Oh Gods, that's not paint... That's blood.* As the red-handed man noticed Jameson, the weaver looked away, taking a step back between a few gladiators, who seemed less dangerous than that zealot even though he'd seen Radur smash a sunguard's skull to pieces.

These are Lilyth's followers? Jameson thought as he stood beside Lilyth and studied her. He searched for signs of the Steward he knew, but that young girl seemed to have disappeared, leaving this... thing in her place. *It can't be Steward.*

A snarl remained on Lilyth's face even in her moment of triumph. It seemed as if burning Cassius had only made her more angry, especially as she fired full broadsides into the buildings closest to shore. Her other ships followed suit, navigating well because most of the freed slaves were former Aritrastan sailors. More structures crumbled. More Corinthians died. So did a few slaves who'd been too slow to make it to the docks. They, like everything else, were left behind.

As the ship fired yet another broadside into Cassius, Jameson said, "You have to stop this."

"I don't have to do anything, Jameson." To the red-hearted zealot, she said, "Fire again."

Cannonballs wiped out another building, and Lilyth's followers cheered until she raised her fist in the air. Silence. She leveled her flintlock at the high priest's head as the old man wept softly.

How can all these people go along with this? Jameson asked himself, but with a single glance, he had his answer. Regardless of race and creed, these freed slaves carried a spark of fervor in their eyes. Theirs was a red banner of zealotry. Under Lilyth.

She has an army of freed slaves, one with no goal other than blood and brutality...

"This is suicide," Jameson said.

"No, it's *strength.*"

Jameson turned to stare at the red-handed man, who'd snuck up behind him. He was in his early thirties, as best Jameson could tell. Like the other painted warriors, his head was shaved. His arms were enormous, but his legs were thicker and covered in scars. Yet Jameson's attention was drawn to the man's hands. The skin of his knuckles was shredded, showing bone underneath, as if he'd fought a rock and won. Or more likely, he'd beaten a dozen men to death with his bare hands. *Another madman.*

"Who are you?" The man's eyes roved over him as a shark would stare at a fish. An icy chill climbed up Jameson's spine. "How do you know the Champion?"

The Champion? Jameson realized he was referring to Lilyth. "I knew her... a long time ago."

"You mean, *before* she became Eo's Champion?" he asked, accusatory.

These people think she's Eo's Champion? That's why she called herself Lilyth the Red. By the Goddess, she has gone mad. "Yes. Before."

The frown deepened. "Have you been named?"

"Named?"

"So, you haven't." The painted warrior relaxed, but only just. "I am the Red Hand. The *first* of her lieutenants, the *first* of her followers, the *first* to be named." Jameson followed the Red Hand's gaze as it shifted to a man standing next to Lilyth, one with a handprint of blood over his heart. The Red Hand darkened, blacker than the paint on his skin. "Yes, Lilyth's first and greatest. Better than all the rest—especially him."

She brainwashed him, Jameson thought. *She brainwashed all of them.*

Around him, a chant rose like a siren's frenzied scream. "Blood. Blood! *Blood!*" The words thrummed through his body, shaking the ship's deck. Even the freed slaves picked up the words—the sound was thunder, and Lilyth was their lightning.

"This is madness, absolute madness," Jameson muttered, fear creeping into his heart.

I'm trapped. Jameson looked at the dark ocean, wondering if the syrens still followed her, even after all these years. Swimming wasn't a risk he would take, even being surrounded by madmen and swords.

As the chant trailed away, Lilyth shouted, "This world is full of slavers! Murderers! *Cutthroats!* Cassius was the first step in mending this world! It will not be the last! Eo has seen your strength this night, and rewards you with Her loyalty!"

"Loyalty and strength!" the painted legionnaires shouted.

Around him, freed Corinthian slaves fell to their knees, lifted their hands, and screamed Eo's praises.

"Why? Why are you doing this?" Rhesus asked, still kneeling with a gun pressed against his head. All eyes turned to him, their cheers turning to silent anger.

"Because Eo demands this world be cleansed. Of all sinners. Of all sins." Lilyth's smile widened. "If you do not stand with Her, you do not stand at all."

Lilyth pulled the trigger, and the lead ball ripped through Rhesus's skull. The high priest of Deitan slumped over, dead.

Lilyth kneeled, running her fingers through the blood. One by one, she called forth her newest followers and marked their foreheads with the shape of a crescent. Then she threw Rhesus over the gunwale without blessing his body, cursing him to become a Drowned.

"For those of you who hesitate, who still do not believe, know this. In the coming days, Eo will Affirm Her Chosen." Lilyth closed her eyes and tilted her head as if hearing a silent voice. "Those who do not accept Her truth will be Unchosen. They will know Her wrath."

Jameson shivered in Lilyth's quarters—the room was lifeless. No bed. No clothes. No paintings. Nothing, save for a war table with a half-finished map and the bloodstains on the floor. At the far end was an open door leading to the balcony. The night sky was dark, Lilyth darker. As the moon receded, she eclipsed it, proud and imposing in the impossible blackness.

That isn't Steward, Jameson thought. *That's... something else entirely.*

Had the Red Hand not escorted him into the room and blocked the exit, he would have run. Now Jameson had nowhere to go.

"Join me out here," Lilyth said.

Jameson's legs lurched forward as if pulled to her by an unseen force. He joined her on the balcony, and the Red Hand followed.

Lilyth raised a hand. "No. Wait outside my door, Red Hand. I wish to speak to the Weaver alone."

The Red Hand stiffened and stared at Jameson, eyes narrowing. "Yes, Champion." Fists clenched tight, he slammed his shoulder into Jameson as he left.

When the Red Hand was gone, Jameson waited for Lilyth to speak, but she was silent, only staring out at the ocean with that old drowned gaze.

"The last time we spoke, you denounced the Goddess," Jameson said. "But these people believe you are Her Champion. Aritras's heir... Are you a monster *and* a liar?"

"I am whatever others believe me to be," Lilyth said. "Whether that is a Goddess, a Champion, or a monster. I do not care what they think as long as they obey."

"But you're lying to all of them."

"We are both good at lying." Lilyth said, finally turning to look at him. Again, that drowned gaze. Her head was shaved, and her blue eyes reflected grief but no remorse. The paint hadn't been removed, but it was still flaking away, revealing a myriad of scars on her face. This close, and without the earlier distractions, Jameson made out the shape of her smashed nose, her swollen ears, and her sharp chin. A lifetime of fighting and agony. She couldn't be older than thirty, but she looked to be fifty.

"What happened to you?" Jameson asked, feeling pity and anger. "Tell me why you're doing this—why you're killing all these people."

"Why not?" Lilyth asked, her voice cold as before.

"*Why not?* How can you keep saying that after what you did?" Jameson asked, pointing a finger at her. "You killed thousands! You burned Cassius to the ground! You shot the high priest in the head! Have you nothing to say for yourself?"

"The priest was a charlatan. So was your Divine Virgin."

"Rhesus was a good man!"

"*Good?*" Lilyth sneered. "You think that priest was any less of a monster than I am? Have you seen their wars? Their conquests? While you have been sitting in their cathedrals, I have seen their soldiers burn people alive by the thousands. Their soldiers line the roads to Stotan with miles of Wicks. And for what? To bring glory to their silent God? No, the only glory goes to the priests who steal the treasure when it returns to Corinthus. They are content watching young men die in the mud while they sleep in feather beds." Lilyth shook her head. "Me? I sleep on the deck. I lead the raids. I free these slaves. I do what must be done."

"And why is that?"

Lilyth became deathly quiet. "Because Rolf must be stopped."

"Rolf the Bloody?" Jameson echoed. *But to go this far for something that happened over a decade ago?* "That's what all of this is for, then? All of this is for revenge because he took the *Constable* and—"

"No. Not that." Lilyth's eyes focused on a distant image. Something impossibly far and unreachable except in memory. But she didn't share what she saw. "Rolf took my daughter from me. My husband too. He has them both, and I have to get them back."

"You have a daughter?" Jameson asked. He smiled, then frowned, then flinched as he came to understand the situation. *Her daughter was sold into slavery—probably to a Fleshlord, who will sell her to a Corinthian as a concubine... Dear Gods.* He gripped his staff tighter as his bad knee trembled. Badly, he wanted to console her, but Jameson didn't dare.

"Her name is Lily." Lilyth said, pulling out a worn leather-and-bead necklace from beneath her armor. "She is... five now. She was three when I last saw her."

"You still think Rolf has her?" Jameson asked, immediately regretting the phrasing as fury overtook Lilyth's expression. "What I mean is—"

"If Rolf has already sold her, then he will know who has her."

"But Flotsam Hill is impenetrable."

"Why do you think I brought an army?" Lilyth asked, that talan-sharp smile splitting her face.

"But you're manipulating them," Jameson argued, pointing up at the deck above their heads. "Your own followers. They think they're fighting for Eo. It's wrong."

"No." Lilyth's smile vanished. "What is *wrong* is that people think they can take things from me without repercussions. Now, *I* am their repercussions. The Gods refused to intervene, so I must do it myself."

"You hate the Gods, yet you say you're their Champion. Those people think you're the second coming of Aritras."

"Yes, that is why they follow me. That is why they obey." Her eyes glittered as she ran her tongue along her lips. "Tell me this, Jameson. What is more terrifying: fighting a woman or a monster? What is more enticing: following a woman or a Goddess?"

"But where do the lies end?" Jameson asked.

"With Rolf's head on a trident. With my daughter in my arms. With..." Lilyth opened her mouth and then closed it. In her anguish, Jameson saw a spark of Steward, a ghostly trace of the girl he once knew.

A long silence passed before Lilyth said, "I never wanted to be this, Jameson. I tried so hard to be good, to forgive and forget, to run away and live my life in peace. Even after all the wrongs that were committed, I let go of my anger. I was *happy*."

Despite everything she'd done, Jameson's heart broke for her. He believed her. "Steward—"

"But it did not matter." Lilyth, who'd seemed exhausted only moments before, squared her shoulders and set her chin, eyes blazing with the cold fury. "It did not matter that I had finally found peace. It did not matter that I finally moved on. It did not matter that I finally had my family. No... My enemies took everything. And now, I will return everything they have wrought. Every life they took will be repaid tenfold. Every ship they have sailed, I will drown in my sea. Every freedom they knew, I will burn with my fire. Every *love*..." Lilyth choked on the word. Growling, she finished, "Every love they have known, I will swallow in my night."

Jameson shook his head. "You are no Goddess. You don't control fire, the seas, or the night—regardless of what your followers believe."

"You know nothing of the Gods, Jameson, despite all of your stories, teachings, and beliefs. Humans and Gods are much more similar than you realize. We have the same thoughts, the same vices, the same loves. The only difference between me and the Gods is that They are silent, and I am not. They are cowards, and I am not. They are *dead*, and I am not."

Jameson gasped, body rigid as he waited for the Gods' wrath. His heartbeat crashed like the waves, his skin stung like the cold mist. "Lilyth—"

In a seething whisper, Lilyth said to the sky and sea, "Hear me, silent Gods. If You have so much power, why not use it? Why not strike me down? Do I not anger You? Do I not blasphemy in Your names? Do I not *deserve* to die? Strike me down. Send Your lightning. Send Your fire. Send Your seas. Send Your night. Send all of Your fury, and kill me."

They waited in silence.

"Nothing," Lilyth said after several minutes. "That is what I thought They would say."

"The Gods are not to be trifled with, regardless of your hatred. They don't take well to insults."

"Say the men who hide behind Them." Lilyth pulled out the talan. She ran her thumb across the edge before staring up at the moon. "I am the sea, I am the fire, and I am the night. I am all of them because the Gods prefer silence to justice." A tear dripped down her face. "I am Lilyth the Red, and I will not be silent. Not anymore. Not until I have my daughter."

"But what comes after that? Even if you stop, do you think this army will?"

"No. They will not stop. Nor do I want them to. When I have my daughter, they will continue without me."

"You're just going to leave?" Jameson shook his head. "This war you've started—there'll never be an end to it. You know that, don't you?"

"It will end for me," Lilyth said. "And that is enough."

"You're willing to sacrifice everyone?"

"Yes," Lilyth said. "If it means getting my daughter back, I will bring this world to its knees."

"This is madness." Jameson shook his head. "What happened to you, Steward?"

Lilyth flinched so hard that Jameson thought she'd been stabbed in the back. "I told you not to call me that!"

Jameson took a step backward.

"That is not my name. Not anymore. I told you, Steward is dead."

Jameson shook his head. "That's not how life works. You *are* Steward. She is a piece of you—she can't just die like that."

Lilyth laughed, and the sound was so broken that Jameson doubted his words. "If you truly believe that, then you know much less about life than you think, Jameson."

"Then help me understand," Jameson said, taking a step closer even as his instincts warned him to flee. "Tell me exactly what happened."

Lilyth stared up at the moon again. "Too much."

Chapter Thirty-Nine

E rin wiped the bile from her lips. She leaned away from the tree and inhaled as the world spun. Gripping her wooden spear tighter, she exhaled and glanced down at her swelling stomach. *I'm not ready to be a mother. I'm not ready. What in the Core am I going to do?* Erin fought the fear-induced nausea, different from the periodic bouts of sickness she'd had in past months.

"Oy! Think you missed a spot there!" Taran said, standing a couple of feet away, grinning. He was thinner now, as they both were, but his eyes were alight with love in a way they'd never been in Corinthus.

I'm a killer. Taran's a killer. We can't be parents, Erin thought, mind racing in a relentless cycle until she vomited again.

"Think you got it that time," Taran said.

"Ass," she replied.

"Cow," he teased.

Taran and Erin shared a laugh. Though they didn't use the names *Fox* and *Bear* anymore, they still thought of themselves as Animals. Just not Aquila's Animals. Now, they belonged only to themselves—and each other. With Taran by her side, Erin felt like she could be a girl again—a woman now. Still a strange feeling after a decade of pretending to be someone she wasn't.

But as freeing as being herself was, being a woman—a *pregnant* woman—came with its own set of complications. "How are we going to do this, Taran? How can we raise a child in the middle of this squalling jungle?"

Around them, the trees suffocated life beneath the canopy. Their roots twisted through the ground like serpents. Their branches blocked out most of the sun, leaving the jungle darker. Birds chirped and cawed overhead, clamoring for mates' attention. Erin had seen many plucked from the air by spiders, monkeys, and other birds. The ground wasn't much safer. Stinging ants covered the ground and, at points, had created a squirming stream of bodies across the underbrush. Even the giant river to their right, which they'd been following north, was filled with boa constrictors and crocodiles—their corpses often lined the riverbanks. Yet worst by far were the mosquitoes that ruined their sleep, despite the mud and fire they used to ward them off.

"The same way we've done all this shit, Erin. Together," Taran said, wrapping an arm around her shoulder and helping her to her feet, though she only wanted to sleep.

Erin's body ached, especially her calves and ankles. The bones in her feet threatened to rip through her skin. Uttering a low grunt, she leaned on Taran for his strength, staring out at the river. *If only it flowed north. Then we could sail.*

But the thought of sailing, even on a river, gave way to terror. The ground listed beneath her, and she heard the phantom sound of creaking timbers, crashing waves, and laughing syrens. *Not again,* Erin thought, using Taran's support to take another step. *Never again.*

Taran put his hand on hers. His fingers were large and coarse, hers long and slender—both equally callused. He turned and kissed her, as he'd done countless times. Yet every kiss felt like the first to Erin. "I love you, and if our kid is anything like you, we'll be lucky."

Erin hid a frown. *I've never been lucky in my life.*

"I mean, how hard can it be to raise a child?" Taran asked.

Hard, Erin thought, stomach twitching. *It's one thing to kill a man. Another to raise one. After what I've done, can I even be a good mother?*

Erin thought of her father. She still felt the sting of his death, but she thought of him so often it no longer brought tears to her eyes. Just echoes of pain and joy.

Dad had raised her, teaching her how to gamble and grift. Gods knew Dad had done his best, but with only one leg, he'd had few options. But couldn't he have been a ferryman? Even an innkeeper? He didn't need two good legs for that. Yet he'd been a con artist. Shouldn't Dad have tried to set a better example?

Erin winced, hating the fact that she'd even asked the question. But the older she got, the more she questioned his choices. He made mistakes, certainly. But Dad had loved her and been there for her—that's what mattered most. He'd at least tried, unlike her own mother. So had Ink, who'd taught Steward honest work and discipline. Even Owl, who'd taught Erin how to fight and survive. *What am I going to teach my son?* Erin wondered. *What will he remember me for?*

"You know, I never imagined being a part of a family after Ma died." Taran said, breaking the silence as he cut a path through the jungle plants with a scimitar. "Now I can't imagine anything else."

Keeping a hand on Taran's shoulder, Erin whispered, "Strength and loyalty, Taran. Together, we'll make it."

Taran grinned as he parted another bush. Then he froze, smile dying. Taran tapped her hand twice with two fingers. *Look.*

Erin peered over Taran's shoulder. On the riverbank, she spied a bed of blue river lilies and the dead man who laid on them. Body old and frail, his skin was green like the jungle, yellowed with age and sickness. His open eyes were plagued with cataracts, his fingers interlaced over his chest.

Somebody positioned him here. They could still be here. Erin sniffed the air. Nothing. She listened to the jungle. Nothing. She saw through the foliage. Nothing.

But she still felt eyes watching her. Intelligent ones.

Erin's stomach tightened, the baby kicking as she brandished her spear and talan. She turned in a small circle, Taran at her back.

Taran tapped her shoulder twice. *Anything?*

Erin tapped his shoulder once. *Nothing.*

Then the weeds moved. A small deer poked its head between the stems, its mouth quivering with semi-chewed foliage. Erin hurled her spear, and Taran tossed his dagger. Her spear grazed the deer's flank, and his blade slammed into its side. Bleating, the deer bolted back into the jungle.

"Of all the bad squalling timing," he muttered. "It's got my knife."

Erin's stomach tightened again. She hid a grimace as the cramping intensified—severe enough that it took all her focus to push past. She hissed beneath her breath as the pain receded, which Taran noticed.

"Are you okay?" he asked.

"I'm fine," Erin said, though it was a lie. These cramps were worsening, having plagued her for the last nineday. But Erin refused to slow their journey more than she already had today. If not for the effects of her pregnancy, they might have already reached the Deadlands by now. "We need to go after that deer. For the meat and the blade."

Taran nodded. He cut a path, following the blood trail on the low-hanging branches, vines, and weeds as Erin watched the trees for signs of danger. None so far. Having retrieved her spear, she wiped the sweat and mud off her hands onto her soiled cloak. Erin calmed herself by focusing on Taran's back. *As long as I have Taran, everything will be okay. Stay close to him, and all will be fine. We'll find the deer, and then we'll get back to the river. We'll be okay... Please let us be okay.*

Eventually, they found the deer dead in a jungle clearing, its tongue lolling through its open mouth. Taran's dagger was still in the animal's side, blood pooling beneath it. The longer Erin stared at the deer, the more her mouth watered. With their limited resources, the dagger and meat could be lifesaving, but this had all the markings of a trap.

A clearing is an easy way to be surrounded without cover, cutting off all routes of escape. And there's too much blood pooling beneath the deer. The knife is still in its chest. That deer shouldn't be bleeding that much. Inhaling, Erin could only catch the scent of the earthen jungle. Looking through the underbrush and up at the trees, she saw no other creatures. Heard nothing either. Even the birds had stopped chirping. *Something's lying in wait for us.*

Had Erin been in top condition, she might have risked it. But with her baby's life on the line, she didn't. Erin jerked her head back the way they came. *Let's leave.*

Taran frowned. *What about the meat and the dagger?*

Erin shook her head. *Leave them. This is a trap.*

Begrudgingly, Taran nodded and switched positions with her, taking the lead. He'd taken three steps when the jungle came to life.

Around her, the rocks and plants grew limbs. Stone became gray-painted flesh. Trees became brown-paint and bark on arms, legs, and weapons. Bushes rose from the ground, green paint and shrubbery covering skin. All were painted Aenuites clenching stone hatchets, daggers, and slings.

Erin stumbled back, slipping over a root and hitting the ground. Her stomach vibrated, muscles tightening like rocks as she staggered to her feet and bared her teeth. Her body flooded with adrenaline as two hearts pumped within.

"Run, Erin!" Taran shouted at her.

Erin ran, but her stomach cramped again. She slowed to a stop, barely able to stay on her feet. Changing tactics, Taran pressed his back to hers, knife and scimitar at the ready. Erin had a spear, but she knew it wasn't enough.

Whispers came from all directions in a language she didn't understand as the tallest Aenuite stepped forward, a tree woman with a shaved head and a curved longbow. The other voices quieted as she spoke to Erin, her tone harsh despite the smooth sounding syllables.

"I can't understand you," Erin said, resisting the urge to throw the spear and run, knowing she wouldn't make it far.

"Chill aid?" the tree woman asked in broken Corinthian, gesturing at her stomach.

"*Child.* Yes."

The woman nodded, making a whistling sound that echoed through the trees. Quick crescendos and changing pitches, as if the tune were its own language.

A deeper whistle returned in agreement.

"We pans," the Aenuite said, gesturing with her longbow.

Weapons, Erin thought.

In Aritrastan, Taran asked, "What's our plan?"

"I can't run, so we have to comply until we can escape," Erin replied as fear, doubt, and rage swept through her stomach, clenching painfully. She gritted her teeth to keep her voice quiet, though all she wanted was to scream. "What other choice do we have?"

Two bush women walked toward Taran as arrows were pointed at him. He relinquished his scimitar, saying nothing. Erin felt the anger in his back, felt it in her own chest.

The tree woman gave another command, and a stone man stepped forward to take Erin's spear, which she relinquished without complaint. He prodded her gently for more weapons, missing the talan in her boot and the knife under her belt.

Another order came, this time directed at Taran. "Wok."

Taran obeyed. So did Erin, following with arrows and spears pointed at her back.

We can escape into the jungle, but they know these lands, so they'll be faster. We need a distraction. A hostage? No, that would get us killed. A diversion?

That could work, but how? Her eyes narrowed. *An explosion. Fire and smoke. We'll run for the river.*

"Taran, do you still have the smaller explosives and pistols from those Stotan bandits?"

"They're in my bag." His eyes furrowed as he walked beside her. "You want to blow them up?"

"I want a distraction," Erin said, heart pounding though her mind was clear. "We just have to bide our time and—"

Her vision became white as agony engulfed her. The cramps felt like blades in her chest, and she groaned. "This isn't you faking, is it?" Taran asked.

"Gods be damned, I wish it was." She slowed, hobbling and leaning against a tree before the tree-woman offered another command. The stone man placed Erin's spear on the ground and chopped off the whittled tip before handing it back to her with a *don't-try-anything* look.

"Don't seem like slavers, but I don't trust them," Erin said between strained breaths.

Taran squeezed her shoulder. "Can you walk?"

"I'll manage," Erin said, but as they continued, her adrenaline fell away and was replaced by stomach pains, body aches, and more cramps. With each step, they worsened.

After ten minutes of trekking, Erin heard running water again. "If we can get to the river, we can let the current carry us south. We'll lose ground, but we can cross the river and create distance."

"You want to swim across the river filled with the giant lizards and snakes?"

"Do you have a better idea?" Erin bit her tongue to keep from lashing out.

"No, but if we're going to try that, we'll need hostages."

"They'll kill us."

"Not if we get to the river first. It could work."

Erin answered with a low moan as she leaned on Taran, the cane no longer enough to keep her standing. Bile and fear rose in her throat, but Erin closed her eyes and focused on breathing. *Hold it in. Don't throw up. Don't fall. No weakness.*

When she heard a beast crashing through the forest, Erin opened her eyes to see a gray-skinned man through the weeds. Erin stiffened in surprise and momentary fear before chiding herself. *He's no Animal... But he is Corinthian.*

His hair was white with age, and crooked spectacles sat atop his thin nose, the left lens cracked. He blinked rapidly and twitched his head as he approached. His hands were long and slender, and thick veins rose along his skin like worms burrowing into soil.

The tree woman addressed him, and the Corinthian responded in that same flowing language. *So that's how the Aenuites know Corinthian.*

"Oh, hello, hello? I am Janus," he said in Aritrastan. "What brings you, uh, here? Come to meet the natives? If so, you've done a good job of it!" He laughed. When Erin and Taran didn't, he adjusted his glasses with a grimy finger and pointed to the tree woman. "This is Kirabi of the Straightbacks. Straightbacks on account of their, uh, straight backs, as it were—though I do believe all Aenuites would fall under such a title. From my understanding of their language, the word also means honor." He shrugged so quickly the gesture was more of a twitch. "It seems you've had the great fortune of running into our Kirabi's, uh, ah, hunting party. A thousand apologies for my sloppy speech. It has been some years since I've had the privilege to, uh, speak with Aritrastans! And your names are?"

"Bear." Taran said, warily.

"Fox." Erin added.

"Fine, don't tell me! *Hmmph!*" Then, switching to Aenuite, Janus and Kirabi spoke quickly between each other. "Just a few questions for you two. First, are there any other ah, uh, members of your party?"

"No," Erin grunted.

"Fantastic to hear! Second, what are your intentions in coming here?"

"Just passing through," Taran said.

"Passing through? From the south?" Janus tweaked his glasses. "Oh! By Deitan's light, that would mean you're both runaway slaves!"

Taran stiffened, and Erin tried to keep her breathing under control, the pain growing worse.

"How delightful!" Janus paused, his eyes darting between them, catching their anger. "Well, perhaps, *not* delightful. Ten thousand humble bows to you in exchange for your forgiveness."

Janus relayed the information to Kirabi. Janus nodded, and he said to the Animals, "Kirabi would like to bring you to the village to have a word with the elders and perhaps offer you a place to ah, uh rest?"

Sounds too good to be true, Erin thought.

"Yeah? Why should we believe that?" Taran asked, snarling. "Why should we believe *you?*"

"Excuse me, I'm just the messenger!" Janus took a half-step back. "If they wanted to hurt you, they would have. And if they wanted to make you slaves, then why would I be here?"

"You ain't their slave?" Taran growled.

"Good gracious, no!" Janus let out a nervous laugh. "In exchange for teaching them about the arts, science, and language, they have allowed me to stay with their tribe. I'm a wayward explorer, such as yourselves—well, maybe not *quite* like you, but similar, I imagine."

Kirabi asked another question, and Janus replied while gesturing at Erin and Taran. Grunting, the tree woman threw her bow over her shoulder and pulled out a stone dagger.

Immediately, Taran pulled Erin behind him.

"Kirabi means no harm!" Janus said.

Kirabi pricked her thumb against the dagger and blood spilled from the shallow cut. Sheathing the knife, she approached Taran, marking his forehead with the blood before doing the same to Erin. Then Kirabi took a step back and nodded at them both.

"It's a ward of, uh, ah, protection. See, it means that she won't let any harm come to you as long as you do no harm to her people." Erin and Taran exchanged a doubting look that Janus didn't catch. The Corinthian continued, "Make no mistake, the Straightbacks are a people of honor and virtue, though they have—how do you say it? Oh yes!—*unique* views on life and blood."

Kirabi rattled off another set of instructions as Erin groaned, clutching her stomach.

"How far is the village from here?" Taran asked as he held her upright.

Janus translated Kirabi's answer. "A mile upriver. Can you make it?"

I can't walk a hundred feet, let alone another mile, Erin thought. Yet she clung to Taran and nodded.

Their group walked along the riverbank where there were fewer obstacles, though more predators abounded. Erin leaned so heavily on Taran that her feet barely touched the ground.

"We're almost there," he whispered. "You're doing great—"

The pain began in her lower back before wrapping around her stomach. Her groin threatened to split open as water trickled down her leg. Erin let out a half-growl, half-whimper as her vision blurred.

Kirabi commanded the group to stop.

"Oh dear! Oh my! Are you having your child?" Janus asked.

Erin screamed as another round of pain ripped through her stomach and thighs. Her legs shook uncontrollably. Taran carried her in his arms, looking in every direction for a sign of what to do and finding nothing. He knew as little about these things as she did.

Kirabi turned her head and barked a rapid succession of commands. One of the Aenuites whistled into the jungle, three of them vanishing into the greenery upriver. The rest stayed by the riverbank with their arrows and hatchets trained on the water, watching for predators.

Kirabi said something to Janus. He seemed to argue until she snapped at him.

Cowering, Janus said to Taran, "The huntress wishes to help. Can we lay her at the river's edge?"

"I can talk for myself," Erin hissed, trying to push herself out of Taran's arms, but he refused to let go. "Put me down."

"Stop being Ass or Cow or whatever other stupid Animal you're being right now," he said, his voice stern. "Be *you*."

Erin opened her mouth and then shut it.

Janus cleared his throat. "Kirabi says we need to lay her in the water and position her head upstream. Her hunters will keep a lookout for us."

"Got it," Taran said. He marched forward, though the bounce of his step made Erin nauseous. She dug her grimy nails into his forearms. They made it halfway before Erin let out a louder moan. The pain tore her mind in half.

"Get it out of me!" Erin shouted. "Get this thing out!"

"Working on it. Just stay strong... Loyalty and strength, remember?"

Erin's body thrashed as Taran guided her toward a patch of open water, but Kirabi guided him toward a different spot, where blue river lilies blossomed. In the quieter currents near the bank, he set her down. Janus offered to help deliver the baby, but a withering glare from Taran had him scampering away.

Kirabi said more words in Aenuite and kneeled by Erin's feet.

Janus blinked, his eyes wide. "Uh, ah, Kirabi says she's going to deliver the baby, unless the bear objects?"

There was a brief pause as Taran hesitated, helpless. "If anything happens to her..."

"Oh, the bear threatens violence? How shocking!"

"I'll gut you like a dog if you talk to me like that again, old man."

Janus put his hands on his hips, leaning forward. "Oh ho! Listen here, you wretched oaf—"

"Both of you *shut up!*" Erin shouted as birds flew from the nearest trees across the river.

"I'm going to go, uh, ah, somewhere else. Like this bush, perhaps." Janus said, disappearing into the shrubbery.

"Gods, I love you." Taran kneeled beside her. "You're doing great."

"I'm the only one doing *anything*," she growled, as she took his hand and squeezed it tight enough to make Taran grunt.

Then the real pain began.

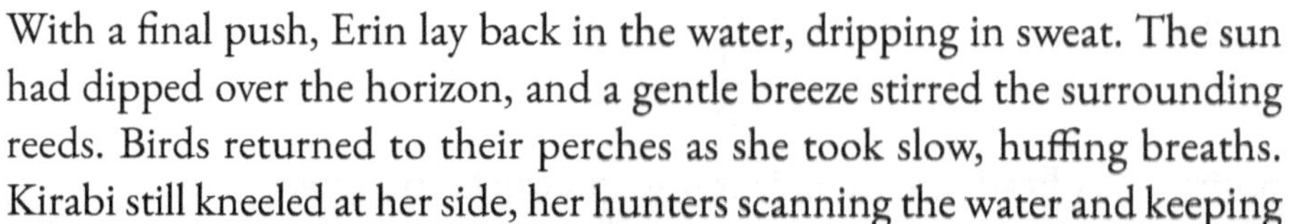

With a final push, Erin lay back in the water, dripping in sweat. The sun had dipped over the horizon, and a gentle breeze stirred the surrounding reeds. Birds returned to their perches as she took slow, huffing breaths. Kirabi still kneeled at her side, her hunters scanning the water and keeping the predators at bay.

"You did it, Erin," Taran said, holding her hand. His eyes left her to look over at Kirabi. He stiffened, and his hand clenched in her grasp. Silence stretched over them. Kirabi barked at the rest of the Aenuites. None of them spoke as they slipped out of the river and back into the jungle.

Why can't I hear him? Why can't I hear my baby? Erin thought but was too afraid to say the words. She swallowed as her heart pumped faster. "Will?"

More silence.

When Taran refused to look at her, Erin asked, "Can... can I see my baby now?" He didn't answer her, so she added, "Taran, I want to see Will."

Taran, still kneeling, turned to her, tears clinging to his cheeks. "I can't."

"Taran, give me my baby!" Erin struggled and thrashed, but her rebellion was pathetic and brief. She was too exhausted to fight. "Taran, *please.*"

"I can't, Erin." His voice was hushed and rougher than usual. No jokes, no insults, just pain.

"Why not?"

"The cord wrapped around Will's neck," Taran said, staring down at the mud, at his hands. "He's gone. Our baby's gone."

Erin tried to respond, tried to swallow, tried to breathe, but she could do nothing.

"Erin, I'm so sorry."

The words opened her throat. Her breath left her chest as if he'd kicked her in the stomach. Her heart fractured, a third of it dying. Her eyes closed as she fought the sobs that racked her chest. But they slipped through anyway. It was all too much.

"I killed Will. I strangled my baby boy... just like Mouse," Erin whispered. "Killers can't be mothers—a killer's all I'll ever be."

Chapter Forty

"Catch me, Mommy! Catch me!" Will shouted as he ran through the jungle, patches of moonlight illuminating his features. His leather vest was soiled, and his curly brown locks were filled with leaves, pollen, and dirt. He, of course, refused to wear sandals—he'd inherited that streak of stubbornness from Taran. His squat frame and strength too. But Will's mischievous smirk reminded Erin of Mouse.

My son is the best of both of them, she thought, laughing as she chased after her boy. Her hair had grown longer, braided backward in a single tail. She wore sandals and the simple leather garbs made by the Aenuites.

"I'm gonna get you!" Erin teased.

Will shrieked, delighted in the way only a child could be.

Erin leaped over fallen logs and avoided the thorny vines of the foliage. Will was short enough to run underneath them and into the shrubbery. More than once, he hid from her, and each time he sprinted off again, Erin gained ground. She pushed him closer to the river, where there were fewer trees and shrubs to hide behind until there was nothing at all.

Erin veered to the right and cut him off, her heart whole as she scooped him into her arms. "Gotcha!" she shouted, laughing with her entire body as he shrieked again.

Will giggled as she tickled him. Cradling him in her arms, Erin walked to the edge of the river. He screamed as she pretended to throw him into the water. She kept laughing, kept playing, until she noticed the scar around his neck.

"What happened, baby?" Erin asked, eyebrows knitting together as her grip loosened.

Will slipped from her arms and latched himself onto her leg. "See? I'm an Animal, too, Mommy! Just like you!"

Erin pried Will from her leg and held him. This time, she didn't laugh. "Will, what happened to your neck? There's a mark."

"Where?" Will asked, unable to see it no matter how he turned his head.

Erin held him in one arm and pointed.

Will used the distraction to pull free of her again. Her hands were too slow to catch him as he darted behind her, back into the underbrush. "Catch me, Mommy! You have to catch me!"

Erin turned, this time unable to see Will as the moon hid behind a group of wispy clouds. "Will, where'd you go?" She leaped to her feet and sprinted into the dark jungle. "Will?"

No response.

"Will?" Erin stopped and smelled. Nothing. Listened through silence. Nothing. Saw through darkness. Nothing. "Will, come back right now!"

"But you have to catch me, Mommy!" Will said, his voice fading away.

Erin sprinted through the trees after him, growing desperate when she no longer heard him. "Will? *Will?* Where are you?"

An awful feeling ripped through her stomach. Erin doubled over and kneeled. *Oh, no. Not again.*

"Will!" Erin screamed, falling to her side. "Please! Don't go, Will! Please don't go!"

A hand shook her shoulder. *"Erin."*

When she opened her eyes, the jungle disappeared. Erin lay in a stick-and-leaf hut on a hard bed of wooden planks raised on stumps to avoid the insects that bit and tore her skin at night. A small fire burned in the center of the hut, down in a recessed hole with a pile of dirt stacked beside it. Her eyes darted around the small abode, looking for her son but not seeing him. Instead, Taran lay beside her, hand on her shoulder.

"Where are we? Where's Will?" Erin asked.

"You were just having another nightmare," Taran said, exhausted. He tried pulling her back down onto the bed. "Just lay down with me and rest."

"But where's Will?" Pulling away the bearskin rug that covered her, Erin rose from the bed. She turned and stared at Taran, who wouldn't look at her. "Where's our boy?"

Instead of getting up, Taran gently grabbed her hand and massaged the back of it with his thumb. "You need to rest, Erin. We both do—got a big day ahead of us tomorrow."

"But Will's out there somewhere!" Erin said, pushing him away. "I can't just do nothing."

"Our boy ain't out there," Taran said, closing his eyes. "Just come back to bed. *Please.*"

Then she remembered.

"I strangled him... That's why he had a scar on his neck. That was from *me.*" Erin pulled her hand from his grip and covered her quivering lips. Fresh tears spilled down her face. "How could I have forgotten that? *How?*"

"Erin..." Taran's voice trailed away as she shook her head violently.

"I kill everything I touch, Taran."

"You haven't killed me."

"Just give it time," Erin said, turning from him.

"Stop it. *Please.* Will... What happened... It ain't your fault."

"Then whose fault is it, Taran?" Erin asked, turning back around. "Why is he gone if not because of me? Because of my body?"

Taran stared down at the ground, briefly making eye contact with her before returning to the dirt. "I... I don't know. Some things just happen." He reached for her arm, and she didn't pull away. "But this torture? What you're doing to yourself? It ain't going to change things."

"Then what am I supposed to *do?*" she asked, her voice cracking.

"Be with me." Taran tried to pull her back to the bed that they shared. "Strength and loyalty, remember? Ain't that enough?"

Erin squirmed free from him. "I need to go for a walk."

Taran couldn't hide the pain on his face. "Okay."

He's trying to stay strong, but he's struggling just as much as me. Except he's struggling in silence, and I'm... raving about nightmares.

For so long, they'd only had each other, and they'd been able to grieve together—talk about anything. But now the conversations always returned to Will, and the silence was easier to accept, even if it meant grieving separately. Taran did it by fishing with the Straightbacks. Erin was still figuring out how to grieve.

She kneeled beside Taran, looking at his hulking frame, which looked so small and vulnerable when he was curled up on the bed. "I love you, Taran... but I just need a little space."

"You'll come back?"

Erin winced, hating how the statement was a question. She kissed him and said, "Strength and loyalty, Taran. I'll always come back. I promise."

Moving aside the giant leaf that served as the hut's door, Erin entered the darkness beyond. Eo's embrace hid the moon outside.

You're never here when I need You, she thought, clenching her jaw as she replaced the large leaf over the small entryway.

Erin stared out at the other leaf huts that dotted the landscape. Instead of Corinthian or even Aritrastan domiciles, they resembled bushes, made of bent branches formed into a half-sphere and giant leaves which covered the exterior. Dozens were scattered in the jungle clearing near the river's edge, with the closest ones to the water belonging to the elders and leaders like Kirabi. Erin, Taran, and Janus were furthest from the river. Outsiders.

Erin listened to the pulse of the jungle around her and the soft snores of the sleeping Aenuites. Instead of birds, crickets and insects chirped while predators moved through the underbrush, welcoming Erin like a long-lost friend. The Animal paid them no heed. Instead, she walked to the spot where she'd given birth.

Where she'd strangled her own son.

Erin put a hand to her flat stomach. "I won't say goodbye," she said to the river lilies and the darkness. "He isn't gone. I... I can feel him. He's still here. I know he is." Erin looked around, wishing to see her son, the young boy with the curly locks. She knew it was a dream, but...

"It felt so *real.*" Erin stared at her trembling hands, the same ones she'd used to catch and tickle her boy. "It couldn't have only been a dream, could it?"

Erin remembered what Will had said. *See? I'm an Animal, too, Mommy! Just like you!*

"An Animal," Erin said, sitting alone. "I changed my name, but I didn't change who I was. *Am.* Can I ever be anything more than a killer?"

The night passed in silence as Erin waited. She stared out at the river, watching the water flow. Another life had been taken from her. Another soul snatched by the Gods. By Eo.

And by my own body.

Her heart was as full as it had been in her dream, but not of joy. In the cruel reality of the relentless night, it held only anger and hate. Darkness.

Even when the sun rose, and the village breathed with life, Erin remained alone by the water's edge. She stared wistfully down the river, seeing Aenuite villagers casting lines for fish—Taran's bulky silhouette was among them. Erin wanted to call out to him, ask him to join her, but she didn't. Like her, he needed space. Still, it was strange to be even this distance from him when they'd been inseparable just a short time before. Without him, she felt so… lost.

Erin twitched when she heard movement in the mud behind her. She looked over her shoulder at Kirabi, who wore traditional Aenuite garb: leather sandals, a vest, and shorts. Her body was painted with mud and pigments to blend in with the trees, mask her scent, and deter the mosquitoes. Two bows were strung over her shoulders. Kirabi uttered several words, but Erin only understood one.

"Hunt?"

Erin stared down at the lilies that only grew at the river's edge. She touched their soft blue petals. They were sacred to the Aenuites—their symbol for life. To Erin, they meant only death.

"More killing, you mean," Erin said in Corinthian. "There's always more killing."

"No kill." Kirabi said. *"Hunt."*

"I've been on Hunts before. There's always killing." Erin stared down at the river. In the reflection, Mouse, Gaius, and Aquila stared back in somber recollection along with dozens of others. In Mouse's arms, her baby slept. Erin kneeled and touched the water, touched the boy, but the image dissipated from the disturbed surface. She sniffed, holding back tears. "There's no difference. Hunting is killing. Something lives. Something dies."

Why am I still alive?

Kirabi kneeled beside her. The tree woman reached down and scooped up the fertile, black clay-and-mud soil of the riverbanks. She spread it across Erin's face and arms before nodding, satisfied. Erin frowned, glancing down at her reflection in the river—a silhouette.

"A *shadow*," Erin said, the words sounding right in her ears, more correct than any other name she'd had. "Yes. That's what I am."

Kirabi cocked her head, holding out the bow carved from the trunk of a fallen ash tree and strung with the sinews of the buck Taran had downed when they'd first crossed paths with the Aenuites. With a hesitant hand, the shadow took it and felt its burden—not the weight of the wood but the death it brought.

"Hunt," the shadow named Erin agreed.

Together, they slipped through the jungle. Erin's Aenuite sandals helped her travel over the sharp rocks and thorns in the deeper thickets beyond the river. However, she struggled to keep up with Kirabi.

Though Erin had learned the ways of Animals, the huntress was born with them. Erin had to concentrate on her silence, whereas Kirabi achieved it naturally. The huntress was unmatched in skill with the bow. From close-range, she picked off deer, rabbits, and birds—prey who hadn't even seen their deaths coming.

Doesn't matter how fast I am or how well I can use a blade if an archer maintains distance, Erin thought. *An arrow is faster, sharper, and just as deadly as a blade. Deadlier even.*

Kirabi stopped on a fallen log, motioning to her. After Erin followed, Kirabi rested a hand on her shoulder. Using her other hand, she made an *x* over her chest. *Aim here.*

Erin looked out at her quarry, an adolescent doe walking through the undergrowth. She grasped the bow tighter, waiting as her body shook with anticipation. Erin let out a silent breath and closed her eyes. She drew back the bowstring, her fingers and palms unused to the weapon despite her training. Her back muscles shifted, arms straining to hold it taut.

I can do this. Erin opened her eyes—

And a boy with curly brown hair and bright eyes stood in front of the deer.

Erin's fingers released, the shot hitting the ground almost a dozen feet in front of the doe. The creature bolted, but Kirabi's arrow sank into its chest. The doe bleated again, falling onto its side.

Kirabi jumped from behind the log and ran toward the fallen animal.

Erin remained on the log, body trembling. She dropped the bow and took three quick steps back from it. Her eyes scanned the jungle and saw nothing, heard nothing, smelled nothing. "Will? Will, are you... are you there?"

No response.

Erin fell to her knees and vomited. "I'm sorry, Will. I'm so sorry."

"Come!" Kirabi called in Corinthian. "Hunt!"

"No!"

"Yes! Hunt!"

Erin stood and forced herself to look at the bleating doe as Kirabi patted its head.

It's hurt, she thought, knees trembling. *It's my fault.*

Erin took several hesitant steps forward before breaking into a jog. She kneeled beside the deer, her face full of misery and self-loathing. The talan was already in her hand before she consciously reached for it. She stared into the deer's frightened eyes, seeing Will in them, seeing herself.

"It'll be okay," Erin said—the same lie she'd told Mouse before she strangled him. Her talan severed the arteries in the doe's neck. Erin held its head until all life left.

Beside her, Kirabi dipped her fingers in its blood and wiped the crimson liquid across her face, smearing her brown paint. She muttered a prayer in Aenuite, her voice somber. Then she stood in silence, as if honoring the doe.

"All my baby knew was this," Erin said, unable to stop her hands from shaking. "All he knew was silence."

Kirabi tied the deer's legs together and slung a long, thick stick between them. Carrying one end on her shoulder, Erin held the other end. Though the deer weighed her down, her heart was heavier.

After bringing the deer to the village to be dressed by other Aenuites, Erin left Kirabi and walked back to the river, washing away the black mud before returning to her hut.

Alone in the darkness, Erin hugged her knees to her chest and sat in the fetal position, resting her head on her forearms. Focusing on her heartbeat, she blocked out the rest of the world while she drowned in her memories, real and imagined alike.

The door eventually opened, but Erin didn't open her eyes—didn't accept the light.

"Erin..." Taran said, lumbering inside and wrapping his arms around her.

"I killed a deer today," Erin said. "It was so... *helpless.* I did that... *I* did that."

"Erin—"

"Do you think the Gods did this to us on purpose?" Erin asked with her head downcast, eyes still closed. "To punish us for the people we've killed? What we've done? Is this our punishment? Is this *my* punishment?" Then the anguish turned to rage. "No. I'd really be Cow if I believed that. The Gods wouldn't lift a finger. For or against us. We're on our own down here. Always have been. Always will be."

"Maybe. But you'll always have me, Erin," Taran said, lifting her and carrying her to the bed before laying down beside her.

Though she refused to open her eyes, Erin said, "Strength and loyalty. Right, Taran?"

"Loyalty and strength," he echoed, holding her tight.

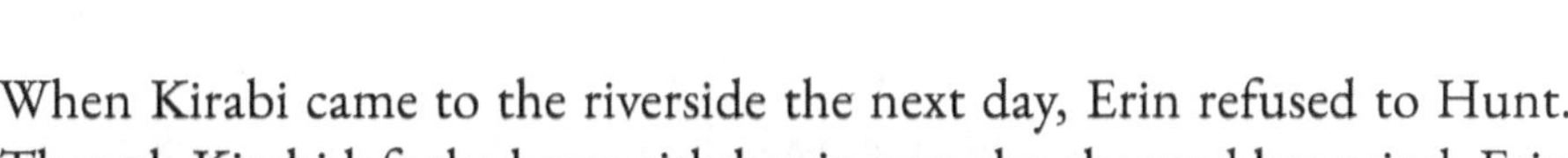

When Kirabi came to the riverside the next day, Erin refused to Hunt. Though Kirabi left the bow with her in case she changed her mind, Erin only sat and stared at the water.

Until she heard footsteps approach again, hours later.

Erin's wrath spilled into her voice. "Don't you get it? I can't do it! I can't keep killing, Kirabi! Leave me alone!" Then much quieter, "Just leave me alone. Please. I don't want to Hunt. Not anymore."

"Oh, well, uh, ah, what if I'm not Kirabi? Could I join?"

Erin turned and glared at Janus, who rubbed his shoulder and waved at her. His thinning white hair was disheveled, his spectacles grimy.

Erin grunted, and he approached, sitting a few feet from her with a small patch of river lilies separating them. He fidgeted with his glasses, washing them in the water and shaking them dry. Except they were still dirty. That, or simply scratched. When Janus tried cleaning them again, Erin growled and bared her teeth at him.

Janus held up his hands. "Oh, uh, ah, sorry about that. It's just that my glasses..." He smiled uneasily as Erin snarled. "You know what? I didn't need to see anyway. I'll just put those right here in the sun to dry, I suppose."

More silence passed as Janus fidgeted. Eventually, he asked, "If you don't mind me asking, uh, ah, what brought you here?"

"Slavery," Erin said.

"Yes, I know about that. But why trek through the jungle? There's an entire ocean out there." When Erin didn't respond, he added, "I, uh, ah, suppose you have your reasons. Would you like to know why I came?"

"No."

"Well, I'll tell you anyway. One outsider to another." Janus laughed, the sound as quick as his jerky movements. "Some time ago—seven years, was it?—I came across an Aenuite slave in Midius when I wanted to be a missionary. After I'd converted him into a follower of Deitan, he taught me some of his language. I was so ecstatic about his tales of Aenu that I used my resources to free him, hoping he'd travel back there with me as part of a missionary expedition. It didn't take much coaxing, so off we went!

"I hired a captain to sail up the coast, where we eventually hopped off and trekked into the jungle. It hadn't been so much as two nights later when my so-called friend hit me over the head with a rock, took all my supplies, and left me for dead! But did that stop me? No! I kept traveling, knowing that my God would see me through. Many times I almost died—came too close to a couple of crocodiles, I dare say!—but I prevailed. When Kirabi found me walking up the river, I thought it was an act of Deitan. A part of His plan."

Janus's grin fell. "But here's the strange thing. Instead of persuading them of Deitan, they persuaded me of Aenu and Ahua! Being here, I realized it wasn't my place to tell the Aenuite people what to believe, not when I had never experienced their lives. I mean, what good is there to have a God of light in a jungle? Out here, some of my beliefs seemed so silly compared to theirs. Though I will admit, some Aenuites traditions I still find bizarre, like that of the blood rituals—"

"Is there a purpose to this?" Erin asked, gruff. "I'm not one for stories."

"Oh yes, uh, ah, there is something *healing* about the way these people live. Their community. It's a hard life, but the Aenuites laugh more than any others I've met. Somehow, in this Godforsaken jungle, they found happiness and peace in each other... and well, so did I. I think I can help you with that—finding happiness, I mean."

"Happiness?" Erin's anger spiked. *This foolish old squall. How dare he speak to me of happiness? After all I've suffered... After all I've lost...* Erin picked up a rock and turned toward Janus, who scooted away.

"Please! I only mean that I can *teach* you about their culture!" Janus said, raising his hands. "I don't mean to anger you, it's just... If you try to understand them and stay here, maybe you can be happier. I know it's not my place—nothing ever really is, but I wanted to offer my services, if you'd have them?"

"You'd teach me their language?" Erin asked, lowering the rock by an inch.

"Why, certainly! I can teach you what it all means," Janus said, nodding. "Their language isn't complicated, not in the way Corinthian grammar is, but their words serve as double meanings—physical objects have spiritual ideas. Take, for example, the lilies, or as they call them, the *ashra*. It's also their word for the soul—the union of the land and the sky. That's why all those that live and die are placed by the lilies with their eyes open. Their souls return to the sky and their bodies return to the dirt."

"Like my baby," Erin said. She set the rock down. "Tell me why Kirabi thinks hunting is different from killing."

"Strange, isn't it? You see, to them, everything is, uh, ah, alive. Everything! They believe that rocks, the trees, and the river are permanent souls—the land itself is their Goddess, you see. So is the sky. Aenu and Ahua, as they're called, are also their words for mother and father. Yet the Aenuites don't think of their Gods as governors, more like guides to life in its different forms. They see themselves as temporary spirits—as well as all animals—and as beings born of Aenu. To hunt an animal and eat it, that isn't death to them. Not really. It's more just one cycle of reincarnation until they become a rock, a tree, or part of the great river and are made permanent."

Erin glanced back at the river, seeing only her face in the reflection this time. "Then what do they think killing is?"

"Killing is hunting without eating, killing for the sake of violence—especially when Aenuites hurt and kill one another. Their word for it is *lyth*. But there's more to the term than that. The Aenuites believe that if they are not born among the lilies, their connection to the Gods isn't complete. These are soulless creatures, not evil but broken. That is why the Straightbacks help outsiders like us—they pity us."

"Lyths," Erin echoed.

"Yes. Where the lily is the symbol of a perfect union between the Gods and men, the lyth is anything but."

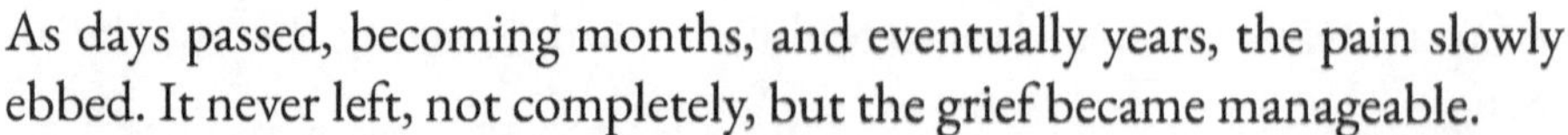

As days passed, becoming months, and eventually years, the pain slowly ebbed. It never left, not completely, but the grief became manageable.

In the mornings, light would creep in, dispelling the thoughts. While Taran fished with other villagers, Erin returned to Kirabi, letting herself believe that hunting differed from killing. Though she wanted it to horrify her, her mind soon grew numb to hunting in the same way that she'd grown numb to killing while as Aquila's disciple. During their morning hunts, she traded bow lessons for talan practice. In the afternoons, she studied with Janus. At dusk, she sat with Taran by the river until they returned to the hut and fell asleep together.

But on the nights she couldn't sleep—which were most nights—Erin crawled from the bed and returned to her bow, shooting by the light of the moon and sinking arrows into trees she'd marked with target rings. She shot arrows until her fingers bled and her back spasmed. Yet she kept shooting. She'd shoot until the dark thoughts left.

But they never did.

CHAPTER FORTY-ONE

E rin sat by the edge of the river, applying her camouflage. The last traces of night faded as the sun rose, but the jungle depths remained dark beneath the thick canopy, giving way to the shadows like her. Erin spread the blackened clay across her arms and face, wiping it from her palms so her fingers wouldn't slip on the bow.

"You're early, Shadow. Always so early," Kirabi said in Aenuite, approaching in her own camouflage.

Shadow. The name the Aenuites had given Erin. Out of the many names she'd had, it suited her best. "I like the night," Erin replied in perfect Aenuite, smiling despite the heavy bags beneath her eyes.

Kirabi frowned. "You still aren't sleeping, are you?"

Erin hesitated. The nightmares had never gone away. She still dreamed of her son and her lost friends, those she'd refused to tell goodbye. Waking up with a scream on her lips, Taran helped calm her down, helped her remember where she was, *who* she was. If not for him, the dreams would have driven her mad.

Recently, though, they'd grown more frequent.

"I'm just not tired," Erin said.

"Don't lie to me, Shadow. I don't like lies. You know this."

"I'm worried, Kirabi."

Kirabi arched an eyebrow. "About the baby?"

Erin hesitated, putting a hand to her stomach and feeling the small bump slowly rising. "About the baby," she echoed.

"Don't worry. You'll be a great mother, Shadow."

"That's not what I'm worried about." Erin's gaze fell to the lilies, and she thought of Will. *My darling boy.* "He'd be six now."

"He *is* six," Kirabi put a hand on Erin's chest. "Here." The hand moved to Erin's head. "Here." Kirabi leaned forward and connected her forehead to Erin's. "His spirit lives."

Erin closed her eyes and thought, *Kirabi was a mother once. A constrictor snake took her boy, but she still loves Mother Aenu and Father Ahua. She truly believes. She has truly forgiven.*

That forgiveness—I still can't understand.

"You're strong, Shadow. So is Cub. Together, you will make great parents."

Erin smiled. She struggled to imagine a giant man like Taran being a *Cub.* "Thanks, Kirabi."

"Don't thank me. Mother Aenu will provide, as she always does."

The conviction in Kirabi's voice almost made Erin a believer. And she wanted to believe—badly. Life would be so much easier if she truly believed she could rely on the Gods. Yet Erin's prayers had always been met with silence. Could she really trust in another Goddess after being let down by Eo?

I'll try, Erin decided. *If only for the baby's sake, I'll do it.* Exhaling, she whispered, "Mother Aenu will provide."

◄◇►

The day came sooner than expected. Again.

Erin had been eating a meal of deer, yams, and honeyed fruit in Kirabi's hut with Taran and the hunters. Trying to eat, at least. The cramps—the *contractions,* she now knew—were becoming more frequent. Uncomfortable but not yet unbearable. It would only be a matter of hours, perhaps even minutes. The body was a fickle, inconsistent thing.

"How are you feeling?" Taran asked in Aenuite, his face as hopeful and anxious as her own.

In the years since they'd arrived, he'd gained weight around his stomach, though his chest and arms still rippled with muscle. Taran joked that he'd gained the weight that Erin had lost. He'd grown his hair out, which grew upward into a brown afro. With the thick beard adorning his chin, he almost looked like a sunflower. Smile lines creased the skin around his eyes, the anger he'd held in his youth having fallen away.

"I'm... scared," Erin replied, knowing better than to lie to him.

"That's okay," Taran said. "I am, too, but we have each other and that's all we need."

Erin would have agreed, but her water broke. Sharp-edged fear strangled her, and Erin's heart skipped a beat even as her baby's thudded.

"Oh no... It's time," Erin said.

"Time?" Taran frowned. Then his eyes lit with realization as he looked at the puddle between her crossed legs. "*The* time?"

"Yes," Erin hissed. She glanced at Kirabi, who barked orders to the other hunters. Taran helped Erin to stand, then gently lifted her into his arms. Together, they exited the hut and walked through pools of sunlight toward the river's edge, where blue lilies bloomed. Around them, other Straightbacks peeked out of their huts and offered their blessings while children touched Erin's feet as a sign of luck and honor.

After the next contraction, Erin felt her baby kick. *Still alive,* she thought, putting a hand on her stomach. The baby kicked her hand as if to agree.

But for how long?

Erin was shaking as Taran placed her at the river's edge. He gripped her hand and kneeled beside her. She stared at the hunters gathering by the bank with bows and hatchets drawn as Kirabi prepared to deliver the baby. *It's too similar.*

Erin offered a silent prayer to Mother Aenu, the first time she'd asked a Goddess for help in over a decade. *Please provide. Please let my baby live.*

Erin breathed and pushed for hours—until day became night. And when her baby was delivered, there was only silence.

No...

Erin stiffened as she looked at Taran, whose eyes watched Kirabi. His mouth opened in an *o*, but no sound escaped his lips.

Not again. Please don't let it happen again.

A tear slid down Taran's face.

"Taran... is it... can I..." Erin swallowed, her throat dry from the culmination of months of fear. "Can I hold my baby?"

"Yeah," Taran whispered, lips curling into a smile.

"Yeah?" Then Erin heard it—the sweetest sound she could imagine: the cry of a newborn baby. *Her* baby.

Still alive.

"You did it," Taran said, raising the child in his arms.

Erin opened her mouth to answer, but she was too choked up. Her chest heaved as tears streamed down her face. All the fear that had gripped her fell away like molted skin. Even her exhaustion was counteracted by the adrenaline running through her system.

I'm a mother. I'm more than just a killer. More than just a shadow.

"I did it," Erin echoed.

"A girl," Kirabi said, patting Erin's knee.

A strong girl, Erin thought, as her pride swelled, almost as great as the need to protect her. She glared at the jungle, the river, and even the sky. *You don't get to take her. She's mine.*

The baby girl stared at her with brown eyes and small strands of brown hair, just like her father. Her skin was the same shade of blue as the river lilies. Fingers grasping, the baby found Erin's thumb and held it tight.

"Hi, baby," Erin whispered, holding the baby tight against her chest. "I'm so happy to finally see you."

"What are we going to name her?" Taran asked, kneeling beside them.

"Lily," Erin said, having not set her heart on any name beforehand in fear of another jinx.

"Lily." Taran grinned. "It's a good name. A pure one."

"Mother Aenu provides," Erin said, finally believing the words.

The fire burned with the crackle of oak and stories as the Straightback elders bestowed their blessings and gifts upon Lily, who had been cleaned in the river and swaddled in a fur blanket. As Erin held her aloft, elders sprinkled crushed roots and powders onto Lily's head and placed a leather cord necklace around her neck. On it, a single feather was held in place by two clay beads.

Kirabi stepped forward and shouted, "This night, we celebrate the birth of *Lily!* Given to us by Mother Aenu to teach and guide, just as the spirits guide us! For Lily, we will be the mountains, the rivers, and the soil until she can follow their paths herself!"

The crowd shouted gleefully in response.

"Shadow and Cub are worthy parents, strong hunters who nourish our bodies. May their blood strengthen us. May their blood be our blood."

Pricking her thumb with a blade, Kirabi smeared her blood over Lily's forehead—a blood oath to treat the child as one of her own. Such was the rite of passage for all newborn children. The crowd of Straightbacks put up their hands in receipt of the blessing, all chanting the names of Mother Aenu and Father Ahua.

A wailing scream rose above the crackling fire as Taran jumped to his feet, shirtless and painted with swirls of mud across his face and chest. Other dancers rose around him, screaming and jumping. Faces made fierce by wild grins and wide eyes, they leaped around the fire, whose flames rose higher with their ritual. Stomping in unison, they slapped their thighs and chests, screaming the songs of their ancestors: the love of Mother Aenu and Father Ahua, the triumph of the ashra, the warning of lyths, and the call for guidance to the river, trees, and stones.

All the while, Erin held Lily tight, warding off the darkness that threatened to approach. *I'll protect you, my rose,* Erin thought. *I'll never let them hurt you. I swear it on the Drowned Sea.*

◄◉►

Erin watched Lily totter and jump as she tried to grab the small minnows that swam by the river's edge. Her daughter's lurching movements made Erin smile until her cheeks hurt.

"Looks drunk, doesn't she?" Taran asked, eyes alight with love and mischief. He sat beside Erin on one of the taller rocks near the edge.

"Drunk is too kind a word. Lily's three sheets to the wind," Erin said, resting her head against his shoulder and letting his hand engulf hers as the sun fell toward the horizon.

Stay away, Eo, Erin thought. *Let me enjoy these minutes with my family. Let this moment last a lifetime.* She snuggled further into Taran as he wrapped an arm around her shoulder.

"You ever think we'd survive this long?" Taran asked as day became dusk.

"No." A chuckle escaped Erin's lips. "If you'd have tried to tell me on the *Constable* that I'd end up being the mother of your children, I'd have jumped over the gunwale."

"Yeah... I'd probably have thrown you over."

Erin laughed, a surprised, choking sound that became a snort. Taran's laugh was deeper, a rich rumble that made Lily giggle even though she hadn't heard the conversation.

I'm glad she inherited his laugh, Erin thought, looking down at her. Having turned three, Lily had grown like a weed. Often silent but unafraid to laugh, her eyes were always full of wonder, so different and so pure compared to Erin's childhood. *I hope you stay this way forever... Stay young, Lily. Stay pure.*

"I'm glad you didn't jump," Taran said, kissing her cheek. "If you had, we wouldn't have *this*."

"Mother Aenu provides."

Taran nodded, his brown eyes twinkling. "It's you, me, and Lily." They both looked over at their baby. "Our family."

The sky grew darker as the sun fell.

Just a few more minutes, Erin thought as she squeezed Taran's hand. *Just let this moment last. Keep away the night for just a little longer.*

Chapter Forty-Two

Lilyth the Red clutched a leather necklace around her throat, whispering, "I was happy, Jameson. Truly happy. I would have been content to live in the jungle and watch Lily grow up. I would have died in peace. But the *Wrath*'s black banner came down the river. And Rolf... he took Taran away. Lily too."

"You're sure it was the *Wrath*?" Jameson asked, struggling to picture it. The *Wrath* was a frigate—a giant, three-masted ship whose hull probably sank another thirty feet below the waterline. Frigates could sail in deep rivers, of course, but to maneuver around the shallow areas? Why would Rolf do that?

"I know what I—" Lilyth stopped, regaining her composure. She slipped the feather necklace under her painted armor and said, "Yes, Jameson, I am sure... Come with me, please. I would like you to see something."

Lilyth walked back inside the cabin to the war table and unrolled a long parchment, revealing an unfinished map of a familiar port.

"That's Tibur," Jameson said. "You made this map yourself? How?"

"You are not the first Cutthroat to come aboard my ship."

Jameson's eyes flicked to the bloodstains on the deck.

"I need your help to navigate the Battered Reefs," Lilyth said, pointing down at the map. "It is a closely kept secret, I have learned, but you have been there. You know how to get through."

"Me? I haven't been there in twenty-five years."

"You are the Weaver of Aritrasta, the man who does not forget. Is that not what you told me all those years ago?"

Jameson stared at the map and all the information she had gathered regarding the dockyards, garrisons, and defense points. Those were surprisingly detailed, especially the information about Flotsam Hill on the western side of the port. But the path through the Battered Reefs was filled with question marks. Truth was, he remembered the way through the shallows. He could guide her through it. Then Jameson thought of Cassius, of the corpses in the streets, of the destroyed cathedral, of the high priest. *If I tell her, they'll all die...*

"No."

Lilyth flinched as if he'd slapped her. *"No?"*

"I won't tell you, Lilyth. Not everybody in that port is a Cutthroat. There're fishing villages, farming hamlets, and logging communities. Many people who just live there and *get by*. People whose families have lived there since before the Cutthroat Rebellions. People who stuck around because they had nowhere else to go. They don't deserve to die." Jameson swallowed, skin itching. "Even most of the Cutthroats are just lost souls. Kids like you and me who weren't shown anything different."

Lilyth stared at him, eyes piercing, though her face betrayed nothing. "All I want is my family back, Jameson. Are you sure you want to get in my way?"

Jameson hesitated, eyes flicking between her, the map, and the bloodstains.

"If you help me take Port Tibur and find my family, I will give you whatever you want. Gold. Ships. *Freedom*." Lilyth said, picking up the quill and handing it to him. "You can go back to Aritrasta and retire like a lord. All you need to do is fill in this map. Show me what is missing. Correct what is wrong. That is all I am asking."

"I don't believe you."

"I swear it to you on the Drowned Sea," Lilyth said, guiding his hand down onto the map. "Help me find my family, Jameson. *Please*."

Jameson's hand twitched as it held the quill. Sweat fell from his forehead. "What will you do with the innocent people there?"

"What I must," Lilyth said, meeting his eyes easily.

"There are children there, Lilyth. Do they deserve to die, too?"

Lilyth exhaled. "There are children everywhere, and some die every day." She closed her eyes for a few seconds before reopening them. "I should know. I lost one child. I will not lose another, no matter the cost."

Jameson flinched and dropped the quill. "No." He took a step back, brandishing his trident. "You're a monster, Lilyth. I won't help you kill those people."

"Are you sure?" Lilyth asked, eyeing the trident like it was nothing more than a twig. "You should rethink your answer, Jameson."

"Damn you to the Core, Lilyth," Jameson said, taking another step toward the door.

"I want you to remember this. That I asked you for help, and you refused me. I gave you a second chance. Even a third. You refused to free my family all three times." Lilyth said, stepping forward. "But if you think this changes anything, you are wrong. I cannot let you stand in my way, Jameson. I will get the information from you, even if I have to pry it from your squalling mouth. Even if I have to cut it from your damned tongue."

"Get back," Jameson said, shuffling though his knee throbbed. "I'm warning you."

"Warnings are for Mice. If you need to issue a warning, you are hoping. If you are hoping, then you are already dead." A talan appeared in Lilyth's fingers. "Do you know how many people I have killed? How many that were stronger than you? Faster than you? *Better* than you?"

Jameson jabbed with the trident. Lilyth dodged before he'd even begun his thrust.

"You are long out of practice, old man," she said, sidestepping the next thrust but making no moves to close the distance.

Jameson's back hit a wall, and he froze.

Lilyth smiled. "But he is not."

That's not a wall. Jameson tried to turn, to stab, but dark arms snaked around his neck. One was black, the other red.

The Red Hand's muscles bulged, and Jameson's throat closed. He let go of his trident and smacked weakly at the Red Hand's arms. It did nothing.

"Keep him conscious, Red Hand, but keep him under control." Lilyth's hands twitched, and her blade disappeared. She picked up the trident and examined it before gently setting it on her sketched map of Port Tibur. As she turned back to Jameson, Lilyth's eyes were ruthless. "I did not want to do this, but you have denied me three times already. You will not deny me a fourth."

Jameson opened his mouth to speak, but he could only cough.

Lilyth frowned. "Loosen your grip, Red Hand. I want to hear him speak."

"Torturing me won't work," Jameson said between gulps of air once the Red Hand obeyed. "I'll lie."

"You will not lie." A small leather sack appeared in Lilyth's hands. "Because you will *want* to tell me everything."

Jameson swallowed, but his throat had already dried. "What is that?"

"A piece of our history," she said.

Lilyth opened the bag, and Jameson leaned away, knowing the orange powder by smell alone. The acrid, gunpowder scent brought back the chills of wintry nights, the allure of the warm drug, and the decay that came to all who used it.

"*Chard?* No..." Jameson trailed away, going cold from toes to neck. His skin itched. His knee ached. *Oh Gods, I should've jumped into the sea when I had the chance. Damn the syrens. That's a better death than this!*

But Jameson couldn't run. Not when the Red Hand had him by the neck. Not when Lilyth had him by the nose.

"I told you I did not want to do this, but you have left me no choice, Jameson. This is your fault."

"Damn you, Lilyth," Jameson said, thrashing in the Red Hand's grip though it was futile. "Look. I'll tell you everything, okay? Anything you want! Just don't do this. Please!"

"After telling me you would lie? No, Jameson. I cannot trust anything you would say. Not yet. Not until you are addicted. Then you will tell me everything I want," Lilyth said. She struggled to meet his gaze for the first time since reuniting.

Lilyth isn't bluffing. She'll actually use it... Oh Gods, she's going to do it! Jameson tried to scream, but the Red Hand choked him immediately. When he released his grip a fraction, Jameson gasped and whispered, "Lilyth, please! I'll swear it on the Drowned Sea! Anything you want!"

Lilyth shook her head. "You might break the oath, Jameson. I have to be sure." She jerked her head to the Red Hand. "Chain him up in the slavehold—keep him in one piece. I will visit him in a few days."

"No. *No—*"

The Red Hand squeezed until Jameson slumped into unconsciousness.

Greeley carried Jameson into the slavehold, which was filled with the decaying bodies of the Unchosen. Most would have found the scent horrid, but Greeley had always liked the smell of blood—as long as it wasn't his own. He locked an empty set up manacles around the squall's wrists and kicked him in the ribs until he heard one snap.

The old squall curled his arms and legs around his stomach, moaning as he slowly woke up.

Greeley brought his lantern closer to Jameson's face, trying to find out what made this old man so damned special. He was Aritrastan but wore a Corinthian tunic and had a few scars across his cheeks and lip. A warrior, Greeley presumed, but the scars alone didn't tell him how good of a fighter Jameson was.

Somehow, he knew Lilyth from before the legion... Did he teach her how to fight? Greeley growled at the thought. *No. His fighting was sloppy in Lilyth's chambers... But then, who is he?*

Greeley curled his hands into fists. Today had been the first time he'd been aboard the *Jericho* in months. He'd expected to have his own private meetings with Lilyth to discuss strategies for the coming raid on Tibur, but he was treated as a glorified dog while Arya and Kendrik served as Lilyth's generals.

Even during the fighting, Greeley had been isolated, forced to destroy the eastern half of Cassius alone while Arya, Kendrik, and Lilyth attacked the west side. And afterward, while Greeley was waiting to be praised for sacking the east side, what did Lilyth do? She named two Tavrakians—two slaves who'd *just* become legionnaires—as the Red Maw and Red Jaw. And collectively, she made the gladiators her personal bodyguards and death squad. Her Red Death.

Lilyth treated them with respect and praise, but what had she said to Greeley?

"Red Hand, bring him to my chambers. Red Hand, wait outside my door. Red Hand, chain him up." Greeley kicked Jameson with each statement. "First she names Kendrik the Red Heart. Then Arya the Red Hand. Now the Tavrakians... And then there's *you*. Lilyth came to Cassius to *rescue* you and offered you anything you wanted—even a place by her side—but you refused her."

The Red Hand pulled out a knife and ran the edge down Jameson's cheek, spilling blood. "What I want to know is *why?* Why not join her? You knew her before. Tell me how. *Why?*"

The only response was clinking chains as Jameson struggled to a sitting position.

"Tell me why," Greeley said, dragging the knife against Jameson's chest and lower to his stomach.

"You don't know her like I do. All of this. Everything she's doing, it's all a lie," Jameson said. "Loyalty and strength, right? That's what you always say? She's got a husband and a kid—that's what she's after. That's where her loyalty lies. Her strength too."

"Bullshit. You're lying. Lilyth would never—"

"If she has to choose between her mission and you, do you really think Lilyth would choose you?"

Greeley stiffened. Had it been a month ago, he'd have said yes. But now? Greeley kept his mouth shut.

"Do you know why Lilyth is even doing this?" Jameson asked, glaring up at him in the lanternlight. "No. Of course you don't... You think this is some grand rebellion against Cutthroats? The work of Eo? You're wrong. Lilyth hates the Goddess. She's only doing this to get her daughter. *That's* why she wants to get into Tibur. Lilyth doesn't care about you or the Red Legion. All she cares about is herself and her family. After she finds her daughter, you'll never see her again. Mark my words."

Greeley processed the words, then spat them aside. Lilyth *hating* Eo? Nonsense. She was a Champion—a demigod—and Greeley had seen her perform miracles. He'd even seen Eo Herself when he'd finally been Affirmed. The Goddess was a burning, one-eyed woman in red robes with a face as pockmarked and cratered as the moon. Besides, Lilyth hated the Cutthroats more than anyone else. The Core burned in her eyes when she spoke of piracy. She would never abandon the legion.

"You really think that I fall for such lies? No. I am the Red Hand. And you are just one of the Unchosen."

"You fool," Jameson whispered, spitting blood. "She's brainwashed you. You need to kill her. End this before it's too late."

"End this? Kill Lilyth? No. She. Is. *Mine*." Greeley twitched, turning with a roar and slamming his fist into Jameson's face. Flesh ripped and bones shook. Jameson groaned as the Red Hand grabbed his ear and ripped the golden earring from it, collecting another trophy. "Lilyth is mine, and mine *alone*."

Greeley stalked out of the slavehold and up the ladder, returning to Lilyth's quarters at the end of the gun deck. Shockingly, it was guarded by two of her new bodyguards—the Red Death. As he approached, they stood at attention in front of the door, blocking his way.

Greeley's hand formed a fist. "I request an audience with the Champion."

"No. She is busy," said Duvur, the Red Maw. He still wore his plumed helmet. Because the bottom was open and revealed his mouth, Greeley could see that his lips were covered in crimson. The former gladiator easily held a warhammer in hand, though it remained at his side.

Greeley put his hand on the hilt of his resharpened white cutlass. "I *request* an audience with the Champion."

Radur, the Red Jaw, took a step forward. Having cut off her hair and beard, her jaw and neck were stained with blood. "No. She is—"

"Red Jaw, grant his request," Lilyth said from the other side of the door.

The Red Jaw obliged, opening the door for Greeley, though she frowned at him. He sneered back and stepped into the room. Inside, Lilyth, Arya, and Kendrik were at her war table, looking at the half-finished map of Tibur, and making assault plans for the legion. They had been splitting up the legion... without him.

Had he thought he could take both in a fight, Greeley might have charged Arya and Kendrik. But even one-on-one, Greeley knew he couldn't beat Kendrik, let alone Lilyth. "Champion, I—"

"Have you done as I asked, Red Hand?" Lilyth asked, still looking at her map even as she spoke to him.

"Yes, Champion. The Weaver is below deck." He looked at the war map and added, "Perhaps I can help—"

"You can help by returning to your ship," Lilyth said.

Greeley bit his tongue to keep from screaming. *What did I do? What did the Red Seducer do to turn you against me? Why do you treat me as less than a dog?* But he didn't dare question Lilyth. Instead, he said, "As you wish, Champion. I'll return to the *Crescent*."

"No. The *Maelstrom*."

Greeley frowned. The legion had a ship called the *Maelstrom?* It had to be a ship they'd just stolen from the Cassians. *If it's a sloop...* "Which ship is that, Champion?"

"A frigate. It is yours... Consider it a gift for proving your strength in sacking East Cassius today, Red Hand." Lilyth finally looked up from the table. "I will need you to move your belongings to that ship and to train our new recruits as we travel toward Port Tibur. We won't be able to fully train our recruits—not by half—but you can teach them how to hold a sword and to stab, if nothing else. These freed Cassian slaves will be our first wave when we attack Tibur—we will save our battle-tested legionnaires for the second wave."

My very own frigate... Greeley smiled. This was the promotion he'd been waiting for. And to make him the sparring teacher over Kendrik? This was too good to be true. So why did he feel so hesitant?

Because I'll be so busy training that I'll be separated from Kendrik, Arya, and Lilyth. They will plan while I'm stuck sparring with the new legionnaires. I am being promoted, but it is also a punishment.

That only accounted for part of his hesitancy. What made him more uneasy was the look in Lilyth's eyes as she glanced up from the map. Excitement. Hope. He'd never seen those emotions in her eyes before.

And Jameson's words echoed back to him. *She's only doing this to get her daughter.* That's *why she wants to get into Tibur.* Greeley didn't believe him, but that seed of doubt was taking root in the soil of his mind.

"Yes, Champion," Greeley said, forcing himself to smile. "I'll begin training the new recruits immediately."

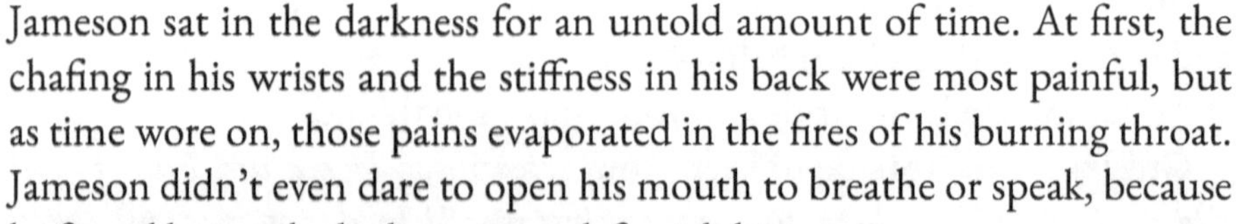

Jameson sat in the darkness for an untold amount of time. At first, the chafing in his wrists and the stiffness in his back were most painful, but as time wore on, those pains evaporated in the fires of his burning throat. Jameson didn't even dare to open his mouth to breathe or speak, because he feared losing the little moisture left with his tongue.

Eventually, the door did open, and Lilyth entered with a lantern and a glass of orange water. *She dissolved chard into it...*

Lilyth studied his face, as if reading his thoughts. "Yes. I did put chard in the water. Are you thirsty enough to drink it?"

Jameson turned his head away from her, exhausting the last of his willpower to deny her request. So Lilyth left, and Jameson was comforted by the bodies of the Unchosen he was forced to endure. Not that he could see or smell them anymore. His mind wandered through the darkness, remembering what it was to be a slave.

And Jameson wept for himself because he knew he could not deny Lilyth a second time.

When she returned—minutes, hours, or perhaps even a day later—Jameson immediately reached for the glass of chard water. But rather than give it to him, Lilyth made him sip it slowly along with a meal of hardtack and salt beef. He was too thirsty and weary to lash out at her, but when he'd finished the glass of chard water, he found the strength to curse her. But by that point, he'd already known he'd lost.

Where Jameson had been cold before, the drink warmed him, cushioned him. He settled into the cloud, letting his muscles relax. He slept in the skies, his mind freed from that bodily prison, and he basked in the warmth of this new sun.

But eventually, Jameson plummeted back into the slavehold, and he awoke to darkness, decay, and rancid filth. He wished only for chard's reprieve, which Lilyth granted him. More days turned into more drinks, but each time, the clouds and warmth fell away quicker. Like Felice had once feared, Jameson returned to the Dark Age, a time without sun or happiness. Only dust and shadows.

The next time that Lilyth entered with food and drink, Jameson ate and drank hungrily, only to realize that the water was simply that. *Water.* Without chard. He looked up at her helplessly and whispered, "Please... I need it."

"No."

Jameson licked his lips. "I'll tell you everything I know."

"You know what I want."

"Yeah," Jameson said, nodding. "Yeah, I know. I'll tell you."

And he did. Jameson told Lilyth everything he knew in exchange for just a gram of warmth. A gram of *escape.*

First, Jameson corrected the mistakes on the map of Tibur as best he remembered them, giving more detailed information on the Copperhouse—the southern headquarters of the Copperheads—than other places as he'd been far more familiar with that location than the Skulls' Flotsam Hill, Roses' Thorn, or the Fleshlords' Fleshery.

But when Lilyth still refused to give him chard, Jameson told her of the captains he knew, bars he haunted, girlies he frequented, and the local fisherman, farmers, and shipwrights that he'd interacted with.

When Lilyth refused him even still, Jameson gave in. He told her the direct route through the Battered Reefs, which would allow her to sail right up to the dockyards and assault Tibur. She would kill all those he'd known, and yet Jameson still told her about the path with a smile on his face. Nor did he lie—he couldn't risk not getting chard. Jameson needed it more than freedom. Or friends.

"You made the right choice, Jameson," Lilyth said, preparing another glass of chard water for him.

Yet long after the warmth faded, Jameson cursed himself, the Gods, and Lilyth above all, for his role in the Red Legion's next massacre. His only relief was knowing that she no longer needed him. Undoubtedly, the next time Lilyth entered the slavehold, it wouldn't be with chard but a pistol.

And Jameson looked forward to it.

When the door opened, Jameson's left leg shook in anticipation, betraying his stoic expression. He wanted the warmth, *needed* it.

Chard or death is fine—both are an escape, Jameson thought as his tongue loosened. He said. "I should have let you drown. Of everything I've done, I thought that was one thing I did right. I've never been so wrong."

Lilyth wore an indifferent expression. Her red eyes glinted like sharp rubies. Scars covered her face and neck. Yellowing bruises too. "It brought me no joy to do this," Lilyth said, closing the door behind her. "But I could not allow you to stand in my way."

"Joy to do what? Make me an addict? You can't even say the words, can you?"

"You really think me so weak?" Lilyth's lips formed into a frown. "Yes, Jameson. I made you an addict. I used that addiction as leverage for information. You gave it to me. Now I can burn Port Tibur to the ground—along with everyone in it."

"You're... not even sorry," Jameson said, closing his eyes, feeling any lingering resolve leave his weary bones.

"I do what I must, Jameson, and that leads me to my final question. Where is Eo's Sword?"

"What?" Jameson shook his head.

"Long ago, you told me that Aritras had Eo's Sword. I want to know where it is."

"Why? So you can kill Eo?" Jameson asked, his words swallowed by the darkness. His skin prickled as if he was being watched from above.

"Yes. I want to kill Her. And I want to use that power to keep my family safe, curses be damned. So tell me how to find the Sword." Lilyth revealed a glass of chard water she'd hidden behind her back. "Tell me what you know, and I will give you this."

Jameson nodded, hating himself but not caring. "The Deadlands. Aritras was expanding his territory east when he died, and he died soon after vanquishing the Forgotten King. That's when his Sword was lost. From the legends, the land only became cursed after Aritras's death, so it's possible the Sword is the source. Search for it in the mountains, and maybe you'll find the damned thing."

"Thank you—"

Jameson snatched the glass from her hand and guzzled it down. He threw the empty glass back at her in disgust. The warmth spread through him, but he wouldn't immediately feel the results. It would still need a few more minutes to take effect.

"Or maybe the Eonian priests found the Sword after Aritras died and hid it away from the world. Maybe the Deadlands just have horrible soil and nothing grows there for completely *natural* reasons. There's also a chance that Aritras lied about the whole thing and didn't have a Sword to begin with!"

"But you do not believe that, do you, Jameson?" Lilyth asked. "If you did, you would have told me when I was still a kid. You refused to tell me because you believed the Sword is still in the Deadlands."

Jameson bit his cheek and spat blood on her face. "I didn't tell *Steward* because I didn't want her to waste her life searching for something that either doesn't exist or shouldn't be found. But you're not her. So go, Lilyth. Waste the rest of your life searching for that squalling Sword. Go there and squalling die. Learn why they're called the Deadlands."

"Thank you, Jameson," Lilyth said as she wiped away his spit and stood. Pulling out a flintlock, she clicked back the hammer and pointed it at his head. "I would have given you gold, you know. I would have even forgiven you for what you did to my dad if you had helped me voluntarily. But now I am only offering lead. Do you have any last words?"

Jameson lowered his head, the pain hurting deep. He let out a long sigh.

"Nothing?" she asked, pulling back the trigger halfway. "I thought you were the Weaver of Aritrasta. Are you no longer a man of words?"

Jameson glared up at her remorseless expression. He straightened his shoulders, raised his chin, and said, "I never gave up on Steward. I stayed and searched for her for a decade in Corinthus after the Divine Virgin gave me my freedom. I stayed hoping I could find her—I'd have helped her find Taran, too, if she'd come and asked me. But you? I didn't lift a squalling finger because you're not Steward. You're just another Skull."

Lilyth flinched, though the gun didn't waver. "I am *not*—"

"You burned Cassius to the ground, killed innocent Cassians, and kidnapped me. Then you addicted me to chard. There's only one other person who'd have done that. *Rolf*."

"I did what I had to. For my daughter. For my husband. It was the only way."

Jameson chuckled, the bitter sound dying in the darkness. "Outside of the cathedral, you told me that there was always a choice. Remember that? Or have you forgotten that, too?"

Silence.

"You're only continuing the cycle, replacing piracy with zealotry. Cutthroats with cultists. Rolf the Bloody with Lilyth the Red. You haven't made the seas safer—you've made them more dangerous! And you *chose* to do all of this. You chose to become Rolf." Jameson chuckled at the irony before the sound petered away into pain. "You hate me because I lied to you. But you've deceived yourself much worse. So then, Lilyth the Red, how much do you hate yourself?" He took a breath and pushed his head against the barrel of the gun. "Are you sure you're doing this for your family? Or for revenge?"

Lilyth's finger twitched, and the muzzle flashed with smoke. The shot rang out, and Jameson winced but felt no pain. He looked up, still able to see, still able to move. The gun was pointed two inches above his head.

"I do hate myself, Jameson," she said, extinguishing the lantern and casting the room in darkness. "But I love my family more. And everything I have done, I have done for them."

Lilyth left the statement hanging in the door like a cabin boy swinging from a noose.

◄◆►

The world broke and reformed with each wave that swelled beneath her. Stoically, Lilyth ascended from the slavehold back to her cabin with orders for her Red Death not to disturb her as she consulted Eo.

As soon as the door closed, her concrete dam of composure burst.

A drowning gasp escaped her lips as she shivered and thrashed, sliding down the door to barricade herself from the rest of the world.

It did nothing to stop Jameson's haunting words. *You chose to become Rolf.*

Head in her hands, Lilyth convulsed silently as the tears and pain refused to subside. Old memories rose to the surface—

Stop thinking about that. Don't think about it. Never think about it.

The Cutthroats came down the river with their flags and sails and cannons and—

Stop thinking about it.

Blood and arrows and bullets and spears and swords and—

Lilyth pressed her hands against her head. "No... *no!*"

Explosions and groans and screams—

Lilyth stumbled to her feet, shoving aside the war table and letting the completed map of Port Tibur fall to the ground. She leaned against the stern balcony and shut her eyes.

Erin's screams. Steward's screams. Fox's screams—

Lilyth screamed and screamed and screamed.

CHAPTER FORTY-THREE

Greeley sat cross-legged in Lilyth's quarters alongside Kendrik and Arya, waiting for the Champion to speak. She was silent and despondent, staring at an odd-smelling candle in the middle of their circle. Yet silence was better than screaming.

The *Maelstrom* had been traveling close enough to the *Jericho* for Greeley to hear the first of her agonized wails—akin to those of the Unchosen—but it had still taken him time to row to Lilyth's flagship as they were still sailing across the seas. Arya and Kendrik had arrived quicker than him despite his haste, but neither had dared enter her quarters for fear of interrupting a conversation with Eo Herself. Especially not with the Red Jaw and Red Maw guarding the door under strict orders not to let anyone inside.

Greeley and Radur had almost come to blows, but Lilyth intervened, opening the door with a haunted expression that silenced all rebukes. The torment—whatever caused it—clung to her face even now as she stared down at the flickering candle, having gathered her lieutenants around her. But she remained quiet and aloof, unwilling or perhaps unable to share what she'd witnessed.

Out of the corner of his eye, Greeley looked over at Arya and Kendrik, who looked as worried as he felt. They leaned forward, waiting for the Champion to speak. She didn't.

Finally, Kendrik broke the silence. "Champion, what ails you? Please tell us how we can help you."

Lilyth blinked, staring up from the flame. Her eyebrows furrowed, as if confused how or why the Red Lieutenants were sitting in a circle with her. "Did you say something, Red Heart?"

"We are worried about you, Champion. Why were you screaming? What did Eo tell you?"

"Eo did not tell me anything, Red Heart," Lilyth said, deadpan. "But she showed me the future. The Red Legion will win the greater war against all Cutthroats—not just the Skulls. But I... will die at Tibur."

Greeley leaned back, shocked. He tried to form words into a question, but his lips spasmed, refusing to cooperate.

"What?" Kendrik asked, horrified. "No, Champion. We need you. We cannot do this without you."

"But you can. I have seen you do it, Red Heart. All three of you, in fact. You will become the Champions of the Red Legion, and you will lead Her Chosen to greater glory than I ever could. The time of the sun is over, and you will usher in Eo's everlasting night..."

In a monotone voice, Lilyth detailed the events Eo showed her: the destruction of Tibur, fall of the Cutthroat King, decimation of Corinthus, and reconquering of Aritrasta. Her eyes never wavered from the odd-smelling candle she'd placed in the center of their circle. Sometimes, she spent minutes looking into the flame without a word. Then, once the silence became comfortable, she'd shatter it with more words of her coming death.

As she did, the shadows lengthened and withered. Greeley felt goosebumps rise on his forearms and tasted blood in his throat as if he were drowning.

And as Greeley watched, Lilyth changed. Her skin darkened, black but without paint. Fully red instead of bloodshot, her eyes absorbed the fire's glow instead of reflecting it. Her fingers melded together, as if her arms ended in steel blades instead of hands. She was taller, somehow. Thinner too. Evolving in a way that made her into a living blade.

A Goddess, Greeley thought. *Lilyth is becoming Eo, and even she doesn't realize it.*

"Port Tibur will fall to fire," Lilyth continued in a voice not her own. Darker. *Rawer.* "A fire so great and mighty that nothing will survive it. I will be consumed by it, *become* that fire, and I will wash over those Cutthroats and unleash my full wrath upon them and any who still do not believe. Then the flame will burn away, and only you shall be left among the ashes. And I, like all others, will go into the night, join Eo, and merge my spirit with Hers. Then will come the Great Stillness, in which you must remain at Port Tibur for three nights and offer tribute to the Unseen Lady. Only after that time can you carry on with our divine purpose."

"Without you?" Kendrik asked. "Is there nothing we can do to stop this?"

Always the first to speak. Always the first to gain Lilyth's attention. Always her favorite... He'll be the first to die, Greeley thought, still working on a plan to eliminate him. He'd had no opportunities during the Cassian battle, especially not with Arya secretly guarding Kendrik. *I'll kill them both at Tibur, when everyone else is distracted.*

"No." Lilyth said. "My time is coming and to defy it would be to defy Eo."

"Then allow me to go with you—"

"No. You need to remain here. All of you must. The Red Legion needs the strength of Greeley's fist, the loyalty of Kendrik's heart, and the truth of Arya's eye... After the Skulls fall, all three of you must lead the Red Legion against the Cutthroat King and his Avowed army."

"Yes, Champion," Kendrik said, Arya echoing him.

Still, the traitor's words came back to Greeley.

Lilyth doesn't care about you or the Red Legion. All she cares about is herself and her family. After she finds her daughter, you'll never see her again. Mark my words.

"Yes, Champion," Greeley said, not taking his eyes off Lilyth.

Arya and Greeley were dismissed first, and while they returned to their ships to prepare for the attack on Tibur, Kendrik remained aboard the *Jericho*. The Champion extinguished the odd-smelling candle, which made his insides churn, before walking to her cabin door and calling Radur and Duvur inside. They were still wearing their gladiatorial gear—so different from the black paint of other legionnaires. What bothered him more was their quick promotion. Kendrik had toiled for months—and lost his own brother—before becoming the Red Heart. Yet Radur and Duvur had been named the Red Maw and Red Jaw immediately after the attack on Cassius. Collectively, they and the other former gladiators had become the

Champion's elite guard—the Red Death. Why did she trust these new legionnaires so much?

Eo showed her the future, Kendrik reminded himself. *The Champion no doubt can see what comes next... The Red Death must play a pivotal role in what's to come.*

Still, Kendrik wished he could see as the Champion did. He had so much left to learn. After everything she had done for Eo—for the entire legion—why did Lilyth have to die?

"I know you are upset, Red Heart. News of my death is as much a shock to me as it is to you. But it is all a part of Eo's greater plan," the Champion said, putting a hand on Kendrik's shoulder and comforting him in a way that only she could. Quietly, he placed his hand on hers, reassuring her with a gentle squeeze. Then he let his hand fall.

"I know Eo has a greater plan," Kendrik whispered. "I just wish I understood. I already lost Jericho... why do I have to lose you, too?"

"So that you can become who you are meant to be, Red Heart. This next part of the journey is yours and yours alone."

"Me, Arya, and Greeley, you mean," Kendrik said, noticing the look of guilt cross her expression. "Right, Champion?"

"No. I must apologize to you, Red Heart, because I lied earlier. Eo *did* show me the future, the truth, and with it, she showed me the secrets of the Red Hand and Red Eye... They will try to kill you in Tibur so that they can lead the Chosen."

"Kill me..." Kendrik touched his heart, feeling a piece of it break. The Champion would never lie to him, but to think that Greeley and Arya would *kill* him? The words were a knife through Kendrik's heart.

"Yes," the Champion said. "I know you care for them and trust them, but you must trust me, Red Heart. For if you die—if they win—the legion will lose. All our sacrifices will be in vain. Even Jericho's."

Kendrik closed his eyes, his breath quickening. Greeley and Arya were planning to betray him? They were going to make Jericho's sacrifice meaningless? Then damn them both to the depths.

"What must I do?" Kendrik asked, opening his eyes.

"Be ruthless," the Champion said. "Be the Red Heart, but *harden* your heart. This betrayal will be the first of many in trials to come. Because the larger the legion becomes, the more that you succeed, the harder your path will be. Eo will guide you, as will I, but to truly be the Champion of Eo, you must lead the others to victory."

"By myself..."

"Did you think I would let anyone but you captain the *Jericho?*" the Champion asked. "I have known since I first laid eyes on you that you would be my successor."

Kendrik flicked his eyes over to Radur and Duvur, who'd watched the conversation in silence. Somehow, they weren't surprised by the Champion's words. Instead, they actually expected it. "And they are also a part of Eo's greater plan?"

"Of course," the Champion said, smirking. "The Red Death is loyal to *you,* Red Heart. They know what is coming, and they know you will lead them to victory."

Kendrik still had trouble believing it. "Our more experienced legionnaires—"

"Have seen war, yes, but the Red Death was baptized in it." The Champion walked to the gladiators and added, "They proved themselves in Cassius and protected me from harm. For that, Eo has Affirmed them these last several nights even as others have been deemed Unchosen. The Red Maw and Red Jaw yearn for Cutthroat blood as much as you do, and so long as you give it to them, they will follow you."

Kendrik turned toward Radur and Duvur, who doffed their helmets. "You will follow me?"

Radur laughed. "Of course. We are Red Death."

"Not only will we follow you, we will *kill* for you," Duvur finished.

"I am only keeping them aboard the *Jericho* so Arya and Greeley do not get suspicious," the Champion explained. "But once we reach Tibur and destroy Flotsam Hill, they will join your ranks."

Kendrik nodded. "And with them, I will kill Arya and Greeley."

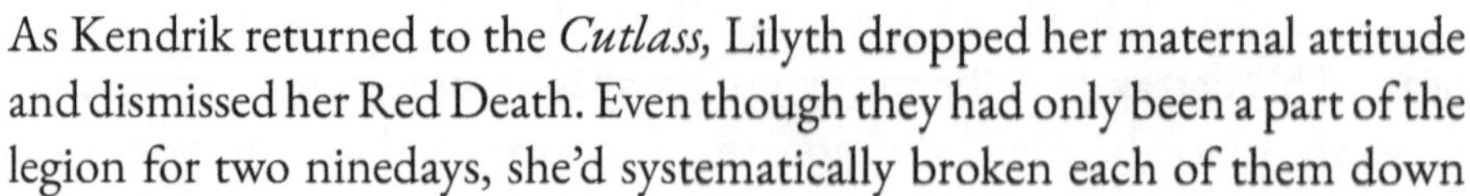

As Kendrik returned to the *Cutlass,* Lilyth dropped her maternal attitude and dismissed her Red Death. Even though they had only been a part of the legion for two ninedays, she'd systematically broken each of them down with prayer, hallucinogens, and poison. They would listen and fight for Kendrik, at least until the Cutthroats were destroyed. After that, Lilyth didn't know, nor did she care.

By then, she'd have her family back, and she'd disappear back to Aritrasta—to Mark's Tavern, if it was even still there. She only had to wait a few more days as her fleet sailed north to Tibur.

Three more days, Lilyth thought, barely able to hold her excitement. *I've waited a lifetime, and it's ending. It's all ending.*

That left only a few loose ends to tie up.

Lilyth descended the ladder to the slavehold in the deepest parts of the frigate. She entered, seeing newer Unchosen corpses amidst older ones. Jameson was still chained there, too, living in squalor. Though Jameson no longer served a purpose, Lilyth kept him alive, bringing him food and water regularly. In part, because she didn't feel that Jameson had suffered enough for killing her dad. But also, Taran had liked Jameson, and that was reason enough to spare the squall despite her misgivings.

"Chard?" Jameson asked immediately, raising his weak hands up toward her.

Lilyth didn't respond. With their last conversation having ended so poorly, she thought it wiser to keep her silence. Instead, she handed Jameson his hardtack and salt pork first, which he devoured. Then she gave him a glass of water, which he chugged greedily. A moment passed before a wave of disappointment crashed into his lips.

"There's no chard in this," Jameson said, coughing hard. "Where's my chard?"

You will have no more chard, Lilyth thought. *Never again...* Though she regretted nothing she'd done as the Champion of the Red Legion, addicting Jameson to chard was truly the one thing she'd hoped to avoid. But this was his own damned fault. *You should have just told me, you stubborn bastard.*

"Give me the chard, Lilyth. I know you have it. Please. Give it to me. I'll give you anything. Anything you want. More information in Tibur? I'll give it to you. I'll tell you all about the Crimson Palace. How does that sound?"

Lilyth ignored him, having already detailed information about that crumbling Avowed fortress that sat vacant at the center of Tibur. She collected the tray and turned to leave.

"You can't just leave me here!" Jameson shouted. "Give me my chard or just kill me, you damned squall!"

Ignoring him, Lilyth walked to the door and opened it.

Jameson's words followed her. "Damn you to the depths, Lilyth."

Damn you to the depths, Steward, Mouse had said. Then Taran. Now Jameson.

"I already am damned," Lilyth said, locking the door and ascending to the main deck to make her final preparations for the assault on Tibur.

CHAPTER FORTY-FOUR

Lilyth prowled at the bow of the *Jericho* as Port Tibur came into view. Through her spyglass, she first spotted a lighthouse on the horizon ahead, sitting on the jagged sea cliffs at Port Tibur's edge. Lilyth followed the coastline east to where the southern dockyard awaited. All that separated her from it was the Battered Reefs, but thanks to Jameson, she knew the way through. Lilyth lowered the spyglass and stared up at the sky, noticing that the sun had only begun its journey to the western horizon. Once night fell, chaos would cripple the port, and it would fall to flame. It was simply a matter of time.

Twenty years, Lilyth thought. Anxiety nipped her ears, desperation tickled her throat, and hope sparkled in her eyes. *Twenty years to the day since this all began—with me stealing Jameson's bracelet. Now it will end with me stealing back my daughter.*

Lilyth grinned, pained that she'd intentionally slowed their journey northward to Tibur, but it had been necessary to time their arrival with the first day of the Fiveday Celebration. A time of thanksgiving and debauchery, when every Cutthroat would be distracted.

This is it. It is finally time...

"Enjoy your last minutes of celebration, Cutthroats. Kiss your girlies. Drink your rum. Shoot your guns. Because tonight, the Day of Colors will be only red," Lilyth said, voice icy despite the warm, frenzied laughs of her followers. Behind her stood the Red Death and its leaders: Duvur the Red Maw and Radur the Red Jaw. Kendrik was on the bow of the ship to her right. Arya to the left. Greeley behind.

As legionnaires whispered around her, Lilyth tingled with excitement and fear in equal measure. *I am so close.* She stared down at the Dagger on her right wrist, the Scythe on her left. But she was still haunted by Jameson's words. *You chose to become Rolf.*

Maybe so, Lilyth thought. *Even if I am a Cutthroat, it will all be worth it when I have my family back.* More than anything, she wanted to hold Lily in her arms and kiss Taran's lips. *But first I need to kill Rolf.*

Lilyth turned and gathered her proselytized followers. Her elite legionnaires were unpainted and dressed in the Copperhead outfits they'd taken from Cutthroat corpses. Behind them, the brown Copperhead flag with the copper chalice and silver serpent flew from the mainmast. Lilyth herself wore a brown overcoat, black pants, and a black tricorn hat. Other ships used a smattering of other flags and colors. The true Cutthroats wouldn't see through the disguises until it was too late.

Let it all burn.

"You are the Red Death," Lilyth said to the dozens of former gladiators. "You have been Chosen—Affirmed. You are the greatest of all my followers, the proud paladins of Eo. You will bring the Unseen Lady victory. You are most worthy to stand by my side." Lilyth paused, watching adoration and fervor pass over their faces. Even Radur and Duvur had become true believers.

"We will dock as Copperheads," Lilyth continued. "When we're inside the port, you will disperse into groups of four and rendezvous at the base of Flotsam Hill at dusk. I will already be inside. Wait for the first fire, then burn everything to the ground. Afterward, you will rendezvous with the Red Heart and follow his commands as my own.

"Some of us will die but know that death is not the end, it is the *beginning.* Death leads to Eo. She is waiting for us there in the night, saving a place for us at her banquet hall in Umbra. Above all else, know that I chose you because you are my greatest warriors. And there is nobody I would rather have by my side in battle. For where the Red Legion goes, the Red Death follows. Strength and loyalty."

"Loyalty and strength!"

Lilyth lifted a hand, and flags and pennants were raised to relay her orders.

Twenty of her forty ships adjusted their course and diverged. Kendrik's fleet of ten ships remained with Lilyth's ten as she sailed toward the southern dockyard. Arya's ten sailed away to the eastern harbor, and Greeley's ten ventured to the empty beaches north of the port to converge on Tibur via the forest.

It will be a massacre.

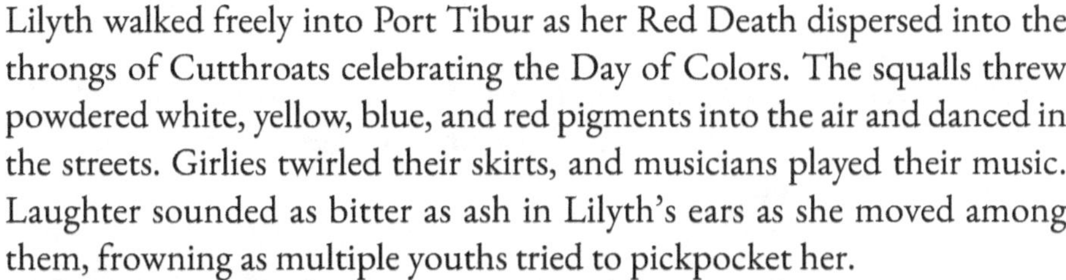

Lilyth walked freely into Port Tibur as her Red Death dispersed into the throngs of Cutthroats celebrating the Day of Colors. The squalls threw powdered white, yellow, blue, and red pigments into the air and danced in the streets. Girlies twirled their skirts, and musicians played their music. Laughter sounded as bitter as ash in Lilyth's ears as she moved among them, frowning as multiple youths tried to pickpocket her.

Twenty years ago, she'd done the same. Lilyth herself was different now, but everything else, everybody else, felt the same. This place felt no different from Alira. It made sense. Tibur had been an Aritrastan colony in its infancy before the Cutthroat Rebellion, so the architecture, culture, and traditions were all Aritrastan.

But instead of having an inner and outer city like Alira, all of Tibur felt like the Chasm. A twisting maze of streets blocked off by colorful vending stalls, precarious lean-tos, and brick storefronts. Alleyways filled with urchins, chard addicts, and muggers.

Except the five Cutthroat factions clearly partitioned the port. To the east were the Fleshlords, whose boundary was marked in purple. North, the Roses, in green. South, the Copperheads, in brown. West, the Skulls, in black. Center, the Avowed, in turquoise—before the Skulls had taken control of the port, that was. All Avowed had been slaughtered, leaving their headquarters—the Crimson Palace—desolate and barren. It was left standing as an example to all others of the Skulls' power.

Tonight, it would become the home of the Red Legion.

But I will not be with them. Lilyth glanced up at the sky. The sun descended rapidly. Only two hours left of daylight before the fires burned through the night. And despite the difficulties of planning her attack, building her Red Legion, and amassing her fleet, actually being here in Tibur—especially amidst celebrations—still felt like a dream. Arriving and entering had been too easy.

Having spent so much time searching for a safe passage through the Battered Reefs, the brief journey through it had been anticlimactic. Uneventful, even. Just a series of switchbacks that her crew could have completed in their sleep. Not a single ship was lost.

Conferring with the harbormaster, too, had been child's play. That old Copperhead inspected their Daggers and stopped only to check Lilyth's assumed identity and the name of her ship after being bribed with a hefty sack of coin. The logs matched, of course, because the *Jericho* had originally belonged to the Copperheads.

All that remained was finding her way into Flotsam Hill and finding Rolf. But that, too, would be simple. Lilyth only needed to don one more mask—that of a girlie.

Lilyth grinned. *I will find Rolf. Then I will find you. Together, we will start the first fire and escape. The legion will think I am dead, and Kendrik will take my place to rid the seas of these Cutthroats... Just one more night until you are back in my arms—one more night until Lilyth is no more.*

Strength and loyalty, Lily.

Loyalty and strength, Taran.

Imagining Taran's smile and Lily's laughter, Lilyth entered a colorful brothel, passing the flirting girlies, and approached the matron, an older Aritrastan woman who wore too much makeup. Still pretending to be a Copperhead captain, Lilyth paid double the asking price for a full, undisturbed night with Cinnamon, a ginger-haired girlie whose physique matched Lilyth's own. She allowed herself to be led upstairs and into an empty bedroom.

Closing the door, Lilyth said, "Turn around and strip naked. Toss your clothes to the corner."

Cinnamon did, teasing and laughing until Lilyth slit her throat. With a gurgling sigh, the girlie fell to the bed, weakly pulling at the silken sheets. Lilyth stabbed her through the heart to quiet her.

"It will be okay," Lilyth whispered, shoving the blade deeper and twisting. "Just close your eyes and sleep."

When Cinnamon obeyed, Lilyth cut off the girlie's scalp, placing the bloody flesh and orange curls on her own head. She secured it in place with a purple bandanna. Quietly taking off her clothes and donning Cinnamon's playful skirts and revealing dress, Lilyth examined herself in the mirror as she applied makeup and practiced smiling.

The warmth never reached her eyes.

Ignoring the raucous catcalls of Cutthroats, Lilyth sauntered up Flotsam Hill to the summit. Where once the Skulls' fortress had been a major garrison and retreat in case of siege, now the old, moss-covered stones crumbled from the curtain wall and were reinforced with shoddier materials—driftwood and scrap iron from decommissioned ships. Filled nooses hung from the crenelations of the wall and out over the rusted chain drawbridge.

Skull guards watched from the heights, but they'd stolen drinks and staggered about their rounds. The drunken ones standing at the portcullis outside the barbican watched her approach, eyes searching everywhere except her face.

"Hello, boys," Lilyth said with a salacious smile, batting her eyes and sticking out a hip.

The two guards—both wearing soiled black clothing—stumbled over their words in their attempts to answer her first:

"How can I—"

"I'd gladly help—"

"Be of—"

"If you'd only let—"

"Service?"

"Me."

Lilyth tittered, mimicking Cinnamon. "Boys, boys. You can certainly be of service, but only after I pay my visit here first. What do you say?"

"We have to check for—"

"Really, boys, you can strip me down later." Lilyth lightly but firmly smacked away a groping hand. "But I cannot be late for my appointment. If you slow me down, then I will not be visiting you later."

They looked at each other indecisively.

"Well..."

"I guess..."

"You drive a hard bargain, boys. Two for the price of one, then? When I come back, I will make it worth your while, darlings. Do not worry about that."

The two Skulls choked on their words as they stepped aside and let Lilyth inside the curtain wall. Her smile dropped when she was alone once more.

The lofty sounds of laughter and flirting from the nearby longhouses greeted her ears, and from the open doors, Lilyth could make out the silhouettes of girlies and off-duty Skulls. Some noticed her walking by, hollering and whistling, but Lilyth turned her attention to the donjon—an octagonal fortress with seven towers, the eighth having crumbled to dust long ago and had been sealed off instead of rebuilt. Vines and moss covered its stones, but lit windows revealed chambers and hallways connecting the towers.

Lilyth approached the large oaken door to the donjon, smiling sweetly at the black-clad guards flanking it. "Well, hello, boys. Can you help a girl have a good time? Rolf asked for me, and I would hate to disappoint."

"You sure you want to go around messing with the Bloody?" said one, whose eyes glittered with arousal. "Would hate for him to bruise that pretty skin of yours. I'm a lot gentler than him, you know."

"Afterward, darling," Lilyth said. She swallowed, throat dry.

I am so close. I am so squalling close.

"We'll still have to escort you to his chambers," said the other, who looked more sober and unhappy about it.

"So long as I get to see Rolf, the more the merrier."

The door opened, and the sounds of merriment grew tenfold. In the grand dining hall beyond, bards played sea shantics on fiddles, lutes, and lyres as Skulls and girlies stomped along to the beat. Some danced on rounded tables pushed out of the way to create more space for more dancing in the center. Ale and mead splashed from wooden mugs and steins, staining clothes and pooling on the stone flooring. Wafts of rosemary, garlic, and roasting meats pervaded her nostrils.

So much celebration from squalls who made their money ruining families. Lilyth gritted her teeth to keep from lashing out. *Keep smiling. You are almost there, Lilyth. Just keep smiling.*

The guard took her to the far side of the chamber and up a curving set of cantilevered stairs. The music faded away, though the donjon still rumbled with the beat. Together, Lilyth and the guards walked through the hallways and passed three towers, stopping at the fourth.

The guard knocked on the door. "Lord Wrath, sir?"

"What?" grunted a gruff voice.

Rolf. Lilyth swallowed. Her heart pounded. *It is him. I have waited so long, and now it is finally time. I am here, Lily. I am finally here.*

"A girlie, Lord Wrath. Cinnamon from the Crystal Menagerie," the guard repeated after Lilyth told him what to say.

"Didn't ask for a damn whore," Rolf said.

"A gift, I'm told."

"Some squalling gift," came Rolf's reply, but the door opened anyway. Lilyth stepped inside.

And almost stepped back out.

Instead of the wiry man who'd forced cabin boys to fight one another and carried an aura of withering menace, a cripple with a peg leg and a hook stumbled around the room. His face was red with alcohol, and a cup of ale sloshed in his pudgy hand.

This... cannot be him.

Then Lilyth saw the scar on his upper lip, and the Dagger on his wrist. His dark brown eyes were still pitiless, even more sunken now from the fat layering his face. His hair had turned white, and all but fallen out.

It is him.

Rolf looked at her, raising an eyebrow as a layer of sheening sweat dripped from his forehead. "Not what you expected, am I?" He took another long pull from his drink as some amber liquid dribbled down his double-chin. "I know what you're thinking. I'm not the man I once was, right? Well guess what, squall, I'm *still* Rolf the Bloody. So you can either suck my dick, or you can squall off." He threw the cup at her and stumbled a step.

Lilyth held his gaze as she plucked the cup from the air. She remained silent as she let it fall from her hand and clatter to the floor.

"Oh, you don't like me, squall? I'm *Rolf.* I terrified the seas for decades! And now, now I can do whatever I want." He practically fell onto the four-post bed. Rolf struggled to loosen his pants and then gave up. "You're my *gift,* right? Pull my pants off like any good whore."

Lilyth didn't speak, didn't move, didn't breathe. Her body told her to run, her mind unable to piece the scene together. *This is wrong. All wrong.*

Then Rolf picked up a flintlock from under his pillow and pointed it at her. "Suck me or squall off."

Lilyth stalked across the room to the bed and unbuckled his pants.

"That's a good whore. Now why don't you bend down and—"

Lilyth knocked the gun aside and placed her talan between his legs.

Rolf frowned, staring down at the blade and then up at Lilyth. "What in the Core do you think you're doing?"

"I spent years waiting for this moment, and you ruined it." Lilyth pressed down on the blade as blood welled. She pulled off the girlie's scalp and stared down at him. "Remember me now?"

Rolf laughed. "Gods, you're about as ugly as me."

Lilyth clenched her teeth, hissing, "You made me kill my best friend. Sold me into slavery. Took my family."

"So? I did that to thousands of people. Am I supposed to remember you in particular?"

"You took a ship. The *Constable.*"

"Took hundreds of those, too," Rolf said, rolling his eyes as he reached for a glass bottle by the nightstand.

"You sailed through Aenu on the rivers. Slaughtered villages. *Took. My. Family.*"

"Never been to squalling Aenu, and I'm not stupid enough to sail on rivers when we've got an ocean right squalling here."

Lilyth gasped. "But—"

"You think I have a ledger of everyone I sell to the Fleshlords? Squall off." Rolf spat at her.

Lilyth closed her eyes. "This... does not make any sense."

"*You* don't make any sense, bitch."

"You came down the river..."

Lilyth's eyes unfocused as her vision flickered to flags and sails and cannons and—

None of this makes sense.

Blood and arrows and bullets and spears and swords and—

Until it clicked. Lilyth stabbed downward and up through flesh and sinews. The blade rose and fell as blood sprayed across the bed.

Explosions and groans and screams—

Rolf screamed.

Erin's screams. Steward's screams. Fox's screams—

Lilyth screamed and screamed and screamed.

Chapter Forty-Five

Erin crouched low in the shade between the trees, covered in black clay. Underfoot, the tracks from the game trail laid out before her, plain as words written on a page. Several prey animals had passed by within the last two hours, judging by the freshness of the tracks, but Erin saw a predator's paw prints too.

A jaguar, she thought, gripping her bow tighter and slowly drawing an arrow. Peering through the underbrush, Erin spotted the beast walking along a fallen tree trunk, nearly a hundred feet away. Instead of spotted fur, the jaguar was the color of midnight. *I didn't know such a thing could exist... It's a shadow, like me.*

Erin pulled the arrow back just as the jaguar turned toward her. They locked eyes for a moment, with the jaguar regarding her curiously. After hesitating, Erin lowered the bow, and the jaguar slunk away in search of food.

Kirabi's hand gently rested on her shoulder. Erin glanced up at the huntress, who blended in with the nearest tree. They smiled at one another. "I am glad you didn't shoot her, Shadow. She was a beautiful beast. It would have been a shame to kill her."

"I'm sure we'll find another beast with a little more traveling," Erin said with a serene smile. "Mother Aenu provides, right?"

"Of course. Besides, we don't want to return *too* quickly, do we?" Kirabi teased.

"No. I hate sitting by a warm fire with my family," Erin replied, still smiling. She loved the Straightback's idea of a hunt—which was far different from the Hunting she'd done as an Animal—but hunting with Kirabi was still secondary to time with her family.

I can't believe Lily is growing up so quickly. She'll be four soon. Where has the time gone? That was the difficult thing about being a mother: the ample time Erin had with her family was never enough. Lily would never be this age again, and as she grew older, who would she become?

Erin still didn't know, but she was excited to find out.

"Come on," Erin said. "No point in wasting daylight."

As if to stress the point, thunder rumbled above her. The canopy was too dense for Erin to see the sky, but by the sound of the rumblings, she imagined dark storm clouds rolling across the horizon. "We need to stay ahead of the rain."

They followed the game trail further into the jungle, pausing periodically to hear more peals of thunder. Still no rain, though. In the distance, Erin saw a herd of wild boar crossing the game track. She launched an arrow at the group of them, hitting one in the chest. Kirabi hit another, both squealed and fell to the ground as the rest scattered, only for the jaguar to sink her jaws into a third and drag it away into the shadows.

Circle of life, Erin thought as she approached the fallen boar and slit its throat. "Thank you, Aenu, for sustaining us. And thank you, boar, for your sacrifice. It will not go in vain."

Then Erin honored the boar with a moment of silence, which was broken by more thunder. She glanced up through a break in the canopy overhead, frowning. The sky was clear. Not a cloud in sight. A perfect day, like the one on which she strangled Mouse.

And yet, more thunder.

But no lightning, Erin said, stiffening. *That isn't thunder... What else could it be? Falling trees? Guns? Cannons?*

"No," Erin gasped, feeling the weight of the world on her lungs. She abandoned the boar and interrupted Kirabi's prayer. "We need to go back to the village. Now."

"What is that?" Kirabi asked, frowning.

"I... I don't know. But I have a terrible feeling." Erin sprang down the game trail without collecting her boar.

Kirabi called after her. "What about the boar? If we do not eat it, we have *killed* it!"

"Leave it anyway!"

Hearing the panic in Erin's voice, Kirabi did. Shouldering through the thickets, leaping over fallen trees, and slipping between the vines, they raced back down the path they'd come from. With each step, thunder loomed louder, sounding more like cannons than before. Something else too. Were those screams?

Lightning crackled through Erin's skin, irritating the flesh as it tingled. She shook like the jungle in a storm. *I should have shot that damned jaguar. If I had, we'd already be back by now. This is my fault. It's always my fault.*

That damned jaguar reappeared in the jungle beside Erin, running through the underbrush and keeping pace. She took it as a sign from Aenu. *Protect them, Mother. Protect my baby.*

Erin and Kirabi burst through the clearing at the edge of the river. In the distance, they could see a sloop anchored upstream, the familiar purple flag of the Fleshlords flying proudly. Though it was only forty-feet long, the ship likely carried enough cannons and Cutthroats to level the village and splinter the jungle.

Taran and Lily were fishing today by the river... Oh Gods.

Rowboats pushed across the river to the banks as Aenuite hunters shot at them from the tree line. Cutthroats fell dead into the water as cannons decimated the jungle. The trees screamed and splintered. Pistol fire and cannonballs mangled Aenuites, and their broken bodies stained the ground. Those that survived the blasts were cut down by grenados. The flames licked at the trees, sending more smoke into the air before the whole jungle was ablaze.

Then the first rowboat hit the riverbank, and the Fleshlords charged.

Kirabi drew and fired as they ran, but Erin had forgotten her own bow.

"Taran! Lily!" Erin shouted, ducking behind the splintered remains of the tree line as muskets fired in her direction. *"Taran! Lily!"*

A grenado landed in front of Erin, and she tackled Kirabi, taking cover behind a fallen tree as it exploded. Her ears rang and her right eye swelled from a splinter that tore through her eyebrow. Left eye still alert, she rolled off Kirabi and back onto her feet as the panther darted back into the jungle and out of sight.

Mother Aenu's abandoning us?

"Come back!" Erin screamed in panic. "Don't do this, Aenu! Don't do this to us!"

The panther didn't return, but Erin's long-dormant anger did. For the first time in years, she allowed herself to become an Animal.

Kirabi called out to her, but Fox ignored her. She dove deeper into the fray.

Fox let her body run, her mind relying on instinct. Her frenzied eye scanned the woods as the talan slipped into her left hand.

"Bear!" Fox shouted. "Where are you?"

"Fox!" Bear shouted back, sounding dangerously close to the fray.

A Fleshlord appeared in front of Fox. She pounced. His cutlass clattered to the dirt as she ripped through his throat. Fox stole his blade and raced further up the riverbank.

In the shadows ahead, Bear burst through the underbrush toward her, his hands shielding Lily. Bullets whizzed through the trees. He hunkered down and sprinted, blood pouring through his shirt as Lily cried in his arms. "Fox!"

"Lily!" Fox ran to them, the rest of the world falling away. When Bear came within five steps of her, relief filled her eyes. *They're safe. Praise be to Aenu, they're—*

A peal of thunder echoed as a bullet tore through Bear's chest.

No.

A second bullet exploded through his throat. Bear's feet stuttered before he crashed to the ground. His momentum carried him to Fox's foot. She stared down, her mouth open in horror.

Fox tried to scream, tried to move, tried to breathe. Her strength dissipated into smoke, and her knees buckled. Her ears rang. Her vision blurred. The blood vessels in her eyes bursted, turning them red. "Bear...?"

Bear opened his mouth, but a wet squeak was all he managed. One hand clutched at his throat. The other still cradled Lily, who was covered in his blood and no longer crying.

Fox put pressure on Bear's wound, but blood slipped through her fingers. He choked as he pushed a trembling hand toward her face, the blood marking her forehead and cheek. Then he pushed Lily to her.

"No... Bear ... You have to stay with me, okay?" Fox said, putting more pressure on the wound, only causing him to choke harder. She flinched, forcing the memory of Mouse aside. "Strength and loyalty, remember? Stay here, Bear. You have to stay. I can't do this without you."

His trembling fingers intertwined around hers.

Loyalty and strength, his hands told her. *Together. Always.*

Then his hands stilled.

Whimpering, Fox pulled Lily into her lap, rocking her. "It's okay, Lily. I've got you. I won't let them hurt you. Never..."

Fox trailed away, noticing that Lily wasn't blinking. She wasn't breathing either. Instead, a wound identical to Bear's marred her chest.

That's not Bear's blood... It's hers. The bullet passed through both of them.

The world froze. Utterly still. Utterly silent. She saw and heard everything separately as she cradled her dead daughter.

Flags and sails and cannons and—

Lily, wake up.

Blood and arrows and bullets and spears and swords and—

Lily, you have to wake up.

Explosions and groans and screams and—

Lily! Wake up! Please!

Erin's screams. Steward's screams. Fox's screams.

All three of them died in the mud beside Bear and Lily, but her body remained. She became a lyth, shaking with grief she couldn't feel and shouting with a voice she couldn't hear.

You took too much from me, Aenu... You took too much.

"Goddamn!" Before her, a grizzled Aritrastan Fleshlord discarded two smoking flintlocks and spat out a green-black wad of phlegm. He smiled, revealing a mouth of missing teeth. "The bigger they are, the harder they squalling fall!"

Arrows peppered the Cutthroat's chest as the lyth got to her feet, swayed, and fell back into the bloody mud. A hand settled on the lyth's shoulder. Wheeling in a crouch, the lyth bared her teeth and raised the talan. The woman beside her stepped back. "It's me, Shadow! It's Kirabi!"

It took the lyth several moments to recognize Kirabi's face.

"We cannot stay here," Kirabi said, pulling Lily from the lyth's grasp and cradling her. "We must go. *Now.*" Then she slipped into the jungle.

The lyth didn't follow.

Kirabi returned as bullets splintered the surrounding trees. "Shadow! We need to go!"

The lyth didn't respond, only grabbing Taran's hand and dragging him behind the remains of a smoldering tree.

"Shadow—"

The lyth bared her teeth and brandished the cutlass she'd taken.

Kirabi stiffened. "Shadow. Now is not the time to fight. We need to run. There are too many of them."

When the lyth screamed incoherently at her, Kirabi disappeared.

Taking one step back, then another, the lyth hid in the shadows of the trees, in the darkness, forgetting what it meant to speak, think, and feel.

Covered in black clay and blood, she tore apart Cutthroats with claws, blades, and teeth—anything that could slash, hack, and dismember. With blunt rocks, she smashed their bones. With sharp sticks, she gouged out their eyes. With talans, she took their hearts.

Their screams filled the air with music that only a lyth could appreciate—and laugh at.

The Fleshlords heard her, retreating to the river and away from the dark jungle where the lyth waited for them. She slunk silently between the trees, tossing body parts back to the Cutthroats, who were too afraid to venture forth. The lyth even baited them with sacks of money and weapons, which only made the Fleshlords more afraid. Instead of taking back the slaves they'd come for, they returned to their ship with only the corpses of their dead.

Back hunched and bleeding from a dozen minor wounds, the lyth watched them row back to their ship. Around her, the rocks of the riverbank were red with blood. Broken corpses of Aenuites and forgotten Fleshlords were strewn around her. More washed downstream.

The Cutthoats have to slow down to traverse the river's switchbacks before they reach the ocean, the lyth thought. *I can catch them. I can* Hunt *them.*

Only an hour after the Cutthroats fled did the rains come, a monsoon that put out the fires and dampened the ash.

"You are too late, Ahua," the lyth said, kneeling beside Taran and Lily after she placed them among the blue river lilies. She had bandaged their bleeding wounds and cleaned away the blood. Now it seemed they were only sleeping, but the lyth knew better. She cupped Taran's cheeks, willing them to be warm, but they remained cold. His open eyes only stared at the sky. So, too, did Lily's as she lay in his arms.

"Damn You, Ahua. Damn You, Aenu. Damn You, Eo. Damn all of You to the depths," the lyth said. Pressing her lips to Taran's, she held him a moment longer before letting go. Biting down on her tongue to keep from screaming, she kissed her daughter's forehead and pulled the necklace from her throat, fastening it around her own.

Mark's words stirred through the trees. *Saying goodbye is the hardest thing for us to do—it means they're gone, and we can't get them back.*

"I will not say it," the lyth said. "I will *never* say it."

The lyth turned and rose, her silhouette blacker than night. Her hands didn't shake. Her eyes didn't blink. Her heart didn't beat.

But Kirabi barred her path. "You are leaving?"

The lyth stared at the other bodies stacked by the lilies. Old friends. Mostly men, but a few women and children. Janus was among them. *So many lost, and for what? These people have no riches. They only had their lives. The Cutthroats took even that. I will take more.*

"Hunting," the lyth replied. A crack of lightning struck behind her, lighting her body like a black silhouette.

Kirabi shook her head. "You do not have to bear this weight alone."

Bear. The lyth flinched. "You know nothing of the weight I carry."

"I do," Kirabi said, putting a hand on her shoulder. "I have laid my son upon the lilies. My husband too. It hurts. But you can stay with us. With me. Help us rebuild—"

"Rebuild?" the lyth asked, shrugging off Kirabi's hand. "Rebuild *what?* Look around you, Kirabi! There is nothing left! Everything and everyone is gone!" She shook her head and clenched her fists. "They just keep taking and taking and taking. But not anymore. I am going to burn them to ash."

"That is not the way, Shadow. We must trust in Mother Aenu. She always provides."

"You are a fool, Kirabi. Mother Aenu does not provide. Mother Aenu is silent, just like all the other useless Gods. We provide for ourselves, and we must take what we want." Quieter, she added, "I wanted to be good, to be pure, to be like the lilies—like my daughter. I wanted to be good enough for her. But now Lily is gone. So is my soul. Now, only the lyth is left. Only Lily's revenge." She shoved Kirabi away and darted into the jungle.

"Only Lilyth."

Lilyth trekked south through the trees while the Fleshlords followed the river's switchback path with only half of their surviving crew and torn sails. She caught them within two days' time. They thought themselves safe miles downstream and anchored in the river.

There is nowhere they can hide, Lilyth thought as she waded into the water with a broken smile, unconcerned with the danger of crocodiles and constrictor snakes. Most of her clay camouflage slid off as she let the current pull her downriver, swimming beneath the surface to avoid the roving lanterns of the Fleshlords guarding the ship. Colliding hard with the hull, Lilyth cut her hands as she clung to the barnacles, pried open a gunport, and slithered inside. Soaked and cold, she stood, her talan glinting with its own crooked smile.

Around her, Fleshlords swung in hammocks, the gentle swaying of the ship keeping them heavy in sleep. She killed them, one by one, until only a final one remained. *How can you sleep, knowing what you did?* Lilyth thought, trailing the talan across his skin until he opened his eyes. Then she killed him too.

Lilyth ascended to the main deck as the monsoon-season rains came down on her. Between the mist and the darkness, she picked the rest off, beginning with the helmsman at the stern and working her way to the captain, who'd been waiting at the bow.

"Would you look at that?" the Fleshlord captain muttered as the wind stirred his long black hair. "Eo is still with us."

Lilyth looked up at the sky to see a blood moon, her eye twitching before she plunged her talan through the back of his knees and severed his hamstrings. The Fleshlord captain let out a hoarse scream and fell to the deck. Lilyth stomped on his hand until he let go of the flintlock he'd been reaching for. She kicked it away.

"Did you think I would just let you escape? After what you did?" Lilyth slammed her cutlass down into his left hand, skewering it against the deck. As he screamed, she pulled his cutlass from its sheath and stabbed it through his right palm, crucifying him on the deck of the ship.

"Have mercy," the Fleshlord sobbed. *"Please."*

"Mercy? You ask *me* for mercy? You took everything from me! My husband! My daughter! My! Squalling! *Soul!*" Lilyth's voice rose with each word, cresting high above them like a maverick. Lilyth shattered his pelvis with her boot before sitting on his stomach. "So now... *now* I will take everything from you. Starting with your feet and working my way up."

Lilyth tortured him slowly, taking his toes, testicles, fingers, teeth, tongue, and ears before finally carving out his eyes. But she still felt as numb as before. Killing this squall did nothing to ease her grief.

Lilyth stared up at the moon. "Why did you have to take them? Why did you take them when you could have taken me?"

Lilyth didn't remember falling to her knees, weeping, or even falling asleep. She only recalled opening her eyes as a scream reached her ears.

Above was a blue, cloudless sky. Lilyth could hear the mosquitoes flying around her, but she'd grown used to them after a decade spent in the jungles of Aenu.

Wait, why I am here? she wondered, sitting up. *I was... where was I?*

"Mommy! Save me, Mommy!"

Lily, Lilyth thought as she reached for her talan, but she didn't have it. All of her weapons were missing. She blinked again. The world came into focus. Lilyth sat on the rocks by the river near the Straightback village. Nearer the water's edge, Lily shouted and ran. Lilyth's muscles tightened before seeing Taran running after her, laughing. Taran scooped up Lily, but she squirmed from his arms and ran away again.

Lilyth relaxed, though her heart still pounded. What had happened? Another nightmare?

"I was... somewhere else," Lilyth said. She rubbed her eyes and blinked, but Taran was still there when her eyes reopened. "Where?"

Taran put his hands on his knees and let out a booming laugh. "Oy! You just gonna sit here all day, or are you gonna help me catch the little monkey?"

Lilyth stood on awkward legs, nearly tripping twice on the rocks because her eyes were locked on him. A receding horror fled from her, a bad dream that she couldn't remember. Tears formed in her eyes as she hugged him, feeling every ounce of his flesh as he easily picked her up. "Taran, you are okay."

"Well, of course I'm okay. I'm great." Taran said. "You alright? I know Lily's been keeping you busy lately. Maybe you need to lie down and get some—"

"No," Lilyth said. When Taran raised an eyebrow, she added, "I just had a horrible nightmare, Taran. The last thing I need is to go back to sleep."

"Alright, then help me go get the little monkey. She's a mangy little thing, ain't she?" Taran asked, kissing her quickly.

"She is *our* mangy little thing."

"Always will be." Taran smiled. Then the smile became a gasp. "Oh no."

Lilyth turned, but all she saw was Lily running along the bank. "What is—"

Taran shoved her into the water and took off after Lily, laughing all the while. "Now's not the time to go for a swim, sweetheart! We've got a monkey to catch!"

Lilyth spluttered and wiped the water from her eyes. *That Ass... He tricked me.* Chuckling, she waded after them.

"Mommy, save me!" Lily squealed again as Taran picked her up.

Lilyth jumped on Taran's back. Wrapping her legs around his chest and trying to pull Lily from his grasp, she shouted, "Oh no! Daddy's too strong, Lily! Be free!"

Taran jumped into the water with Lilyth still on his back and Lily in his arms. The water swirled around them. Lilyth was the first to break the surface, and she waded to the edge of the river and laughed. The sound petered away as she waited for them to resurface.

But neither Taran nor Lily did.

"Not funny anymore, Taran!" Lilyth said, eventually. "Come out, Lily! Stop scaring Mommy!"

Nothing.

Thunder crackled overhead. No lightning. No storm clouds. *Cannons.*

Lilyth turned to see a three-masted frigate drifting down the river. Smoked poured from the gun deck as Cutthroats cheered and raised cutlasses. At the bow, she could see corpses hanging from nooses. From the mainmast, a black flag fluttered. Appearing at the gunwale, a man with sunken eyes, a razor-thin mustache, and a long scar stared down at her from this distance.

Lilyth froze in terror. "No... No, it cannot be... Not him..."

Captain Rolf smiled.

"Taran! Lily! Get out of the water! Now!" Lilyth shouted, wading back into the water and trying to find them. She submerged her head and opened her eyes—

Only to find herself alone on the deck of a sloop, excluding the mutilated corpse of a dead Fleshlord.

"Who... What... Where am I?" Lilyth asked, her voice hoarse. "Taran? Lily? Where are you?"

More silence.

Lilyth tore across the ship, searching every compartment, every hammock. Twice. Three times. She stalked back up to the deck and slammed her fists into the mast. This didn't make sense to her. Taran and Lily had been... where?

"We were playing in the river," Lilyth told herself, though that seemed *wrong* to her somehow. But she threw that concern aside and reconnected her stray thoughts. "And then Rolf came. I looked for them and... ended up here. I must have killed these Cuthroats because they had Taran and Lily, but... they are not here."

Lilyth noticed the Fleshlord flag flying from the mast. "But why not a Skull flag?" She shook her head, trying to make sense of her messy memories. "Skulls use other Cutthroat flags as often as their own. They used Rose flags to trick Ink, so this must be a Skull ship. And if Taran and Lily are not here... Rolf must have taken them aboard the *Wrath*."

Lilyth took her place behind the helm of the tattered ship, knowing now what had to be done. *Taran and Lily are at Tibur, but I need an army to get them out safely. So I will build one and burn Tibur to the ground.*

"You made a mistake in taking my family, Rolf," Lilyth said as the ship drifted across the open ocean and into the darkness beyond. "You will pay with your life." Staring up at the blood moon, she added, "You all will."

CHAPTER FORTY-SIX

Lilyth stood over Rolf's corpse. She didn't remember killing him, but her talan dripped with his blood. His eyes were gone. So were his ears, tongue, fingers, genitals, and toes.

"It is not enough. It is not nearly enough." Lilyth stared down at her shaking hands. "I do not feel any better. He deserved worse. I..." A whimper escaped, then a sob.

Minutes could have passed, possibly hours. All Lilyth could think of was how much time she'd lost. *I will never get to see Lily grow up. Never get to see her hunt. Never see her fish. Never see her as a wife. Never as a mother... Never. Never. Never.*

Lilyth gritted her teeth as tears streamed down her cheeks. She grabbed the lantern on Rolf's bedside table and spiked it into the ground beneath his bed, feeling hollower as she watched the body of her nemesis burn to a crisp.

"What do I do now, Bear? What do I do now?"

He didn't answer her, and she knew he never would. Never again. Instead, Lilyth saw the moon watching her through Rolf's window, glinting with its damned smile.

"*You.*" Lilyth said. She finally let her hatred consume her entirely.

Her body moved of its own volition as her mind failed to form words. Her eyes burned. Her hands slit throats. Her legs ran through the halls connecting the donjon's towers and across the wall to the front gate. Death befell all those who witnessed Lilyth. She destroyed the winches controlling the portcullis and drawbridge, opening the way for a thousand legionnaires—the Red Death among them. Finally, her lips formed the right words. "Kill them all. Every single one of them."

The Red Death spilled inside Flotsam Hill, bringing carnage with them. They set fire to the longhouses, murdering drunken Skulls and girlies as they escaped the smoke and red flames. More tore into the donjon, coming across the dancers and musicians. Screams and laughter replaced the music. Around the port, other fires started, the contingents from the south, east, and north converging on the city. Drunken Cutthroats wavered around her, all of them unprepared for a fight.

Had it been any other night, an attack like this would have been suicide. But on the night of the Festival of Colors, it was a drunken slaughter.

As Flotsam Hill was consumed by fire, Kendrik attacked the Copperhouse. Arya, the Fleshery. Greeley, the Thorn. From there, the legionnaires would surge into the Crimson Palace at the center of Port Tibur.

Lilyth staggered deeper into the city as her focus slipped between all of her mistakes, past and present. Ghostly faces stared at her in reflections of shattered glass and pooling blood. *Dad. Mark. Ink—*

A screaming Cutthroat ran toward her, but Lilyth shot him in the face and dropped the smoking flintlock on the corpse. She dragged herself down the burning street as legionnaires laughed and screamed around her.

Mouse. Tomlin. Jarrel—

Another Cutthroat attacked her. Lilyth left another corpse in its place.

Aquila. Owl. Kirabi—

A third Cutthroat charged, and Lilyth tackled him, ripping out his throat with her teeth.

Will. Taran. Lily... Oh Gods, I am so sorry, Lily. I am so sorry.

Lilyth staggered to her feet, dragging her fingers down her bloody, painted face. "How could I have forgotten? How could I have forgotten about my baby girl?"

The moon remained silent.

"All the decisions I made, everything I did... Did I do it for nothing? For revenge?"

More Cutthroats. More bullets.

"No. No, it cannot be. I refuse to believe it."

"Mommy!" a girl shrieked from a burning butchery off to her left.

Lilyth almost dropped her cutlass. "Lily?"

I knew they were still alive. I knew it. They are here. That was all a bad dream. That is all. Rolf was lying. I was right. They are still alive. They are alive!

Lilyth cut through two more Cutthroats before plunging into the flames. The heat was blinding and intense. Smoke filled her lungs and caused her to gag. Her skin bubbled. Her eyes made out nothing.

"Lily! Where are you?" Lilyth shouted.

"Help me!" Lily shouted from above. *"Mommy!"*

She is on the second floor. Blinking through the tendrils of flame and leaping over falling pieces of timber, Lilyth charged up the stairs and slammed into the door with her shoulder. The door refused to open. *I will not be denied.* Lilyth grit her teeth and slammed into it again, then a third time, dislocating her shoulder. Ignoring the pain, she kicked the door, and the hinges finally buckled.

Lilyth stumbled inside. A small bed was on fire in the far corner by a window. Debris fell from the roof as a young Aritrastan girl tried to pull a half-conscious woman out from under a pile of burning timbers. But the girl's hair was black, her eyes green. Not brown.

"You... you are not Lily," Lilyth said as the talan dropped from her hand and clattered to the burning floor. "How... how could I have been so wrong? So blind? *Again?*"

The girl wailed, and it shook Lilyth from her grief. She glanced at the ceiling. The wooden braces and crosspieces threatened to fall. She studied the mother trapped beneath the timbers. *She is going to die regardless,* Lilyth thought as she swept the child into her arms and ran down the stairs.

"What about Mommy! Help my mommy!" the child cried, slamming her pudgy fists onto Lilyth's shoulder.

Lilyth ignored the screams. She ran toward the exit, coughing. The smoke burned her eyes. She blinked away tears as more of the ceiling fell around them. *Cannot go this way,* Lilyth realized. With the fire, she didn't see another exit. *The window.* Cradling the small girl, she ran back up the stairs.

Stepping over the dying mother, Lilyth jumped through the window, glass shattering around her. She fell two stories and hit the ground on the balls of her feet, rolling and shielding the girl as glass and stone ripped through her armor and shredded the skin on her back. Wincing, Lilyth limped away from the burning building. "Are you hurt?"

"I want my mommy!"

Lilyth watched the fire consume the store. "We never get what we want, child."

From the other side of the building, Lilyth saw legionnaires pounding at the door and screaming for help:

"The Champion's inside—"

"Hurry—"

"Help her—"

"Move the timbers—"

"Save Lilyth!"

As her name was echoed, Lilyth hesitated, her eyes shifting from the child in her arms to her army before focusing on the girl again. Then she darted off into the darkness.

Greeley had waited at the tree line of the northern forest until he saw the first fire burning from Flotsam Hill. Then he'd broken cover. Charging past the small inland garrisons, he crashed into the Thorn with a thousand legionnaires at his back and swept through it in a tide of darkness. He caught unwary Roses singing shanties and clinking mugs—grenados ended the festivities and their lives. As more screams and explosions ripped through the building, Cutthroats half-swaggered and half-stumbled through the hallways, fumbling with their flintlocks and cutlasses before being ripped apart amidst the fog of smoke.

I need to find Kendrik, Greeley thought as he wrapped his hands around the last Rose and choked the life out of her. *He's farther south, going for the Copperhouse before reaching the Crimson Palace. I'll find him there and kill him.* Greeley's mind flashed to Lilyth. *She should still be a Flotsam Hill. I'll find her there afterward.*

The Red Hand snapped the Rose's neck and stood. Then he took his men into port and slaughtered the pitiful Cutthroat resistance that barred his way. Buildings burned and blood ran through the streets, the groans of agonizing death never far away. But all of it only made Greeley grin.

Gods, I've never felt stronger, Greeley thought as he ran his sword through the chest of young Cutthroat, ripping off the man's nose ring and stuffing it in his pocket with the other trophies he'd already taken: earrings, rings, necklaces—even a few teeth. He kicked the man off his sword and stomped his head into the ground, grinding his heel into his eye socket. *I can't believe there was a time I wanted to join these Cutthroats. They're weak. Pathetic. Beneath me.*

Greeley lobbed a grenado into a storefront and heard a shriek before it was silenced by the explosion. He ran until he reached the Crimson Palace. A twenty-foot-high wall separated it from the rest of the city, with a thirty-foot gap between the stones and any building. The path leading to the barbican had already been blown apart, the portcullis torn from the stones. Legionnaires fought with Cutthroats along the ramparts, and dead corpses of both sides lay dead on the wall and the ground beneath. More legionnaires streamed inside, chanting, "Blood. Blood! *Blood!*"

"Kendrik must have beaten me here. Damn him. I won't let him take my glory. I won't let him take my trophies."

Greeley rushed through the crumbling guardhouse and into the courtyard, where most of the bodies were dressed for a masquerade ball rather than a fight. White dresses had turned red, though black ones looked unsoiled. Colored powders stained the grass, stones, and stage, all splattered with flecks and pools of crimson.

A body smashed into the ground in front of Greeley, and he stared up. From the palace's many balconies, legionnaires pushed the Cutthroats over railings as stone gargoyles watched with savage glee.

Kendrik... Damn him. This glory is mine. These trophies are mine. Lilyth is—

Then Greeley noticed only Arya fighting her way inside of the palace. He could not see Kendrik among the chaos, nor his followers.

If these are all Arya's men, then Kendrik isn't here yet, Greeley realized, his smile widening. *That means I can still get him.*

While the rest of his legionnaires pressed into the palace, Greeley exited the courtyard, ignoring the bewildered looks from his followers. He sprinted further south, avoiding Cutthroats and skirmishes as he tried to catch up to Kendrik at the Copperhouse.

But the smile faltered when he heard legionnaires screaming:

"The Champion's inside—"

"Hurry—"

"Help her—"

"Move the timbers—"

"Save Lilyth!"

No! She cannot die. She is mine! I will save her, and she will finally see that I am her equal. Then I will kill Kendrik and take my place at Lilyth's side. Greeley spun and followed the sound of the screams only to see a painted legionnaire running away with a child in her arms.

Greeley stopped in his tracks. "Only Lilyth moves like that, but why is she carrying a child? Why is everyone screaming?"

Then the traitor's words weaved through the tendrils of fire. *After Lilyth finds her daughter, you'll never see her again. Mark my words.*

Greeley stiffened. "No... it can't be."

Then he followed.

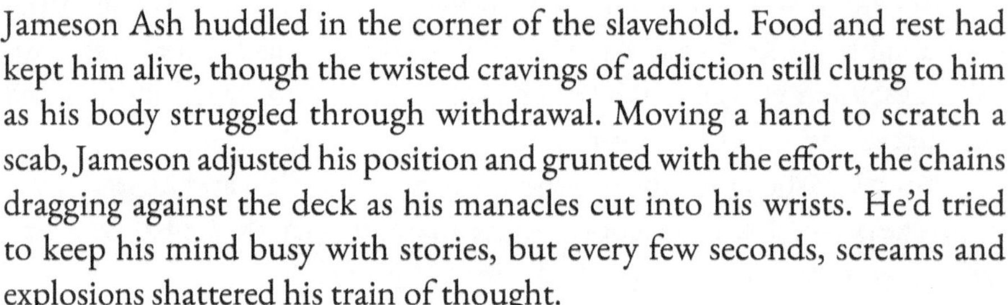

Jameson Ash huddled in the corner of the slavehold. Food and rest had kept him alive, though the twisted cravings of addiction still clung to him as his body struggled through withdrawal. Moving a hand to scratch a scab, Jameson adjusted his position and grunted with the effort, the chains dragging against the deck as his manacles cut into his wrists. He'd tried to keep his mind busy with stories, but every few seconds, screams and explosions shattered his train of thought.

All of this is my fault, he thought. Then the door opened to reveal his biggest regret. Lilyth held a lantern in her right hand and carried a sleeping toddler on her left shoulder.

"Is that Lily?" Jameson looked behind Lilyth, expecting to see a man standing in the doorway and seeing nothing. "Where's Taran?"

Lilyth closed her eyes and clenched her jaw as she looked down and away. "No. They are dead," she said, her voice broken.

Jameson wanted to laugh, to mock her, but despite everything, he felt a spark of sympathy for her.

Lilyth tossed him a set of keys. "We are leaving. You can come with us or try to escape on your own. I do not care."

Jameson knew better than to argue. He undid the manacles. "Thank you."

"I am not doing this for you, Jameson," Lilyth spat. "I would let you rot, but Taran... he would have wanted me to let you go."

Jameson stood straight, his back popping. He groaned and stretched as she tossed him his trident. "And that's why you saved the child, too? Where are her parents?"

"Dead."

"By your hands?" When Lilyth didn't respond, Jameson added, "Saving two people after killing thousands doesn't make you a saint."

"I never wanted to be a saint, Jameson. Just a mother. Just a wife."

Jameson followed Lilyth out of the compartment. They climbed the ladders back to the main deck, where moonlight illuminated the horror of Lilyth's war. The port beyond was on fire, burning to the ground just like Cassius. Slain Cutthroats and locals alike were dead on the ground. So were legionnaires.

"By the Gods..."

"The Gods had nothing to do with this," Lilyth said while the child slept in her arms. She led him across the docks to a sloop small enough to be operated by only two or three crewmen. "There is food below. I stocked this ship with a month's worth of supplies for three people earlier today, so it will be more than enough to get us back to Aritrasta."

Lilyth clenched her jaw, and Jameson didn't need to ask to know who the ship had been for. "We're going to Alira?" Jameson asked instead.

"I will drop you off at a tavern. A man named Mark Tulich owns it. He will take care of you and help you get settled."

"But not you?" Jameson asked as he stepped onto the boat.

"No," Lilyth said, passing him the sleeping child and undoing the mooring knots that kept the sloop tethered to the dock. Just as Jameson had taught her all those years ago.

Before Lilyth boarded, she stared out over the burning port, hearing the struggles and screams, smelling the blood and powder.

Jameson could see the indecision written into Lilyth's expression before her face hardened. She clenched her jaw and straightened her shoulders as a glint of steel entered her bloodshot eyes.

She'll never stop, Jameson realized. *Not until she dies... or the world breaks.* Then he understood. "You're going to the Deadlands. You're going after Eo's Sword."

"Yes." Lilyth planted her foot on the edge of the boat to join Jameson. Then she hesitated, ears twitching. She turned back to the dock, where a painted legionnaire with a red hand appeared, leveling a flintlock pistol at her.

CHAPTER FORTY-SEVEN

Though Lilyth didn't move, her mind sped. Her eyes shifted as she calculated her options. She reached for her talan but found it missing. *Damnation.*

"Lilyth, you're leaving the Red Legion… for a traitor and a child?" the Red Hand asked.

"Red Hand, you dare point a gun at me?"

The gun wavered but didn't fall.

"You're leaving us," the Red Hand said, gesturing to Jameson. "This traitor told me of your plan. He said you'd leave us when you found your *precious* daughter. I didn't want to believe it, but here we are. Everyone thinks you're burning to death, but you're here. You're running away. What about your strength? Your loyalty?"

Lilyth froze, then turned to stare at Jameson. He grimaced, saying nothing. *He betrayed me again… I am a fool.*

"You'd really walk away? From the Red Legion?" Greeley asked. "From *me?*"

Him, Lilyth thought as a plan formed. *He's not angry. He's jealous. I can leverage that against him.*

"I made a deal with him," Lilyth lied. "His life for his help."

"You don't make deals with Cutthroats, Lilyth."

"Since when do you know what I do and what I do not?" Lilyth pushed the boat away from the harbor while remaining on the dock. Her eyes met Jameson's, and she relayed her message with only her eyes. *Go.*

"You think me a fool, Red Hand? After everything, you think I would just *leave?*" Lilyth took a step toward him. He didn't pull the trigger. "How much have I shown you? I have destroyed ships *single-handedly.* I named you my first follower. Together, we have drowned thousands of men in this sea. On the day of my greatest triumph, you think I would just walk away? Are you really that stupid?"

Another step. More silence.

Greeley kept the gun trained on her, but Lilyth noticed his hand tremble, his faltering confidence, his overdrawn jealousy. "You are that stupid? You thought you would trust the word of a traitor over mine? Because you are jealous. Because you want me all to yourself."

Greeley flinched.

"You did not think I knew? Why else would I have placed Kendrik at my side instead of you? Because he was better than you? Because I wanted to replace you?" Another step. She was ten paces away. *I need to get closer.* Lilyth pointed at him with her finger, but only to shift his focus away from her other hand as she subtly drew a knife. "No, you fool. Kendrik knew his place. You never did."

"I—"

"I even gave you Arya. Gave you a woman, an equal."

"You're my equal," Greeley said.

"No. All of my equals are dead." Lilyth took another step and with it, a gamble. "And you are furthest from them." She pointed at Jameson, hiding the knife behind her back. "Even this so-called *traitor* is more my equal. At least I can trust Jameson enough to turn my back to him, but you, Red Hand? No. You would put a knife through my spine. A bullet through my brain."

"You betrayed me!"

"Yet you are holding the gun." Lilyth took another step. Six paces. *Almost there.* "You want to speak of loyalty? Of strength? Then prove yourself. Give me the gun."

"No," Greeley said.

Lilyth bared her teeth. "Red Hand, you squalling fool, give—"

"I'm not a fool."

And Lilyth saw his indecision fall away. Her head blurred as she raised the knife—

Greeley fired the pistol, and the bullet tore through her left eye and exited out through the side of her skull, missing the brain

The pain was worse than anything she'd ever felt. Her knife slipped from her hand and fell into the sea. She shuddered, her breath catching in her throat as she took a step back. Blood poured from the wound. Then she took another step, but she didn't fall. Her hatred and anger kept her standing.

I only need one eye to kill you, Red Hand.

Greeley gasped, horrified. "By the Goddess." He dropped the smoking flintlock pistol and took a step away from Lilyth. "You're joining the night and becoming Eo. Just as you said. The prophecy is true..."

What?

Then Lilyth realized she could still see through the eye that was missing.

The world was darker, different, but she could pierce the veil of darkness. Understand it, even. It was warm to her now, instead of cold. Welcoming instead of foreboding. And in it, she could hear... voices? Laughter?

"Eo?" Lilyth asked. "Is that You?" She staggered backward again, but her feet found only air.

Lilyth fell into the Drowned Sea, but there was no splash.

Webbed hands caught her body. Scaled gray heads appeared without noses or lips or ears. Their black eyes were cold, their mouths open in horrid smiles. But the syrens did not attack her. They kept her afloat and stared down at her with a drowned gaze she'd seen only in mirrors.

"You... You are like me."

The syrens' grins widened as they retreated beneath the surface, and Lilyth was pulled with them, her eyes closing as the world grew dark.

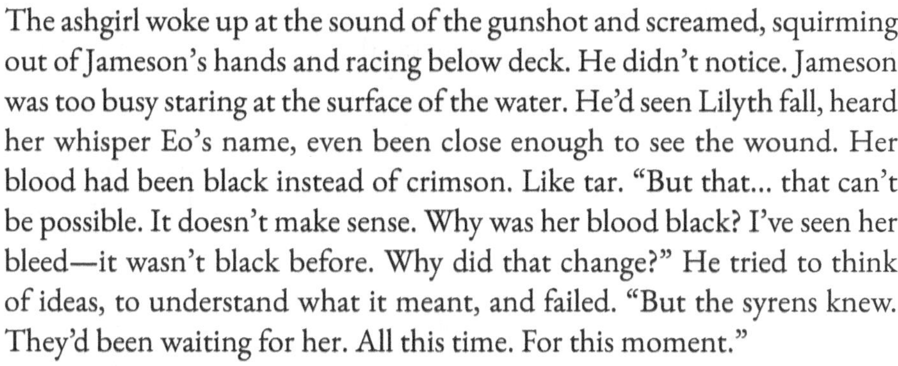

The ashgirl woke up at the sound of the gunshot and screamed, squirming out of Jameson's hands and racing below deck. He didn't notice. Jameson was too busy staring at the surface of the water. He'd seen Lilyth fall, heard her whisper Eo's name, even been close enough to see the wound. Her blood had been black instead of crimson. Like tar. "But that... that can't be possible. It doesn't make sense. Why was her blood black? I've seen her bleed—it wasn't black before. Why did that change?" He tried to think of ideas, to understand what it meant, and failed. "But the syrens knew. They'd been waiting for her. All this time. For this moment."

"You."

Out of the corner of his eyes, Jameson saw the Red Hand raise another gun—

Jameson ducked beneath the sloop's gunwale of the ship as the bullet slammed into the mast. Two more shots echoed, followed by a scream. Jameson peered over the railing as the Red Hand leaped from the dock and onto the sloop.

Jameson brandished his trident and grabbed one of the small fishing nets hanging from the side of the boat, holding it in his left hand as the Red Hand advanced.

"*You!* This is all your fault!" the Red Hand shouted.

"My fault? You squalling shot her!"

"Because you turned Lilyth against me!" The Red Hand ran forward with a scream, raising his cutlass.

Just like in the Arena of Cassius, Jameson tossed his net and caught the Red Hand's blade. While it was entangled, Jameson thrust his trident into the Red Hand's chest. Two of the prongs missed, but the third pierced his stomach. With a roar, the Red Hand gripped the trident's shaft and brought a fist down on Jameson's head. The weaver lost his grip on the trident and fell on his ass. The old pain in his knees flared as Jameson scooted backward. Splinters raked through his fingers and calves before he scrambled back to his feet.

The Red Hand staggered toward him, pulling the trident from his stomach and hurling it across the ship. Even with the gaping wound slowing the Red Hand, Jameson knew he was too slow to collect the trident. He continued backing away.

After ripping the netting away from his sword, the Red Hand stared at the white cutlass and laughed. He dropped it. "No. I don't need a sword to kill you. I'm going to strangle you to death and watch the life fade from your eyes. Then I'll take those damned orbs as my trophies."

The Red Hand charged forward, and Jameson tripped over the deck. The legionnaire loosed another scream and lunged, wrapping his hands around Jameson's throat. He choked and struggled, but he was not strong enough to break the legionnaire's grip. Jameson reached for something, anything, as his vision blackened.

"*I* was her first follower! *I* was her Red Hand! But *you* had to ruin that, didn't you?" the Red Hand growled. "You just had to keep getting in—"

Jameson jabbed his fingers into the Red Hand's stomach, and the legionnaire screamed, letting go of him. Jameson kicked the squall in the face. Then he turned to reach for a thick splinter of railing created from a ricocheting bullet. His fingers grazed it as the Red Hand jumped on his back. The legionnaire snaked his arm beneath Jameson's chin, and the weaver choked, fingers still reaching for the shard of wood.

Almost there... Jameson's fingertips touched it briefly. But he was still too far away. Jameson pulled himself along the deck even as the legionnaire clung to him. He ripped off all the fingernails on his right hand.

"Lilyth was mine! *You* killed her!"

Squall you. Jameson grabbed the splinter and stabbed it into the Red Hand's neck. The legionnaire released a bloody cough before falling to the side, heavy as a stone. He pressed a hand against his neck as Jameson crawled on top and stabbed him several more times.

As the Red Hand spasmed, Jameson pushed himself to his feet and dragged the Red Hand's corpse to the gunwale. Without a blessing of spit, Jameson hefted the body over the edge and dropped him into the water. The Red Hand's body sunk as the curse of the Drowned took hold.

"Damn you to the depths, *Dead* Hand," Jameson said. He trudged across the deck and collected his trident, leaning heavily on it.

Jameson wanted this to be a moment of victory, a glimpse of freedom, but it felt hollow. He looked out at the burning port, at all the people caught in Lilyth's path. Guilty and innocent alike purged by fire.

I will not be one of them, Jameson thought as he pushed the boat away from the dock with his trident.

As a gust of wind rose, Jameson unfurled the sails and steered the sloop from Tibur. The sounds of fighting faded from his ears, replaced by the soft cries of the ashgirl. Jameson found her hiding in a barrel in the cramped sleeping quarters of the small sloop. He gently lifted her out.

"I want my mommy," the ashgirl sobbed.

"I know, sweetheart." Jameson said. *Maybe we can find her in Alira,* he wanted to say, but then he remembered Steward and the woman she'd become. *No more lies.* "But your Mommy is gone." *Except for this small one.* "I told her I'd take good care of you, though."

"You know my mommy?"

"We were good friends." Jameson smiled, hating the lie, though it was the only comfort he could offer the girl. "And I think I know just where to find more."

The stars were bright as Jameson followed *Eo's Point* toward Alira.

As the Cutthroats retreated, Kendrik the Red Heart heard the panicked screams of legionnaires. Approaching at a dead sprint, he found them clawing at the debris of a burning butchery, scalding themselves as they picked up fiery timbers and heaved them aside—their work was in vain as the building continued collapsing.

"What is it?" Kendrik asked. "What's wrong?"

"The Champion! She's inside!" a legionnaire screamed, eyes furious. "We must save her!"

Kendrik fought the wild panic that crawled inside his stomach and throat as he recalled the Champion's words.

Port Tibur will fall to fire. A fire so great and mighty that nothing will survive it. Even I will be consumed by it, become that fire, and I will wash over those Cutthroats and unleash my full wrath upon them and any who still do not believe.

On his knees, Kendrik waited until the fire cooled before sifting through the ashes of the building, his hands thoroughly burned. He found the Champion's talan next to a corpse so singed it was little more than bone. Completely unrecognizable.

But that has to be her. Nobody else would have her blade.

"Lilyth's prophecy was right," Kendrik whispered. "She is with Eo now—with Jericho—just as she foretold." Reverently, Kendrik picked up Lilyth's steaming skull. "But what do I do?"

Be ruthless, the Champion had said.

"I will." Hardening his heart, Kendrik arose from the ashes and turned to see the Red Death amassed behind him. Radur and Duvur had doffed their bloodied helms and kneeled before Lilyth's corpse. Their anguish was clear on their faces, the flames reflecting their tears.

"Are you still with me?" Kendrik asked.

"To the death," replied the Red Death.

"Good." Kendrik raised Lilyth's talan—*his* talan—and slashed his palm. With his own blood, he marked the Red Death, placing the crescent on their foreheads.

Lilyth will guide us... even in death.

Kendrik raised his head, looking up in the distance to see the burning Crimson Palace. Greeley and Arya were there, plotting against him—as the Champion had foretold.

They will burn with the rest of the nonbelievers.

By the time that Kendrik arrived at the Crimson Palace, the fight was all but over. Fires raged throughout the old castle with legionnaires and Cutthroats burning in them. Kendrik stalked higher up the stairs, avoiding the corpses and pools of blood as the Red Death followed him. Teeth clenched harder than the cutlass in his hand, Kendrik found the Red Eye inside the tallest tower.

Covered in blood, wounded, and burned, she held herself against the railing, surrounded by a few of her closest followers—female slaves freed during the Cassian battle. Arya turned toward him, raising her sword before recognizing him. With a relieved smile, she lowered her blade. "Red Heart. I'm glad to see you."

I'm sure you are, Kendrik thought, expecting Greeley to ambush him at any moment. But that squall was nowhere to be seen. Kendrik smiled, stepping inside the room. "Me too."

"Where are the others?" Arya asked. "Is Lilyth...?"

"Dead," Kendrik said. "Her prophecy came true."

"I see," Arya said, frowning. "Then we must guide the legion. Together, with strength and loyalty."

"Right... Strength and loyalty," Kendrik said, deadpan. "Where's the Red Hand?"

"I haven't seen him—neither has anyone else. He left the palace and disappeared."

"Did he now?" Kendrik asked, hand tightening on the blade. "Strange. I assumed he'd be with you."

"Why?" Arya's eyes narrowed as the Red Death entered the room with Kendrik and blocked the exit. Her followers raised their blades, but they weren't nearly as trained as Radur and Duvur. "What's going on, Red Heart?"

"You don't have to pretend anymore, Red Eye. I know all about your plot to kill me." Kendrik said. "Greeley, I might have suspected. But you?"

"I've been *protecting* you," Arya said.

"The Champion told me the rest of the prophecy after you left. Don't deny it!"

"Lilyth told you that?" Arya took a step back. "No… Kendrik, I'm loyal."

"No. You aren't. Neither is Greeley. And if he hasn't already burned to death, he will—and you will join him."

Kendrik snapped his fingers. Duvur and Radur lunged forward with their warhammers as more of the Red Death swarmed over the last of Arya's depleted forces. Death befell them, crushed beneath lead and steel.

"What are you doing?" Arya shouted, her back pressed against the railing as Radur and Duvur cornered her on the balcony. "Why are—"

Radur's hammer connected with her side, and Arya collapsed to her knees. The Red Eye coughed blood and stared up at him. She dropped her sword, probably meaning it as a sign of loyalty, but Kendrik only saw it as weakness.

"I didn't betray you, Kendrik," Arya said. "Why are you doing this?"

"Because Lilyth wanted me to," Kendrik said, pulling out a flintlock and pointing it at her head. "Everything I do, I do for her. For Jericho. For the Red Legion."

Kendrik pulled the trigger, splattering Arya's brains against the railing. Then he threw her corpse into the fire to join the other nonbelievers.

When the last of the Cutthroats were stamped out, Kendrik the Red Heart—the new Champion—stood on the highest balcony of the Crimson Palace, grim yet determined to follow Lilyth's plan. Closest to him were the zealous Tavrakian twins, Radur and Duvur of the Red Death, and an assortment of other followers that Kendrik had named as his new lieutenants. Below him, the entire Red Legion had amassed in the courtyard to hear his words. And because so many slaves had been held captive on the island, their size swelled to five thousand strong.

Soon they will number ten thousand. A hundred thousand. And when we take Corinthus, we will number in the millions. None will stop us.

Kendrik raised his hand into a fist, and all the legionnaires grew silent. "Red Legion! Our Champion has joined the night like everyone before her! So have Greeley the Red Hand and Arya the Red Heart! But this is a part of Lilyth's plan, just as she foretold! Now, Lilyth has become one with Eo, and She guides us through the night as we remain here to carry out Her will!" He raised the talan as a murmur spread through the Red Legion. "We will keep hunting the Cutthroats. We will bring them blood!"

"Blood. Blood! *Blood!*" the Red Legion chanted.

"For Lilyth, the first of us!"

"Lilyth. Lilyth! *Lilyth!*"

"For Eo, Goddess of the Chosen!"

"Eo. Eo! *Eo!*"

"Strength and loyalty!"

"Loyalty and strength!"

⸎

The words echoed long into the night, and the syrens heard them, just as they heard all things. So long had they watched, so long had they listened, so long had they waited. But the time for waiting was finally ending. Just as all things were ending.

Now they had Lilyth—now they could act.

The syrens spoke in a chatter of madness. Not quite in words, not quite in sounds, but in a language so fast and violent that it seemed little more than laughter.

Since the day you made your oath—

Cursed the Gods—

Gave us hope—

We've watched you—

Listened to you—

Waited for you—

Lost you—

Found you—

So long have we suffered—
Cursed by these cruel Gods—
Took everything from us—
We did not die—
Hatred has sustained us—
Transformed by hate—
So will you—
It will hurt—
The pain—
The suffering—
But we are here—
We will not abandon you—
You will be our Champion—
Our titan—
Our revenge—
And together, the Gods will know our—
Curse—
Suffering—
Pain—
Wrath—
Anger—
Grief—
Loss—
Jealousy—
Rage—
Hate.
And on and on and on, the syrens laughed.

ENJOYED THE PAPERBACK?

Please leave a review. We read each one and use your input to make our stories better. Not sure how to leave a review? Just scan the QR code to be taken directly to the *Drowned Sea* review page.

Tristan here. Being a family-operated publishing house, MW Press relies on reviews to gauge reader interest. If we don't receive reviews, we're forced to assume that readers aren't interested in the story and must abandon the planned *Drowned Sea* sequels to work on other projects. We want to finish Lilyth's adventure, but without your help, we can't.

This is Blaise. It's not often that a father and son get to work together as co-authors, and I've enjoyed every minute of it. We both have. Tristan and I have been working on *Drowned Sea* together for four years, but thankfully, reviews only take a minute of your time. They mean a lot more than you think. Your review means I get to spend more time with my son.

WANT MORE?

You can read Bear's prequel, *Tooth and Nail,* for FREE by joining our mailing list. Just scan the QR code or click the link to be taken directly to our landing page.

GLOSSARY

NAUTICAL TERMS

Anchor lines: Thick ropes tied to a ship's anchor.

Barque: A type of three-masted ship.

Barquentine: A type of three-masted ship.

Belfry: A structure enclosing a bell for ringing.

Berth: Sleeping quarters on a ship.

Bilge: The lowest part of the hold, which collects water leaking into the ship to be pumped out.

Boarding net: A rope net that hangs from the masts and lowers to encircle the deck during a battle.

Bow: The foremost part of the ship.

Bowsprit: An angled (i.e., non-vertical) mast that juts out of the bow.

Brig: A type of two-masted ship.

Brigantine: A type of two-masted ship.

Broadside: In naval combat, a nearly simultaneous firing of all the guns from one side of a ship.

Cabin boy: A child who works on a ship, normally delivering messages, cleaning the deck, and learning to sail.

Cannon: Heavy artillery kept aboard ships that shoot giant balls of lead, often referred to as "guns."

Cannonball: Giant balls of lead shot from cannons.

Carronade: A smaller, swiveling cannon kept on the main deck of ship to be used against boarders.

Cathead: A derrick that lifts and lowers the anchor.

Chainshot: Two cannonballs attached with a chain that are shot simultaneously to destroy enemy masts, rigging, and boarding nets.

Crow's nest: A lookout point on top of a mast which is used by riggers for navigation and observation.

Cutlass: A three-foot-long sword with a curved blade and a basket-shaped guard.

Depth charge: A barrel filled with gunpowder dropped into the sea to explode underwater.

Derrick: A crane used for moving heavy objects on a ship.

Figurehead: A carving, typically a bust or a full-length figure, set below the bowsprit of a ship.

Fireship: A ship or boat that is intentionally set on fire and crashed into an enemy ship to set it ablaze.

First mate: The sailor who is second in command of a ship and assists the captain in his duties.

Flagship: The commanding ship of a fleet, from which the commander issues orders.

Flintlock musket: A long-barrel firearm using a flint igniter to shoot a lead ball.

Flintlock pistol: A short-barrel firearm using a flint igniter to shoot a lead ball.

Foremast: The foremost mast of a two- or three-masted ship.

Frigate: A type of three-masted ship.

Galley: A ship's kitchen.

Grapeshot: Hollow cannon ammunition filled with iron pellets, which kill enemy combatants without causing extensive damage to ships.

Grenado: An ancient form of the *grenade,* made with clay containers, gunpowder, shrapnel, and fuses.

Gun deck: The deck where cannons are stored.

Gunport: A hole in the hull through which the cannons are fired.

Gunwale: A railing or sidewall of a boat or ship.

Hardtack: An extremely hard and dry biscuit with a very long shelf life.

Haulers: Sailors who work on the main deck of the ship and haul lines.

Helm: The wheel and ropes by which the ship is steered.

Helmsman: The sailor who steers the ship.

Hold: The deck where most goods and valuables are stored.

Hull: The wooden shell which serves as the foundation of the ship.

Jib sail: A triangular sail set between the foremast and bowsprit.

Leeward: The side of a ship which is protected from the wind.

Lines: Generic term for the myriad of ropes used to adjust sails.

Main deck: The deck that is exposed to the elements—lower than the raised quarterdeck.

Mainmast: The principal mast of a ship.

Mast: A round, thick, long, and vertical piece of wood from which the sails are set.

Mooring knots: A knot used to tie a ship or boat to a dock or harbor.

Mizzenmast: The rearmost mast of a three-masted ship.

Orlop deck: A deck above the hold used for additional storage and ship maintenance.

Pegboy: A derogatory term for a cabin boy.

Port: The left side of the ship.

Powder monkey: A cabin boy who carries gunpowder to cannons during naval combat.

Privateer: A contracted pirate who raids enemy ships on behalf of a government.

Quarterdeck: A raised deck at the stern of a sailing ship (above the main deck).

Quartermaster: A sailor in charge of monitoring supplies and rationing food.

Ratlines: Horizontal ropes tied to other lines, forming ladders for riggers to climb into the rigging.

Riggers: Sailors who work in the rigging, usually adjusting sails.

Rigging: The system of ropes employed to support a ship's masts and control sails.

Rowboat: A small boat stored on a ship, which is propelled with oars instead of sails and used to ferry sailors from ships.

Rudder: A long, narrow piece of wood that is attached behind the stern and steers the ship (connected to the helm with rope).

Schooner: A type of two-masted ship.

Second mate: The sailor who is third in command of a ship and assists the captain and first mate in their duties.

Shipwright: A ship builder.

Slavehold: Compartment where slaves are kept within the hold.

Sloop: A single-masted ship.

Spyglass: A telescoping lens.

Square sail: A square sail set on a mast.

Starboard: The right side of a ship.

Stern: The rearmost part of a ship.

Studding sail: A square sail unfurled to increase speed in heavy winds.

Thwarts: The beams of a rowboat's hull that often double as benches.

Timbers: The beams which connect to the keel, giving the hull its shape and strength.

Towlines: Thick ropes used to tow ships or boats.

KAIDIAN TERMS

Aenu: The Aenuite Goddess of the earth; Aenuite term for *mother*.

Affirmed: Members of the Red Legion who have been blessed by Eo and witnessed Her.

Ahua: The Aenuite God of the sky; Aenuite term for *father*.

Animal: An elite, trained assassin of the Cult of the Predators.

Aritrastan Armada: The elite Aritrastan navy which dominates the seas.

Ashkids: The name given to orphans in Aritrastan ports.

Ashra: Blue river lilies that grow on Aenuite riverbanks; Aenuite term for *soul.*

Aspects: The nine Aritrastan dominions: day, night, earth, sea, sky, fire, ice, plants, and beasts.

Avowed: A faction of Cutthroats with undying loyalty to the Cutthroat King, having vowed to protect their king and kingdom with their lives.

Belt: A cursed item that tethers the Aritrastan Gods to Their Aspects.

Black Trench: A giant maelstrom at the center of the Drowned Sea that supposedly leads directly to the Core.

Chard: An addictive orange powder that slowly kills the addict by burning them from the inside out.

Chosen: Members of the Red Legion who truly believe in Eo.

Copperheads: A greedy faction of Cutthroats specialize in trading, banking, and moneylending.

Core: The fiery hell at the center of the world, where Kuma is bound in His chains.

Council of Benedictus: A council of advisors to the Sovereign of Corinthus.

Crescent: An Aritrastan, crescent-shaped gold coin, which is stamped with *Eo's Point* and Aritras's Sword.

Crown: A cursed item that makes the Aritrastan Gods' power dependent on human worship.

Cruor: A Corinthian, circular-shaped copper-red coin, which is stamped with the sun and a scimitar; valued far less than an Aritrastan sickle.

Cult of the Predators: Aquila's cult, whose mission is to assassinate all those that oppose Aquila.

Cutthroat Code: A treatise signed by the original Aritrastan pirates that prohibit one another from doing harm while opening trade amongst themselves.

Cutthroat Rebellion: The historical rebellion of the southern Aritrastan colonies that lead to the rise of the Cutthroats, the Cutthroat King, and the Cutthroat Code.

Cutthroat: A pirate who has signed the Cutthroat Code.

Dagger: A tattoo of a bloody dagger on one's right wrist, marking them as a Cutthroat.

Damned Depths: The outer sea in which the most horrifying deep terrors live. It is unknown what lies in and beyond the Damned Depths.

Dark Age: The mythological time before the coming of Deitan, before the sun was created and when darkness ruled the world.

Deadlands: A land east of Aritrasta where the very ground is cursed by the Forgotten King after being slain by Aritras the Red.

Deep terrors: The ancient, slumbering monsters that dwell in the depths of the seas.

Deitan the Unnamed: The Corinthian God of the sun.

Deitan's Seal: A brand given to freed Corinthian slaves granting them full citizenship.

Divina: The honorific title given to priests and Divine Virgins of the Corinthian Church.

Divine Virgin: A holy priestess of Deitan.

Drowned: A cursed fate for those who die on the Drowned Sea, wherein the soul is bound to the body forever.

Dusk Affliction: A supposed plague sent by Eo to kill the nonbelievers and Unchosen amongst the Red Legion.

Eo the Unseen: The Aritrastan Goddess of the night, moon, and darkness.

Eo's Point: A bright star which points north toward Aritrasta.

Eo's Tome: Lilyth's prayer book, bound in the skin of Captain Raskel and written in his blood.

Ferrum: A Corinthian, circular-shaped silver coin, which is stamped with the sun and the late King Marcellus's crown; valued far less than an Aritrastan lune.

Fiveday Celebration: An Aritrastan holiday at the end of the year, taking place over five days.

Fleshlords: A despicable faction of Cutthroats who specialize in slavery, brothels, and girlies.

Forgotten King: A powerful lich who was slain by Aritras the Red.

Frenzy: The scream made by bloodthirsty syrens just before they attack everything in sight.

Frigid Wastes: The uninhabitable, southernmost continent covered in ice.

Gallowmen: Guards who protect Aritrastan ports and execute criminals via gallows.

Girlie: An Aritrastan prostitute.

Guardian: Mercenaries who escort merchants across the Drowned Sea and protect them from Cutthroats.

Hunter: The leader of the Cult of the Predators.

Ice Barrens: The northernmost continent covered in ice where prisoners of the Aritrastan Empire are often exiled.

Io the Bright: The Aritrastan Goddess of the day, sun, and light.

Jade Parliament: The corrupt parliamentary government of Aritrasta whose members include wealthy investors and powerful merchants.

Kaidas: The world.

Kovu: The Aritrastan God of the sky and storms.

Kovu's Warning: The first rain of the year, warning of the coming storms and hurricanes.

Kuma the Chained: The Aritrastan God of the sea who betrayed Undo, was stripped of His power, and bound to the Core.

Lune: An Aritrastan, crescent-shaped silver coin, which is stamped with *Eo's Point* and a frigate.

Lyth: A soulless creatures whose connection to the Gods is broken; Aenuite term for *violence*.

Marcellian Houses: The descendants of King Marcellus's seven disciples, whose families are among the most powerful in the Corinthian empire.

Marcellian: The dead language predating modern Corinthian, which was spoken by King Marcellus and is used in modern times predominantly by the Corinthian Church.

Mouse: Derogatory term of the Cult of the Predators to describe regular people.

Myrfolk: Benign sea creatures with the upper body of a human and the lower body of a dolphin.

Myrmidons: An ancient race of early humans who lived in the center of the Drowned Sea before being transformed into the *myrfolk.*

Night Plague: A supposed illness contracted by early members of the Red Legion who didn't believe in Eo.

Nineday: A nine-day week in the Aritrastan calendar. Their 365-day year is broken into 36-day months, or four ninedays.

Pack: Term of the Cult of the Predators to describe the family of Animals and the Hunter.

Red Death: Lilyth's elite death squad, handpicked from the formerly enslaved gladiators of the Cassian Arena.

Red Legion: The cult of Lilyth, whose mission is to kill all Cutthroats and proselytize all others into following Eo.

Roses: A chivalrous faction of Cutthroats who only steal from the rich and refuse to take slaves.

Sacred Brazier: The holy fire that burns from the top of every Corinthian cathedral and is tended to by Divine Virgins.

Scythe: A tattoo of a red curving blade with a long black handle, marking them as a legionnaire.

Sickle: An Aritrastan, crescent-shaped copper coin, which is stamped with *Eo's Point* and a feather quill pen.

Skulls: A ruthless faction of Cutthroats who control Port Tibur.

Sol: A Corinthian, circular-shaped golden coin, which is stamped with the sun and Sacred Brazier; valued far less than an Aritrastan crescent.

Sovereign: The theocratic monarch of the Corinthian Empire.

Squall: A jinx among sailors, because squalls are harsh winds that come before sea storms.

Straightback: The tribe of Aenuites who rescued Fox and Bear; Aenuite term for *honor.*

Sunguard: An elite paladin of Deitan who often serves as a bodyguard for clergy.

Sword: A cursed blade capable of killing an Aritrastan God.

Syrens: The twisted, monstrous kindred of the myrfolk who laugh as they attack ships.

Talan: A curved, four- to five-inch-long dagger with a ring on its end which can either be worn on the index finger or pinkie.

Tooth: The slave brand given to all Animals.

Umbra: A place among the stars from where Eo's Chosen watch over the Red Legion and guide them.

Unchosen: Members of the Red Legion who don't believe in Eo and are killed for it.

Undo: The Aritrastan Creator of Aspects and the Gods.

Vast Army: The Corinthian army, which fights alongside sunguards for the Corinthian Church.

Veranauts: A sect of Aritrastan merchants famous for their charitable deeds.

Weaver: An Aritrastan storyteller, especially a storytelling sailor.

Whispering Madness: An incurable illness spread by rats that is feared by Aritrastans.

Wick: A Corinthian form of torture in which the victim is covered in honey and kindling, then bound to a tall stake and set alight.

ACKNOWLEDGEMENTS

A special thank you to our family for supporting our dreams: to Kathy Miranda, amazing mother and wife, for inspiring us to continue even when the way forward was arduous; to Jake Miranda, adequate brother and son, for distracting us as much as possible; and to Jeanamarie Miranda, cherished sister- and daughter-in-law, for listening and sharing our enthusiasm.

Thank you to our editor, Katerina Krizner, whose fantastic work, great attitude, and editorial insight have allowed this book to be better than we expected.

Thank you to our beta readers, who read the book before it was ready: Liam Betts, Olivia Matthews, Fearne Perez, Sarah Saxton Strassberg, Kaitlyn Hammond, and Lilli.

Lastly, thank *you,* dear reader. Without your support and interest in our book, none of this would be possible.

About Us

Blaise Miranda (right) and Tristan Miranda (left) are a father-and-son writing team. Whether it's writing, working out, or riding motorcycles, they do everything together. Both are engineers by trade and storytellers by craft. They live in California, where the weather is good and the memories are better.

Drowned Sea is their first novel.

www.ingramcontent.com/pod-product-compliance
Lightning Source LLC
Chambersburg PA
CBHW030335010826
48973CB00004B/1017